Stephanie Zia was born in Dorset in 1955. In 1972 she joined the Russian Section of the BBC World Service. Moving to television, she spent fifteen years in the Music and Arts Department, working on arts documentaries for *Arena*, *Omnibus* and *Bookmark*. She began writing after directing her first film for BBC Bristol, *10 x 10: Applause*. She lives in West London, writing between school runs.

Praise for *Baby On Board*:

'Any mother will identify with the depiction of Molly's moving and funny struggle to get her life together after the birth of her baby. A really good read, with strong, well drawn characters and lots of wry humour' Louise Voss

Baby On Board

STEPHANIE ZIA

Copyright © Stephanie Zia 2003

First published in Great Britain in 2003 by
Judy Piatkus (Publishers) Ltd of
5 Windmill Street, London W1T 2JA
email: info@piatkus.co.uk

The moral right of the author has been asserted

A catalogue record for this book is available from the British Library

ISBN 0 7499 3366 6

Set in Palatino by
Phoenix Photosetting, Chatham, Kent

Printed and bound in Great Britain by
Mackays of Chatham Ltd, Chatham, Kent

Grateful thanks to Judith Murray at Greene & Heaton and Gillian Green at Piatkus. I'd also like to thank the creative writing staff and students of Richmond Adult Community College, especially Diana Morgan, Barry Brooks, Joy Isaacs, Jeff Trollope, José Hacon, Linda Buckley-Archer, Louise Voss, Jacqui Hazel, Jacqui Lofthouse, Susan Kerr and Ann Vaughan-Williams. Thanks also to Gilly Fuest, Rosy Voss, Stephen Arneil and Steve McDonnell. Last but most, all love and thanks to my family, especially Natasha.

To Rebecca, Jane, Katie, Melanie, Helena, Emma,
Maria and Judy

My own Kew mum gang, whose friendship and
laughter over endless cups of tea in that first year of
first motherhood inspired the story that follows

CHAPTER ONE

When the alarm bells rang on Molly Warren's biological clock she bit the bullet and stopped popping the Monday to Sunday tabs which had kept her moods swinging, her body available and her life stagnant.

At seventeen, she'd taken to voluntary sterility like the pill had been a free gift from Cosmo or something, but by the time she was thirty-eight her life had become dominated by a voice yelling from deep inside, 'Switch me off!'

'You're what?' Max Boyd spluttered into his raspberry gratin eleven months later. 'How the...?' His voice petered out. The waitress came to take the empty wine bottle away. 'Another one,' he growled as if it were her fault, 'and fast.'

He glanced over his shoulder before leaning forward across the table, his eyes popped in disbelief.

'It's all right, Max.'

'All right? What do you mean, "it's all right"?'

'I mean, no one can hear us.'

'How long?'

'Eight weeks.'

1

'You've kept this to yourself for eight whole bloody weeks?'

'No, Max, I've known for three.'

'Well, why the hell didn't you say something?'

'I've been looking for the moment, Max. It's not exactly easy. I didn't know how to tell. I, I – didn't know how you'd react.'

Max put his head in his hands and looked at her through his fingers, his eyes shadowed by a deep frown.

'Bloody.' He looked down at the table, 'bloody, *bloody* hell.'

Molly sat up straight and looked directly and confidently into his eyes. 'It's due on the fifth of January. I've got my first hospital appointment in two weeks' time.'

'It's due? What d'you mean, it's *due*?'

'Max.'

'You have a career, Molly! What about your flat? Your mortgage? Your....your figure. Your arse will drop, you'll be ... I'll be ... I. Veronica, for Christ's sake! Molly, you can't possibly in a million *years* think ...'

'I take it you're not happy, then.'

'It would be insane,' he said in his deep, authoritative, discussion-over voice he used to such effect when interviewing politicians on the radio.

'I did tell you, Max.'

'Tell me what?'

'When we got back together. Don't tell me you don't remember?'

Max looked at her blankly.

'No. You don't, do you. I suppose you've conveniently forgotten all those weeks of fumbling with the condoms as well.'

'Too right.' He ran his fingers through his hair over and over. Molly watched, fascinated, as his white-blond curls unfurled and sprang back one by one.

He looked up suddenly. 'But you went back on the pill after that. Surely.'

Molly shook her head.

'But you *know* my situation, Molly.'

'That's not what you said at the time.'

Max sighed deeply.

'We've been together for six years, Max.'

'Five.'

'All right, five, not counting the year we split up. Well, six years is long enough to wait. Far too long.'

'What is this with waiting, waiting, waiting? I'm not a bus! What's wrong with just enjoying all the good times we do have together?'

'Living for the moment,' said Molly wearily.

'I don't understand it. You say you're waiting for me and look, I'm here. I always have been here, haven't I?'

'Not all the time, Max.'

'I see you more than I see Veronica, Molly. You know that.'

'She's still your wife.'

'No one gets anyone "all the time", Molly. Wake up! This is London. 2001, and you're acting as if you're living in a Mills & Boon lino land circa 1950.'

'I'm not going through that argument again, Max.'

3

'You've always known my position, Molly. As does Veronica.'

'Hurray for Veronica,' said Molly drily.

'She doesn't ask for or expect me to be faithful. She knows what I'm like!'

'And you know what *she's* like!'

'Yes!'

'Then if you're both off with other people all the time, why the hell bother staying together at *all*?'

Max opened his mouth then paused.

'NO!' Molly raised her voice. 'Don't answer that, we've been through this too many times.'

'You've just got to be *realistic*, Molly.'

'Like Veronica, you mean?'

'She doesn't have the jealous gene.'

'Puh!' Molly threw her eyes up. 'Well, I happen to be human and I *do*. It's not enough, Max.'

'It's not enough,' Max sighed, 'all the meals out, the weekends away, the shopping trips to New York?'

'NO!'

'Keep your voice down. Do you realise what lengths I've had to go to?'

Molly splatted her spoon down into the middle of her raspberry gratin. 'You just said she didn't mind!'

'So long as she doesn't know too much, she turns a blind eye.'

'It's. Not. Enough, Max. Can't you see? It's all champagne. Froth and bubbles. I'm *fed up* with champagne, Max.'

Max laughed. 'Since when?'

'I want vegetables, and … Vim! I want beans on

4

toast and, and ... saucepans hanging on hooks and, and...'

'A box in the suburbs full of damp washing on the radiator, screaming kids and stinking nappies.'

'Yes, yes, YES! '

Max turned his head sideways and looked at her curiously out of the sides of his eyes. 'You've gone mad!'

'I've had enough, Max! Enough of all this empty, deceitful froth on the road to nowhere.'

The totally bemused expression on Max's face made her want to jump up and hug him and tell him it'd all be all right, except it didn't look like it was going to be all right.

'It's just that there – there's something so satisfying about chopping an onion.'

'Chopping an *onion*?'

'At least it *leads* somewhere.'

'*Leads* somewhere?'

Molly dreamily fingered the petals of the solitary white orchid in the silver-steel vase between them.

'Are you telling me that all the time I've been bringing you champagne, you'd have been happier with a bag of onions?'

'You know what I mean.'

'No, Molly, no, I don't know what you mean. *Onions?*'

'For a man of forty-six you've got a lot of growing up to do, Max.'

Max spoke slowly and softly, 'Just let me get this straight, Molly. Because you'd prefer to chop an

5

onion rather than sip champagne, you decide – *by yourself* – to have a baby?'

Despite the chasm of earthquake proportions tearing open between them, Molly felt a flush of warmth ripple through her. It was the first time she'd heard anyone acknowledging her big secret. Growing inside her. Slowly, slowly, turning from a condition into a human.

'Stop trying to twist everything I say, Max. I'm not one of your smarmy-clever politicians. I can hardly believe it myself.'

'That is so selfish, Molly.'

'I *told* you, Max.'

'You decide. Totally by yourself.'

'You "conveniently forgot", Max, and you know it.'

'You could have reminded me!'

'Oh come on! That sex happens to be, in no small way, related to reproduction?!'

'You know what I mean. I *trusted* you, Molly.'

'Trusted me never to really matter.'

'That's *not what I'm saying.*'

'While you're happily trolling along with your head stuck in the sandpit of your oh so cool "open" marriage. Open, my foot. Open so long as nothing else affects it too much. Nothing as inconvenient as, as . . . real life.'

'What about the sex? Has that been all empty froth and bubbles too?'

'Keep your voice down, Max.' Molly glared at the group of suddenly silent businessmen at the next table.

'Well?'

'Technically speaking, yes. All froth and bubbles is precisely what it is. I mean was.'

Molly could feel a new strength in her voice. A fierce protectiveness. A pride which had little to do with holding her side of the argument. Poor bloke, he doesn't know what's hit him. He came here for a normal evening meal and he gets his whole future thrown in his face. Splat.

'Though it *was* good sex,' she added sweetly.

'Come on, it's been amazing. The best ever.' He reached over for her hand.

She quickly pulled it away, 'because it was the real thing, Max. Or so I thought...'

'Look – I don't think you've quite thought this through, Molly,' he said gently.

'There's nothing to think through, Max. I'm all thunked out. Nature, as they say, will take its course.'

Max's voice hardened. '*Listen*, Molly, nobody gets everything in this life.'

'I'm sick of it, Max. I'm fed up with the world around me changing at the rate of knots, fed up with everyone else's lives going forwards. Going backwards even. At least *moving*. Changing. Life! At least I'm going to be *in* it now, Max. Not just a, a – spectator!'

'There are other ways of changing, Molly. Anything, *anything* would have been better than this.'

'You've made yourself clear, all right?'

'I'm not a domestic creature, Molly. I never have

been and never will be. You *know* that! And as for –
babies...' He said the word with disdain.

'I've got your drift, Max. There's really nothing
left to talk about, is there?' She put both hands on
the table to get up and leave. 'That's how it is. It's
facing up to reality time. I'll go. I mean we. *We'll* go
without you.'

'Go? Where?'

He leant forward to fill her glass. Molly covered it
with her hand. He looked at her in bemusement
before hurriedly refilling his own.

'I don't know. The country. Anywhere. We can't
stay here, can we? I'll sell my flat. Find somewhere
cheaper. Everywhere's cheaper than London, isn't
it? And I should get a good price. They've shot
through the roof round here, haven't they?' Molly
tried to keep her voice steady. 'No need for you to
worry, Max. We'll get by. We'll be happy. I expect.
Once we've adjusted. And you know? I really quite
fancy living in the country.'

'Phff, you'd last five minutes.' Max twisted sideways in his chair and crossed his legs.

'I could grow cabbages. And make soup. I could
sew, and knit even! I'd be very happy. Extremely
happy probably.'

'Molly ... come on now, don't cry.'

She wiped away a tear with her finger. He took
hold of her hand and held it between his. She didn't
take it away.

CHAPTER TWO

Molly hopped from one leg to the other as she watched the porter fiddle with the key to her suite, gorging on the sweet anticipation of not knowing what was behind the door while her heart beat a hey-ho-life's-a-hotel dance with her ever-present hope and optimism. She was in hotel heaven and her expectations were high. For not only was she in one of her hotel 'moments', as she called them, she also happened to be in one of her favourite hotels in the world.

As the porter fussed, Molly pondered the unknowns. Had she gauged the next few moments accurately? Was she in for a pleasant surprise? Or mild disappointment? Not likely. This was suite territory. Almost unheard of in Molly's hotel history except for a few, memorable, upgrades.

A suite at the Portobello Hotel had to be good.

The only question was how good could good get?

Once she got behind the door, the pattern was always the same. A computer-like systematic rundown clicked into gear as her brain automatically divided the hotel's star rating by its position.

(Categorised into country, international city, nowhere city, beach resort, airport, etc.) After the split-second overall summing-up would come the immediate, almost unconscious, bed analysis and check for the big three: phone, TV and fridge. This would be followed by a more general summing-up, taking in view and proximity of big noisy things like roads and runways. If all that passed and didn't throw up the bothering, but nevertheless essential, request for another room, the porter would be tipped and the sniffing out of the room could begin in earnest. First the bed-bounce, then the fridge. Would it be stocked with overpriced, suddenly highly desirable, miniature goodies or a sad, cold corner of emptiness? A mean hint at what might have been.

Then a thorough bathroom survey. First, the smellies. Tiny replicas of Parisian posh? Or a few trashy sachets? Then the shower. An English country-life speciality dribbler or a proper power job?

The hunt continued.

Just the five TV channels? (And in the provinces, even this was pushing it.)

Or satellite?

If so, which package and did it include porn?

Was there twenty-four-hour room service?

Nickable stationery?

Fruit?

Decanters full of free booze?

Were there any nasty sneaky surprises lurking? Like stopping breakfast before nine? (Usually related to an uncivilised kicking out time.) When *was* kicking-out time?

She'd amused herself with this little game count-less hundreds of times – a small compensation for a life lived on the road managing TV documentaries. Not least because choosing location hotels had been part of her job. And film crews were a discerning lot when it came to their creature comforts. If the slight-est thing was wrong they wouldn't complain to the hotel but would get straight on to Molly like a group of whingeing children.

But this was different. The next twenty-four hours at the Portobello Hotel were for pleasure and plea-sure alone. She watched the key twist slowly in its lock. The young porter turned and gave her a crooked smirk, as if he knew her game. Open the box, open the bloody box, can't you? She jumped from one leg to another as he pushed the door open with his shoul-der. She smiled back at him, holding her head coyly to one side as she bent down to pick up her holdall.

'No!' he lunged for her bag. 'Don't you touch that, now.'

Molly patted her stomach lightly. 'That's my baby,' she whispered.

Although the usual excitement was there, her basic comforts were uppermost in her mind. Her ankles had swollen up, her feet were killing her and she was desperate for a wee. She was looking for-ward more than anything to a good lie-down on any bed of any shape or form. The walk from her nearby flat had taken its toll. To come by taxi all of two blocks had seemed just too decadent, but she felt more knackered than if she'd travelled thousands of miles on the overnight non-stop to LA.

The floorboards beneath the afghan carpet creaked as she stepped into the quiet stillness of a small, dark inner hallway. She was just thinking how little it gave away as to what lay behind the second door when it flew open by itself. Molly leapt back in surprise. Instead of stepping into an oasis of first-class London hotel squidgy calm, there was a loud explosion as the room, or rather the contents of the room, came out to greet her.

Dozens of pink and white helium-filled balloons and poppers exploded from all angles into the tiny space, as the minuscule hallway filled with her friends throwing silver and gold streamers at her.

'Sur – pri – hi – ise,' said an already half-gone Sukie.

'You sneaky lot!' Molly looked round at them all in astonishment.

'Happy birthday, Moll,' Amanda planted two big sloppy kisses on both cheeks, put a champagne flute in her hand and clunked it heavily. Molly, her mouth still open in amazement, put her fingers up to touch the sticky red lip marks on her face.

Katie and Gayle, giggling as always, hugged her, one each side.

'Hey! Be careful, you two,' said Molly, almost losing her balance.

The porter stood transfixed with a stupid grin on his face as he gazed at Amanda's long, slender legs protruding from her tight Lycra miniskirt.

'Come on in and have a drink.' Sukie grabbed her by the hand.

'You too, hon,' said Amanda to the porter, pinching his cheek.

'Amanda, don't, you're making him blush!' giggled Sukie. 'And how's this little one,' she asked, as she wrapped her other arm round Molly's neck and bent down to her bump, half using her for support.

'Fine, everything's fine. Er, excuse me a minute.' Molly raced for the bathroom.

'How the hell did you lot get in anyway?' she called out through the open door as she pulled her enormous knickers down carefully over her bump.

'Who pays says, as they say,' said Amanda.

When she got back, the porter had dumped Molly's bag on the bed and was backing away nervously towards the door, his arms held stiffly out at an angle.

'Now look how you scardied him,' said Gayle.

'He didn't even wait for a tip,' laughed Molly, as the door clicked shut behind him.

'I'd like to do more than tip him!' said Amanda.

'Oh do shut it, Amanda,' said Katie and Gayle together.

'I mean, this is my . . . I mean it's lovely to see you all, of course, but we weren't supposed to meet till later. In the bar.' Molly sank into a chair, her hand on her bump, legs apart. She sighed and without any warning farted loudly.

They all looked at each other for a moment. Then laughed.

'You're only supposed to do that in company you've been dating steadily for at least two years!' said Katie. 'I read it in a quiz just the other day. "How Intimate Are You and Your Lover?" The fart stakes were quite high, I seem to remember.'

13

'It just goes to show, you lot are my most intimate partners in this world.'

'Come on, you can do what you like when you're pregnant,' said Gayle.

'Doing what you like doesn't come into it. You do what you have to,' said Molly, suddenly feeling more like their older sister than a mate.

She leant back and closed her eyes for a moment. All she wanted to do was have a lie-down, a long bath and put her feet up for a few hours to build up some energy for the evening. They'd wanted to do something special for her fortieth. Coming so soon after she'd broken up with Max, and now, seven months pregnant with no income. She hadn't told them she'd jacked her job in yet. Coping with their questions and emotions was going to be an extra strain. She'd tell them in the bar, when they'd all be so pissed they'd barely register it.

Amanda picked up Molly's glass and held it up to her. 'Now come on, drink up,' she said, standing over her in mock hurt. The two thin black lines that were supposed to be her eyebrows disappeared into her heavy ink-black fringe.

How was she going to boot them out when they were just trying to be kind?

'Just a tiny droplet,' said Katie.

'So we know the real Molly's still in there,' said Gayle.

'It's your birthday all day, you know,' said Sukie.

'You can't have gone off champagne as well?' said Katie.

'Come on, pretend, if nothing else,' added Amanda.

14

Oh, thought Molly. I'm going to shout at you all in a moment and I don't want to do that. You lot are all I've got.

'Don't worry,' said Gayle, sensitive as always, 'we're not staying. We just didn't want you to be on your own when you got here.'

'It's so kind of you all,' sighed Molly, ' but if I took even just one sip I'd throw up over all this – opulence!' She looked around, noticing for the first time the oriental carved wooden shutters, the enormous dark pink velvet sofa, the four-poster draped with thick tapestry throws and piled with huge square pillows and white linen cushions. The stillness of the air, unique to hotel rooms everywhere, was the only giveaway it wasn't some rich boho's lavish home.

'Oh, look.' She smiled weakly, noticing a banner with an enormous silver '40' tied to the ends of the four-poster.

'If you want to throw up, you throw up,' said Gayle.

'They must get it all the time,' said Sukie. 'They have enough rock stars staying here, don't they?'

'That's what hotels are for,' said Katie, 'making as much mess as you like and not having to clear it up.'

'Just tell me first, so's I can leave the room,' said Amanda.

'Amanda, you're such a squeam-bag,' giggled Gayle.

Her laugh tailed off.

The room suddenly stilled. All eyes were on Molly. She gazed at them all, slow-panning across their faces, one by one. Gayle and Katie looked down. It was a moment she wanted to freeze-frame in her memory for ever. She'd stepped outside, and knew in that moment that she wouldn't be able to get back in. She had the horrible feeling she was losing everything and everyone all at once.

Her eyes rested for a moment on the half-empty decanter of port on the mahogany desk in front of the Victorian bay window. The weak Winter sun illuminated the dark, still liquid making it shine like an oil painting. She longed to climb inside the rich burgundy and stay there forever in a deep, warm sleep. Protected from the world by the hundreds of tiny sharp shards of cut crystal.

She took her glass. Gayle and Kate looked up again. She looked around at them all, then down at her glass.

Then she threw it all over her bump.

'To it!' she said.

After a pause, Amanda chucked her glass at Molly's stomach as well.

'To it, Moll,' said Sukie, following suit.

Then Katie and Gayle, giggling, did the same.

While Molly undressed, Gayle ran her a bath. A sweet, high smell came wafting out of the bathroom. Shalimar! They'd remembered her favourite bath oil. The thought was almost immediately replaced with a faint memory of something she'd read in a baby book about some perfumes not being good for pregnant women? Or was that aromatherapy oils? Oh sod it. I'm having that bath.

'Of course you are,' said Gayle gently. Molly

16

looked at her, not realising she'd spoken the last few words out aloud.

'Thank you, all of you.'

'You're all right,' said Amanda.

'Just look after that bump of yours,' said Katie, 'and have a good rest.'

'And we'll see you later,' said Gayle.

She watched Katie and Gayle, their identical slick, scraped-back ponytails swinging below fluffy fur ties, follow Amanda and Sukie out of the room. To be so free! thought Molly. She shook her head, marvelling at how she'd been just that only a few months before.

After her bath, she wrapped herself up in a thick white towelling robe and sat at the dressing table. If only her life could be as clear and uncluttered as a hotel room, she thought wistfully as she pushed the bowl of fruit to one side and arranged the side mirror so she could see her profile. She took a childish pleasure in seeing her reflection from a different angle, her movements once removed from her direct image. She moved the other mirror until they were reflecting back on each other, so she could see herself repeated over and over into infinity. She brushed her hair out to a thick golden shine, drying it slowly, turning her head to examine her newly rounded face from different angles. Plumper, prettier, though. Her lips were redder, and fuller. Her skin glowed and her green eyes glistened with something. What was it? A new knowing, so secret she hadn't worked out quite what it was yet. And, despite her problems, the serotonin flowing through her brain gave her a cat-like feeling of contentment.

Giving up work had, in the end, been nothing but a relief. Early on in her pregnancy, she'd been transferred from location work to a desk job and she'd thought she'd somehow be able to work it out, keep her mortgage, her job. But all thoughts of seeing out her maternity rights and going back after the baby soon disappeared as resentments in the office had grown. Too many noses had been put out of joint by her transfer. A busy TV production office was the last place to find a nurturing environment. They had enough to worry about keeping to tight budgets and impossible schedules just to stay in business. She couldn't begin to think about what it would have been like after she'd had the baby, presuming she'd manage to navigate through all that childminding stuff.

Then there'd been all the speculation. She'd felt more like a fallen sixteen-year-old in an Edwardian village than a mature woman in the most happening part of the most fashionable city in the world. Scandalous half-whispers had followed her around like a second shadow, there, but invisible. When she'd started to get clumsy and forgetful they'd really laid into her and that was that. There was no such thing as a scatty, forgetful production manager, at least not an employed one. Her old efficiency had gone, along with her capacity to work sixty-five-hour weeks any time of the day or night. The job she'd once loved had turned into a nightmare.

She found a buyer for her Ladbroke Grove flat

straight away and, not even daring to think about contracts and the rest of it, had resigned. Then it all seemed so obvious what the right thing was to do. The more she thought about it, the more the idea had grown on her.

She put the hairdryer down and opened the drawers of the dressing table. From each, she pulled out bits of stationery, laundry bags, pens, a Bible and a magazine list with instructions to ring down to order at any time. Hmm, nice touch, she thought. She took it over to the four-poster, piled the goose-down pillows together in front of the carved wooden headboard and leant back.

She curled her toes contentedly as she skimmed the titles. She'd already read her usuals, *Marie Claire* and *Elle*. She'd got through both of them in minutes. None of the articles seemed relevant to her any more.

'Ah, this is what I need.' She smiled to herself as she ticked off *Good Housekeeping* and *Country Living*.

That was another bombshell she had to drop on her friends that evening. Molly was leaving town.

'Surrey!' they all chorused in a mixture of alarm and dismay which reverberated around the Portobello's cosy basement bar.

'Never!' said Katie.

'You can't,' said Gayle.

'Surrey's not you, Molly. You must know that.' said Sukie. 'Don't you?'

'It's just some weird joke, ' said Amanda drily.

'Well, only just Surrey,' said Molly defensively.

'You *can't* be serious, hon?' said Amanda.

'She'll be taking up golf next!' said Katie.

'And wearing Laura Ashley,' added Gayle.

There was a silence as they all looked down at Molly's pale-blue checked maternity dress.

'It's Monsoon, actually.'

'Monsoon! She's halfway down the A3 already,' said Amanda, grimly shaking her head.

'Look' said Gayle, 'we know, I mean I know we, we can't exactly share your problem...'

'Problems,' Molly corrected her.

'But we can help. You can't just take off into the wild blue yonder on your own, Moll!'

'Green yonder,' Amanda pointed out.

'What the bloody hell else can I do?'

'We can all dig in – help! You know...'

'What? Let me, I mean us, take up residence in your non-existent spare room?'

'Of course I'd...'

'Don't worry. I don't expect anyone to put up with – it. I don't know how the hell I'm going to cope with it myself. I don't think I've ever touched a baby, let alone held one.'

'Yarrrgh.' Amanda scratched down her face with her pointed red fingernails in mock agony.

'I had to chuck in the job. Even if I wasn't pregnant. It really wasn't working out any more.'

'It was a job, though,' said Amanda.

'I was beginning to feel like a *granny* with all those media-studies students around. And as for the crews ... I've had enough of spending my life looking after groups of spoilt sodding great big men.'

'And travelling all over the world,' Amanda went on.

'And getting paid for it,' said Katie and Gayle together.

'It's just as well I've had enough. How would I ever be able to go off at a moment's notice with a baby? Let alone work all those daft schedules.'

'Well, why not just keep your desk job?' said Sukie. 'They can't fire you. They have to keep you employed.'

'Oh great, thanks.' Molly reached for Gayle's Marlboro Lights at the thought of it, immediately taking her hand away as if she'd touched a hotplate. 'Cooped up all day with that lot. It was bad enough getting time off for hospital appointments. You'd think I was off on three-hour lunches or something the way they reacted.'

'But Molly. Surrey?'

'Don't be so bloody – bloody *metropolitan*, Amanda. What's wrong with Surrey?'

'Come to think of it, I don't think I've ever been there.' Amanda frowned as she took her cigarettes out of her tiny patent handbag and picked up a packet of matches from the bar.

'Come on then, tell us more,' said Katie.

'Yes,' said Gayle. 'So you've really got it fixed it already?'

'I've had to, haven't I?' Molly looked down at her bump. 'There's only two months to go. Just pray for me the exchange of contracts goes through all right.'

'You've *sold*?' said Sukie, horrified.

'Come on then. Where is it?' said Amanda.

'Finding somewhere to rent anywhere was a nightmare.'

'When did you *do* all this, Moll? said Amanda.

'It was crazy. No agency wanted to know,' Molly continued. 'They don't seem very keen to rent to pregnant women without jobs. Funny that, isn't it? None of them would even register me!'

'So how did you...?' said Sukie, popping a peanut in her mouth and looking at Gayle.

'My old school friend, Julie. Her brother lives in Nice. His tenant back here just happened to be moving out. It's really not bad. Well, it's not a palace but...'

'WHERE?' they all said at once.

'Kew.' Molly looked around at them triumphantly. They all looked at each other.

'Oh, well, that's not so far away, is it,' said Sukie.

'Kew Gardens? That's on the District Line, isn't it?' said Katie.

'Green,' said Amanda, like it was a disease.

'Half an hour to Sloane Square door to door,' said Molly proudly. 'It's easier to get there from there than it is from here.'

'If a train ever turns up.'

'Amanda, stop being so Zoneist,' said Sukie.

'Originally I was thinking of further out. More, you know, the real country. Devon or Somerset or somewhere deep and rural.'

'Oh no no no, all that fresh air'd kill you!' said Gayle.

'Or the locals would. They hate Londoners,' said Katie.

22

'I'm not surprised, with your prejudices,' said Molly.

'And it closes for the winter,' said Amanda.

'I can't believe it! You lot are so full of clichés, ' said Molly.

'So. You've seen it, then?' said Gayle.

'The flat?' said Katie.

'It's really not bad. I'd almost made up my mind before I'd seen it. Well, I didn't exactly have a lot of choice, did I? When I looked it up in the *A-Z* I could see it was virtually countryside anyway.'

'It's in the *A-Z*?'

'Shut it, Amanda,' said Gayle.

'Well, let's face it, darling, it won't be like living in the middle of the O of Notting Hill, will it?'

'You just go and look up Kew. Almost the whole page is green blobs. Green bits without cowpats has got to be better, hasn't it? And Richmond Park's massive. I think it's going to suit me fine. It's going to have to suit me fine.'

'But what are you going to *do* with all that green?' Amanda shivered.

'I don't know – walk?' said Molly. 'With – it, you know ... It'll beat pushing a buggy around Shepherd's Bush precinct, won't it.'

'What's wrong with Shepherd's Bush precinct?' said Amanda, turning on the defensive.

'Nothing, so long as you're not pushing a buggy.'

'Go on then, what's it like?' asked Gayle.

'Well, you're not going to believe this, but the first thing I saw when I stepped off the Tube at Kew Gardens station was a pub!'

'So?' said Gayle.

'There are quite a few pubs in London, Moll,' said Amanda.

'On the station?'

'Tell me more,' said Amanda.

'A proper, full-sized pub right on the platform. Now, this is my sort of a place, I thought. And, as I didn't have much option anyway...' Molly trailed off.

'What's it like then? The flat?'

'Well, it's a bit *small*, but I'll manage.'

'How small?' said Gayle.

'Two rooms? Plus a bathroom and kitchen – of sorts.'

'There'll be two of you.'

'I don't think a tiny baby's going to take up much space, do you? When it's a teenager it might be different. And it's got a garden, quite a big garden actually. And it's cheap.'

'Oh, well that's all right then,' said Gayle, eyeing Katie unconvincingly.

'You must all come and visit.'

'How?'

'On the Tube, dummy. Honestly! You must come and see. It's a different world out there.'

Amanda took a deep drag of her cigarette.

'So Max's completely out of the picture, then?' said Gayle.

'Right off the bloody edge.'

'But if you move right out. I mean, you've really, you'll never get back together, will you? Max'd never go further south than Chelsea.'

'Precisely.'

'But I thought you wanted…?'

'What you want and what you get aren't related.'

'So you haven't seen him at all then since.'

'We've had a few meetings,' said Molly. She smiled wryly. 'And he thinks I did this to him!' she patted her bump. ' "I can't believe you're doing this to me, Molly," is what he said.'

'But you are, aren't you?' said Amanda.

'Don't *you* start!'

'Well, I mean of all the men in all the world, Max Boyd must be one of the most un, un, er…'

'Unfatherlike?' said Sukie.

'Undomesticated?' said Gayle.

'Unattractive, not!' laughed Katie.

'All lifestyle and no life, that's his problem,' said Molly. 'He'll grow up. One day. I don't know how long it'll take him, mind you, but there you are. There's nothing I can do about it, is there? Except get on with my own life and,' she patted her bump, 'this one's here. It'll be for the best. Better to do that somewhere else. Start again and all that.'

'What if he *wants* to see er – it?' said Gayle.

'He can come whenever he likes. I've made it clear, it's up to him. But what I'm *not* going to do is fall back into a half-baked relationship. I *know* he'd make a really brilliant father, though.'

'You're still hoping, aren't you, hon?' said Amanda.

'Of course I am. But at a distance. That'll be the difference now. And my little – it – here. I think it's called getting real.'

The others all looked at each other.

'You won't get *too* sensible, will you, Moll?' said Katie.

'Like they all do?' said Sukie.

'I'm *not*! But ... how can I explain?'

'Let's face it. You can't.'

'Oh, you're right, Amanda. I'm on this track now, aren't I? I've just got to get on with it. And the base instinct right now is survival! That's all. Crazy to talk about that from the bar of one of the swankiest hotels in London when I have a perfectly good bed a couple of blocks away.'

'You're only forty once, hon.'

'Thank you, all of you. This'll probably be my last taste of luxury for a long time to come.'

'Hey, yes, let's lighten up. It's your night, Moll! Another drink, anyone?' said Amanda.

'You go ahead.'

'Talking of which, where's all the talent?' said Amanda, looking around. 'I mean, it's not exactly heaving in here, is it? Where is everyone? Where's Johnny Depp? Gayle? This was your idea.'

'Too early,' said Gayle.

'I knew we should have gone to Woody's.'

'It doesn't get going till eleven or twelve some nights. It's a twenty-four-hour bar.'

'Ah, right!' Amanda brightened.

'Oh, wrong,' groaned Molly.

Molly's thoughts turned longingly to white goose-down pillows, a crackly-clean duvet, a room-service hot chocolate, the Toffee Crisp in the fridge and *Country Living*.

'It'll get wild later, I promise. It depends who's in town of course,' said Gayle.

'Oh,' groaned Molly. Thinking of a bit of satellite trash telly in bed and room-service breakfast with the papers before back to the real world.

'What are you going to *do* then, Moll. Once you get to Kew?' said Gayle.

'What do you mean, what am I going to do? I think I'll have my hands full, don't you?'

'I mean, for work.'

'I haven't a bloody clue.'

'Are you going to ask Max to support you?'

'Of course not!'

'Why not? He could afford it.'

'I've been independent all my life, Amanda, I'm not suddenly going to stop now. Besides, he's got enough problems just getting used to the idea.'

'Imagine,' said Amanda, 'if it was the other way round?'

'If he'd suddenly told me I was going to be a mother? That's what I mean. It's up to him. I'll have enough from the flat sale to keep me going for a while. For the whole of the summer if I'm careful. You will all come and visit me, won't you?'

'Too right we will.'

'Just try and stop us.'

'Now. Who's for another slammer?'

'St Clements for me,' said Molly.

'Oh Molly.'

'I've done quite well on the giving up front, haven't I? My whole life evolved around a married man, smoking and drinking and suddenly pham,'

27

she banged her hand on the bar, 'all my bad habits go at once!'

'Molly,' said Amanda, deeply serious. 'You will promise me one thing, won't you? For old times' sake. Just for me?'

'What?'

'You won't get one of those stickers, will you."

'What stickers?'

'"Baby on Board." '

Katie put her head in her hands and groaned, 'Baby, I'm bored already.'

Molly laughed. 'Of course not.'

'Yeah, weird, aren't they? Like, hey, don't crash me, crash some childless trash instead,' said Gayle.

'Listen, you lot, I may be about to have a baby. And we all know what happens to people who have babies. But I won't. I won't change. I'll still be the same old Moll. I will. I promise.'

Even as she said it, she felt that unknown knowing lurking behind her eyes telling her she was lying through her teeth.

CHAPTER THREE

Molly reversed her battered orange Beetle into a space beside Kew pond, deeply regretting her premature scoffing at the Baby on Board stickers. Her drive, all of three-quarters of a mile from one side of Kew to the other, had been a nightmare. Every other car on the road had loomed up towards her like a terrifying potential threat. It wasn't the thought of a gory accident which worried her as much as betrayal. The betrayal of trust her tiny, fragile baby put in her.

She tried to calm down as she rummaged in her blue flowery Boots changing bag, which had unceremonially evicted her compact leather Prada from her life, and seriously wondered if she should get some stickers made up just telling the truth: *'Paranoid, Brain-dead New Mother on Board – and DRIVING!'*

For a few moments she stared at the piece of paper in her hand, desperate to turn round and scuttle home, but, as this would have involved driving the car again, she stayed put. Since Daisy's birth she'd hardly been out at all. Let alone mingled and small-talked with a bunch of strangers.

The name was enough to make her feel edgy: Tamara Worstenburt, East Surrey Health Trust, Postnatal Coordinator. Below the address was a neatly drawn map of Kew Green and the names of five women, printed in green ink. Nothing to distinguish her name from the others, nothing to say she was any different; she'd even been called a Mrs like the rest, and, despite her lifelong independent bachelorhood, it fell into her head like some kind of a fake promotion.

She heard the voice of her health visitor in her head. "It'll be good for baby's progress, dear. Just give it a try ... You can have a cuppa and a lovely chat with some other new mums!"

Yerk.

If her antenatal experiences were anything to go by: double-yerk.

She twisted the rear-view mirror round and pushed her hair back off her face, horribly aware her free-falling hormones had caused a Frankenstein's-monster-like overnight transformation from a, just about passable, slim slick townie into a fat and forty sleepwalking tramp. Her hair, which had shone pure gold in pregnancy, was lank, dank and falling out and her blotched skin, which had glowed so serotoninly bright, was screaming out for some seriously expensive resurfacing.

Neck-down it just got worse. Her carefully and expensively accrued wardrobeful of bottom-hugging jeans, Lycra T-shirts and Jigsaw dresses had become as laughably useless as a shoebox full of Barbie clothes. Citing her new economy rather than a reluctance to purchase a size fourteen, or, perhaps, dread, even a sixteen, she was still in full maternity gear, which meant a rotation of fabric tents sporting pinprick clusters of flowers or red woolly checks. Their only saving graces were their complete concealment of her nappy-like underwear. While pregnant, she'd revelled in the baggy feminine flowingness of it all. She'd even got away with Heidi plaits on some days. But now? Now there was almost something supernatural about the way the dresses so perfectly completed her overall post-natal bedraggle.

She looked down at Daisy, fast asleep in her backward-facing pink elephant car seat, looking for all the world like a miniature version of Max, with his bumface chin and turned-up nose. Her thick crop of curls, though jet black rather than white blonde, had the same twist to them. She even had his long fingers and two tiny versions of his funny big toes which bent in the middle.

She yawned and stretched, savouring every rare moment of her precious baby-sleep peace in a place where she was in a sitting-down position which wasn't the loo. She thought about whether she should just give herself a break and sit there for an hour or so, staring across the pond to the Green beyond. Why put herself through another ordeal? She didn't *have* to go, after all, and it was the first day with any warmth in it for a long time. The February day had at long last shed its winter grey. The birds and the planes stood out in sharp definition against the white-blue sky. The trees fringing the Green had lost their deathly winter brittleness and seemed to be softening in the sun before her eyes.

A young girl with a baby in a pushchair and a toddler stopped to feed the ducks. Molly watched as the child laughed and threw bread everywhere except the water, while the girl sat cross-legged and hunched on the wall, puffing on a cigarette. A pair of Canada geese skid-landed on the pond and muscled in on the ducks as a flock of shrieking gulls circled and dive-bombed the bread from above. When the girl stood up to leave, the boy didn't want to go. She pulled him away by his arm. He began to scream. As they crossed the Green, his yells got fainter. It wasn't until they were crossing the cricket pitch beside the old church that the sound faded. But Molly could see by the shape of his body that he was still crying. She sat mesmerised, her mouth half-open, until they became two tiny dots disappearing into the distant gates of Kew Gardens.

How the hell? she wondered, glancing at Daisy, how the hell did mothers give their babies up to nannies? How was *she* going to do it? She pushed the thought from her mind, telling herself it wouldn't be till later. Preferably much later. If she was careful, she wouldn't have to go back to work till the end of the summer. If motherhood at forty wasn't going to be an easy swim, single motherhood at forty was already panning out into a constant struggle to stay afloat. She unclipped the car seat and Daisy opened her eyes.

'Hello, little one! You're just in time for a social.'

Molly bent over and looked into Daisy's face, a careful Penelope-Leach-prescribed twenty centimetres away. Daisy lay very still and studied Molly intently, moving her turquoise blue eyes slowly up from her mother's chin to her nose to her eyes. Then back down again.

'Are you ready to party then?'

Daisy looked across Molly's face again. Suddenly, her serious, intent frown cracked into a big gummy grin.

'Oh,' said Molly, tears welling in her eyes, 'so you're a party girl, are you? Just like your mum. Was,' she added ruefully.

Molly hummed as she gathered all her stuff together and smiled exaggeratedy down at Daisy again. After the momentous occasion of Daisy's first smile, the ordeal ahead didn't seem nearly so bad.

Daisy stared back blankly.

'Serves me right, trying for a repeat performance. Sorry, babes, I'm becoming a pushy mother already, aren't I?'

She looked down at the address in her hand, took a deep breath and opened the car door.

'Here we go, time to go and meet the locals,' she said as she crooked the car seat tightly under one arm.

They've all just been through the same experience as me, they'll probably be in much the same state, she thought happily as she walked down the narrow lane which led from the Green to the river, wishing she didn't feel so much like a strange form of walking Habitat cushion. They might not even all be Mrs-es, who could tell.

Molly flip-flopped along in her battered old Dr Scholls, trying to push the feelings of resemblance to an overweight duck from her mind. As it was February she wore thick socks, which added nothing to her foot-appeal. She'd been really shocked and annoyed that the weight of her pregnancy had made her feet grow a size. Not something any of the dozens of books she'd read had warned her about, so she'd become a shoeless person, as well as a clothesless one. Just the thought of a cheap and nasty shoe shop with Daisy in tow was enough to bring her out in a cold sweat.

The soft wind floated on her skin as she passed high back-garden walls on her right and a terrace of tiny whitewashed cottages to her left. Each little bay window, like nearly all the houses in Kew, was fringed by its triptych of window boxes. Some still contained their worn-out winter pansies and heathers, others had already had their spring makeovers and bulged with fresh earth, snowdrops, crocuses and sharp spears of daffodils in buds. There seemed to be birds everywhere, singing at the tops of their voices. Despite the looming meeting, Molly couldn't help but feel high on the promise in the air.

She shoved the piece of paper in her bag and headed for the large, dark green canvas pushchair which stuck out of the porch of a cottage bulging with flowerpots and hanging baskets near the end of the row. She moved it clumsily out of the way, trying to steer its front, almost bicycle-sized wheel with one hand away from the jumble of terracotta pots around the doorway.

'Oh sod it!' she cursed through her teeth as the front wheel went off in its own direction, careering straight through a small pot of freshly planted purple pansies. 'And I don't know what you're staring at,' she said to a large, white fluffy cat which was looking at her with hostile round yellow eyes from its window-seat perch.

'What the bloody hell are Land Rover doing making oversized pushchairs, anyway? You wouldn't see a bloody car going around calling itself Baby Buggy,' she muttered as she turned the pot back up and scraped the spilt earth off the ground. She took a few deep breaths of the rich, hyacinth air, trying to stem the surge of sheer hatred for the unknown, though soon-to-be-known, Land Rover owner.

The turquoise door opened, making her jump. She found herself looking up at a large woman in a long, flowery silk dress and dangly daisy earrings who filled every portion of the doorway and Molly's vision.

'Ah, you must be Molly,' she said, completely ignoring Molly's strange crouched position as she stretched out her arm. 'Tamara Worstenburt. Last one's here, ladies,' she called behind her shoulder. 'Do come in, dear.'

Molly stepped into a narrow hallway dominated by black wallpaper sprawling with gigantic lilies and climbing roses. She followed Tamara through to the back sitting room where four women sat stiffly in a circle on wooden chairs. Three of them had their babies in car seats at their feet; the fourth had a Mel Smith *Spitting Image* puppet lookalike lying back on her lap. Molly found herself staring fixedly at Mel Smith's feet, drawn to the familiarity of the pattern on its booties while at the same time desperately trying to place it.

'Ah,' she said, unsure if it was aloud or to herself, as an image from her recent past pulled up the Hermès logo like an old cash register into her addled brain. As her confused thoughts juxtaposed perfume counters, duty-free but still outrageously expensive silk scarves and babies' feet, she looked up at Mel Smith's owner and became equally, if not more, fascinated by the neatly folded rectangle of muslin draped over her shoulder, looking convincingly like a must-have fashion accessory. As the woman glared back at her, Molly, unsure whether it was in defence, defiance or disgust, became instantly self-conscious about her own muslin, lurking about her shoulders betraying its function, a sick and spittle rag full of sick and spittle.

'Right,' boomed Tamara in a high-pitched voice, 'shall we begin?' She edged sideways behind them to her seat, her silk dress rustling as she moved.

Molly slowly sat down in the empty chair.

'As I expect you've all gathered by now, I'm Tamara, your post-natal coordinator.' She smiled, lips closed, around the room. She spoke in an exaggeratedly overcaring voice which belied her previous shout. 'During the coming weeks we shall

36

go over all the things which may be worrying you. Breastfeeding, nappies, weaning, teething. I myself have two children, both grown-up now,' she laughed cynically. 'Thank goodness. Right, ladies, shall we begin by introducing ourselves? And,' she added as if she'd just thought of it, 'why don't we share our birth experiences with each other? That's usually a good warmer-upper.'

Molly glanced at the door, wondering whether to make a run for it straightaway. Tamara leant forward and looked directly at muslin-throw accessory woman. Curiosity kept Molly in her seat. Tall with gold lumps on her ears and expensively streaked hair, she wore matching ponyskin hair band and boots. Boots expensive enough, Molly noted, to be smart rather than tart. And, she was staggered to see, with heels.

The woman's eyes widened and hardened slightly. She flashed a broad smile at everyone. Molly caught the look before it vanished and didn't quite believe it.

'Of course,' said the woman in a firm, assured voice. Sure enough, as soon as her smile had gone she looked annoyed again. 'I'm Caroline Symes, and this here is Charles Anthony Nigel Symes.' She poked her tongue out at Mel Smith. He looked at her, round-eyed, for a few seconds before opening his mouth and poking his tongue back at her. Caroline looked around the room proudly.

'They all do that,' muttered the woman with frizzy ginger hair and glasses sitting next to Molly.

'He was born by elective Caesarean section. Weren't you, darling?' She gave him a noisy kiss on the cheek, squashing his rubbery lips to one side of his face for a moment.

'Queen Charlotte's?' asked Tamara.

'The Portland.'

'Where else?' muttered the woman next to Molly under her breath.

'It was so quick, and utterly without pain. I really don't know why everyone doesn't do it. I do honestly believe it was worse for my husband. Poor Theo. He had to wait outside and imagine it all. He couldn't possibly have stayed to watch, the poor darling can't even pass a butcher's shop without feeling queasy. It was all over in minutes.'

'Was he a breech, Caroline?' asked Tamara.

'Breech? No, oh no. We didn't want to take any – risks. And we liked the idea of being in control. None of that messy unpredictable...'

'Agony,' said the young girl in the white tracksuit next to Caroline.

'So I gather,' said Caroline, for the first time looking genuinely happy.

'Hmmm.' Tamara looked frostily into space.

'While we're on me, as it were. I might just add that we live in Riverside Drive, just behind the Green here. We've lots of space.' She looked round Tamara's sitting room through lowered eyes. 'I suggest we have the next meeting at mine, save us all being squashed up together like this.'

Land Rover owner identified, thought Molly, adding control freak to her first-impression résumé.

38

'Thank you, Caroline,' said Tamara, 'that's very generous of you.'

She turned and looked expectantly at white track-suit girl, clear-skinned with a cute blonde crop and unlived in-face. This one looks more like she's come out of a fortnight at a health spa than childbirth, Molly thought as she quietly slipped her Scholls off and pushed them underneath her chair with her heels.

'I'm Jenna? And this here is my little Lavender Iona Clouds?' She bent down and stroked her baby's quiff of black hair which stuck straight up in the air, making her look like a small fully-formed punk. 'We call her Lulu for short. You know? Lav? Loo? She was born at home?' Jenna's voice rose with an Antipodean inflection at the end of every sentence. 'I really wanted a natural birth. They don't like it when it's your first but we really really held out for it. We chose whale music...'

You would, thought Molly.

'We ended up having her in the kitchen, that's our centre for health and harmony? My partner Jason helped with the delivery? He completely chilled out. He didn't freak once. It was awesome. I yelled at him, called him all the names I could think of, just to stop me thinking of the pain. You know? '

'I still remember my first,' muttered the woman next to Molly. 'felt like he was coming out with a car seat already fitted.'

'But Jase was so, so cool. I can really really say he did as much as me.'

Molly's toes curled involuntarily inside her socks.

'I lived it, I lived the pain, I wanted to take responsibility for it. I embraced it and talked to it and we gave it a name.'

Don't tell me, thought Molly. Just don't ...

'Jason was right there, though. Right inside the moment with me, *and* he videoed it at the same time? He and Lulu bonded right away. Oh, *Lu*.'

Oh, where's the sick bag? thought Molly as they all politely concentrated on Lulu's distorted face which, without warning and within seconds, had disintegrated into a full screaming fit. Jenna picked Lulu up and lifted her tracksuit top. She unzipped one side of her pristine white bra and put Lulu to her breast as if she'd been doing it for years.

'Lulu's a Sagittarius, aren't you? With the sun rising in Virgo. That means she'll be bold, intelligent and so, so psychic? I'm already getting those vibes from her ... aren't I, Lu, hey?' Jenna looked down, Madonna-like, as her baby sucked greedily at her chest.

'Jase and I aren't even married yet,' she continued, 'but I didn't want to get spliced with a bump up my dress. I'm glad we waited. Now she can be part of it. We're getting married in Kew Gardens? This summer. When all the roses are out?' She laughed. 'A flower wedding. Oh,' she added, 'and she's sleeping through the night already.'

Everyone's jaws dropped.

'Till four anyway. They say it's quite common with home births?'

'That's very impressive, Jenna,' smiled Tamara while the others tried to wipe the jealous frowns off their faces.

Molly wondered who the mysterious 'they' were and whoever they were she wanted to slap them hard. Extremely hard. All of them.

'I hope you've all noticed I'm the only one with any make-up on today,' said the frizzy-haired woman. She smiled around the room. 'Underneath this lot I'm as pale and worn out as the rest of you look.'

Caroline and Jenna glared at her.

'Only joking. This here is Bob. He's my third. I have two others, Bradley, who's four and Gordon who's seven.'

'And you must be?' said Tamara pointedly.

'Izzie. Izzie Appleby.'

'Yes. Izzie. I expect you'll be teaching the rest of us a few things, won't you, Izzie?'

'There's always something you don't know, when it comes to kids, isn't there? Each one's different.'

'Little surprises full of surprises,' sighed Tamara.

'The best advice I ever had was, listen to all of it, read all the books. Then ignore it.'

'Ah yes,' said Tamara. 'So much of it is instinct isn't it? But I've also found in my career, you new, sorry, Izzie, most of you *new* mothers have so many questions you want answering. And that's why we're here, isn't it? To bond with each other. To help each other. To learn. To experience...'

'Yeah, right. It's good for the babies though, isn't it. They have a little social group of their own to grow up in. Little buddies. That's why I'm here.'

Tamara frowned.

'Anyway, this here is Bob.'

41

Two little round button eyes peered out of the midnight-blue car seat at Izzie's feet.

'He was born at Queen —

Izzie paused with her mouth still open. Someone's handbag was ringing.

'It's me,' said Caroline.

Izzie closed her mouth.

There was a silence while everyone listened while she listened. 'Yes? Hmmmmm, look – I'm in a meeting ... hmmmmm, no!' Molly caught the glint in Izzie's eye and smiled at her. Izzie threw her eyes up in a bloody-hell-who-does-that-woman-think-she-is look.

'Oh?'

They turned their eyes back as Caroline's voice dropped dramatically.

'I don't. Now, listen...' Caroline leant back and crossed her legs, rearranging Charles onto one knee.

'We are all listening,' muttered Izzie.

'Go further down, further down, three shelves down, see it? No – not there,' Caroline looked up at the ceiling and round at them all witheringly.

'No, Ulé. Now, listen. Get the assistant onto me. What do you mean? Yes – that's it! That's *it*, Ulé. At last,' she said to the group.

Tamara sat up straight.

'How many do they have in stock?' said Caroline, ignoring her. 'Oh, how annoying. Buy all of them. Now, must dash, 'bye, darling. See you later ... oh – tell them to keep some back for us next time.' She clicked the phone back and flashed her smile again. 'Nannies! You have to tell them every little thing or it simply doesn't happen.'

'What's she doing?' asked Molly, who *had* to find out or she knew it'd annoy her for days.

'Buying stockings.'

'For Charles?'

'For me. I don't know why I bother. Whenever I send her shopping she calls me at least three times.'

'Are you going back to work then, Caroline?' asked Tamara.

'Work?' Caroline looked at her blankly.

'As I was *saying*,' said Izzie very loudly and pointedly, 'Bob was born at Queen Charlotte's.' She paused for a moment. 'It was a quick in, out, wham-bam-thank-you-mam sort of a birth. I had the full painkilling works, of course.' She looked firmly at Jenna. 'And I was home as quick as I could after the epidural wore off. Had to be. So much to organise with three. He sleeps well. Not all through, mind you, but not half as bad as the other two. My husband, Carter, he's very good. He gets up in the night as much as me. We take it in turns. Strict rotation. Otherwise I couldn't do it. I just couldn't do it.'

Molly bit her lip. She felt like she'd nosedived into some *Woman's Own* utopia. Where did all these young, cared-for, nurtured, married, or as good as, women, *come* from?

As the next woman introduced herself, Molly switched off and thought back to her own experience. What should she say? Should she tell them about the sheer panic when her waters burst on a Sunday afternoon right in the middle of her third Toffee Crisp and a western? Of how she'd tried to get hold of Gayle, Katie or Sukie on their mobiles, and how all of them were switched off? Of how she'd then tried Amanda's number in desperation, even though she'd been emphatically upfront about not wanting anything to do with that side of things? Of how, between contractions, she'd dialled the obvious restaurants before a tidal wave of a pain came along and crippled her double? Of how she'd got herself to the hospital in a cab?

She'd even phoned her mother in Spain. Sounding like she was just down the road rather than Pedreguer, she'd told Molly to hang on, be brave and be sure to visit her soon, like she was just off for a massage or something. Should she then tell them of how she'd hung up on her when she'd made a joke about being too young to be a grandmother? And of how she'd cried and really wanted her mother to be there? Despite everything.

Should she tell them of how she'd called Max's answerphone? Even though she knew he was away on business in California. Of how it wasn't even Max's voice any more, but Veronica's? Of how she'd hung up quickly?

Should she tell them of how the cab driver had taken her in to the hospital and handed her over to reception like she was a parcel? Of the whole bloody awful build-up? Of how she was left on her own for what seemed like hours at a stretch? Of how the sheer bloody agony brought on strange, previously unheard, deep-throat screams and primal yells as she'd bawled the hospital down? Of how she'd needed to do that? She'd needed to scream that

44

loud. She'd needed to do it for years and years and years.

And then.

Then.

Of how it all turned round.

The sudden, overwhelming peace.

The end of the pain and the immediate, instantaneous entrance into a new existence. Like someone had heard her screams and had come along and wrapped her in the softest cotton wool. Had stroked her. Held her. A cocoon where only the tiny damp little creature she held mattered. She just hadn't been prepared for it. She'd heard about it and read about it in countless articles but it still came as a complete surprise. A love without all the questioning, anxiety, trauma and insecurity that had been such an integral part of her relationship with Max. A worse love. A love full of the deepest, darkest fear. Fear of harm, of the danger, of the big, cruel world out there her vulnerable little living thing was going to have to get by in. Was this the fear that Max had felt? So much earlier than she? Was it more than a horror of three-piece suites and Sunday barbecues? Of course it was. This thing went straight down to the depths of existence.

She'd had to concede that it was, after all, she who had changed. Not he. It was hard for her; for Max it had to be as difficult in a different way. He couldn't just dump Veronica. She knew that. He owed so much to her. Even though she was younger than him, the same age as Molly, she'd started him on his career proper, the most important thing in Max's life. Making him leader of her team. Her star reporter. Now he was stuck there, suffocating beneath her feathers.

Should she tell them of how she wondered where he was? What was he doing in those moments? Missing it all. *Where was Max?*

'So,' the woman was saying, 'that was it really. I was back home before I knew it. I had to be, my husband was going off to the States the next day.'

'Thank you, Becky.'

Tamara looked at Molly, smiled and nodded.

They all looked at Molly.

Get me out of here, she thought. She stuck to the birth without the frills and found, with careful editing, she enjoyed the telling of it. When Gayle, Katie and Sukie had finally arrived at the hospital, they were kind and tried to be helpful. Overbusying and fussing, squabbling over the CDs with arguments about whether James Taylor, Aretha Franklin or The Clash were the most appropriate. Lighting candles and mopping her brow, while Amanda, on her mobile, paced up and down from a safely distant pub. As much as she loved them, they weren't Max. They went off and brought back presents and said polite things, as she herself had done when her friends had gone through it. She'd known what they were thinking because she'd done it too. Another chum down the tubes. Another one who wouldn't be coming out to play any more. Another one who'd just willingly handed her soul, body and life over to someone else.

Now she was the one who'd gone over to the

other side. Like a death. But what kind of a strange world had she got herself into? How was she going to cope with all of this?

'Of course they'd be married,' said Amanda on the phone later. 'It's a post-natal group, you dummy. Most people with babies, you are going to find, are married.'

'That's not what the statistics say. But where did they *find* them, Mand?'

'Find who?'

The men. I mean, there are men, there are men here who will get up in the middle of the night to change a nappy. There are men who will sit through seventeen hours of labour. There are men —'

'Have you met any of them yet?'

'No, but —'

'Well, there you go.'

'Are you saying they don't exist?'

'No, no. But then maybe I do mean that. On one level.'

'But, I mean, Mand. We think we've hit the jackpot if we find one who's ...'

'Not married?'

'Of course not married. Say, vaguely single.'

'Not a thicko?'

'Not a thicko, well, hopefully vaguely intelligent, and not on the skids, let's say.'

'Not ugly?'

'Not actively ugly, say, you can't have everything, who'll deign to stay the whole night if we should get so lucky as to ...'

47

'Speak for yourself, hon.'

'Oh come on, Amanda. You know what I mean.'

'Why don't you ask your new friends where they found them and I'll be right over.'

'Friends? I'd have more in common with a bunch of Senegalese scaffolders. They don't even know I'm on my own yet.'

'Whoa-ho. You'd better watch it then, hon. When they find out your baby's got a married dad they'll be getting their balls and chains out.'

'I wish I'd never gone, Mand. I was really very happy here until I went to that wretched meeting.'

'How's it all going, then?'

'Daisy is utterly, totally adorable. I never knew it would feel like this. You must do it, Mand. You must before it's too late.'

'Molly darling,' she said in a completely different tone of voice, 'do you remember, not so long ago, how you used to say that what you've just said to me is the most annoying, irritating, patronising, *pissing-off* statement any woman can make to any other woman? EVER!'

'Yes, but . . .'

'So cut it. It's not for me, hon. Now respect – OK?'

'OK, I'll stick to the drawbacks, shall I?'

'Stick to what you like but never say it again.'

'Would it make you happier if I told you it's like walking around balancing a pile of bricks on your head with your hands tied behind your back, forbidden to sit down, eat, sleep, let alone read – ever?'

'Sounds more like the truth of it, hon.'

'That *Coronation Street* and the *Countdown*

conundrum are the highlights of my day, that my figure is that of an orange, that my legs are like tree trunks and if you really want to know the intimate stuff, I'm still wearing M&S mega-sized cosy-cotton huge baggy knickers. And I won't go into any more detail than that. It's something you may never have to know about.'

'All right, all right, enough. You'll be telling me about the birth next.'

'Well, actually, that's what we did at this meeting! And—'

'Don't you *dare* or I'll cut you off. What's that noise?'

'Sorry. Hang on a minute.' Molly pulled the flex of the phone out to its full length and moved from the hallway, next to a violently rumbling, vibrating washing machine, into the kitchen. 'That better? And I've aged, Mand. Oh, how I've aged. You know all those hormones that make you glow and breathe beauty? They drop out with the baby. Instantaneously. Still. She's the beauty now. She's utterly stunning, Mand.'

'So Katie and Gayle said.'

'*Did* they?' She felt a proud lift in her chest.

'Yes, yes, yes.'

'Well, I'm sorry you can't make it with Sukie tomorrow. When do you want to come? The week-end? Next week, any day's fine by me.'

'I, er, yes, I will come.'

'Soon?'

'Soon. It's this presentation. It's taking all my time. I *so* want to, of course I do.'

'You've got to, Mand. She *is* gorgeous.' Molly moved back into the hall and hooked the phone under her chin while she crouched down to empty the washing. 'Oh, I'm sorry, I'm beginning to sound like one of those things I promised I wouldn't.'

'A mother, Moll. You're a mother now.'

Oh dear, Molly said to herself, momentarily overwhelmed by a sense of loss as she put the phone down. She looked across the hallway through to the front-room window. Outside, yards from where she was standing, stood three lanes of static traffic. The nightly weekday jam. More like Watford Gap than Kew, she thought, as she tucked her hair behind her ear with one finger.

She tried Max's office again. She was more worried about him than angry now. Supposing he'd had an accident? Before he'd even set eyes on Daisy. He had to at least see her. Even if it was only the once.

CHAPTER FOUR

'Fridge, freezer, vegetables, cupboard. Fridge, fridge, freezer, cupboard. Vegetables, fruit, freezer, fruit,' Molly recited like a wonky mantra as she hurriedly emptied the blue and white Tesco bags piled up on her tiny work surface.

'And that was Leapy Lee, there ... leeeaping along there with his Little Arrows. And now, here's Buddy Holly with 'True Love Ways'.

'That's more like it, Jimmy,' she said as she shoved the bags under the kitchen sink, picking at a Mr Muscle lid at the same time. It seemed now so clearly, laughably impossible for fastidious, steel and chrome, all-Conran, black leather-sofa Max ever to fit into her cluttered jumble of an existence. She'd already had many moments of extreme gratitude that she didn't have to make any kind of effort at keeping herself presentable, within her four walls at least.

She surveyed the sparse, botched-together kitchen. It was just as well he hadn't come round. He'd die! But then, it was beginning to look as though he'd been and done that already. Molly's mother-

worrying thoughts flashed between various scenarios. Maybe the car back from Heathrow had crashed. Maybe he wasn't on the plane? Perhaps there'd been a car accident in LA; perhaps Veronica was in the car as well. Molly pulled her Mr Muscle trigger really hard and squirted a big one. Maybe *she'd* died and he survived? Or had he died and she survived?

She aimed at the sink and fired.

She was still pondering which way round the fates had intervened, revving up to put the kettle on, when she stepped into something wet.

'Damn, damn and bugger-damn,' she said, looking down at the small ice-cold pond forming in front of the clapped-out fridge. She poked around the little hole at the back with a chopstick, singing along with the radio at the top of her voice to try and make herself feel better. The bounciness of 'I'm A Believer' turned her dim, gutter-poking slimy chore into a happy-clappy healthy breeze, perversely satisfying even, as she picked out the grey browny gunge and tattered stray strings of spring-onion leaf with her stick. In mid-poke, she suddenly stopped. As if from the dead, Max's rich voice was booming out of the hallway.

'*Molly. Are you there? Hello. Hell-oh-ho...*' all bright, then a serious, slightly deflated, '*OK ... I'm er, I'm leaving this message at eleven thirty and...*'

She snapped the radio off and raced out of the kitchen, skidding on her wet feet and falling halfway to the ground as she went.

'I didn't hear it ring!'

'What's happened?'

'Didn't you get my messages?'

'Is everything all right?'

'Fine,' she said, unable to resist a loaded pause at the end.

'Look, I'm really, really sorry I haven't got there.'

'Are you?' Flat monotone.

'It's, there's, I've been insanely busy, Molly, I've only just got your messages. What's happened?'

'What do you mean, *what's happened*?'

Another silence.

'I – I really don't know how to...'

'I know, I know. But, Max. You've *got* to see her. You've got to. She's looking even more like you now than she did when she was born.'

'Really?'

'Max, you must.'

'Molly, I can't.'

Molly suppressed her gut response and pushed on. 'Well, we could come up to town then,' she said breezily. 'Meet somewhere?'

'It's not that – it's just I'm—'

'It's really important, Max. Even if it's just the once. She's *smiling*.'

'Look, it's—'

'Max, look, just for five minutes? No strings, I promise.'

'I'm in Venezuela, Molly,' he said quietly.

'Venezuela?! But you've only just got back from the States!'

'That's why I didn't call. As soon as I got back I literally had to turn straight around and go back to Heathrow again.'

She suddenly felt very, very tired. 'I see.'

'It's a breaking story so I had to get here fast. Molly – I'm the only London reporter here, it could be a coup. For me, I mean, not Venezuela. Well, I do mean for them too. It looks like it's all turning pear-shaped here in a big way.'

Molly swallowed hard. Arguing was pointless once he was onto a lead.

'The revolution's revolving, Moll. The middle classes are all leaving Caracas by the planeload!'

'I don't know anything about Venezuelan politics, Max, and I don't *want* to know anything about Venezuelan politics. When are you coming back?'

'I'm – I'm not quite sure. Look – there's a cheque in the post?'

'I don't want your money, Max.'

'You're not back at work already, surely?'

'Of course I'm bloody well not back at work, unless you call being on twenty-four-hour … Oh, forget it!'

'Then you need money.'

'I'm all right for now. It's Daisy, she needs…' Molly's voice trailed away before it wobbled into oblivion. The last thing she wanted to do was cry all over him.

Molly let the silence ride as the exclamation marks in Max's brain fired across the Atlantic static.

'Listen, I am thinking about you, about it all, Molly. Believe me.'

'Well, thanks. I *know* it's difficult for you, Max. But it's *you* who's missing out. Look, you just get on with your coup, all right? And don't worry about us.

Just come and see us soon. And remember. No strings, OK?'

She put the phone down slowly. Well, stuff him. It was he who was missing it all. He'd come. In, it had to be, his own way, his own time. Once he'd got that head unstuck from the sand. Max didn't like being told what to do any more than she did. For all their differences they had so much in common.

She heard Daisy stirring. She went into the front room of the flat, which, apart from the unspeakably horrible plastic stone fireplace dominating one wall, she'd managed to turn into quite a decent baby room.

'It's all right for your dad, isn't it, he's only got a South American coup to deal with, not a big tiny baby like you!'

Daisy screwed up her face crossly as she bent down to pick her up.

Vaughan Munro was on the radio singing 'There I've Said It Again' in the scratchy, distant 1940s. She turned the radio up loud and, with Daisy under one arm, danced around the kitchen, determined to get a cup of tea in before Daisy's next feed.

'Never mind. We'll be all right won't we. Hey? We'll get along just fine. And today we're in an extra hurry. Shall I tell you why? Your Auntie Amanda'll be here soon.'

'I thought you said you lived in Kew!' Amanda marched straight through the hall and plonked a long, thin Oddbins carrier on the kitchen worktop. She looked back sharply at Molly, who was still standing with the front door open.

'This, Amanda, is Daisy,' she said sternly.

Amanda put her hands on her hips. 'Molly, you didn't tell me you lived on a *motorway*.'

'Dai – SY, it means Day's Eye.'

'It's the effing M3 out there, Molly!'

'Or Eye of the Day and it's not motorway till after Feltham.'

'Molly, how could ...' She leant over the sink and looked up again as a plane flew directly overhead, drowning her last words.

'I told you. It was all I could afford. This,' Molly repeated, ' is Daisy.'

'Oh, Molly.' She slapped her hand to her forehead, 'I'm sorry. I'm supposed to do the cooing noises now, aren't I?' She peered down at Daisy, not saying anything for a while. 'I mean, if they had *fur* ...'

'Amanda! At least try to show some interest, can't you? Things are tough enough as it is.'

'You want me to put it on a bit, do you? Come on Moll, where's your sense of humour gone? Does that go too when you reproduce? Remember your promise at the Portobello?'

'How I swore I wouldn't become a baby bore? How I'd never in a million years get one of those ridiculous Baby on Board stickers?' said Molly meekly.

There was an awkward silence.

'Molly, you haven't, have you?'

'No, Amanda. I have not. Not quite. But, well, it's all different now. Things do change. It's amazing.'

'Molly.' It was Amanda's turn to sound stern.

Then she laughed. 'Come on, put that baby down and let's have a drink.' She pulled out a bottle of champagne and started opening all the peeling brown melamine cupboards which still had doors on them.

'Do you have any glasses? Now, come on, tell me, Moll. Why?'

'Why what?'

'This!' She waved her arm around the kitchen. It's a classic "Ghaad, who on earth would live in a house like that?" house you pass on the motorway.'

Molly laughed; she always found Amanda's directness refreshing.

'It's very handy for petrol.'

'You're an original, Moll, I'll give you that,' Amanda said, reaching up to a top cupboard.

'I had no choice, Mand. Anyway, I *like* it.'

Amanda held each glass in turn up to the light.

'It's home now. And it's lovely out the back, come and see. I always wanted a garden.'

'But you had a garden in Ladbroke Grove. One and a half acres of it, I seem to remember.' Amanda rinsed the glasses out under the tap. 'Where're the tea towels?'

Molly went to the airing cupboard in the cramped hallway between the kitchen and the back bathroom and threw her a clean but crinkled red-checked cloth.

'That was communal. Here I can grow things and Daisy can play out in the summer. You'd never know there were three lanes of traffic on the other side of the house. And then Kew Gardens is just ten minutes' walk away. It's just bliss to walk in there with the pram. They've even got sea horses.'

'Sea horses! You need a decent flat, Molly, not sea horses.' Amanda held the glasses to the light, inspecting them closely.

'When did you last see a sea horse in Holland Park?'

'You'll have an allotment next, and a compost heap. You'll start watching all those gardening programmes and growing hairy legs.'

'Oh I do. I love them. Gardening programmes I mean, not hairy legs. Though actually ...'

'I don't want to know, Moll.'

Molly laughed. 'Come on, come and see the garden. I'll just put Daisy down; I timed your visit for naptime, you'll be pleased to hear.'

While Molly put Daisy in her bed, Amanda tiptoed around as if the flat were going to bite her. She stood stiffly, hands on hips, looking suspiciously at the expanse of grass before stepping down awkwardly in her heels from the crumbling mossy concrete patio onto the lawn. Low wire fences separated rows of gardens dotted with fruit trees and spring flowers beneath a big, open sky.

'Normandy skies, aren't they?' Molly threw some cushions onto the lawn. 'This was all one big orchard once, before the houses were built. That's why there're so many trees. That one there at the end, that's a pear, and this one we're under is a cherry.'

'It's not Lansdowne Crescent though, is it?'

'Oh stop comparing everything, Amanda.'

Amanda sat down carefully, sliding her black-stockinged legs to one side of her pencil-thin skirt. 'Let's make this a big one.' She sat upright and pointed the bottle of champagne away from her. The cork exploded into the air.

'Shhhhhh, you'll wake Daisy.'

'Oops. Sorry, Moll. I forgot.'

She offered Molly a cigarette before withdrawing the packet quickly, 'You don't mind if I smoke?'

'It doesn't bother me now.'

'So there's something to be said for childbirth after all? A bit more of a result than a double dose of Nicorette?'

'I'm worn out but not stressed out. It's a big difference.'

'You win that one, hon. I've given up giving up now, the strain was killing me.' She took a long, slow drag and blew the smoke into the air.

'At least it keeps you thin.' Molly looked Amanda up and down enviously.

Amanda ignored her. 'Big BIG changes since you left.'

'Don't tell me! Who's moved in now? Marlon Brando? Or has Madonna changed houses again? No – I know, the Lark Bar's replaced its coked-up star-spotters with a new breed of hetero single men in their forties?"

'Down-dating,' said Amanda triumphantly, taking a long whiff of her cigarette.

'Nnnn?'

'Everyone's doing it.' Amanda stretched her legs out in front of her.

'Come on, I've only been gone a few weeks.'

Amanda laughed.

'Stop it, Amanda, and tell me what you're on about.'

'Do you remember that cute porter at the Portobello?'

'Yeees,' said Molly slowly.

'Suddenly we've all got dates. *All* the time. Sukie's with CS, her plumber, he's a bit short but, as she says, it doesn't matter when you're lying down, does it? And Katie's found a postman – in Acton of all places, and you should see him! My dear.'

Molly felt a pang of hurt.

'They kept that quiet! Why didn't they tell me?'

Amanda half-closed her heavily mascara'd eyes dreamily. 'And I've found Vince.'

'The porter?'

Amanda leant forward excitedly. 'It's the *answer*, Moll. They get food and sex on a plate and think they've died and gone to heaven. They're so grateful! We went to a Debbie Donald dinner party the other night and he was the biggest hit, I can't *tell* you.'

'Has it really got to that?' asked Molly in a queer lemony voice.

'And my dear, the sex!! I took him to the Venice Biennale last weekend, I thought he was twenty-six but I got a look at his passport and he's only twenty-*three*!'

Molly shook her head. 'Desperate!'

'It's a darned sight better than the shamble of gays and marrieds we've been used to. Besides, my job gives me enough brain exercise. I don't *need* to discuss the latest Saatchi acquisitions when I get home from work, all I want is food, a fuck and a cuddle.'

'Amanda, you're sounding like a man!'

'Why not? They've done it for years.'

'I think I got out just in time.'

'And into what?'

'Max phoned this morning,' said Molly quietly.

'And?'

'He's in bloody Venezuela, isn't he?'

Amanda gave a low whistle. 'So he *still* hasn't seen her?'

'Give him time.'

'Still hoping?'

'He's confused.'

'Ah.'

'It's like, you know, how men have a compartment for everything in their brains? He doesn't know where to put us, that's the problem.'

'Hon, he needs to open a whole new bloody filing cabinet.'

'He's scared.'

'That's one way of putting it.'

'Scared to see the face of his own future staring back at him.'

'You're too kind to him, Molly.'

'What the hell else can I do?'

'Call him a few names, get it off your chest. It'd do you good.'

'At least he's totally reliable in his unreliability.'

'Puh!'

61

'I *know* him, Amanda. And what's more I know what has happened is good.'

There was a squeak and a click of the gate at the side of the house.

'Hello, who's this?' Amanda looked across.

'Oh, just Mrs Constandavalos from upstairs,' said Molly, nodding and smiling. The old Greek lady smiled and nodded back, her ancient lawnmower tinkling along behind her as she dragged it up the side path to her back half of the garden.

'You could claim maintenance, you know?'

'Declare war, you mean. No way. I'll manage. It's not as if I'm the only single parent in the world, is it? Though it bloody well feels like it here. Meantime I'm free to date other men. Har har.'

'Just stay away from those husbands!'

'Phffffff!'

'Haven't you sent him a photo?'

'God, no.'

'Why not? He's got to be *so* curious.'

'He'll come. I know he will.'

Amanda shook her head pityingly.

Molly ignored her. 'It's like when men spend ages in the loo. They haven't all got dysfunctional bowels. They go off there to think, don't they? That's what Max is doing. He's having a big long sit on the loo.'

'As opposed to a big long shit.'

'All right, all right.' Molly laughed and took a long sip of champagne, 'Mmm, I'm so glad booze doesn't taste like vinegar any more.'

The rhythmic whirr of blade against ground was

soon filling the air, followed by the sweet fresh-pea smell of cut grass.

'When are you going back to work then?' Amanda refilled Molly's glass.

Molly swallowed hard, '*How* am I going to go back to work again? I wouldn't even have the energy to get there, let alone be of any use to anyone. Not till the end of the summer anyway. If I go carefully. I've paid off all my credit cards. Can you believe that? And I've cash in the bank; I've never been so well off.'

'It'll run out, hon.'

'I'm on a big economy drive, as much as you can be with a new baby. And I don't exactly go *out* any more, do I?'

'It'll still go, hon. Money does that, you know. You only had one flat to sell.'

'I know. I know. But this place is dirt cheap. Especially for the area.'

'For the *area*?'

'If you go five minutes down the road you're in a different world, Mand. There's a village, a pond, a Green, cricket—'

'Since when have you been into cricket!'

Molly ignored her, '. . . everything. It's heaven. And the Gardens, Mand, you should see the Gardens.'

'What'll you do when you go back then?' Amanda screwed up her face and looked up as a JAL jumbo flew over. 'Look at that, you can almost see what they're having for lunch.'

'Something bland and local,' said Molly, ignoring it, 'enough to pay the rent, you know. And a child-

63

minder,' she added slowly. 'Ugh, I hate even saying that word. A quiet office job at the Gardens, maybe,' she went on brightly, 'or the Public Records Office or something.'

'Molly, it sounds like you're retiring! You can't have given up on life that much.'

'My life's just beginning, Mand.'

Amanda grunted and lit another cigarette.

'I wish I hadn't gone to that bloody meeting, though. I felt such a freak.'

'It's them who are freaks, darling. Believe me.' Amanda stubbed her cigarette out on the lawn, the end of the filter covered in red lipstick.

'Apart from anything else they're all at least ten years younger than me. Do you realise one of them could be *twenty* years younger than me! I'd been doing a good job of forgetting I was actually forty till I met them. Now I'm reminded of it all the time. Even on the bloody road outside here there's a little round "40" stuck onto every lamp-post. And then if I told them Daisy's dad's married, they'll immediately think ...'

'Don't tell them. Lie. Say anything. Say it was a one-night stand or something.'

'Amanda, that's *terrible*. I'll probably never see them again anyway. Penelope Leach'll see me through.'

'Who?'

Molly sat up. 'Why a one-night stand?' she back-tracked, 'Come on, tell me, what's everyone been saying about me? Has there been any kind of talk going round?'

'If you want to be frank about it,' Amanda said without a beat, 'did you? Did you have the baby for yourself? Or for Max?'

'Of course I had her for myself! But because I *love* – loved Max. I wanted *his* child.'

'But he didn't.'

'Maybe he *will*. It was something I had to do, Amanda.'

'You didn't *have* to.'

'But that's it. I did! And I *know*, I know it even more now she's here, and I'm here, looking like I do and with my bank account in free fall.'

'There's no taboo about not falling for the biggest con trick in the world any more, you know. It's not called childless, it's called child-*free*.'

'It's scary but it's put everything into perspective somehow. It's, like, I know I've got nothing but I've got everything at the same time.'

'What about Veronica?' said Amanda quietly.

'All right, a wobbly perspective. But everyone knows Veronica Bulford-Boyd has a *string* of lovers.'

'Do you *know* that?'

'Come off it, Amanda, you know it's true. So, people have been saying I've been selfish, have they?'

'Well, it is a bit, isn't it?'

'Having a child is selfish whoever, however and whenever. If you're broke and on your own or if you're here in functional fucking family land. It's just what it's all about. All this *stuff* ...' Molly waved her arm around at the garden. 'And, you can tell them from me as well that whatever happens, no one's going to feel sorry for Daisy, ever.'

'All right, all right.'

'I just don't know how the hell I'm going to fit in round here. It's like one of those ghastly Caribbean resorts which doesn't let anyone in except couples. Stopstopstop! Why are we discussing this? I need never see them again if I don't want to.'

'You're not forced to go, are you?'

'No, of course not. At least you're still *out* there, Amanda.'

'Out where?'

'The world of tormented relationships.'

'The satellite world of the Gate? Come on, you're not telling me you're missing that snakepit, are you?'

As the bottle got emptier the chat got lighter and sillier and Amanda was just saying it was almost like old times when a little whimper came from behind the white muslin curtain, followed by a bellowing yell that got louder and more urgent by the second.

Amanda sighed and lit another cigarette.

Molly rushed inside, picked up Daisy and took her into the kitchen. She wasn't going to come in for more scat by feeding Daisy in front of her. She switched on the radio and the kettle and jiggled Daisy around, ignoring the music, moving to no song but the baby's heart and hers. Jig-a-gig, jiga-jiga jerky jig. Daisy glared up with Max's beside-himself furious frown on her face.

'Moll,' Amanda said as she rushed into the kitchen, 'I've just realised what time it is. I have to go, hon, I should have been at a preview, like, ten minutes ago.' She bent over to Daisy. 'Bye-bye-bye little one, look after your mom.' She stood back and looked at her with her head on one side, 'You know, she does look like Max, doesn't she?'

'They all do, apparently,' said Molly crossly.

'Look like Max?'

'Like their dads. Something to do with the bonding process.'

'Typical,' said Amanda.

'What?'

The kettle whistled.

'They would go for little copies of themselves, wouldn't they.'

'They might if they could be bothered to find out they existed.'

'Perhaps that's what he's scared of.'

'What do you mean?'

'Bonding. If he sees her and falls for her, he's done for, isn't he?'

'Thanks very much.'

'Sorry. But you know what I mean.'

'We'll be all right. We'll get by. Millions of children get by without their dads. It's not exactly rare any more, is it? Loads even find new dads,' she added faintly, aware she was open to argument there. Molly hadn't taken to her own stepfather at all.

'If anyone can do it you can, Moll. You'll come out the other side laughing, I'm sure of that.' Amanda took her lipstick and compact out of her tiny patent handbag and went across to the window. 'Got to dash.' Amanda pressed her shiny red lips together. She took one last look in her mirror before snapping it shut with the flourishing movements of finality. 'I'm gone.'

Amanda looked at the radio, then quizzically at Molly like she was, for once, lost for words. 'Bye, darling.' She kissed her on both cheeks.

'We'll speak on the phone then,' said Molly brightly, escorting her to the door, with a strong feeling they probably wouldn't. Not for quite some time.

Molly took her cup of tea through to her back room and settled back on her bed to feed Daisy, humming along to the final refrains of 'Swinging on a Star'.

She thought about the different universes of Amanda and her old friends and the Kew women. It wasn't just her flat that was in no-man's land. It was her whole life.

Where was she going to fit in?

She couldn't go back to the Gate for a pint and a fuck with a bit of rough any more than she could share in the cosy, pampered lives of those Kew mothers. The other option, to join the tough but mutually supportive world of single mums on benefit, wasn't only daunting, it was impossible. They'd be even younger – hang on, their *mothers*'d be younger than her!

As she looked down at Daisy, suckling contentedly, she decided. She'd give it one more try. She'd go to Land Rover Caroline's. If just to see how the other half really did live.

CHAPTER FIVE

Molly slapped her moisturiser on by memory rather than facing the shock of what might lurk in the mirror. It was four thirty a.m. and Daisy had only just dropped off after hours of middle-of-the-night alertness.

'All on half a bottle of champagne,' she muttered as the cream slid across the surface of her skin, 'and to think I used to get away with twice that for lunch.'

She gave in to gravity and let her eyes close as she brushed her teeth and her tongue over and over until the taste of the toothpaste made her feel sick.

Four hours later, as they crossed Kew Green, Daisy woke up. Starving. Molly stopped by the pond, rocking the car seat in her arms.

'Look, Daisy!' she said with exaggerated excitement, waggling her at the flotilla of ducks, geese and moorhens who, knowing that miniature people and food came in a package, were gliding confidently across the pond towards them. Daisy couldn't focus that far yet and wasn't impressed. Her screams ricocheted across the water, stopping even the birds in their tracks. She wanted only one thing, which was tucked away in a 38D inside Molly's dress.

Molly stopped outside Caroline's to check the number against her list. Most of the late Georgian houses had been converted into mini blocks of flats, but this one was all on its own with an in-out gravel driveway and a big, bossy sign saying No Circulars.

She pressed the round bell in the middle of the wide black door.

'Sorry I'm late, bit of a hangover, I'm afraid. On top of everything else, that is.' Molly indicated to the screaming car seat.

Caroline looked at Daisy approvingly, ignoring her screams. 'Gooood. I'm so glad there's someone around here who's still got a life.'

Her fully formed opinions of Caroline began to shift and change as she followed her down a long, broad parquet-floored hallway. Her eyes squinted in the light as she stepped into an enormous glass room which covered the entire back of the house.

Tamara was sitting on a piano stool in front of the others who were sprawled on two huge, sun-baked tapestry sofas. Outside, stripes of freshly mown lawn sloped down to the willow-fringed river where a turquoise-tiled, kidney-shaped swimming pool glistened in the sun.

'Excuse the mess.' Caroline threw her eyes towards the vast expanse of emptiness. 'We've only just got rid of the builders.'

Izzie turned round. 'Don't talk to me about builders.'

'No, I won't,' said Caroline crisply.

Daisy was still in full yell. Molly put the car seat down next to Charles, who was reclining regally in his baby bouncer.

'Sorry, guys,' said Molly, crouching down in front of Daisy, 'she's had no breakfast. We've had a bit of a night.'

She picked her up and sat down next to Jenna, who was already feeding Lulu. Molly tucked the unzipped cup of her already greying feeding bra awkwardly into her dress.

'I'm glad to see so much breastfeeding,' observed a beaming Tamara. 'Did they all clamp on without any difficulties, ladies?'

Jenna smiled smugly at Molly as she pushed the top of her breast down delicately with two fingers to clear Lulu's nose from her bosom.

'Remember, ladies, look after your nipples! They're all you've got. They can get sore just like baby's bottom. Think baby's bottom. Mummy's nipple. Dry and flaky, damp and soggy, both unpleasant. Do dry both carefully after feeding and cleaning. A few sacrifices from you will see baby's immune system set up for life.'

'Sacrifices?' said Molly. 'It's got to be easier than bottles with all the sterilising, measuring, scoops and fumbling around in the kitchen in the middle of the night.'

'You know, ladies, I expect some of you enjoyed a drink before your little darlings came along. Of course you can't have any alcohol and you should watch your diet as well. No curries!' she laughed, 'or baby will have some decidedly peculiar poos!'

Molly swallowed deeply.

'Which brings us neatly on to our subject for this week,' Tamara continued in the hazy background of Molly's thoughts. 'We'll be doing poos and wees now and then get on to solids next time. They kind of follow one another, don't they, ladies?' She laughed. It was a mocking laugh, as if to say that life's a joke, but not a funny one, a sick one.

Molly felt the fizz in her nose which meant she was blushing. She looked across at Caroline, who winked, then down at her irreversibly contaminated child. Guilt consumed her as she watched Daisy, eyes half-closed, glugging away at the undoubtedly undiluted Moët flowing from her bosom. No wonder she'd had an unsettled night. Molly had introduced her baby to all-night boozing at the tender age of two months.

Caroline leant over to Molly and whispered stoically, 'Start 'em young, that's what I say.'

'Excuse me?' said Tamara.

Caroline ignored her, 'Who wants tea? Hippy or ordinary?' She went to the door and called into the hall, 'Ulé, darling, can you come down?'

'Do you have any herbals?' Jenna stood up and put the blissfully zonked Lulu in her car seat. Molly and Izzie stared as she tightened her thick black patent belt across her hollow stomach.

'Jenna!' said Izzie accusingly. 'Ten weeks ago you gave birth!'

'Yeah, I'd noticed?' she said, not noticing.

'Typical thin person,' Izzie confided to Molly, 'doesn't even appreciate what she's got.'

Molly's heart sank at this sudden confirmation of her inclusion in the world of thin-envy, a future of diet hell looming before her already restricted existence.

She turned back to Jenna. 'Are you sure your Jason didn't have that baby for you? How did you get your stomach back?'

'Don't tell me, you go to the gym twice a day,' said Izzie.

'A little, mainly yoga and t'ai chi?'

'No Pilates, then?' Molly said over-seriously.

'I tried that but I'm just starting balletcise, it's more fun. I've just found a great class in Richmond, the teacher's fantastic...'

'Enough, enough, you're making me feel knackered just talking about it.' Izzie looked at Molly in collusion. 'Some of us are too far gone to bother now.' She vibrated in a low machine-gun-like laugh while Molly concentrated hard on keeping her expression polite.

'Where do you get the *time*, Jenna?' she said conversationally. Jenna ignored her as they all turned to look towards the door. A young girl appeared. She had a slight stoop, which made her thin, centrally-parted dark hair fall down in front of her face. A voice murmured hello from beneath the hair curtain, a deep, husky voice which belied her fragile frame.

'This, everyone, is Ulé. My nanny.'

'Au pair,' said the voice.

'I may as well introduce you now as she'll most probably be bringing Charles to some of the meetings. Later on. After we've got through these first few months. Of course.' She smiled at Tamara. She didn't introduce them by name to Ulé, who sat down on the sofa looking straight ahead with wide expressionless eyes.

'Where are you from, Ulé?' asked Jenna.

'Poland,' she replied sullenly.

'Cool,' said Jenna, bending over to play with Lulu's feet. 'Come on, Lu, give us a smile.'

'What does your husband do, then, Caroline?' Izzie said casually, voicing what Molly was dying to ask but wouldn't have dared.

'Theo? He's a lawyer.'

Izzie looked at Molly and mouthed, 'Big dosh.'

Alarmed at Izzie's directness, Molly smiled at Caroline pleasantly. 'That's nice,' she said pathetically.

'Ulé, would you come and help me in the kitchen?'

Molly turned her smile to Jenna, who raised her pretty arched eyebrows but didn't smile back.

I want to go home, I want to go home.

'Right, ladies,' said Tamara, 'while we're waiting. Does anyone have any particular problems they'd like to share? Molly? Jenna?'

'Isn't it a neat garden?' said Jenna to no one in particular.

Izzie stood up and went over to the glass wall. She gave a low whistle. 'Will you just look at that!'

Molly went over to join her.

'Imagine having one of *those* at the bottom of your garden.'

'All I've got in my garden is a pond,' said Molly

74

wistfully, 'I used to love ponds, too. Now, every time I look at it, instead of water lily and newt thoughts I have attacks of *Titanic* horror-drowning imaginings.'

'Not the swimming pool – *that*!'

'*What?*'

'Him!' Izzie grabbed her arm and pulled her closer.

Molly, whose eyes had been naturally drawn to the sparkling turquoise tiles, followed Izzie's gaze to the octagonal summer house tucked beside the river.

'Oh, *that*.'

They both stood and stared. He was crouched down with his back to them, one knee up, sorting out rows of pots on the wooden terrace.

'I don't know how you can even think of guys,' said Jenna.

'We don't have to, there's one here,' said Izzie.

'Just the idea of sex makes me want to puke.'

'Speak for yourself,' said Izzie.

As if some sense told him he was being stared at, he turned and looked back.

Molly came away from the window quickly, leaving Izzie rooted to the spot. She took off her glasses and wiped them on her T-shirt, put them back on and leant forward as if she was looking through a pair of binoculars.

'He's waving at me!' said Izzie. 'Cooee.' She waggled her fingers.

'The pool's a bit of a worry, too, don't you think?' said Tamara.

'And the river,' added Molly.

'I'm sure Caroline's got that in hand. She seems such an efficient sort of a person, doesn't she?' said Tamara.

'I see you're admiring my garden,' said Caroline as she put the tray of cups down on the upholstered tapestry coffee table.

'It's beautiful,' said Molly.

'Isn't he?' laughed Caroline. 'My latest student from Kew. We get one every year. Ulé, would you mind, sweetheart?'

'From the Gardens?' said Tamara, obviously impressed, as Ulé began handing out the teas.

'Theo's an Associate,' she said, her voice going softer as they all looked out of the window, 'one of the perks. He's French.'

'Theo?' said Molly.

'No, no, my gardener, Christophe.'

'*Is* he?' said Izzie.

'Yes,' said Caroline slowly, running her tongue over her pink-glossed lips, 'yes indeed.'

'Right, ladies, shall we get on? said Tamara brightly. 'Where were we? Wees and poos. Now. Nappies. I want to have a little chat with you all about real nappies ...'

'Pah, as far as I'm concerned God made disposables for a reason,' said Izzie, 'just like he made epidurals, microwaves and Disney videos.'

'These might make you think again,' said Caroline. She unpopped Charles's Babygro to reveal his heavily embossed designer kookies. A dank, phosphorous farmyard smell wafted into the air.

'Charles *darling*!!' Caroline hastily pulled down his Babygro. 'Ulé. Would you mind?' she handed him over to Ulé who stomped across the room to the changing table. 'I'm *so* sorry.' Caroline smiled. 'Hobnob anyone?'

'I don't know how au pairs do it,' said Izzie. 'I mean, it's all right changing your own child. But changing someone else's.' She screwed up her face.

'They're like little flowers, aren't they?' said Tamara.

'Each with its own pong,' said Izzie. 'Anyway, if anyone's interested in trying Sainsbury's own I'll give you a couple – *bloody* hell Norah!' A look of horror silenced her in mid-sentence.

'What the –' said Jenna.

Tamara, in a whoosh of rustling silk and shriek, had flung herself in a dive to her left. A stream of liquid was jetting above their heads and landing right on her lap.

'Charles Charles CHARLES!' Caroline cried, rushing across the room.

They all looked round at the changing table.

Ulé, her mouth dropped open, was standing back with both hands in the air as the baby, looking like a cross between a cherub and a garden hose, spouted. Caroline rushed over and tried to stem the flow with both hands, which sent the jet stream off into different directions.

As one, they all ducked.

Caroline grabbed the clean nappy from Ulé. 'I'm so so sorry, Tamara.'

Tamara smiled tightly. 'Only a little bit of wee-wee, nothing to worry about. Anybody got a Wet Wipe?'

She left soon after, with mutterings about missing *Gardeners' Question Time*.

'Before we all go I want to take a photo of all the babies?' said Jenna, taking her camera out of her rucksack.

'Why don't we go in the garden?' said Caroline.

'Oh *yes!*' said Izzie, suddenly sitting up straight and looking out of the window.

'More tea, anyone? Ulé, can you get the picnic rug?'

With one eye on their babies, and another on the gardener, who kept his back firmly turned away from them, they chatted on and on about all the baby things they couldn't talk about to anyone else. Molly found herself knocking back the cups of tea like they were the Tequila Slammers of the old Bar Blanket Babylon days. Even the dads, they'd discovered, glazed over when it got to bodily functions. Molly, who'd had no one to discuss these things with laughed properly for the first time in a long time.

'I wish Tamara wouldn't use those *words*,' said Molly, 'they send a shiver right down my spine.'

'Like what?' said Jenna.

'Like *soggy nipples*, and "clean the folds of skin on the *groin* behind the *anus*". Ugh!'

'*Ointment*,' said Izzie, '*scab . . . CLINIC . . .*'

'*Stop* it!'

Charles's hosing seemed even funnier in retrospect,

and when Molly told everyone about her hangover, Izzie laughed so much she wet herself.

'Oof, I've sprung a leak,' she spluttered.

'Which end?' said Jenna.

'Bottom up.'

'Who's not been doing her pelvic floor exercises then?' said Caroline.

'It's all right for you Caesareans, isn't it.'

'And that's *another* thing the books gloss over!' said Molly with feeling.

'What,' said Izzie, 'saggy fannies?'

'I'm *amazed* we haven't had the pelvic floor lessons yet from Tamara. "Now ladies and after three – one, two and *squeeeze* your organs,"' said Caroline.

'Give your crotch a good clench, girls,' laughed Molly. 'And big feet are another one. Why don't any of these zillions of books *warn* you your feet grow a size so all your shoes will be useless forever after?'

'Good excuse to buy some more,' said Caroline with feeling.

Jenna moved her hand from side to side in front of Lulu's eyes. 'Look, she's following it! Clever Lulu... clever *girl*, yes!'

'I think it's time we offered Christophe a Hobnob, don't you?' said Caroline.

'He could hob my nob any time,' said Izzie.

'Come on,' said Caroline standing up. 'I'll introduce you.'

'Not *now*,' said Izzie, 'can't you get me a spare pair of knickers first? I don't want to meet him with a soggy crotch.'

'Of course darling, that comes later, doesn't it? Come with me.'

Caroline stood up, hugging herself inside her violet pashmina. 'Don't you find the spring so *annoying*?' Her voice faded as she went up the garden. 'Too warm for wool in the sun and too cool for cotton in the shade. I've got *both* wardrobes running and I never know which one to go to in the morning; even if it *looks* warm it might be *freezing* and vice versa. Theo's having to use one of the guestroom wardrobes.'

Molly felt she should say something to Jenna but couldn't think what. It all had gone very quiet.

Jenna lay back and soaked up the sun. 'This is one hundred per cent neat, isn't it?' she said. 'One hundred per cent.' She closed her eyes.

Molly tried to stem the surge of panic as she looked at the four babies suddenly under her sole supervision. She caught Bob's button eye. As soon as he'd focused on her his face screwed up in fury. Seconds later he was in full flood. She looked up the garden in vain for Izzie to come rushing. No Izzie. She picked him up. He cried harder. She cuddled him tight and walked around, feeling the resistance in him, amazed at how different he felt to Daisy. Though only slightly larger he felt so different to Daisy: heavier, but bonier. And his skin was pinker and more—folded—somehow.

What seemed like an age later, Izzie came running down the slope towards them. Molly gratefully handed Bob back.

'Christophe looks like he's ready for a tea break,'

said Caroline, 'come on, girls. Can someone bring the tray?'

They all stayed where they were and watched as Caroline approached him. He took his gloves off and wiped his brow.

Jenna, Izzie and Molly looked at each other, pausing in a bonded moment, before following Caroline down to the summer house.

Caroline introduced them. Molly noticed her cool veneer had evaporated into coy giggles as she twisted a strand of hair round her finger.

He politely shook hands with them then turned back to Caroline.

'I can now?' he asked.

'Of course.' She smiled.

He buried his face in her neck. Izzie put her hand to her mouth and squeaked. Caroline was visibly flushing. He stood back quickly, put his head in the air, closed his eyes for a second, sniffing the air like a mouse.

'Red Rose – Jo Malone.'

'Correct.' Caroline laughed delightedly.

'It's a little game we play,' she explained in a patronising, lower tone of voice to the others.

He went over to Jenna. Jenna jumped back.

'Ah, this is easy, the pure essence, lavender and bergamot,' he said without getting any closer.

'Right on!' said Jenna, visibly melting.

Aware she was just about to be identified as old sweat and baby vomit, Molly had to think quickly. In a life where going to the loo had become one of the luxuries of the day, a quick squirt with the plastic shower hose before it fell off the taps was as much as she could manage in the mornings. She was relieved to see Caroline handing him a mug of tea.

'How do you do that?' said Izzie admiringly.

'Christophe's a *nez*,' explained Caroline.

'Funny name for a gardener,' said Izzie.

'Let me explain,' he said, touching Izzie's arm lightly as he sat down on the step of the summer house and took a sip of tea. Molly had to consciously take her eyes away from his thighs as he spread his legs and leant on his knees, his hands dangling.

Whatever it is, just switch it *off*, can't you? thought Molly, obediently sitting down with the others around him. She absent-mindedly stroked Daisy's head before laying her gently on the soft pink rug with the other babies.

'I am a student here.'

'Really?' said Izzie, as if she hadn't been told already.

'I am on attachment. From my laboratory in Grasse.'

'A gardening laboratory?' said Molly.

`You could say in a way. It is a factory of the senses. I am a perfume student.'

'Oh,' said Jenna, 'cool. So, what are you doing here at Caroline's?'

'Like all students, I need the money.' He smiled.

'Christophe is an artist,' said Caroline firmly.

'And of course, being close to the plants,' he continued, 'is all. At Kew we each get some land to grow the vegetables. But I have to work with flowers. And I make the extra cash as well.'

'What's Kew got that Grasse hasn't?' asked Molly.

'Apart from sexy English girls?'

Oh come on, thought Molly.

'Apart from *beautiful* English girls.' He addressed Molly directly.

He's realised he's not got me, he's going to go for me now, old trick. Can't bear to have one not succumb. Even an old bat like me. Oh, being an old lady could be fun I guess, might make up for the huge dollop of naivety I've had all my life.

'I am studying especially one of the central ingredients to complete my perfume, the orchid,' Christophe turned and dug his trowel into a blue plastic bag of earth.

'To make a *new* perfume?' Caroline asked in a low, deeply interested, deeply serious voice. This was obviously news to her too.

He patted the earth down gently around the plant, before swiftly putting the pot to one side and picking up the next. His movements were quick and firm, but with a deft, authoritative elegance. A simple band of solid silver dangled from his left wrist. Fine-boned, delicate wrists, Molly noticed, but large hands, large competent hands.

'What will it be like – er, this perfume,' said Caroline.

'I will be taking the raw scent, the real essence of the flower. The essence is its blood, its personality. How can the chemicals take the place of the heart? Hein? The blood of the nature herself?'

No one spoke. Molly watched the fountain of rich, crumbling earth fall from his clenched fist into its pot.

'Isn't that what making perfumes is all about?'

He looked up sharply. 'Today there are too many computers, too many chemicals.'

'Gosh,' said Caroline.

'I will take the best of the new technology, but only for the orchid. For the orchid you have to do this.'

He took a tiny plant from a large white Perspex tray and transferred it to its new home in a skilful movement so swift he barely touched it. Molly felt a surge of ridiculous envy for the newly bedded pansy, knowing it would thrive under his expert eye.

'Look at you. You are all mothers. All of you. The most important thing, you have your babies. Irreplaceable? That is nature. Simple but not at all. And that, that will be my perfume. That is how it will be. I will squash the chemists back inside their test tubes with this. I will beat them.'

Molly believed him. Though young there was a strange maturity about him. Having just prided herself on seeing right through him, within those few minutes her fascination grew.

'The smell, it is so important in life, you know? Did you know your first bond with your babies?'

'That first look into their eyes,' said Izzie.

'Smell?' said Molly.

'Of course. But it is the smell of your scalp, did you know that?'

'Yuk,' said Izzie.

'Every part of your body has its smell.'

'*Don't* go there,' said Izzie.

84

'You don't smell with your nose, you smell with your brain. The nose is just the thing which leads to there. Smell is more important, more than sight, more than anything else. It probes the world always. For the bee the flower is its world. It is the same part of the brain which is to do with your emotional life and your memory, your love –'

He stopped, as if he was going to say something else but had then changed his mind. He had his head slightly to one side as he returned his concentration to filling the pots with earth. The note of liquid hitting cup was the only sound as Caroline poured more tea.

After what seemed like an age, he looked up. Directly at Molly.

'Do you, er, have a name for your perfume?' She kept her voice on an even keel.

Christophe laughed and gave her a mocking smile. Was she imagining he was paying her more attention than any of them? To make sure he'd won her over as well? She knew, he knew, he knew she knew, it was one of those looks. No. She had to be kidding herself. Jenna would obviously be the one he'd go for.

'If I did it would be one of my biggest secrets. A good perfumer has to be a good spy. We all spy on each other all the time, it's part of the job. But no, not yet. I am missing the final ingredients. This is why I am here. To find the last pieces of the puzzle.'

'I'd *no* idea!' said Caroline.

'It's why I know all your perfumes, of course. We break all the brands down into their individual pieces, to find out how they did it. It is like a writer has to read many books to find out how to write.'

He pulled out a packet of Duma tobacco from his shirt pocket. There was an elegant deftness to his fingers as he rolled the blue Rizla paper. He casually leant forward on his knees and crouched down over the lighter cupped in his hands.

Smoking suddenly looked so, so desirable again.

'I know,' said Caroline. She stood up and raced up the lawn.

'Where's she going?' said Izzie.

'This woman. She likes to test me.' Christophe smiled.

Caroline returned with a handful of perfume bottles. 'Now, Christophe, show us your stuff.'

She lined them up on the baby mat.

'Hey, mind the babies,' said Jenna, picking Lulu up. She turned her back to the group and unzipped her top.

Christophe watched her with no sign of embarrassment.

'What can you tell us about these?'

'You want me here all day?' he said, looking from Jenna's breast to Caroline to Molly. Molly quickly looked away. 'I cannot do too many in a short time. Did you bring the bread? Yes? Good. OK.'

'Just a couple then. You choose.'

She handed the bottles to him.

He went over to Caroline and took her arm.

'*Away* from the babies!' shrieked Jenna.

'Of course, of course.' He held up the green bottle and sprayed her wrist. Caroline rubbed her wrists together. 'No!' Christophe shouted. 'Never. Never never rub it in. You destroy the balance.'

He turned to Izzie. 'Here.'

Izzie held out her arm, straight, closed her eyes and screwed up her mouth like she was going to be injected.

He sprayed it in the curve of her arm.

Izzie jumped. 'Oooh, I wasn't expecting it there,' she laughed.

'This is where your skin is warm, your blood is near to the skin. Now, listen.' Christophe looked serious.

'Listen?'

'Shhhh. Let it evaporate,' he whispered.

'Listen to *what*?' Izzie persisted.

'This is Poison. This is not a pretty one, no? It is bold and daring. It is outrageous, this one. But it gets away with it. It is clever, a very clever Dior invention. Very creative.'

'What's this one got in it then?'

'Coriander and cinnamon. It has a cheek. You must be careful what to wear with this.'

'Wear?' Caroline jumped in.

'When you dress, you should begin with your perfume. Then you decide what to wear.'

'Chance would be a fine thing!' laughed Molly.

'Is that what French women do?' said Izzie.

'Of course,' he he replied with a shrug, 'this is something they grow up with.'

'I *knew* there was more to it than scarves,' said Caroline.

'So what do I wear with this one?' said Izzie.

'Your most exotic outfits.'

Izzie smothered a laugh.

'Your best jewels, fur, even.'

'Fur!' said Jenna, horrified.

'He means fake fur,' said Caroline, 'don't you?'

Christophe laughed and shook his head. 'You English!'

'I could run to my best leggings,' said Izzie. 'Never been worn, fresh from Primark last week. Would they do?'

'Otherwise, the perfume, it will wear you. People will say, ah she is not wearing that perfume, it is wearing her. This is what we say in France. It is the biggest insult.'

'So now what have you done to me?' said Izzie.

'A perfume tells a lot about you. Your personality.'

'This one's not for me, is it? What goes with leggings and T-shirts then?'

'You need something active.'

'You can say that again.'

'Like you are going for a run, no?'

'You must be bloody joking. Just so it'd *look* like I'd go for a run.' Izzie erupted into her rat-a-tat laugh as she turned to Molly for confirmation.

'L'Eau d'Issey might be good for you,' he said.

'Eau d'Izzie! It's on my Christmas list.'

'There are so many things ... so many. Then there are the bottles, the boxes, when you have your fragrance.'

'Try another,' said Caroline, handing him a bread roll. He broke the bread and sniffed it hard.

'Neutraliser,' said Caroline knowledgeably.

He took another bottle and went across to Molly.

'Your turn.'

She smiled gleefully. Damn!

He sprayed her arm.

'Oh, I know that one,' said Izzie. 'What is it?'

'Joy. Very expensive. Bulgarian rose and Grasse jasmine, such extravagance. It is rightly very famous, many women wear it, but many do not succeed. You must have supreme confidence, you must be ravishingly beautiful.' He paused and looked into Molly's eyes. 'It outdoes any other in its class, it is the top class, the first class. A secret combination of a hundred essences.'

'A bit like Maids of Honour?' said Izzie.

Caroline laughed scornfully. 'Maids of Honour!'

Christophe and Molly exchanged a puzzled look.

'Made from from a secret recipe hundreds of years old. You can only get them in Kew.'

'Puh, you obviously haven't read Nigella!' said Caroline.

'What do I wear with this one?' said Molly, screwing up her nose.

'Very, very bright pink.'

Molly screwed up her face, 'I don't think so somehow.'

'Or scarlet ...'

Izzie laughed. 'We're all going to have to get new wardrobes after this.'

'Or black. Black and white is good with this. Or metallic. A snappy Chanel suit. Party clothes. Be bold, very bold. Or it will overtake you and you will be left shrivelling in its wake.'

'I don't think it's quite me somehow.'

'What is your favourite perfume?' He sprawled out on the grass next to her.

'Shalimar.'

'Ah, Shalimar. Inspired by a shah's deepest love for his favourite wife. Did you know he built the Taj Mahal for her?'

He was addressing just Molly now.

Molly cleared her throat. 'No...'

'It's been around a long time.'

So have I, honey. 'Since when?'

'Since the 1920s. It was one of the first perfumes to use vanillin. It is one of the only synthetics I will use. It smells more like vanilla than vanilla itself. All the oriental perfumes have this.'

'So yours will?'

'Of course. Now I know you love this, I will remember that.'

'Oh, Molly,' said Izzie romantically.

Caroline looked at the sky.

'Oh, come off it,' said Molly, completely confused. If there was electricity zapping between them, it had to be her imaginary electricity. It couldn't possibly be real.

'Everything is an influence, no? The weather, the moods, the beauty you see ... if you are creative it affects your creations, it has to. Shalimar,' he said again. 'And remember, perfume is like a memory. It is something, when you pass by it comes after you. It touches something deep. It has the most influence.'

'She's not exactly dressed for Joy, is she?' said Caroline bitchily.

'Shalimar is a good choice for you,' he went on. 'It is a powerful aphrodisiac. Like Opium.'

'Too strong for me,' said Caroline.

'What would you wear with Shalimar, then?' asked Jenna.

'Black silk.'

Oh please, thought Molly. Stop it. Stop it, damn you, at the same time as thinking her crystal-clear credit card might just have to have a tiny little outing to the shops.

'I think it's time you got back to work, Christophe?' said Caroline coolly.

'*Donc – voilà!* ' Christophe slapped his thigh and smiled at her. 'I don't want to be in the, how do you call it, in the sack!'

'Yes, Christophe.' Caroline smiled back, in spite of herself, and gave Molly a raised-eyebrow, chance-would-be-a-fine-thing look.

'So. Next week then?' Christophe said to Caroline. 'You will be wearing a different test for me, yes?'

'The obscurest scent I can lay my hands on, Christophe. I promise,' said Caroline, a genuinely thrilled girly smile cracking her eyes as well as her mouth.

'Well, what about *that* then,' said Izzie as they walked back up the garden.

'All right,' said Jenna. 'If Jase wasn't in the world and if I ever felt like shagging again, which with my stitches I reckon is never at this rate, then I guess that one'd be in with a chance.'

'Shhhhh,' giggled Izzie, 'he'll *hear* you! Bloody hell Norah! Talk about son of Ginola!'

Molly said nothing, concentrating on getting her breathing back to normal. Why? It was odder than odd, he'd paid barely any attention to hollow-stomached Jenna and, she hadn't been imagining it, most of the flattery had gone *her* way! Could he smell it? Could he smell Jenna's double-whammy celibate unavailability? Could he smell *her* single-ness, and her mourning for her own sexuality?

'Would you like a tour of the house before I kick you out?' said Caroline.

'Oooh, yes,' said Izzie and Jenna together.

With babies in arms they went through the play-room to the steely, granite-surfaced kitchen which looked more equipped for surgery than cooking. The floors squeaked and the doors creaked in the hushed quiet as they followed her around her home.

'We had such a rush to get it all finished before Charles came along,' said Caroline, as they followed her past pots full of squiggly twigs to an enormous living room full of white sofas and lilies.

'That'll have to go, then,' said Izzie, nodding at the massive low square glass coffee table.

'Oh, this is all baby no-go area.'

'That won't last either,' Izzie whispered in Molly's ear.

'You could get my whole flat twice over in that room,' Molly muttered to Izzie as they went up the stairs.

By the time they got to Charles's interior-designed nursery complete with hand-painted Pooh murals, mini-bathroom and nanny quarters at the top of the house, they were all talking about schools. Molly switched off and went to look out of the window.

'There's no guarantee we'll get him in, of course,' Caroline was saying.

'Even if you get them down at birth?' said Jenna.

'We tried. We tried,' she sighed. 'New rule. No foetuses.'

Molly jumped and stifled a gasp. Flushing, she moved quickly away from the window.

Going down the stairs, Molly held onto the banister firmly with one hand, feeling like she'd been puffed up and then suddenly let down, squiggling and writhing into her true identity, a deflated bit of nothing. Serves you right, she told herself, mentally climbing back inside her forty-year-old body. It had just been a casual glimpse out of the window. To see the garden, the river from high up. That's all. At first she couldn't see him. But then she spotted him beside the river, lying back, leaning on one elbow smoking a cigarette. The girl had popped out of the grass skirts of the still-bare winter willows like a witch at a panto. She'd stood over him, laughing and talking. The sudden unbidden feelings of rage and jealousy took Molly so completely by surprise, the colour seemed to drain from her vision. She felt like she was watching an old French film. Or was it Polish? He'd leant back and looked up at the girl, laughing. She'd finished her cigarette and had thrown it to the ground, treading it out with her pointed toe like a ballerina resining her shoe. As Ulé laid herself down next to him Molly could bear it no more and turned her gaze back to the room where

Jenna was giving Caroline a *feng shui* lecture on picture pillows, spelling out the dangers of how a child's identity could be stolen and weakened in the night by any Winnie the Pooh or Buzz Lightyear images lurking in the bedclothes.

'Come to mine next time,' said Izzie on the doorstep.

'No, mine!' said Jenna.

'I got in there first!'

'Maybe we should meet more often, then we'll get to come back here faster,' laughed Izzie.

'All right, mine after you then.'

They all looked at Molly. 'Then it's your turn, Molly!' said Jenna, smiling sweetly.

CHAPTER SIX

Molly sank into the mundane through the timeless haze of motherhood. A permanent jet lag fuelled by an all-encompassing love which helped to seal, or at least cover, the cracks of the problems which held her existence together by a thread.

She'd quickly dismissed her attraction to Christophe as a hormonal rush of post-natal motherlust brought on by Amanda's down-dating stories. A massive overreaction caused by the severe cut-off from any form of social life whatsoever. Max, on the other hand, was a continual presence in his absence as she watched the tiny replica of him growing before her eyes.

She pulled the old Hoover out from under the stairs, stopping in mid-crouch to catch her breath as the next wave of tiredness hit, her emotions lurching through the problems of her past, future, past. She wearily knelt down to jerk out its old brown lead from the clutter of wires and bin liners which had spilled out into the hallway.

Disentangled and plugged, the Hoover shuddered into life.

'Look at me, all of you,' she couldn't help saying above the roar to the static rush-hour traffic just yards away from the squat bay window, 'Molly Warren! Born-again housewife. Minus the husband, mind you. With only half a house, come to that. What does that make me? A flatmistress?'

The Hoover droned on as she stared vacantly out at the cars. Countless pairs of headlights shone yellow beneath the low grey slab of sky, lighting the drivers trapped inside outside in their own sealed world. United in one thing. Wanting to be somewhere else. Anywhere but there.

'Poor sods,' she said, exchanging glares with a woman in a blue Jag before clicking the venetian blind shut with a sharp, bossy flick.

She took some sheets out of the airing cupboard. Molly loved airing cupboards. Spaces full of warm, safe air and fresh, folded neatness. Nothing hostile, dirty or harsh in there. A pair of warm knickers first thing in the morning was one of the small but exquisite luxuries which still existed in her life. She padded through to her back room. It was darker in there and the rain noiser on the window-panes. She switched on the light before punching the pillows, one by one, hard with her fist.

The sheet cracked as she threw it into the air, its folds flying inside out. She stood back and watched the puff of white, floating slowly and satisfyingly down to cover the tatty, rose-pink mattress. Of such small things, she thought as she gazed at the expanse of crispy fresh bed. Of such small things.

Stifling a yawn, she took herself away quickly

before she succumbed to the lethal combination of sheer gravity and a desperate longing to be horizontal. She ignored the phone ringing in the hall. There was a lot to get through before Daisy woke up.

Then the usual telephone thought came. Was he back?

She listened to her outgoing message, grabbing it just before the machine clicked in.

'Tamara asked me to ring you all. With three, I need to get it all on the calendar. If it's not on the calendar with me then it doesn't happen, do you know what I mean? Would we be all right to come to yours in May?'

'Yes, I *think* we'll be here, Izzie,' she sighed half-sarcastically.

'Want to come round for a cup of something wet before then? I'm only just round the corner.'

'Tomorrow? Tomorrow would be great!'

Molly smiled to herself as she put the phone down. Perhaps she'd be all right. Perhaps she'd be accepted in functional-family land after all. Parts of it anyhow.

She went into megadrive for the big one. Trying to get her lunch in before Daisy woke up for hers. She took a lasagne out of the freezer, holding the box to the dim grey light at the window. She looked down the list of flags, scrunching up her eyes till they were wrinkly slits as she struggled to read the tiny writing next to the Union Jack.

'Four minutes, shake, four minutes, stand,' she said over and over, confidently flipping the packaging into the pleasingly empty bin.

'Veronica, Veronica, Veronica,' she said, stabbing at the lid more times than was necessary, thoroughly enjoying the satisfying cracking sounds at each hit of the taut plastic cover.

She paused as she reached for the microwave door, standing for a few moments as suspended in time as her lunch. She looked up at the control panel then back down at the yellowy plastic rectangle in her hand.

'Damn,' she cursed, stretching down to rummage through the darkest depths of the bin, 'not only is my bloody eyesight going, my memory's up the spout as well. Four shake four stand, four shake four stand,' she repeated, carefully balancing the packaging on top of the flip-lid for future reference.

She switched on the radio. *'But when you say neurons that fire together or wire together...'*

'Oh shut up, Melvin.' She turned the dial to the left stopping abruptly as Kevin Ayers, a forgotten voice from the distant past, filled the kitchen. Molly looked at the radio in astonishment, a teenager again, standing on a Sussex cliff holding a tiny transistor to her ear.

If Christophe's banging on about the nose being a route to the memory was right, then music must have another short-circuiting direct line, she thought, amazed at how very long ago her past suddenly seemed.

The kitchen filled with the comforting smell of supermarket bolognese.

But then again, the near past had become an even stranger place, in many ways, than those far-off days. Just a few weeks ago she couldn't for the life of her imagine how she was going to be able to manage looking after a real, live baby. And look, here she was, doing it. Getting on with it.

Ping!

She jolted out of her musings. Now it seemed like she'd been dressed in rags and lunching on lasagne-for-one all her life.

'Yeowch!'

In a split second, Molly snapped into, out of and far ahead of the moment. She'd forgotten about the hole in the oven glove.

J-clothing more or less all of the yellowy orange meaty splodge off her dress, she ran her finger under the cold tap and tore up some iceberg leaves all at once, mixing them in olive oil before chucking in a handful of cherry tomatoes.

The opening guitar riffs of 'Brown Sugar' pulled her forward a decade and back by two.

'Jimmy, your taste in music is *exquisite!*'

Molly danced like a trombone. She was happy. She was nearing her daily big aim in life. A sit-down and something to eat. Time for *her*.

A few minutes later she was there. Lying back on her bed, neatly covered in its daytime sofa-throw combinations of old sarongs from long-ago beach holidays, her plate on her lap, bolting her food, transfixed by Dr Phil on *Oprah*.

She wasn't worried about the sound of the TV waking Daisy. There was only one way to do that. After lunch, when she put the kettle on, not a murmur would come from the cot. When she dunked the tea bag, not a sound. When she put the tea bag in the flip-top bin, trying not to dribble it – total silence. But when Molly's bottom hit the cushion . . . that was it. She'd tried taking her mug to the furthest corner of the flat possible. She'd tried moving a chair into the kitchen. She'd tried taking her tea into the bathroom, locking the door and sitting on the loo lid. She'd even gone down to the far end of the garden. But it was useless. Before cup had time to touch lip, Daisy would start her wriggling and revving up for the first wail. She made a mental note to discuss it with Izzie the next day.

After her meal she hurried on. She filled and clicked on the washing machine and went for the bathroom. Back in the kitchen, Jimmy Young introduced 'Reeling In the Years'. Via Vim's much-better-than-cream thoughts, Molly reeled, gaily sprinkling the lemon-scented powder all over the green plastic bath.

Steely Dan and the mid-seventies were suddenly there in her bathroom, with Molly standing, Vim in hand, like she'd zapped into her future on a past, long-forgotten trip.

Her mother. She'd longed for her own mother to be at home for her but she'd always been out working. Till she'd bunked off altogether. Her friends' mothers had always been there. Shoving endless piles of washing into their machines and cooking big teas with fat chips fried in baskets.

Was *she* her mother now? She looked suspiciously down at her yellow blubber rubber hands. Was she? But no. Her mother had never, ever worn Marigolds.

Quite the opposite.

As the women's liberation movement revved up into fourth gear, so, not far behind, had her mother, finding her G-spot via Colin, a blacksmith from Hull, and promptly leaving home. But instead of heading North, they'd gone to the land of bottomless jugs of sangria without much more than a wave goodbye for Molly and her dad.

Her father, taking advantage of the new divorce laws, had remarried embarrassingly quickly while Molly, following the family tradition, took the opportunity to slip quietly out of the back door, decamping to a nearby squat in Leatherhead.

There she'd found kindness, of a sort, and friendship, of a sort, among mutual lost souls in an exotic world of joss sticks, Rickenbackers and over-sized Rizlas. She'd commuted to an Oxford Street office every day, bringing back a modest salary in her embroidered Greek bag which somehow kept them all in spag bol and curries with enough left over for pub crawls and soft loo rolls. All without a credit card in sight. Life, and love, was all about sharing then. There were jamming sessions, lots of visitors, wild parties full of beautiful, friendly, some of them *very* friendly, strangers.

Molly sang along as she rubbed the Vim into the bath, completely transported. The white powder suddenly looked like a different sort of white powder which Molly began forming into little lines with her J-cloth, its lemony bleachy smell turning into a blend of Sharwood's Extra-Hot, patchouli oil and the heady pong of goaty wet afghan. A full-colour

101

centrefold, at the tail end of the deeply embarrassing seventies. After a winter of squabbles about loo paper and milk-ownership, she'd decamped to a bedsit off the King's Road and had been fiercely independent ever since.

Steely Dan gave way to 'Duelling Banjos', the smell of lemon returned leaving just a faint metallic taste at the back of her throat. Molly scrubbed pointlessly at the bath stains. As Jimmy began an in-depth discussion with a man from Aberdeen about how to clean dogs' teeth, Molly returned to the kitchen, snapped her rubber gloves off and filled the kettle with water through its spout.

Innocent days. Naive days. She'd still been a *child*. She was, what? barely twenty when she'd left there. Only a couple of years younger than Jenna and Christophe! But they all seemed so grown-up. Was it her or was it them? Or was it just the times that'd changed? *Were* those women all as sensible and well padded as they appeared? Were their lives as neat and planned and manicured as the flower beds in Kew Gardens?

Hmmmm, Christophe, she thought as she squashed her PG Tip with the back of a teaspoon and poured the hot water onto it, unwrapping a fat new pack of plain chocolate digestives as quietly as she could.

No sounds of stirring.

Strange?

She sat down on the bed, took a sip of tea, a bite of biscuit, another bite of biscuit. Another?

Silence.

She lay down.

Seconds later she sat bolt upright.

She raced to Daisy's cot in the front room. Daisy lay. Still. Peaceful, so peaceful.

Too peaceful.

She put her finger beneath her nose, only allowing herself to breathe again when she felt the tiny puffs of breath on her skin.

She turned away from the cot only to stop breathing herself, this time preceded by a large, loud gasp.

There was a car reversing into Mrs Constandavalos's parking space and it didn't belong to Mrs Constandavalos. It was Max's shiny black Audi.

'Why the hell didn't you *ring*?'

'I've just got back, Molly. I was on my way from Heathrow.'

'What's wrong with your mobile?'

Max stood beside his car, holding onto the open door.

'I thought you'd be *pleased*.'

'You've had all the way from Venezuela to think about it. One tiny little phone call would have been in order, don't you think? Anyway, you can't park here, it's Mrs Constandavalos's space. She'll go ape if –'

'I can't stay long, Molly,' he said softly.

'Oh no – no – no – of *course* you can't. Whatever was I thinking? That you'd come to spend the *day* with us! Or just for a long, impromptu boozy lunch perhaps? Oh, silly me. Silly, *silly* Molly as usual.' Molly marched up towards the traffic speeding by and back, shaking with rage.

'Cut the sarcasm, Molly.'

'Me! Cut the – How *dare* you just turn up like this, Max.'

'I've got to go to Geneva tomorrow, really it's been more than hectic. You know what it's like.'

Molly's eyes widened as she free-fell in a quarry between confusion and anger. 'Oh yes, I know what it's like, of *course* I know what it's like. Well, do *you* know what it's been like, Max, do you want me to tell you? Because I think it's time for a little...' She stopped in full flow. It took a few moments for her body to follow; she waved her arms about silently for a moment.

She stood and looked at him. He looked petrified. Absolutely bloody petrified.

'Come on in then, come on in.' She turned and walked towards the front door. 'Just don't say a thing about the mess. OK, I know it's a mess, I'm a mess, we're struggling here, all right?'

They both stood awkwardly in her tiny hallway. He was waiting for her lead. She'd never seen him looking so lost. He gazed at the ground.

Through her anger her heart ached. He was *there*. And boy was he present. He seemed taller, and more – defined, somehow. Sharper round the edges. As always, devastatingly smart in his own scruffy way, his blond curls just touching the collar of his soft brown leather jacket. He still had the tang of the flight on him. That cellophane-wrapped, expense-account Dunhill and Tobleroney smell of the big wide world on his skin.

She longed to touch him, to feel the familiar softness of that leather wrap itself around her, she ached to be in the clench of those arms but she fought it. Hard. She wasn't just fighting for herself here, she was fighting for all of them.

She breathed deep and stepped back, out of the tidal pull of him, trying to follow her instincts but not trusting them. She had to throw logic out of the window now, let whatever was about to happen happen.

This poor man, the man she loved, was up a bloody creek without a paddle. He was looking nervously into Daisy's room. Molly followed his eyes to the two white ducks embossed on the wooden headboard of the cot.

'She'll be waking up soon. I'll get you a drink,' she said calmly, turning away from him and going into the kitchen.

How would she feel if it were *her*? If she hadn't gone through all the pregnancy stuff and was just about to be presented with a completely formed child? *Her* child? She would have known about all the bad things, certainly, all the noise and mess and the clinicy, Tamara, ointmenty, wees-and-poos side of things. All the stuff that put her off ever wanting a child for so many years. But she wouldn't have had a clue about the sheer force of the other side.

She took two glasses out of the cupboard and gave them a quick polish before pouring a generous slug of gin into one. The Schweppes spat and hissed as she unscrewed the lid. How would she feel if she hadn't felt her own body changing and transforming literally beneath her nose? Bloody terrified. Worse, it had to be worse trying to imagine what was going on than living it. When you were in it there was no escape. No dumping your bump in left luggage and disappearing across the Atlantic for weeks on end. She dropped in the ice. The warm tonic made deep crackling sounds as the cubes melted in a muffle of underneath explosions.

He was standing with his hands gripped tight to the bars of the cot.

'Still asleep! I'll wake her up,' she said quietly, slipping his drink into his hand.

'No, no, don't do that, she's happy.' Max turned his head to one side.

'She's well over her four hours, if I don't wake her up now she won't have her nap later.'

'You sound like an expert,' he said nervously.

She was standing very close to him now.

It was no good.

She touched his arm.

He turned towards her and looked down at her. 'Molly.'

Within seconds she was where she wanted to be. But there was an awkwardness about his hug, a gap between his arms and her body. Though it could only have been a fraction of a millimetre, it might as well have been the Grand Canyon. He was holding back. She rested her head on his shoulder and let the tears come.

'It must be a bit of a shock, huh?' she said eventually.

He turned towards the cot. Daisy opened her eyes. She looked around for a moment, wide-eyed and startled, before breaking into a toothless, innocent smile.

Laughter seeped through Molly's tears as she picked her up. 'Here we are then!'

Max looked at her intently.

'Don't worry, I'm not going to ask you to hold her.'

An uneasy smile crossed Max's face. He stroked Daisy's cheek.

'I don't know who's the more nervous about this,' said Molly as Daisy kicked and bounced in her arms.

Max looked around as if for the first time.

'And this is the flat!' said Molly brightly. 'I haven't had time to clear the clutter, yet. But I suppose I'll find a few spare moments one day.' Was it a trying to escape look? 'So – now you can see, we're doing all right. It's up to you, Max. It's completely up to you.'

'Things are so complicated, Molly.'

'How *is* Veronica these days?'

'I don't know – I haven't seen her, have I?' Max looked at his watch, which sent a surge of anger raging through Molly again.

'Expecting you home for dinner, is she?'

'Look – I ...'

Calm down, Molly, she told herself. Give him time. Time.

'I'm sorry, Max.'

Max was looking at Daisy with a pained, distant expression on his face, 'She's lovely, Molly.'

Molly softened again. 'She's *yours*, Max.'

'I'll write you another cheque.'

'No! This is about *you* and *Daisy*. You can come and see her whenever you like. OK. And no strings.'

'Nonsense.' Max put his arms round both of them. This time it was Molly who stiffened.

'We've just got to keep away from each other,' she warned him as she twisted out of his hug. 'Keep in touch with the realities. This is real life now, Max. If I ever meet ... whatever my future, her future, her *past*, will always be yours. It's down to you. You can see her whenever you want. It's important you know that. For her as well as you.'

Max swallowed hard and nodded.

Daisy revved up into a food kick.

'I'd better warn you, Max, I'm going to feed her now.'

'That's fine, and I'd better feed you, hadn't I?' He reached into his jacket and took out his wallet and a pen.

Molly laughed cynically. 'I thought you were going to take us all out on a jolly to the River Café for a moment!'

'Look – Molly ...'

'I know, I know, things are difficult, Veronica's your wife, you both love each other very much.'

'It's not that simple.'

'I've enough problems to deal with right now, Max. I simply can't take yours on board as well. Basically we're fine, but it's tough, bloody tough.' Max opened his mouth. 'No no no, but she's brilliant, isn't she? She is the best. I've never been happier.'

'Well, at least take that.' He threw a cheque on the

108

cot. Molly stood up, with Daisy still at her breast, and snatched it away. 'That's Daisy's cot, if you don't mind, not a bloody casino table!'

A series of sharp loud raps on her front door interspersed with Greek swear words stopped Daisy's sucking. She lifted her head and turned to look towards the sound, leaving Molly's exposed nipple glistening like a beacon.

'She's got your frown, Molly!'

'Really?' Molly looked down. 'You'd better get that, Max, I think it's for you.'

After Max had gone Molly looked at Daisy with different eyes. 'So there's some of me in you as well, is there? I've been so obsessed with seeing your dad in you. I just hope you don't get my sarcasm, that's all. I hope you don't get that.'

She threw Max's untouched drink down the sink and tore up the cheque.

CHAPTER SEVEN

'Talk about life being full of shit.' Izzie ran down the stairs with a startled-looking wide-eyed baby gripped sideways under one arm and a large white bottle of economy bleach under the other.

She plonked Bob on the play mat, hurried past Molly and disappeared into the kitchen.

'I'll get this Plug-In in and I'll be there.'

Molly sat at the high stool of the breakfast bar which separated the kitchen from the large knocked-through living room and looked outside. Three boys dangled off a steel and blue climbing frame at various angles, shouting urgently to each other.

'My fingernails are too short, can you get this? Here,' she put the packet in Molly's hands. 'And I'll get the kettle on. I'm not normally this tidy so don't go opening any cupboards or you'll get a mountain of stuff on your head.

'Not now, Gordon,' she said without turning round from the sink as the patio door slid open and a small boy, with a face full of freckles and Izzie's shock of ginger hair, slipped through into the room.

'Visitors is the only thing that gets me tidying,'

she continued in the same breath as she took the packet from Molly. 'When we know each other better it'll be back to normal. Then watch where you tread. I said *no*, Gordon, your tea's nearly ready, now get out of here.'

'Aw come *onnn.*' The boy screwed his face up as he opened a battered round biscuit tin with a picture of two cherubs on the lid.

'Do you have any help?'

'Gordon, I said no!'

'Ow, *muuuuum...*'

'Help? More trouble than it's worth.' She carried on talking as she shooed Gordon out and took a sideways swipe at the patio door which slid shut with a clunk. 'More trouble than they're worth, another body coming and going with the dirt. I like seeing my own dust going into my own Hoover. And do you know how much a cleaner costs in Kew!' She turned to look at the opening patio door. 'All right, just the one each then. Gordon, I said *one*! These women. They pay a fortune for a cleaner then they go and spend a mortgageful of cash a month on a gym.'

Molly couldn't help feeling an envious twang as Izzie opened the freezer section of her massive two-door Zanussi. Nothing grungy about that, she thought as she got a glimpse of the clear icicle-cool within.

'They tidy up before the cleaner gets there anyway, most of them. Then jump in their cars to go off and walk the treadmill or bike on the bloody spot to nowhere before coming back and paying for the exercise they could have done by cleaning up after themselves in the first place.'

Molly watched Izzie lay out a pattern of chicken nuggets, slowly and with a contented kind of a concentration, on a large grill-pan.

'Who needs a tread machine? I get enough exercise going up and down my stairs.' She slid the nugget-filled pan noisily into place and wiped her hands on the sides of her leggings.

'Now, what'll it be? Tea, instant or gin,' she looked at her watch, 'no, I suppose it's a bit early for that.'

'But then, if you had a place the size of Caroline's . . .'

Izzie laughed. 'That's not one of our problems, is it? Every now and then Carter gets this stupid smirk on his face and goes on about getting an au pair. He reckons a couple of hours overtime at the weekend rate and we've done it, but I tell him it's not like he thinks. Chicken nuggets, boys, in ten minutes,' she yelled towards the garden. 'He won't get the idea out of his head that they're all Swedish and French lovelies who don't know how to lock bathroom doors. I keep telling him most of them are big-boned girls from Eastern Europe with tattoos everywhere, rings through their noses . . .' She poured a bagful of frozen chips onto a baking tray before moving over to the washing machine. 'And who the bloody hell knows where else on them. Apart from most of the rugby players of Richmond, if gossip's to be believed. It's more like having another child in the house than having help. A bloody hormonal teenager at that. And then they get the boyfriends, of course, and before you know it you've got more strangers in the house than your own bloody family...talking of which...' She pulled at a lump of matted clothes.

'Mine does that,' said Molly happily.

'What do you make of that Christophe, then?'

'What do you mean?' Molly shifted on her stool.

'Do you think he's for real?'

'I'd never thought of it,' said Molly. 'Why?'

'I don't know. Seems funny to me. A perfumer who smokes.'

'All Frenchmen smoke, don't they? Do you want a hand?'

'Naaah.' Izzie unpicked the twisted damp ball of fabric back into identifiable items of clothing.

'He certainly knows his perfumes.'

'You know something?' Izzie looked up at Molly. 'I think he fancied you.'

'Phfff,' Molly said a bit too quickly, 'if he fancied any of us it wouldn't be me, would it?'

'Why not?'

'I'm old enough to be his mother. Oh dear, I never thought I'd hear myself saying that.'

Izzie laughed. 'You know what they say about these Latinos.'

There was an overlong silence. They both listened to the calls and shouts from the boys in the garden.

'I was probably just a decoy to make Caroline jealous. Look at the state of me.' She bunched up her long limp hair. 'This used to be my pride and joy. Now look, it feels like a frazzled shawl lurking around my shoulders.'

'You're probably not rinsing enough.'

'One shampoo, then a quick squirt of the shower is all I have time for.' Molly looked at the small boy fiddling with his trousers at the top of the climbing frame.

'No wonder then.'

Izzie flattened a T-shirt against her chest and smoothed it out. 'This is my ironing,' she said before taking a sheet of Bounce from a drawer, putting it in the tumble-dryer with one hand and pouring the tea with the other. 'Jeans and T-shirts for Carter, leggings and same for me, keep it simple and stretchy, that's what I say. Doesn't do much for the figure but I don't have time for all that. I seem to put on a chin a child, that seems to be the habit. Still, it's one of the sacrifices, isn't it? Look at this baby's *curls*!' Izzie plonked Molly's tea in front of her and picked Daisy up. 'And soft *soft* skin, haven't you, sweetheart?' She stroked her arm gently.

'She's got her dad's curls. Funny, though, I'm dark blonde, or *was* once upon a time. Max is an almost white blond but she's coal black.'

'She'll be a little blonde Ulrika then, won't you.' She rubbed her cheek against Daisy's face before putting her back on the play mat.

'Most newborns have black hair.'

'So she might be *fair*.'

'If your husband's blond and you're fair, then she'll be fair, of course she will.'

'And I thought I'd read every book and magazine article in the hemisphere on newborns. Why didn't I know this yesterday?' Molly remembered Max gingerly touching Daisy's hair. Remembered the unasked question lingering in a dark part of the air she didn't have the emotional energy to go to.

'What?'

'Oh, never mind.'

'No one's the expert.We're all fumbling along, aren't we. Though I used to be a hairdresser, so I suppose you could say it's my subject. You wouldn't know it though, would you?'

She touched her hair.

Molly didn't know quite what to say for a moment, 'Oh, I don't know. Finding the time for yourself is pretty challenging.'

'Tell me about it. Trouble is my hair's had so much done to it it's just given up and so have I most days. I've got a cupboard full of serums upstairs but then I think what the hell, is the checkout girl at Tesco really going to worry about whether my hair's sticking up or not. I do keep the boys in trim though, that's handy. I do a little sideline in kids' hair if you're interested.'

'Do you do adults?'

'Used to,' said Izzie, pulling a Wet Wipe out of its tub and wiping down the washing machine.

'Do you think you could do − could you have a go at this? ' Even if she'd had the time, the last thing Molly could have faced was a hairdressing salon, looking apologetically at her shadow of her old self while some stranger, who'd be vigorously if voicelessly agreeing with her, tried to put her to rights.

'We could do it now if you like.'

Molly looked at the boys outside, the two babies on the play mat, the hissing grill-pan, then back at Izzie, who was scraping the clutter on the pine table over to one end – a pink lizard with a green blob on its back, a TV remote control, a sticker strip with tropical animals, a bottle of tomato ketchup and an assortment of empty loo rolls and plastic building bricks.

'A bit later, I mean. Carter's on overtime tonight.' She retrieved the tomato ketchup from the clutter and plonked it in the middle of the table. 'Won't be back till nine. Hang around while I get the boys bathed and off to bed. We can do it then if you like. *Come and get it, boys!*'

'Are you sure?' said Molly, not sure if she was sure as the room filled with noise and mud and ketchup and chips. She looked sideways at the boys' hair. 'Of course, I'm not quite Mark at Westbrook,' said Izzie, catching Molly's look, 'but even if I say it myself, I don't do a bad cut. I only do it to keep my hand in now. I was bloody glad to give it up when I was pregnant, I can tell you.'

'Actually, so was I,' said Molly.

'What about that Caroline then? That's the life, isn't it, no work and a live-in nanny.'

'And a cleaner.'

'And a gardener.' Izzie took a stack of coloured cups from a shelf and plonked them noisily in a line on the counter.

'Ye-ess,' said Molly slowly, unable to suppress a girlish desire to talk about him, speculate about him, with Caroline, with Ulé – with her?

'That's the way to do it, isn't it. Get yourself a bloody rich husband. Who wants orange? Calm down, Bradley, if Thomas wants the the blue cup he can have the blue cup, he's the guest, OK?'

'A husband would be a start,' laughed Molly.

'You're one of those "partners" couples, are you?'

'Nope.'

Izzie stopped pouring the juice for a moment. '*No one?*'

Molly shook her head. 'Her father *exists*, of course. We saw him yesterday in fact. We – we don't live together. We're *not* together,' she added as a firm afterthought.

'Oh.'

'He's married ...' Molly's voice tailed off.

'Gordon, shut your ears, open your mouth and get on with your dinner.' Izzie zapped the small television on the counter into Blue Peter mode.

Amanda, why didn't I listen to you? 'It's not what you think.' She kept her voice low. 'He's a *journalist*,' she said, as if that explained everything, which, in her old world, it quite often did.

'Oh?' Izzie pulled a Wet Wipe out of its tub and began wiping the kitchen floor.

'So is his wife. She's an editor actually. She runs a newspaper. She has her own li –'

'Gordon, what homework have you got tonight?' Molly took the cue and changed the subject. 'That's fascinating!' she said unconvincingly as she watched Izzie loading her dishwasher.

'What's that?'

'How you're loading your cutlery.'

117

Izzie looked at her blankly with a new coldness in her eyes.

'Well I, I load mine, *used* to,' she babbled, 'I don't have one any more but when I did I always put the handles up and you're loading yours handles *down*.'

'Spoons and forks up, Knives down.'

'Well, I never knew that!' said Molly in genuine admiration.

'No – Bradley, I've not got any bananas with a blue O on them. Thomas, your mum's here.' Izzie went to get the door.

Thomas's mother, another fresh-from-the-gym-looking blonde woman, in a blue tracksuit with white stripes down the side, jogged by the front door as Izzie, surrounded by a swirl of boys, searched for Thomas's reading folder and lunch box.

'Did they play nicely together?' the woman asked, smiling and nodding at Molly.

Molly smiled back and turned to look at the large black and white portrait of Bradley and Gordon hanging above the mantelpiece. Their soft-focus angelic expressions bore little resemblance to the noisy scamps racing about the house.

'No problems at all, though it's getting to that time of day now, isn't it?' Izzie was back to her old warm self, chattering and laughing. As she ran through everything Thomas had put in his mouth since being there, Molly picked up Daisy and took her to read the fridge door, feeling like she was sitting inside the freezer tray. She held Daisy closer. She picked up one of Daisy's curls and twisted it slowly around her finger.

She was going to have to be a lot tougher than she thought. It was a relief, though, to get it out. Now Izzie knew where she was coming from. Better to be honest and upfront with them straightaway; she'd been strong all her life, she'd be strong now. She was a single mother. So what? Nothing so unusual about that. She'd deal with it. She'd learn to deal with it. And – who knows?

The door slammed.

'Good score!' Izzie called across the room.

'What's that?' Molly carried on pushing the brightly coloured letters around.

'It's a little game I play. Now get upstairs and do your *homework*, you two, and NO ARGUING.'

'But we haven't had pudding!'

'Leave Kathy *alone*. You can have your yogurts in a minute, now scram. Scoot. Go on – off.'

As the sound of their footsteps on the stairs receded, Izzie seemed to be her old friendly self. 'It's a little game I play with myself. If they're not watching a video when the parent arrives, add five. If they're playing quietly on the computer upstairs, add five. If they're finishing off tea and there's vegetables on the plate add twenty. If there's chips deduct ten. If they're quietly playing Pokemon, add ten. A board game, add twenty. If they're fighting, deduct fifty. Playing with guns or swords, deduct twenty. If you're all playing a game together or doing something educational or musical, add a hundred. Or it might as well be a hundred thousand.'

'What were they actually doing over there?'

'Oh, just torturing the hamster.'

119

Izzie took a fresh Wet Wipe and went over to the hamster cage. 'Just another poo corner to sort out, as if I didn't have enough of the stuff in my life. . . .'

'Look, I'm sorry for talking about my situation in front of the boys, I didn't think.'

'Oh don't worry about that, you should hear what they talk about at school! So – what happened to this bloke then?'

'Max – he's still coming to terms with it, with her, he'll – he's been abroad, he does work a lot.'

'So,' Izzie nodded down to Daisy, 'was she planned?'

'She wasn't unplanned. Let's put it that way. I had to either get on with it or accept it'd never happen. And I couldn't do it. I mean, we *were* together for six years,' she added, wanting to explain the whole thing but not sure how far she should go.

'I've never come across an unwanted baby yet. Unwanted pregnancies? Ten a penny. Unwanted babies? Zero.'

Izzie rummaged through her fridge.

'By the mums that is,' Molly added wryly.

Izzie plonked a pack of yogurts on the sideboard.

'Peach yogurts. Why?' she said as she snapped off half the tubs and threw them in the bin.

'I never realised it'd be such hard work, though.'

'Constant, isn't it.'

'How the hell do you cope with three?'

'It's time you started learning,' laughed Izzie. 'I'll leave you in charge of these two while I sort out those boys.'

*

'Are you sure it's all right to drink this?' The house had finally fallen silent, Molly's chair had been turned to face the television. The cups of tea had been replaced with two large glasses of red wine.

'Listen, if Tamara and all that health crowd had their way they'd stop us drinking PG Tips.'

Molly laughed and took a grateful guilt-free sip.

'So, Carter works long hours, does he?'

'Does he ever,' said Izzie heaving a large, pale pink vanity bag onto the table and noisily snapping open the catches one by one. Molly sat stiffly as she watched her setting the combs and scissors out in a line.

'Some nights he could be back earlier but he knows he's banned.'

'Banned?'

'Too right. Just when I've just got the boys down and settled, up pops Daddy and gets them going again. I've lost my rag one too many times. He stays down at the Firkin for a couple when he gets off the Tube. Suits everyone that way.'

'So he only sees them at the weekends?'

'Same in most houses, isn't it.'

'What does he do?'

'He's a film editor. Do you want to wash it yourself, then?'

Molly cleared her throat. 'Yes. Shall I go now?'

She returned, towel wrapped turban-like around her head, and sat down in front of the television. 'Now that beats a mirror any time,' she said as she settled cosily in front of the *Coronation Street* opening titles. 'Where does your husband work, then?'

121

'Carter's up in the West End.'

'I used to work in television.'

'Did you? What as?'

'I was a production manager, on *Holidaytime* mostly.'

Izzie did a low version of her machine-gun laugh. 'What – going on holiday all the time?'

'Sort of.'

'For work?'

Molly nodded.

'You lucky cow.'

'It's *so* not how you imagine. Believe it or not, working when everyone else is on holiday is the hardest thing, twenty-four-hour turnarounds mostly,' she said, thinking maybe for the last time that explaining this over and over to people had also been the hardest thing. No one seemed to be able to grasp it. 'And that was it. That was *me*.'

'What do you mean?'

'I'm not that any more. And it doesn't matter. People are so identified by what job they do, aren't they? That's *them*. Isn't it?'

'How do you do? What do you do? Wipe poo,' laughed Izzie.

'And suddenly, it all went. It's a strange feeling.'

'So you're not going back to work then?'

'Not in television. You never know what's happening from one hour to the next let alone days – or weeks.'

'So, what's it to be,' said Izzie, taking a roll of black bin liners from her bag, and untwirling one from the end. She ripped a hole in the top and put it over Molly's head.

122

'Short.'

'Short?'

'I mean. Not short. I mean...' said Molly quickly, remembering that short to most hairdressers meant bald.

'Not a crop? Is that it?'

'Exactly. Not nearly a crop. Long short, so it's still got long bits hanging down.' She stopped to look over at Daisy, who'd started wriggling her arms and legs and screwing her face up. 'I think a bob. A straightforward shoulder-length bob.' Molly was thinking damage-limitation thoughts while a fantasy image of a new self began to form in her mind. A smooth, shiny brown bob swinging just off her shoulders, showing off her neck. A camel coat. Maybe glasses wouldn't be such a bad idea. Tortoiseshell perhaps ...

'Yes. Definitely a bob. A long bob. Still short but long. A long short bob.'

Daisy began to whimper. Molly picked her up.

'Put her on underneath. She'll be all right. Spread your legs out, let plenty of air in. That's it,' said Izzie, gathering Molly's hair into a ponytail.

Molly braced herself as the old hair went in one snap of the scissors.

'Look at it,' laughed Izzie, holding it up for Molly to see, 'like a dead ferret,' she held it at arm's length as if it were a live ferret, before letting it drop to the floor, 'that needed doing, that did,' she said happily.

'I should have done it years ago.'

'You know what they say,' said Izzie, 'better late than never.'

'I should have done lots of things years ago.'

'You remember Becky?'

'Becky?'

'The one at Tamara's who didn't come to Caroline's?'

'Oh yes.'

'I rang her up about the rota, but she's dropped out. Gone back to work already.'

'Wow. What does she do?'

'Banking or insurance, something like that.'

'How can she do it?'

'They have to, lots of them, don't they? Their maternity leave comes to an end and they have to go back. They can't chuck it in when they've had all that paid time off.'

'Just *thinking* about it makes me panic.'

'It's practicalities, isn't it? We only get by on Carter's overtime. Without that we'd be up shit creek. And it's getting less. There's not the demand for film editors any more. Carter's struggling with the computers now. The work's getting harder to nail down. It scares me to think about it sometimes...'

'What gets me is how do these working mothers find the *time* to work? After seeing to Daisy, the flat has to be sorted out, then me last. Me last? I wish. Me not at all because by the time it's my turn it's Daisy's turn again. *Where* does fitting in eight hours of work a day come into it?'

'Even with the childminder they only do that, don't they, mind the child. They don't do the ironing and a million other things at the same time like we do.'

'And they must get woken up at intervals through the night, just like us.'

'That's it, isn't it. That's why a lot of them go back. To get out of the house,' said Izzie.

'Away from the mundane. It's not mundane, is it? I mean it is but it isn't. Every time she wakes up, she's different.'

'They grow before your eyes, don't they? I reckon it all depends on what you do. If you're a high flier with people running around after you getting your teas and coffees, arranging your diaries and all that, then it's got to be harder to stop. To run around after a baby. Apart from the huge salary drop. They're the ones I feel sorry for. They're really stuck. However much they want to give it up, they can't.'

'I'd rather run around after a baby than a big hairy film crew,' said Molly with feeling. 'Though I don't know how I'll be able to go back to work when the time comes. I don't even know what I'm going to do. I don't want to leave Daisy with anyone, let alone a stranger. *How* can I ever do that?' She could feel Daisy getting heavier in her arms as she dropped off to sleep.

'Cooking's another one,' said Izzie. 'If you hate cooking you're up shit creek before you start, aren't you?'

'Oh, I'm looking forward to that.'

'Huh, you wait. Over and over, every day, that's the real slog of it. There's only so many McDonald's you can get away with in a week. That's what I'd have if I could,' she said dreamily, 'Just someone to do the cooking. Nothing else. I can cope with the rest. I wouldn't care if I never saw another chicken bloody nugget in my life.'

Back home that evening, Molly swung her head in front of her bathroom mirror. It was what she'd asked for. A sleek bob that turned under at the ends. She flicked the ends. They flicked back. She ran her fingers through her hair. Swung her head, feeling the odd sensation of air against neck.

'Shorn like a sheep,' she said to the prim woman staring back at her.

'You're not a girl any more, Molly, you're a woman. Get it? Now get real with it, girl. I mean, woman.' She scrunched up her nose, not sure about the word, it sounded grown-up and periody and all that yucky stuff. Woman – woo-man, wombman. But then, would seeing the world through dark tor-toiseshell frames be so bad?

CHAPTER EIGHT

The roar of traffic on Molly's road faded into back-street birdsong, the extensions of the houses on Marksbury Avenue grew in size and ingenuity and the wisteria became more abundant until it dripped off every wall and windowsill in massive purple tails.

She crossed the deserted road beside the old Barn Church to the broad, grass-fringed pavement of Pensford Avenue and pushed on down into deepest Kew. The four-minute intervals between the planes underlined the deathly quiet and still. The only sounds came from the birds, the wheels of Daisy's pushchair clunkety clunking over the paving stones and a leaf left over from autumn, scudding along in the breeze like a piece of tumbleweed.

After her cramped flat, Molly loved the feeling of stillness and space and just being out in the day. She slowed down to an amble, peering in at the detached mock-Tudors with their mock-Tudor garages and mock-Tudor cats, dozing in their individual patches of sunlight.

'See you soon,' he'd said as he'd left in the Greek

storm that was Mrs Constandavalos. Soon? What did soon mean?

Pensford was odd. *Twin Peaks*-y and somewhere else. Though each house was different, they were all the same, with their driveways, cedars and, cartoon-like, fluffy pink and white blossom trees. A few years ago stifling, dull bells would have rung out loud and clear but the note had changed into the muffled thud of safety, security, warmth and peace. As she passed the tennis club a jumbo flew low but she barely noticed it. Apart from the five o'clock Concorde coming in to land, which she didn't mind at all, the planes had become part of the background, as much a part of Kew as the weekend buzz of lawnmowers.

The houses began sprouting names burnt in sloping writing onto slivers of wood dangling on tiny hooks over porches, gateposts and garage doors. She wondered about the lives behind those heavy wooden doors. Lives so different from her own.

Kew Village extended in a horseshoe shape from the Tube station and its pub. Nearly all the shops spilled out onto the pavements, giving it a market-like feel. They were there to entice the ever-flowing stream of tourists on their way from the Tube to the Gardens, and there, also, for people like Molly with pushchairs who had yet to master the steering in and, usually more complicatedly, out, of small shops.

She liked to have a good linger in the village while Daisy, from her pushchair vantage point, tried to make sense of the world with her ever-sharpening eyesight. After the bookshop would come the green-grocer's, via the delicious-smelling hardware store. The hanging baskets outside the chemist's were the picture of restraint compared to the displays of cut flowers and the strange plants and shrubs outside the three florists. Though even they failed to compete with the greengrocer's, completely hidden from the road by its racks of high-turnover seasonal bedding plants, daffs and tulips. Only the cool, serious exterior of the bank separated this from the rock shop where a guy with waist-length dreadlocks sat, surrounded by dinosaur eggs, crystals and fossils, giving away organic fruit with every purchase. Outside, his dog, with dreadlocks as dramatic as its owner's, watched over the second-hand new age books, cheap pretty rocks and stone eggs.

'Do you take Sellotaped cheques?'

Molly swallowed hard as the cashier thumped his stamper on the cheque. She straightened up and tried to sound confident and rich. 'And a balance statement please.' She scrumpled it in her hand without looking at it and made her way to the cash dispenser.

'Would you like £10, £20, £30, £50 or £100?' the screen enquired. If she was going to fit in at all around here, she'd have to make more of an effort with herself. That was all there was to it. Such a radical haircut had to have new clothes. And Max could help with that at least.

His last words to her surfaced in her head. 'See you soon.' Soon? When was soon?

After she'd pressed the '£100 please' button, she

took a quick sideways squint at the little slip of paper in her hand. She left the bank, glad she'd done it that way round. Her collateral was crashing. Fast.

She had some hard decisions to make on the back of her shaky determination not to rely on Max. That was just a one-off, she told herself as she left the bank. Otherwise she might as well be carrying on as before. Worse, hope would be right up there on the front line. Even if he really wanted to, he couldn't just leave Veronica. She knew that. How could he leave someone he was never with anyway? But she didn't want to leave Daisy. No. Not yet anyway. If she wanted to spend the whole of the summer...

For Sale. VW Beetle Convertible. Orange. One lady owner for ten years ... that always gets them, the lady owner bit, she thought, nibbling distractedly at the end of her green Bic. She settled back in her window seat chair and looked out through the greenery of the Greenhouse Café. She took a sip of her hot chocolate through the stiff mountain of cold cream and took a delicious, anticipatory bite at the Flake sticking out of its swirly peak.

The Greenhouse Café, a miniature version of a Garden hothouse, was, like everywhere else in Kew, stuffed full of plants, inside and out. Spanish guitar music played quietly. She looked down at Daisy, parked comfortably next to her, kicking her legs happily.

She gazed absent-mindedly out of the window at the steady stream of people walking from the Tube to the Gardens. Tourists and lovers, removed from their daily grinds for the day. On their trips as much as Molly was, sitting there, grounded into one of the better parts of her own reality.

'Oh no,' she said out loud, suddenly sitting straight in her chair. She didn't know where to look; she averted her eyes but then had to look again. Striding across the road, a green rucksack over his right shoulder, the other arm swinging, was Christophe, coming straight towards her. Their eyes met but he showed no recognition. She quickly turned away.

She knew without checking that he'd come into the café. What was it about him? She crouched over her postcard, glad she had a proper distraction but immediately feeling like she was acting.

'May I sit here?'

She looked up. He'd already put his bag down.

'Of course,' she said as her eyes did an involuntary slide down from his eyes to his thighs.

Stop leering, woman, she told herself as he scraped back a chair across the tiled floor. But it was no good, involuntary thoughts about how soft and delicate he was in his movements, while at the same time having such a firm, strong physique were swirling through her mind. As he sat down he held his gaze on her for a few seconds.

'I'm sorry, you are writing a postcard.'

'No, no.' Molly cleared her throat, 'No, I'm, this is an ad. I'm selling my car.'

'Oh.' He smiled awkwardly and sprawled in his chair. He was wearing a dark blue T-shirt with the Kew Gardens logo embroidered on one side. A pair of secateurs hung in a pouch on a leather belt slung round his hips, as sexy as a cowboy's six-shooter.

A maturity, yet he was so young, shy even.

'What is it?'

'Sorry?'

'The car, what is it?'

'A Beetle. Convertible.'

'Convertible. Really?' His eyes held her as he leant forward and sipped at his tiny espresso. One last pull, you old bug you, she thought.

'What's wrong with it?' he asked.

'Nothing, what's wrong is I can't afford to keep it any more.'

'You must ask your husband for more money?'

'I don't have a husband.' For the first time since Daisy, she was truly glad she could say that.

'Boyfriend?'

This is pathetic, she thought. 'No.' Molly smiled a motherly don't-be-so-obvious smile. It was all she could do to resist saying, 'Take me, I'm yours...'

'You mind?' He patted his pocket and took out his tobacco. He had short, dirty fingernails. The fine silver bangle shouldn't have worked on hands like those. But it did.

'No, of course not. I used to smoke. Before I had Daisy,' she said, cringing at her own ingratiating-ness. But it was so, even the tobacco smelt exotic on him. She imagined kissing him. 'I used to do a lot of things before I had Daisy.'

'Ah.' He smiled again.

Woops. Bigbigbuggerup. Subject. Subject, change it quick.

'That was quite a party trick you did – with the perfumes. At Caroline's.'

'It is not a trick, it is my work.' He leant forward and tickled Daisy's tummy. She laughed loudly. Her giggly laugh was beginning to become her trademark. Christophe laughed too.

'She's cute.'

That's right. Get to me through my baby. Oh stop being such a crowey old slimebag cynic, Molly. Why should he want to get to me anyway? Why on earth? You're imagining it. He's just being friendly. Normal. Acquaintance. Caroline's gardener. That's all. Could be canvassing for work for all you know. Cool it and don't fool yourself.

'I'm not working now, you see.'

'So you are broke.'

Molly laughed and nodded. 'Getting there! And I don't want to go back to work! I really don't.'

'You are right. You are following your instinct.'

'Instincts don't, unfortunately, pay the bills.'

'When you have a baby, everything changes, no?'

'Yup!'

'Your boyfriend. He has left?'

Soon? What did soon mean?

'He, he's still coming to terms with it, with her, let's put it that way.'

'Sometimes your life has to change. It is natural for that.'

'Yes, but there's change and there's change, isn't there? I mean, I didn't realise how *biological* it all was. Of course I knew having a baby would change my life. But I didn't realise that it – I mean she,

133

would change *me* in quite this way. I mean, the bottom line is we're just lumps of biology, aren't we? Programmed to respond ...'

'This is something boys discover when they are twelve,' Christophe told her, taking a drag of his cigarette. 'No control over our bodies,' he continued. 'A man sees an attractive woman. Bam.' He crooked his finger from floppy down to up.

Molly looked at her Flake, sticking up out of her hot chocolate. Keeping her eyes on him, she leant forward and bit the end off. She kept her voice level. 'It's like, having children doesn't change your life, it changes *you*.'

'It has to, of course.'

'A woman responds, well, usually, a woman will respond – er...' Oh blimey, come back brain, where are you?

'To your baby's cry?'

'How do you *know* all these things, Christophe? Yes. I mean I would *kill* for Daisy, I would happily, cheerfully kill myself if it meant she survived.'

'This is nature. What I study all the time.'

'It must be very interesting.'

'I am trying.'

'Isn't the perfume industry all about marketing and packaging? Isn't the actual smell a bit of an afterthought? I mean, everyone's doing them, aren't they, all the models and so on.' She stopped. He was looking cross. 'Er, sorry I ...'

'Mine will be different. I promise you that. But you are right, of course. The market changes all the time, just as the woman changes all the time.'

134

'And men.'

'In the 1950s fashion was only a woman's business; they did not buy their own perfume, it was bought for them as a gift. As a romantic gift of love by a man. Only in the sixties with the sexual revolution did the woman change. Then of course she was free to make love to who she wanted and to buy what perfume she wanted. But now, phffff, now we are in the world of Aids and safe sex and this is why we have all these unisex. They have no sex, no passion. Even the basic nature of attraction is different for men and women, no? For a man, an attractive woman means he wants to go to bed with her! For a woman an attractive man is a mixture. It is his overall charisma, his voice, his movement...'

'And women are more loyal – to their perfumes I mean.'

Christophe laughed. 'They mate for life? No – not any more, not now, they have a big range to choose and they choose, one this for this, one that for that.'

'So how will yours be different?'

'It will take me a long time to explain.'

Daisy wriggled and began to fret. Molly looked down at her and then at Christophe.

'She's hungry. It's OK, you go ahead. I can leave.'

'No! Don't go!' She said it all too quickly.

He shrugged. She turned away from him discreetly while she undid her top and put Daisy to her breast, turned back to him and carried on chatting as if pulling a breast out in a café in front of a man she barely knew and, what's more, fancied, was the most normal thing in the world.

'I mean, I feel, not only have I got bigger feet and all that, it's like I'm someone else but I don't know who yet.'

'You change chemically on the inside.'

'It's like I'm this – woman – and I don't know who she is and I don't know where she's going to live, how she's going to survive, I know very little about her. And she's me!'

'I am envious. Your future is very exciting.'

'I hope I have a future.'

'Aw, come on.'

As they chatted, thoughts were short-circuiting and firing off again if he as much as stepped outside the words which were being said. If he crossed his legs. Hinted at his attraction for her. If he laughed. If he paid attention to Daisy. If only for that moment it was a bolt of energy she sorely needed.

She saw a passer-by looking in at them through the window. Two lovers, their baby. Laughing. Who'd know they'd just met? She didn't want it to stop. She let her drink go cold, sipping it as slowly as she could. When he offered to buy her another she felt overwhelmingly pleased, though the grown-up inside her was telling her over and over it was nonsense. But she needed a boost. She'd go for it and then be grateful. She'd keep it in perspective. A meaningless flirt with a flirt. What harm was there in that? At least he wasn't married. She double-checked his ring finger, just to make sure.

When he stood up to leave it felt like she was being abandoned. When he touched her arm she nearly exploded on the spot.

Not looking up again, not wanting to see him go out of the door, she held Daisy over her shoulder and patted her back softly.

'Here we are, love.' Molly looked up as a waitress handed her a green paper napkin.

'Oh? Thanks.'

'It's all right, love, I know what it's like,' she said.

Do you? Do you really? Molly wondered as she wiped the sick off her shoulder.

After dropping her postcard at the newsagent's, she nodded a hello to the *Big Issue* seller outside. She felt a warm affinity with another financially challenged person living on the tides of life in a place like Kew. She crossed the road to the chemist's, unable to resist looking up at the windows above Oddbins, where he had told her he lived, wondering which was his bedsit.

'That was just what we needed, wasn't it, Daisy? Now, let's go and get you some real food.'

She spent ages in the shop, picking up and putting down all the paraphernalia of baby foods, bowls, bibs and spoons, completely absorbed in her new shopping experience. Then, when she'd left with her purple striped paper bag with her box of baby rice, there he was again. With his back to her outside the newsagent's. He was writing something down, copying a phone number from an ad.

'Yes!' she said quietly to herself as she turned to go home, 'yes, yes, yes!'

CHAPTER NINE

'Kiss of life and solids today, ladies, I hope you all remembered your teddies.' Tamara, all black silk and large purple petals, burst through Izzie's front door, a gust of wind blowing in behind her, followed by Caroline.

'All this hot, cold, hot, cold is *so* annoying' she grumbled. Even with her car seat under one arm and an enormous fluffy panda under the other she looked effortless in apricot suede.

'I forgot my teddy,' said Molly in a meek, failed-mother voice.

'S'all right, I've got roomfuls of the bloody things,' said Izzie. 'Plonk your babies on the play mat and come and have some tea. We might as well make the most of it. Once they start rolling they'll be off like Exocets all over the place.'

'Daisy's rolling already,' said Molly, almost jumping back at the force of Caroline's face suddenly right next to hers.

'How old?'

'Pardon?'

'Age. What age is she?'

'Thirteen weeks. That's three months, isn't it? I must start counting in months now.'

'Lots of counting in motherhood,' said Tamara. 'Before you know it, it'll be years.'

'That explains it,' said Caroline with obvious relief. 'Charles is just eleven weeks yesterday. She's a full two weeks older.'

'Now, now, ladies. It isn't a race, you know,' said Tamara. 'They all do different things at different times in their own different ways.'

If you think that, you're on another planet, honeybunch, Molly thought as she took Daisy out of her car seat and put her on the floor beside Bob.

'There we are, Daisy. This is Bob. Remember Bob?'

Four new blue eyes looked up, trying out their focusing skills, blissfully unaware of the social expectations which lay ahead.

Go on, give a roll, can't you? she said to herself, wanting to show off Daisy's newly won pole position.

'Come and get your teddy, Moll,' Izzie called from the back of the room.

Molly followed her behind a large découpaged screen.

'Here, I might as well get a few of these things out,' said Izzie, pulling at a jumble of red and yellow plastic monkeys. 'You look in that blue box over there.'

Molly pulled around inside at a collection of toy bears, penguins, ducks and dolls. She pulled out a naked Barbie with legs askew.

'That's Gordon,' said Izzie. 'Loves girls' toys.

He'll only get them out when he thinks no one's looking, mind you.'

As Molly held a brown teddy in dungarees in one hand and a clown in the other, she heard Jenna call out, 'Look at Daisy go!' sounding like she was at a racetrack. 'Excellent one!'

Molly looked at the two toys, threw the brown teddy back in the box, returned the clown's big grin, and rushed back to bask in her moment of reflected glory.

Daisy, lying on her side, looked up and smiled.

'Has she found her feet yet?' asked Jenna.

'No, I don't think so.'

'Lulu has.'

'*Clever* Lulu,' said Molly; without her bidding, her voice came out in exaggerated ecstatic happiness at this news.

Jenna picked up Lulu's foot and waggled it. 'What's this, Lu? Hey?'

'Could you please all come over here with your teddies now,' said Tamara. 'Leave your babies getting to know each other where they are.'

While they sat themselves around the table, Tamara took a chair and moved it to the centre of the room, facing them. She pulled out a large, orange tiger from her bag and sat it on her lap.

'Right, ladies. I want you to watch me carefully,' she said, earrings dangling as she looked down at her tiger then up at her audience like a ventriloquist from a seaside show. 'Can anyone tell me what's the first thing you would do if you discovered your baby had stopped breathing?'

'Ring for an ambulance,' said Molly.

'Panic like crazy?'

'Yes, Jenna. That's why it's important for each of you to act out the correct procedure in turn.'

'You'll be *calling* for an ambulance *at the same time as* administering the kiss of life. You have to do both at once, ladies. Does anybody know what is happening inside when a baby stops breathing?'

Molly and Jenna looked at each other blankly. It was the friendliest look she'd received from Jenna so far.

'Your baby has *stopped breathing*. What is going on inside his tiny body? There is no oxygen going into his bloodstream. You only have moments before he'll be brain-damaged. And not much longer before he'll be dead. Now, pay attention.'

They watched silently as Tamara looked at her tiger and gasped with exaggerated shock-horror. She stood up and went across to an invisible telephone. Picked up the receiver and punched the air three times, miming nine, nine, nine.

'Wouldn't a mobile be quicker?' said Caroline.

'It depends where your mobile is, Caroline,' said Tamara crossly. 'You go to the *nearest* telephone. So. You have your baby on your lap, and with two fingers you find out where his heart is. First across,' she measured, 'then down three times. Hold baby's little nose, remember they have tiny, tiny lungs so no blowing them up like balloons. Blow short and sharp. You're transferring your own oxygen to keep him going until help arrives.' She blew into the tiger's mouth. 'Then puuuush

141

gently.' She pushed its chest. 'Blow. Push. Blow. Push.'

'Remind you of anything?' said Izzie.

'Shhh,' said Jenna.

'Right, ladies. Shall we all do it one at a time? Molly, up you come. Miming's important, ladies. Makes it stick in your mind more. Remember, you'll be panicking, anxious, worried. There'll be no time to read instruction manuals.'

After they'd all taken their turn, with Caroline doing an exaggerated mime of rummaging in her bag for her mobile, Izzie went off to make the tea.

'It's a good idea to teach your partners, your parents, anyone who'll be spending time alone with baby.'

'I'll show Ulé as soon as I get home,' said Caroline.

'If she's a trained nanny I'm sure she'll be well versed in the techniques.'

'She's only an au *pair*,' said Caroline, 'she's there to help me, not to take charge. Though I'm so furious with her I can barely bring myself to speak to her. And as for Christophe . . .'

'Why's that?' said Molly a bit too quickly.

Caroline turned sharply to her. 'In my home! The two of them. Doing – doing – *it* . . . .' The tiny pupils of her large, steel-grey eyes bored into Molly.

Well, at least that put an end to her trying to work out whether having two men not calling was better than having one not calling or none not even possibly going to call, ever.

'It's her home too, is it not?' said Tamara.

'Ulé is a *guest*, Tamara. A *paid* guest.'

'What exactly happened, Caroline?' said Tamara, in her low, caring voice, sucking in her cheeks like she knew what the reply would be.

'You know. I found them.'

Molly looked down at her clown. It smiled back at her, mockingly.

'In her *room*!'

'What she does in her room's her business, isn't it?' said Jenna.

'No, it isn't! She's next to Charles's room. He was in there having his afternoon nap at the time! *She* was in charge!'

'Well, that's a bit naughty, isn't it,' said Tamara.

'I'd been tipped off Vivian's would have the new pressings in and had gone into Richmond.'

'Pressings?' said Tamara.

'Olive oil on draft. Harvey Nicks quality without the parking problems. I'd gone over, only to have to go back home for my credit card. The house was completely quiet. Much too quiet. So I went up to see if Charles was all right and there they were!'

Molly remained silent.

'It was *disgusting*! I nearly fired them on the spot, but then how could I let two staff go at once?'

'What did you do?' said Jenna, pushing her legs together and lying Lulu on her lap, her head furthest away from her, then pulling the baby up towards her with her hands.

'Super head control, Lulu,' said Tamara.

'Closed the door quickly, of course.'

'Have I been missing something?' said Izzie, coming back from the kitchen.

'Ulé's shagging Christophe,' said Jenna.

Caroline glared at her.

'Well, that was on the cards, wasn't it?' said Izzie matter-of-factly.

'In the next room to Charles?' said Caroline.

'We have them in the bed next to us when we're at it.'

Caroline gave Izzie a sharp, disgusted look.

'When they're *babies*, Caroline.'

'Even so ...'

'I don't think we want to hear about your sex life, Izzie,' said Tamara.

'You're a married couple, Izzie. It's utterly different. Utterly.' Caroline sipped at her tea with little pecks and rolled her eyes around.

'Do you think if he'd woken, Charles would have demanded a certificate?' laughed Izzie.

'Let's get on, shall we?' said Tamara briskly, 'Are you all right, Molly?'

Molly looked up and nodded, trying to get the hurt, the stupid, childish, hurt, out of her.

'While we're in our tea break, I have a suggestion.'

'Yes, Izzie,' said Tamara.

'Are you all Friends?'

Molly and Jenna looked at each other, not sure how to take it.

'Of Kew Gardens?' she added.

'I've got a season ticket,' said Molly, trying to brighten up.

'That doesn't count.'

'Oh.'

'We're Associates, as you know,' said Caroline. 'We're going for canapés and a trip up the Pagoda tonight.'

'I can get you in, Moll, if you want,' said Izzie, ignoring her. 'The advance booking form is through for the Kew Gardens Summer Swing picnics.'

'Oh, they're excellent,' said Jenna.

'So I was wondering. Shall we get a group together? We fancy the Bootleg Beatles this year. Our other halves could all meet each other.'

'I'll have to check my diary,' said Caroline.

'We normally go to Jools Holland, everyone does, don't they? But none of the music's our scene, really, so I guess we could change nights,' said Jenna.

Izzie turned to Molly. 'You have to come. It's the height of the Kewite season.'

'Ahem,' said Tamara, 'after the Horticultural Show you mean.'

'That's a matter of opinion, isn't it?' said Izzie. '"Hey Jude", gallons of wine and a hundred tons of fireworks or a few shallots and radishes fighting it out in a tent.'

'Really, Izzie!'

'Only joking, Tamara. So – anyone up for it? It sells out bloody fast so you'll have to be quick.'

'We're on,' said Jenna. 'Jason'd love to meet you. He's heard so much about you, and Lulu's little friends. Hasn't he, Lu?'

'I'll be in Tuscany,' said Tamara curtly, 'but thank you all the same. Now really, ladies, we must get on.'

'Yes,' said Molly slowly, 'if you could get me a ticket, that'd be great.' She was dead curious to meet nappy-changing Carter, wealthy lawyer Theo and cord-cutting Jason. 'Can we bring the babies?'

'If you want to,' said Izzie, 'though I'll be buggered if Bob won't be weaned by then. I want my tits back.'

'Solids, ladies, *solids*!!!' Tamara frowned at her watch.

'I wanted to invite you all to something too,' said Jenna. 'We're having a full-moon barbie? For me it's the full moon, anyway. For Jason it's some cricket match or other. He and his mates are getting together in the afternoon? We thought the wives and girlfriends could come along in the evening? It'd be neat, so long as the men aren't too pissed by then. I could do with some girly support?'

Tamara looked at her with an expressionless stare. 'I'll – check my diary, Jenna. Now, ladies. Has anyone had any peculiar poos lately?'

Molly didn't pay much attention to Tamara's lecture on solids. After she'd gone they got to frenzy pitch talking about Jenna's flower wedding and she tried to block her ears completely. She couldn't stop thinking about it. She remembered Ulé, stamping her cigarette out on the ground. Ulé, half her age. Ulé, less than half her age. No wonder he hadn't phoned. Served her right for thinking like a lecherous old woman.

'You've got all of this wedding stuff to come, Molly,' said Izzie kindly.

'I don't think so somehow, I think I've managed to

146

leap across that one, and divorce, in one go,' laughed Molly.

'Aw, come on . . .'

'I'm too old now anyway. I feel about ninety next to you lot.'

'Come on, you're all right,' said Izzie.

Caroline was looking at her in a strange way.

'Yes,' she said to Caroline, 'I'm single.'

'Oh *dear* . . .' said Caroline, as if she'd lost a glove.

'I don't know,' said Izzie, 'there's not much difference once you've had kids, is there? To be honest. The number of times we do it I might as well be single. Wish I had that Christophe hovering about, Caroline, that might perk me up a bit.' She laughed her machine-gun laugh, stopping abruptly as she caught Molly's expression.

Jenna leant forward and spoke softly. 'That's my big worry about the wedding. I'm so right off sex. I only hope we're doing it again by the time our honeymoon comes. He's a sex and sport man. That's Jason. Thank Christ for the Internet, that's what I say, or he'd've exploded by now. Or gotten himself a mistress or someth...' She looked at Molly as her voice faded away. 'I've bought the underwear already? From that shop in Church Street?'

'They have *fabulous* stuff in there, don't they,' said Caroline.

'Don't they just? It took me ages to decide between La Perla and Passionata.'

'Oh you'll be all right by then,' said Izzie confidently.

'I'm going to have to be, aren't I? Lie back and try not to scream in agony.'

'It's still *sore*?' said Molly.

'Sore doesn't come into it.'

'Stitches?'

'Tear,' she whispered.

Molly shuddered.

'It's perfectly normal to go off sex after birth,' said Caroline. They all looked at her. So was she not doing it either? She leant forward, looking behind her quickly. 'I'd be interested to know if any of you have this problem but in my case, it's not so much my, er, undercarriage, as *Theo*. He's just not interested.'

'Oh dear,' said Molly sympathetically.

'I don't mind. I'm not that, never have been that – what's the word? – physically – shall we say – driven myself. Nor Theo come to that. Not like that Ulé. We have more of an *understanding* relationship. It's really all right. We know all there is to know about each other.'

'*Do* you?' said Molly.

'I should think so, we've known each other since we were twelve.'

Izzie, who'd gone uncharacteristically quiet, sat up.

'Let's face it. Now three babies have gone through there, you could get the Millennium Dome up my fanny. Chance would be a fine thing, that's what I say. With our houseful, getting to do it at all is bloody impossible.'

Caroline looked up at the ceiling.

'We get two goes at it a week,' said Izzie. 'On the outside. I'd just got Gordon and Bradley trained, too, then this one comes along. Typical.'

'What do you mean, trained?' said Jenna.

'At the weekend, they get themselves up, get their Monster Munch from the crisp cupboard and head straight for the cartoons. When we hear the *Rugrats* jingle we know we've got about eight minutes. When we hear them both yelling "I want that! I want that!" we know the commercials are on and we should be about halfway by then.'

'Do they *know* what you're doing?' asked Caroline, twisting her bottom lip.

'No questions asked or needed when crisps and cartoons are online. The bigger, or not as the case may be, problem with my Carter is will he get it up or not?'

'I thought all men woke up with erections,' said Molly.

'Speak for yourself, darling,' said Caroline.

'If he's been hard on the booze the night before, that means Mr Softy's come to stay. We'll have a good *cuddle*, mind you. To be honest, I think I prefer it that way. And sometimes, downstairs, if there's a new commercial for something they really really want they don't let up on the shouting for me.'

'What do you do then?' said Jenna.

'If they keep yelling, I call down – "Comiiiing." That shuts them up for a few minutes and gives Carter enough time to do what I said we'd do. Come. Well, at least he does.'

*

149

Molly set off home feeling quite bright. Christophe and Ülé wasn't really a surprise. At least he'd shown her she hadn't completely shut down in the erotic department. As for the others, she'd been horribly glad to hear their lives weren't entirely without problems. And never the kind of problems she'd ever had with Max. Soon? When was soon?

After the brilliant April morning, a strong wind picked up, obliterating the sun with one big, thick swipe of cloud, as if it had never existed. Molly put out the ironing board, happy to be inside listening to the wind rattling through the budding branches and dying daffodils. She didn't really mind ironing then. The warm thudding and senseless folding waste of time of it all harmonised with the outside gloom. She'd turned the lights on early, the orange glow bringing back the cosiness of deep winter. Leaving spring, like so much else, just a memory.

CHAPTER TEN

Molly lurched forwards as she slammed on her brakes hard.

'Sorry!' She casually repositioned herself into a cooler, arms-draped-on-top-of-steering-wheel mode as she sat staring at the two deer hanging nonchalantly about in the middle of the road. '*Now* I know why there are so many four-wheel drives in Kew. They all come here at weekends to practise for their winter safaris.'

They were on their third circuit of Richmond Park and she was still without a hint of a clue if it was the car Christophe was interested in, or her. Accelerating, she returned to her neutral car-selling mode. 'Well, at least that showed you saw how good the brakes are. Its body's a bit bashed about as you can see, but it's in very good condition for its year.'

'What's it like underneath?'

Whaaat?

'Like steel, and it had a new roof, oh, when was it? About two years ago.'

While she prattled, she couldn't help marvelling

at the fact that here he was, sitting there, in the same little space, just behind her left ear.

'It's got six months' MOT left but it always sails through. If it's taken care of, it'll go on forever, I'm sure.'

Christophe leant forwards and rested his arms on the back of the front seats. 'I can see that,' he said, millimetres away from her ear.

Momentarily struck dumb by this, she allowed herself to speculate as to the meaning or non-meaning of his sudden shift in proximity. All she could be sure of was that the presence of his right hand dangling a hair's breadth away from her left shoulder was making her skin prickle all over.

'Whenever I drive through here I, er, tell myself I really should come here more often.' She concentrated on keeping her voice level and wobble-free as she gestured across the vast open grasslands.

'To drive with no roof is so good. To feel the sun,' said Christophe.

Just to feel your bum, thought Molly.

'There are no seat belts in the back, as you see. That's another reason I have to sell. When Daisy grows out of this seat, she'll be going in the back. I mean I *could* get them fitted but...' Stop waffling, woman, and get on with it. 'So – why, exactly, I mean, what use is a car like this to you? Don't you need your 2CV van for your, um, gardening stuff?'

Christophe laughed. 'The attraction is obvious.'

Arrggh, it *is* me.

'To be in the open air.'

It's it.

'I'm beginning to feel a little bit dizzy. Shall we stop for a coffee?' she said as they drove past Richmond Gate for the fourth time, 'Pembridge Lodge is just up ahead. It has lovely views.'

'Can we keep going?'

'I'm thirsty.'

'Just a little longer, please.'

'OKaaay.' She put both her hands on the steering wheel and pressed her foot down. Let's get round and out of here.

'Here, just here!' he said half a circuit later. 'Pull in at the next car park.'

After parking, she made a big show of putting the roof up, taking it down and putting it up again while Christophe prowled around, looking at the tyres, poking the wheel arches.

'There's a beautiful wood just over there, shall we go for a little walk?'

'Yes, all right then. Why not?' Yes, she thought. *Yes!*

'It's magical!' said Molly in hushed tones. They were following a narrow, twisting woodland path, crossing a series of miniature slat-bridges over a tiny stream meandering through an ever-changing vista of blossom and magnolia.

'The English spring, it's better than I dreamt.'

'Oh, I don't know, Provence has pretty perfect weather, doesn't it?'

'But we have nothing like this – this fresh, lush, all this pent-up energy, it's fantastic.'

'How did you find this place?'

'From the students at Kew.'

'Of course, silly me.'

'They know everywhere round here.'

Daisy shrieked with glee, kicking her legs furiously as a group of startled rabbits scuttled into the bushes right in front of her pushchair.

'But how did you get to go to Kew Gardens? I mean, how did you get into all this perfume stuff?'

'Stuff?'

'Sorry – I mean ...' She touched his arm lightly, quickly withdrawing before it could be taken for anything but a chummy gesture. The path was narrow enough but they were keeping a studied, platonic distance.

'It's the family business.'

'Making perfumes?'

'Growing. My father has a farm. His jasmine is famous in Grasse. It's my job to make it famous in the world, before it disappears.'

'Why should it do that? '

Christophe huffed. 'It almost has already.'

'Why, there's more perfumes around than ever, aren't there?'

'Not so many made with flowers.'

'What do they make it with then, carpets?'

'It's a thing we call les *lignes de force*. Any smell can be broken down by computer into its chemical components.'

'Wow.'

'It is very clever, yes, so that is the way it has been going. Of course the industry still uses many real flowers, but, apart from the best, like Chanel and Jean Patou, they are not French flowers.'

'Really?'

'We used to grow tuberose, lavender, mimosa, *fleur d'orange*, violet, and of course the rose and the jasmine. Now eighty per cent of the jasmine is from Egypt and the nearly all the rest of it from India. France has only a handful of farms left.'

'But why?'

'You can ask! There are many reasons. My father, he has the best land and he's keeping it for me as long as he can but, even for him, the temptation to sell...'

'Why on earth would he want to do that? If he's got the best land, the best jasmine, the best – a son in the business ...'

'For centuries people say the streets of Grasse smell of the flowers, their scent coming in from the fields all around, in each breath you take.'

'Just like here.'

'Today, that is a sick joke. All you can smell is the traffic, the suntan oil and the money coming from the Côte d'Azur.'

Molly shook her head sympathetically. 'These property booms.'

'It's happened already. Most of the farms have gone. All you will see if you go and look across the plains of Grasse is condominiums, villas, apartment blocks, going all the way to Cannes.'

'With Cannes prices?'

'When I was born there were over two thousand growers in Grasse.'

'And when was that?' Molly asked casually.

'In the mid-seventies.'

Hmm, twenty-five then, bit older than he looks. Still, *twenty-five* ... wait till she told Amanda.

'Now there are less than a hundred, and then they grow the rose, most of them, not the jasmine. Jasmine is a delicate flower, it needs care all the year by human hands, not machines, it has to be picked by hand and looked after by hand.'

'And I guess labour's a bit cheaper in Egypt and India.'

'Also, it flowers at night-time, so it has to be picked early in the morning or phmmm,' he waved his hand, 'the smell evaporates, eaten by the sunlight.'

'So you've got a bit of an overtime problem there as well.'

'But you don't have to be a *nez* to smell the difference between the French jasmine and the foreign jasmine. That's why the best still use it. Like Chanel has bought from the same family for generations.'

'They'll be all right then.'

'Grasse jasmine, it's one of reasons Chanel No. 5 is such a classic.'

'I like the box myself.'

'The box, yes. On top of this we have to compete with the world market. The Americans, the Japanese.'

'Jo Malone.'

He nodded. 'All the time the property tycoons make my father bigger, bigger offers, and all the time I tell him to wait a bit more. The good thing is the boutique perfume is becoming the fashion now.

People want unique perfumes and will pay for them.'

'Well, it sounds like you've got the right credentials to make a go of it, Christophe. But what's going to make yours stand out?' Blushing hard, she quickly tried to backtrack. 'I mean...'

'It's OK. I know what you mean.'

She laughed nervously.

'Flowers have a cycle of fragrance, they smell different, they *are* different through the day, through the season, but, more important is, just like women, through the phases of the moon. At full moon they are bursting with what we call their esters, their odours. This is when you get them at their most powerful. Most potent. So, for my perfume, we will be harvesting our jasmine only at full moon.'

'Won't it be a bit – dark?'

'You haven't seen a full moon in Provence?' He laughed. 'It's like the lighting of a football stadium! And then, of course, I have to find the orchid.'

'It does all sound very expensive?'

'The best is always so.' He did one of his shrugs, turned and smiled at her. 'But this is all me. What about you? What do you do?'

'Did I do you mean.'

While she went through all the usual stuff about working and holidays, her mind was elsewhere. Shouldn't she just be taking the lead here? Being the eldest, the grown-upest one between them. The *woman*. Should she risk all and make a grab? *Don'tbesoridiculousMolly.* She kept both hands firmly clamped on the pushchair. She'd never made a first move in her life. She couldn't start *now*. Could she? But what if he was waiting for that? Maybe he was used to girls making the first move? Isn't that what people did these days? Bloke like this, he had to be. She could miss out altogether by being so behind the times here. But – no. She wasn't a twentysomething propping up the All Bar One. Her car might be having a good hair day but that didn't mean Molly was too. She didn't look quite so bad as in those dreadful first few weeks, though she could hardly have got any more dishevelled, but she shouldn't kid herself. She had to be careful, she couldn't cope with any more rejection.

She turned the questions back to him.

'So – you learnt it all from your father? How incredibly romantic.' She dropped it in. A gently-gently, token gesture of a hint, which came out with all the subtlety of a breeze-block landing in a puddle.

Deep in the wood now, they came across a small lake fringed by bushes.

'So – he taught you all you knew,' she tried again.

'I had to go to perfume school as well. Look at these.' He cupped a bud in his hand.

'What are they?'

'Camellias. In a few weeks' time, this will all come out, but this is the most beautiful time now. Can't you feel the energy of it? There but hidden away in these tiny bombs. The waiting? The anticipation? It's like the force of the whole forest is about to explode. Here, touch it.'

Molly obeyed, her finger millimetres away from

his as she stroked the bulging fat bud. She left her finger dangling, waiting for his to curl over hers. But he let the branch drop back down and walked on.

She clenched her teeth and cursed under her breath, lurching Daisy in her chair as she pushed forwards.

'It's the reason I'm here, to find the right orchid.'

'Why the orchid, I mean I know it's exotic but...'

'One of my selling lines is this: the perfume for the woman whose inner beauty is as complicated and mysterious as the rarest orchid.'

'Orchid and moon jasmine, sounds good,' Molly murmured, not daring to look at him.

'Also, wild flowers, and weeds.'

'*Weeds?*'

'Weeds I predict will be the new exotic. Look at them! Wild, free, indestructible. Weeds and wild flowers. Like all wild flowers the woman who wears my perfume will be strong and independent.' He stopped and smiled into her eyes. 'But,' he added, 'perhaps not as inaccessible as may first be thought,' before walking on towards another little bridge, leaving her standing stock-still. She clenched her fist, Henman-like, behind his back. Yesss – *now*! Go on, Molly, go for it. Pounce, girl. Just a peck. At the bridge, he stopped, stepping way back and out of her orbit as she reached him.

'And then, for my undercurrents.'

'What *undercurrents*?' She stomped across the bridge, unable to hide the fury in her voice. As if picking up on her tone, Daisy started fidgeting.

'I will have myrrh for mysticism, leather for

sophistication, and vanillin, a powerful aphro-disiac.' He caught her up.

Only half listening, Molly was looking down at Daisy's legs, kicking like crazy, wondering how the hell she was going to go about getting a soggy tit out of its milky hell-hole.

'Christophe, do you really want this car or not?' came out of her mouth all by itself. She managed to close it just in time before it added, And if not, what the *fuck* are we doing here?

'Are you in a hurry to sell?'

'Yes, I'm desperate. Now, would you excuse me for a moment?' She hurried quickly on ahead to a bench.

And how's this for a passion-killer, honeybunch, she thought as she unzipped her bra.

She was glad to see there was no one else around apart from a painter, sitting on a tree stump in front of his easel in a distant clearing. Christophe settled down next to her and began talking about his mother. There we are, she thought. Great. That's breastfeeding for you. Just great. His mother. How very fond of her he was. How much he missed her. She was beginning to feel seriously depressed. She wasn't a potential lover, she was his *surrogate bloody mother figure!*

She kept her eyes on Daisy's half-closed, blissed-out ones, till she heard him asking her about her mother. He was shocked when she told him she had-n't seen Daisy yet. She tried to explain about her mother's animals, which stopped her coming over from Spain, and Colin, her ghastly stepfather, who stopped Molly going there, but she really didn't have the energy. It was getting chilly and she felt very tired. The solo calls and responses of the birds' evensong, echoing through the treetops, made it feel even colder and later than it was, and the reflexive side of her body began to wonder what the hell she was doing there. Why was it sitting on a hard, wooden bench in a chilly forest without any form of refreshment whatsoever nearby, instead of being in its normal spot at that time of day, which was on its back on her bed, revving up for *Countdown*, with a cup of hot steamy tea and a dunky digestive or three as Daisy passed out into blissful oblivion.

Beyond caring, she rummaged for a tissue and shoved it down her bra. 'Out like a light,' she said, tucking a slumbering Daisy into her pushchair.

'All the fresh air is good for her.'

'It makes me feel knackered, too,' said Molly, sighing loudly as she leant back on the bench with the satisfied feeling of another job done.

'Awf!' she yelled. A split-second bolt of lightning had shot down her spine and up again before stopping somewhere around her solar plexus where it had dissolved into a meltdown of every nerve ending in her body. Instead of leaning back onto hard wooden slats of bench she'd come into contact with a soft squashy arm. An arm with a silver-bangled hand at the end which, as she struggled to take the situation in, moved forward to drape loosely and heavily down across her left shoulder. Oh, the weight of it. The heavy, comforting weight of it. She took a deep breath and quickly grabbed his hand.

Partly to confirm she wasn't imagining it and partly in case it had any ideas about going back from whence it had come.

Sensations of fear and anticipation engulfed her as they sat quietly, listening to every note of the suddenly incredibly meaningfully beautiful birdsong. Her hand caressed his. His caressed hers. Then together. They squeezed. They stroked. Each finger in turn. Exploring touch. Feel. They watched the artist pack away his easel, giggling quietly together in their new camaraderie at the way he kept his head down, deliberately, it seemed, not looking over at them. She didn't want to move. She dared not look at him.

Finally, 'So, how long are you going to be in Kew then?' she said quietly.

'As long as it takes to finish my research.'

'Have you got much left to do?'

'Oh yes.'

'Oh, good.'

'I have time on my side to do this. All the best things. They take time. No?'

'Yes,' said Molly, 'unfortunately, yes, they do.'

CHAPTER ELEVEN

'*Gordon* – come here. *Now!*'

Molly could hear Izzie before she could see her.

'*I'm warning you!*'

A small boy in an orange fleece raced up the spiral staircase of the Temperate House in Kew Gardens.

'I'm counting! One, two, three … RIGHT, you little rascal.'

Izzie plonked a small hand in Molly's. 'Here, hold on to this for a moment, will you.' Before she had time to say hello, Izzie was off and Molly and Bradley were left looking at the contours of Izzie's leggings-clad bottom disappearing up the white wrought iron steps and into the treetops above. She felt the fine bones of Bradley's fingers gripping hers.

'What's your name?'

'Molly.'

'That's nice.'

'Thank you.'

'When I get my next pet, I don't know if it'll be a rat or a horse, but I'm going to call it Molly.'

'Well, thank you,' said Molly, flattered. 'You were right, I had no trouble finding you,' she said, as a red-faced Izzie clattered down and around the spiral, dragging a wailing Gordon behind by one arm.

'What was it I said?' said Izzie, puffing as she put her two forefingers between her glasses and her eyes to wipe the steam off. 'A quiet Sunday afternoon stroll and chat?'

Gordon's crying started Bob off, which started Daisy.

Molly looked down at Bradley, still standing quietly beside her, his little hand holding hers with all the trust in the world. It was only when people passed and glared that she realised the level of noise coming from their little group.

She recognised the look.

A glare from another world.

A few months earlier, it would have been her.

'I think we'd better get out of here before they call the plant police or we'll be chucked out for disturbing the fauna,' said Izzie.

'I don't know how you cope,' said Molly admiringly.

'Cope?' Izzie laughed. 'That's a good one. You just get on with it, don't you. Let's get out of here. I'm sweating like a pig.'

'Wanna see the fish,' Gordon wailed.

'Fishes!' Bradley piped up.

'Fish, fish, fish,' they choroused.

'They're not in here, they're in the Palm House,' said Izzie, oblivious to the passing glares. 'Listen, if we go and see the fishes, are you going to be good boys for Mummy?'

Gordon, his head held low, nodded.

'Pardon?'

'Yes,' he muttered.

'I didn't quite hear that?'

'Yes.'

'Come on then,' she said in a high voice, before lowering her tone an octave to murmur out of the corner of her mouth, 'never waste a bargaining opportunity when it's looking you in the face.'

They left the Temperate House behind in a clutter of pushchairs and children. The hot dry air was instantly replaced by a soft, warm breeze.

'Ah, this is better,' Molly breathed in deeply as she gazed across the acres of thick spring grass stretching away luxuriously all around them beneath a powder-puff sky.

'Where's the Orchid House?' she asked as casually as she could as they walked along. Though bumping-into possibilities were highly unlikely, they had come within the realms of possibility, enough to make her insides glow with a delicious churning of 'what-ifs?' Knowing she was making a prat of a fool of herself to no one but herself, she couldn't stop herself pushing her just-washed hair back and walking tall. Only in case, of course. Just in case. When she'd dropped him off, it had all been very polite. Too polite. Like nothing had really happened. He hadn't asked when they could meet again. Neither had she. He'd kissed her. Lightly, on the cheeks, leaving her with the horrible feeling he might just have been humouring her.

'Oh, right over the other end ... hey, I nearly forgot, the bluebells are doing their thing, aren't they?

Come on, kids. Bluebells for us, tree-climbing for you – then fishes, OK. Shall we go cross-country?

'Are you coming or what?' Izzie called back as she set off in the opposite direction to the Orchid House. Molly momentarily felt heavier as her body did an involuntary slump of a missed opportunity.

While they pushed and chattered through the bluebell woods, the boys ran wild, climbing, hiding and seeking amongst the cedars, larch and Californian redwoods.

'I don't often come here at weekends.'

'Too crowded, isn' t it. It's not so bad round here though.'

'It's not that. It's just in the week everyone's doing their own thing, aren't they? At weekends suddenly everyone's *with* someone.' Molly let off mentioning that what really got to her throat was how all the children seemed to have a dad's shoulders to ride on.

They sat down on a bench in the heart of the bluebell woods, parking Daisy and Bob side by side. Bob immediately hit Daisy with his rattle. Daisy looked at him in astonishment before giving him a swipe back with hers.

Molly held on to Daisy's arm. 'Daisy?'

'Just look at them,' said Izzie adoringly, 'best of mates already, aren't they?'

'They change so quickly,' said Molly, trying to stay calm as Bob gave Daisy another swipe across the cheeks.

'Bob's just cut a tooth, that's why his cheeks are so red. Daisy got any yet?'

'I thought that was at five months,' said Molly quickly, bringing the other arm in to full referee mode.

'Ha! Got you. You sounded just like that Caroline. Four to five months, some a bit earlier, some a bit later. Take that look off your face, it doesn't mean she's backward. It's when they understand the word "no". That's a day worth waiting for.'

'When's that?'

'About seven months. *Supposedly*. I'm still waiting for my two at four and six. And Carter at thirty-four come to that.'

'More a girl thing, I suppose,' said Molly.

Izzie laughed. 'I don't think any male ever gets the meaning of that, do you?'

Molly didn't reply. 'You caught me out there,' she said brightly, 'though you can't help comparing them, can you? What gets me wondering is if they are all so programmed to do these things at certain times. Like at three months you will roll, at five months, sorry, at four to five months you'll get your first tooth, at seven months you'll crawl ... where does it all stop?'

'At thirteen you'll get pussy spots and deep crushes,' said Izzie. 'And at sixteen you'll be madly in love with some spotty guitarist.'

'DJ.'

'At thirty not going out on a Saturday night suddenly isn't the worst thing any more.'

'At thirty-two it'll really bug you that you won't know half the names in the top 20. At thirty-four it won't worry you any more. At forty, high-heeled *shoes* suddenly seems like a contradiction in terms.'

'A bit pointless,' laughed Izzie. 'Yeah, I can see that one now. I must be getting old before my time.'

'How old are you?' said Molly.

'Thirty-four.'

Before Izzie could return the question, Bradley and Gordon came racing over from the depths of the wood. 'Here, Mum, these are for you,' Bradley said proudly.

'*Bradley!!!*' Izzie gave Molly a not-knowing-whether-to-laugh-or-cry look as she took the bunch of freshly picked bluebells from his tiny hand.

'I think we'd better get out of here, don't you?' Izzie stood up quickly, shoving the flowers between the folds of her pushchair hood.

'Who lives *there*?' said Molly as they approached a thatched cottage nestling in a clearing surrounded by bluebells, 'Snow White?'

'It's Queen Charlotte's,' said Izzie, 'No, not the maternity hospital. It's the queen's old summer house. Gordon and Bradley, *away*,' she hissed loudly as they caught up with the two boys at the front of the cottage.

A teenage Indian couple were sitting on the steps, in deep snog. Standing right in front of them, completely unself-consciously, were Bradley and Gordon.

'What are they doing, Mum?' said Bradley.

'What does it look like? Eating each other, stupid,' said Gordon.

'GET away from there, you two.'

The two boys ran off towards the tall curved glass dome of the Palm House rising from the treetops in the distance.

'Nothing like it to make you feel you're past it, is there,' said Izzie dreamily, oblivious to the couple's furious glares.

Oh I hope not. I do hope not, thought Molly to herself. Her body was telling her otherwise, back on happy full-glow alert as they walked in the direction of the Orchid House.

'*Get* up off that grass,' Izzie yelled as they rolled on top of each other, 'there's goose shit all over the place!'

More looks. Molly was beginning to get used to them.

'Bloody geese, they should shoot them all,' said Izzie.

Molly looked across to a large flock of geese grazing. 'Dogs aren't allowed, why bloody geese?'

'How could they stop them?'

'I don't know, there must be … aahhh, look at them.' Izzie's anger had dissolved into proud affection, then deep laughter.

Gordon and Bradley were running into the middle of the flock of geese, sending them scattering, their necks held ostrich-tall.

'Look at the stupid things.' Izzie was laughing more and more.

It was all Molly could do to stop herself running over and grabbing them herself. It wasn't the way to introduce children to animals. But she couldn't say anything. Her instincts had already picked up on one of the new rules in her new world. Telling friends' children off was the quickest way to gain an ex-friend.

All she said was, 'Poor geese.'

'Poor geese! They're bloody vermin! Like the squirrels.'

'Now, squirrels I can go along with,' said Molly.

'Rats with tails.'

Molly pushed on, looking across at an invitingly shady copse of hazel and birch. 'We should have brought a picnic.'

Izzie patted the bag dangling in front of her pushchair which crunched with the sound of crisp packets.

'Never without. That's the kids sorted. I thought we'd go to the Orangery after the Palm House. It's on our route. How long before Daisy's next feed?'

'An hour or so.'

'We always do the same. Temperate House, Fish, after the fish they'll start yelling for the Teletubby hill, then I do a deal with them on the Orangery – lollies for them and tea for me before home, all knackered.'

'You've got it all worked out.'

'Boring old bag, aren't I, everything planned.'

'What's the Teletubby hill?'

'What it sounds like. A hill. They love it. I think it's something to do with the sign next to it that says "Peace and Tranquillity Garden, would parents please ask their children to be quiet in this area." It's their joke. Putting that sign next to a socking great playhill.'

They strolled across the grass.

'Does Carter do a lot of overtime, then?'

'Tell me about it. GORDON … BRADLEY. Come here NOW!' Gordon had opened the door of the Palm House and had disappeared inside. Izzie began to run.

Inside, they were nowhere to be seen.

Molly began to panic as she pushed her way through the jungle of giant bamboos, rubbery spiky leaves and giant hibiscus flowers.

'It's all right, I know where they'll be,' said Izzie calmly, taking her glasses off and wiping them on her T-shirt before disappearing herself behind a gigantic bush of crimson-pink berries. Molly followed quickly before she lost her too, pushing her way through a forest of hairy old African palms, smooth date palms and bendy Madagascar palms.

They parked their pushchairs by the wrought-iron stairs and went down to a dark basement lit by fluorescent fish tanks. Gordon and Bradley were standing in silhouette, stock-still on plastic steps, their faces squashed against a tank ful of angel fish.

Molly and Izzie held Daisy and Bob up to the sea horses.

'Do you know the special thing about sea horses?' said Molly.

'What?'

'The men have the babies.'

Izzie gave a low, cynical laugh. 'Now why would they want to go and do a thing like that?'

'They're the only males of any species who

actually know a hundred per cent their children are their own.'

'It must be the lady sea horses who shag around then, mustn't it? Gordon, don't think I haven't got eyes out the back of my head because I have. Still, Carter could have that little piece of certainty if it meant he took on all the rest of it.'

'At least he's around.'

'Giving up booze for pregnancy would have finished him off for starters.'

Molly tried to picture Max back in the restaurant, suddenly dropping the news of Daisy's arrival out of the blue onto her. How would she have felt? Gobsmacked, certainly. Touched? Definitely. But then, powerless? Or powerful?

'When another one's on the way, I don't know what Carter gets more obsessed with, extensions, au pairs or getting a bigger motor. Though maybe there's a link there somewhere.'

'Think yourself lucky you've got him there.'

'Phffff, when he's not on overtime. Thank Christ for my mum, that's all I can say. Leave that little girl's step alone, Bradley. Bradley? Right, that's IT.'

Izzie disappeared in a waft of fight-referee mode.

Daisy gurgled. 'Mooo, moooo,' she kicked her legs happily.

'Nearly Daisy! Nearly. Neeeigh neigh ...'

'Oooohhh, boooooo.'

'BOO! Daisy, YES!' That was a new one.

Molly held her a little higher and put her cheek next to her daughter's. She was changing from a

Max-lookalike to a Molly's mum lookalike. And she hadn't even seen her yet. 'How can I leave the animals?' had been her refrain for as long as Molly could remember, though it was as much that husband of hers, Colin. If *he* wasn't around she'd have been over there like a shot. She had to go though. She'd look up some cheap flights to Spain, have another tiny tuckette into her virginal Visa.

Molly studied the sea horses, trying to spot any differences between them. A glint, perhaps in the females' eyes, or a world-weary expression in the males'. She tried to recall the exact moment when she'd realised a baby was something she wanted after all. She remembered how she'd debated this desire with herself over and over, questioning whether it was a positive want, or a negative, not wanting not to have. On top of the questioning of her own selfishness, which had, for years, been the perfect excuse not even to begin to worry about it. But then somehow, in all of it, the thought had transformed into something more solid that wasn't going to go away. A quiet fantasy. A what-if? To a real fancy, to a pesky nag. From a pesky nag to a real desire. She wanted to. She did. She really did. From the real desire into an unignorable obsession. And so, from obsession to a possible reality. The mad excitement of stopping the pills. The unexpected feeling from this that her body was her own again. Its destiny, her destiny. The realisation that that was it. That her fertility had rested, not on the all-positive sensation of the male climax, but on the negative, not popping those tabs. The decision to

173

throw away the tiny day-to-day dots she'd swallowed all her adult life. That was it. And so the possible reality became a real bump. Her 'it'.

She'd gone through all of that but for Max it had been bam.

Wham bam thank you mam. You're ON.

What other way to tell the news, except out of the blue? She watched Daisy watching the jewel-like creatures, chins tucked down into their necks, gliding along in their unfishlike way. Even when it was expected and wanted or, like dying from illness, anticipated, it was still a hell of a bloody shock. How would she have felt if, like Max, her body hadn't told her all those things first? Hadn't begun to prepare her, physically and mentally, for all that would follow. She could hardly have expected him to say, 'Oh, jolly good, another glass of wine, dear?' and carry on with his raspberry gratin, could she? Especially not Max.

She remembered the day she'd discovered she was pregnant. She'd been taking her lunch in the office and had been in the middle of a conversation with Louise, an American producer. A pleasant woman, not too many sharp angles like a lot of them. They'd just got their new transmission times through from Channel 4 and were talking about the press launch for the new series. Molly had swivelled round in her chair to look at the chart behind her. She remembered the red-bordered calendar vividly. Months pinned side by side. A whole year's-worth of days, with filming and editing weeks highlighted in fluorescent pink and yellow.

As she'd looked at the rows of red boxed numbers, one to thirty-one, it hit her. She tried to remember the last time she bought Tampax. She couldn't. As she listened to Louise talking about stills and press packs, it was as if a veil had come down across her face, the first gossamer of the invisible screen she'd never be able to get round again. She remembered how grateful she was Louise hadn't noticed and, even then in that moment, how incongruous and unrelated the two things were, the work thing and the baby thing. What had been so important moments before had become completely and utterly irrelevant. She remembered taking the last cherry tomato from its transparent supermarket tub and popping it in her mouth, absent-mindedly rolling the little red ball around with her tongue before piercing the skin with her teeth. As the dozens of tiny sweet pips had exploded in her cheeks, she'd looked down suddenly and accusingly at the empty cherry-tomato carton and there and in that moment the knowing had silently taken up its position in her mind. It took root immediately and began to grow and in the space of a few moments it had become as large, was as unmistakably there, as Charlotte Street was outside her office window. She slotted the nauseous feeling and her recent weight gain into the empty tomato box. She put those beside the fact that her breasts had started to feel like they'd been injected with several tubs of syrup and had to be virtually carried wherever she went. The impossibility of it all had become not only a possible, but a definite.

She'd never forget how, in that same moment, she was thrilled to pieces and devastated. Absolutely bloody terrified.

'Little buggers.' Izzie came back to join her. 'It's a constant battle. Think yourself lucky you've just got your gorgeous little one to think about.'

'If it were that simple.'

'Imagine being me, then, four against one, what did I do to deserve that?'

'At least you've got a husband, and you don't have to go to work.'

'*Work*!'

'I mean out to work.'

'I think I'd be better off sometimes. No – no, not really. I wouldn't want to leave you in a million years, would I, Bob,' she said, giving him a squeeze.

'I'm going to have to go back soon,' said Molly, as they set off up the stairs. 'Sometime soon.'

'Try not to think about it.'

'I am,' laughed Molly, 'I am! The problem is the less I think about it the more I'm reminded every morning when the bloody bills come dropping through the door.'

'A rich husband. That's what you need,' said Izzie. 'We should ask that Caroline to set you up.'

'It's not money that makes you happy, is it, it's the lack of money that makes you unhappy. That's the killer. Shall I tell you what a really good day is in my book now? A no-post day. No post is good post.'

'Come on, you two, keep up.' Izzie stopped. The pow-wow of boys, crouched down sticking leaves through the metal floor grid, ignored her.

'NOW!'

'I'm hot, Mummy,' said Bradley as she pulled him to his feet.

'It's not even funny and I'm not impressed.'

'I don't know about you but I'm knackered!' said Izzie a couple of hours later. She leant forward in her plastic seat, hunched over the table and took a large bite of chocolate cream cake.

'It's just a state of being for me.'

After the fishes and the Teletubby hill they'd finally reached the Orchid House. After a quick Christophe-less glance inside they'd gone on to the Orangery. Between the white brick columns, marble statues peered invitingly out of tall, arched windows, but inside it had been packed with straggly bad-tempered queues.

'Bloody Sunday afternoon, isn't it. Hang on a minute, it's Sunday afternoon!' Izzie had grabbed a couple of lollies, dropped the money at the till and left before the queuers had time to complain.

'Let me tell you,' Izzie had said, almost in a drool as they crossed the Green, heading for the old church in the middle, 'If you like cakes. If you like cream. This is one of the best caffs in all of London. Fresh cream. Thick, thick chocolate...'

They were sitting at a table amid the gravestones and semi-wild flowers of St Anne's. Spread out in front of them, a pot of tea and green china cups were surrounded by sandwiches, cream scones, walnut treacle tarts and enormous, crumbling wodges of home-made chocolate cake and organic lemon cake.

In between sips of Coke and handfuls of crisps, Bradley and Gordon played hide and seek among the gravestones. To the side of them, a cricket match was in full swing on the Green. Daisy and Bob, already fed, had passed out in their pushchairs. Molly felt her shoulders loosen and go down as she relaxed in the warmth of the sun beneath the screeching swifts and gently rustling plane trees.

'It'll be Jenna's barbie soon, won't it,' said Molly.

'I wonder if her house is as perfect as she is,' said Izzie.

'*Feng shui'd* to bits, probably.'

'Why is it people with flat stomachs are always so cool? I can't help thinking they're being smug all the time when they're probably not.'

'And as for Caroline!' Molly laughed.

'What a gaff, hey?'

'What a life! Though she seems to be just as busy as the rest of us. It must be unbelievably wonderful, though, to be able to have someone like Ulé there and take a few hours off every now and then whenever you feel like it.'

Molly watched a fielder, waiting motionless, legs apart, concentrating, cat-like, on a batsman hitting the ground with his bat.

'Her dinner party should be something else.'

A thwack echoed across the Green, followed by a short, sharp shout as the fielder leapt sideways.

'What dinner party?'

The umpire, in his black trousers and straw hat, the only one not in white, marched across the pitch. There was some kind of dispute.

'Didn't you get an invite?'

Molly looked at her blankly.

'All posh and proper? On thick white card? Oh, you're bound to. It'll probably be in the post, I only got mine this morning, yours probably got delayed.'

'Or stuck in with all the bills I shoved in a drawer this morning!' Molly tried to sound light. 'When is it?'

'Friday.'

'Soon!'

'Getting one in before Jenna if you ask me,' said Izzie.

'Perhaps I'm not invited, though. Not being a couple and all that.'

'I'll give her a ring later if you want. Check it out if you can't wait for the morning post.'

'Oh, I can wait for that all right.'

'Grab your moments, Moll, that's what you've got to do,' said Izzie, leaning back in her chair and holding her face up to the sun.

'You know, I think I could quite get into watching cricket.'

'Rounders in a straight line. That's what it looks like to me.'

Molly allowed herself to close her eyes. 'Oh to sleep, to sleep.'

'It's like walking through fog all the time, isn't it?'

'Do you know, I think I'd sell my house for a good night's sleep. Except I already have.'

'The rushing never stops, though, does it. That's the bad news. Even rests are done in a hurry.'

'I'm beginning to realise that.'

'The little buggers are the best and the worst thing that ever happens to you, aren't they? All wrapped up in one. Bradley – don't pick the flowers. Bradley, stop it this instant! God, I hear myself sometimes, like a bloody tape recorder, don't do this, stop it, stop, stop. All I say is no and stop.'

'But at least you're being *you*, Izzie.'

'What? A screaming old hag, you mean?'

'You're running your show.'

'When are you going back to work, then?'

'I wish people'd *stop* asking me that.'

'*You* said...'

'I know I said.'

'No one says it to *you*, do they?'

'No, of course not. But what'll you do then?'

'I don't know. What comes first. The childminder or the job? Whatever it is I do, I'll be spending all my time worrying about Daisy, that's one thing I know for sure. I mean, look at her. She's so tiny!'

'You'll get used to it. Worrying's what mothers are for.'

'When the time comes, God forbid, how do I get to interviews?'

'I can always take her.'

'Really?' Molly felt overwhelmed. 'That's very kind.' Then she added quickly, 'I wasn't looking for, hinting at...'

'No probs. My mum's often round helping. She'd love her. Till you get yourself sorted.'

'My, all my old friends, you see, they don't have children. They, the ones that did fell away years ago.'

'Like they do.'

'Apart from my old schoolfriend Julie, that is. But she's in Dulwich. It might as well be Birmingham the number of times we can get together. She's been a great help, though. She gave me this pushchair, and mountains of nought to six months stuff.'

'You do find out who your real friends are, don't you, when you have a baby.'

Molly went quiet. The picture of Gayle, Sukie, Katie and Amanda, all standing round her at the Portobello, gazing at her like she was off on a long trip. Cornered. Confused. Like Amanda's, their visits to Kew had been short and polite; as her refusals of their frequent invites out on the town had been the same.

'Oh, it's not them, it's me who's not up to the old nightlife any more.'

'Yeah, I think they do go in cycles, don't they? Most of them. You'll find that here too. When she starts nursery, us lot'll be like your oldest mates and the nursery mums'll all be the strangers. When she starts school, then you'll be hanging out with all the old nursery lot.'

'Like gangs?'

'Mum gangs. Terrifying. Then when she goes to school, the mums with the older kids'll seem like the big seniors to you too. Playground politics, phhh,' she threw her eyes in the air, 'they're not just for the kids to run around in, you know. And as for schools . . . you'd best start going to church now. And not just for scrummy cream teas either.'

Molly laughed. 'I don't think they'd have me.'

She only half listened as Izzie got onto her favourite subject, schools, gazing at the cricket, mesmerised by the amoeba-like spreading and gathering of white on green, till the sky changed and it began to feel cold and late and time to be inside.

As they were packing their stuff to go, a round of applause went up from the small crowd outside the pavilion across the Green. Two batsmen were passing each other, their white clothes turned to cream against the weakening light. One with head bowed, stooped and finished, hitting the ground with his bat, the other striding for the wicket, his head up, as they passed in and out of the long tree shadows which had crept right across the pitch.

Izzie went to round up the boys, licking the chocolate off her fingers one by one by one. Molly watched her fondly.

'What on earth is THAT?' said Molly to Bradley as he returned, grinning from freckled ear to freckled ear.

He held his hand up to her face. Inches from her nose, a lime-green caterpillar was working its way across his palm, bunching its behind up until it doubled then stretching its front out.

'Little boys' toys,' said Izzie with a sigh, pulling woollies out of her bottomless pram bag and glancing fondly at Daisy, fast asleep in her white floppy hat.

Bradley picked up the caterpillar and put it on a gravestone. They all watched it climbing up. Just before it reached the top, Gordon picked up a stone.

'Gordon! Don't you *dare*!' said Izzie. But before

she could stop him, he'd brought the stone down on the caterpillar, squashing it in the middle.

'GorDON!'

Its insides spurted out from both ends.

Molly and Izzie parted at the village. She stopped to see if her ad was still there. An excuse to linger for a while. She'd felt cheated at not seeing Christophe in the Gardens. The best things are worth waiting for. Puh! Since when?

Above her ad, another card caught her attention.

Part-time Help Wanted in Village Estate Agent's. Good pay for good computer-literate applicant. Flexible hours.

She needed to do things. Get back on track. Get a dress. Go to Spain. Pull her life together again. With the reality of her disappearing bank account to the fore of her mind, she deliberately avoided looking at Daisy as she scribbled down the number. Could that be it? A gentle kick-start back into the big wide world?

She hung around a while longer, staring at the ad, then up at the flats above Oddbins. Which one was his? Then back at the ad. Should she go for it? She only turned to go home when she noticed the *Big Issue* seller had started giving her funny looks.

CHAPTER TWELVE

'Darling, how *are* you?' Caroline, all strapless and thigh-hugging in bubble-gum pink, turned both cheeks generously to be kissed.

You don't want to know, thought Molly miserably as she padded, dog-like, along the parquet behind Caroline's diamanté clack. Trying to forget Max's cold, almost laughing rejection. It had been a daft last-minute casual invitation anyway. A piercing of the silence as much to stave off her own dread of going alone.

'Theo darling, come and meet Molly – and Daisy!' she called across acres of white sofas and cashmere cushions in the baby no-go room.

Molly looked across at the others gathered around the fireplace, drinks instead of babies in hand.

'I'm so sorry, I haven't even got a babysitter sorted.'

'Don't worry, but – remember what I said. For tonight baby talk is up there with religion and politics! We don't want to bore the men to death, do we? We're here to get to know each other. Now, if you'll excuse me for a moment...'

'I'll try not to look at her. Could we add schools to that list?'

Caroline looked at her blankly for so long, Molly thought she was going to slap her. 'Good idea,' she said at last. 'Theo darling, could you?' she called behind her as she left the room in a cloud of Mitsouko.

Molly hovered close to the door, her supreme tiredness compounding her feeling of other-worldliness. So, there they were. The husbands. She felt like she was there but not there. Belonging but, then again, not. An intruder on the housewife scene.

An elegant, balding man in pink check shirt and baggy brown cords left the group and marched across the room, his arms swaying and swinging out from his sides.

'Theo Symes.' He smiled at her with crinkly eyes and held out his hand. 'Now. What'll it be? G&T? Good, good!' he said, rubbing his hands together and disappearing off to the other end of the room.

Molly joined the group.

'Look at me!' said Izzie, holding her hands up tri-umphantly, 'Bob's a bottle babe, official!'

'Just like his dad,' said the man with the black beard and watery spaniel eyes standing just behind her.

'My tits are mine – all mine!' she sighed happily.

Carter grinned and nodded and held his drink up.

'We expressed, didn't we, Jase?' Jenna mimed a squeeze at her nipple, its outline clearly visible through her antique batik sarong. Jason, a tall, sporty big-bloke blond, just as Molly had imagined, grinned and put his arm around her. Jenna smiled up at him lovingly. 'Hold up, here comes Caroline, cut the baby talk, right, guys?' she said, almost fearfully.

'Molly, Ulé's agreed to take Daisy.' Caroline swept in, followed by the stooping Ulé.

'So, where's everyone going for Easter?' said Theo warmly.

A seizure of panic and fear gripped Molly as she watched Ulé leaving the room with her baby. An awful new sensation. Out of the door. Away. Towards the stairs. Stairs!!!

'Excuse me!' Molly darted out of the room after her.

'That should keep Ulé out of mischief,' she heard Caroline saying, 'with Christophe in the house. Where *is* Christophe, anyway? He's late.'

Molly took Daisy from Ulé before they walked up the stairs.

'It's not that, it's – I haven't left her with anyone before, you see. And ... the stairs ... look, they're steep here ... no?' She stopped.

'Is OK, no problem,' said Ulé, in her monotone voice which left Molly none the wiser as to whether it was or not.

Molly held Daisy and the banister tight as she went up. Christophe coming? Dinner party. Man/woman/man/woman. For her? Ulé! Ulé's room, where they...

When she returned they were all in the dining room scrabbling around reading place cards. There was no sign of Christophe.

'What's a goldfish got that a cod hasn't, that's

186

what I'd like to know,' Izzie was saying to Theo as she settled herself down next to him.

Molly caught a resigned look in Theo's eyes and turned her gaze quickly away. She sat herself down and concentrated on nibbling at a tiny piece of lettuce filled with pâté, letting the conversation go on around her.

'I mean, why does one get mashed into rectangles, covered with gold crumbs and stuck in the freezer and the other gets all the treatment. The tubs of food, the bits of weed, miniature castles, holiday homes, the lot?'

'It's the colour, isn't it,' said Jenna.

'What's wrong with shiny silver *cod* colour?' Theo put in.

'Gold is a sacred colour?' said Jenna, ignoring him, 'has been for zillions of years. It's pagan? It's why we have gold wedding rings, isn't it? Oh, we've set the date, haven't we, Jase?'

'Orange, actually. They're orange,' said Carter next to her.

Molly looked at the baby listener, gripping her chair against the sudden urge to rush upstairs. She slipped her gaze to the empty space on her left and down to the place card. De Mausigny? Christophe de Mausigny. She read it over and over.

When she tuned back in, Caroline was complaining about the blue ice rose in the middle of the white linen tablecloth.

'I ordered cerise, not turquoise, I told them to replace it immediately but they said another wouldn't freeze in time.'

187

Poor Caroline, in control of everything but not, Molly thought. The gap in the seating plan next to her seemed to be getting larger and more uncomfortably – there.

'I wonder where Christophe *is*?' said Caroline, who'd followed Molly's eyes.

'Maybe he's sneaked upstairs for a quick shag with Ulé,' joked Izzie.

'IIIiiiz,' said Carter, filling everyone's glasses.

New images. Daisy's there! Now?

'If they did, we'd hear the jolly lot on that thing,' said Theo, nodding to the pink plastic elephant baby listener sitting incongruously on the drinks cabinet.

'Mmmm, delicious, Caroline,' said Izzie. 'What is it?

'Rosemary and grapefruit granita.'

'Is it organic?' said Jenna.

'I don't think there's any such thing as organic *ice*, Jenna. If you mean is it tap, I haven't a clue, go and ask the caterers if you want. Do start, everybody, Christophe will just have to catch up.'

When Christophe arrived they were still on polite starter talk. Various ice sculptures I have known, with much attention paid to the rapidly melting ice rose vanishing into its silver plinth.

'An improvement on real flowers, what?' said Theo.

'What do you mean?' said Jenna.

'Cut, Theo. You mean cut. Theo hates cut flowers,' said Caroline.

'Flowers should stay where they belong. Who was

it? George Bernard Shaw, wasn't it, who said, "I love children but I don't chop their heads off and stick them in pots," hey?'

'Pah, you English,' said Christophe, grinning at Theo in a jovial faux-English way as he sat himself down next to Molly, not looking at her.

Hoping against hope she looked calmer on the outside than she felt on the inside, Molly concentrated hard on controlling her expression, keeping it to the fixed half-smile she'd mentally rehearsed, but immediately feeling that every tiny movement she made was exaggerated out of all proportion. And why *hadn't* he called, anyway?

'Of course,' said Theo, 'they're fine for certain occasions.'

'Weddings!' said Jenna, smiling across at Jason.

'Weddings. Funerals. Though these days people prefer to donate to charity, don't they.'

'But you *need* the flowers for the ritual. You have lost this. With your religion,' said Christophe.

'No religion, please.' Caroline held her hand up like a lollipop lady.

'How would it be at the end of the ballet, if the ballerina said "No flowers, please donate to charity on the way out." Not everything is to do with money,' Christophe protested.

'All right, at the end of the ballet, then,' said Theo. 'And the opera. But to have them chopped willy-nilly around the place. Doesn't do me any good at all. Who was it, D.H. Lawrence, wasn't it, who said flowers were innocent beauty.'

'He was wrong,' said Christophe quietly.

Theo raised his eyebrows challengingly.

'D. H. *Lawrence*? Wrong?' said Caroline.

'Flowers are weapons, fakes. They are sex. Ruthless sex.'

Caroline wriggled round in her chair towards Christophe. 'Tell us more.'

'They exist to fight for the attention of the lover, the insect. Take my study at the moment. The orchid. Have you ever looked at an orchid? I mean *really* looked?'

Caroline glanced at the others. 'I can't say I have.'

'They are full of tricks, these orchids.'

'What kind of tricks?' purred Caroline.

'OK, take the mirror orchid. It is disguised as a bee and smells of a female bee ready for sex. He tries to fuck it, but as he's fucking he realises he's made a mistake and goes to the next one.'

'I know the feeling,' said Jason.

'*Jase* ...'

'Orchis – Greek for bollocks, did you know that?' said Theo. 'Used them for healing testicles apparently.'

'And an aphrodisiac,' said Christophe.

'Kind of medieval Viagra, what?' laughed Theo.

'They are the biggest sex teasers, these orchids.'

'Like lap dancers,' said Jason.

'How would you know that?' said Jenna.

'Only joking, Jen.'

Molly smiled.

Jason grinned back at her.

Jenna turned her glare from Jason to Molly.

'So where are all the female bees when this is going on?' said Molly.

'Back at the hive, doing the ironing,' laughed Izzie, digging Theo in the ribs.

'We're having a flower wedding, aren't we, Jase?'

'I think we all know that, Jenna,' said Caroline, verbalising Molly's thoughts.

'Maybe we should change it, now we know what they're up to,' said Jason.

'In Kew Gardens?' said Jenna.

'You told us that,' said Izzie.

'Yes, but it's all booked now? The last Saturday in August? We've just got to find a place for the reception.'

'Have it here!' said Caroline. 'In our garden.'

'Aww no, we couldn't possibly put you to any trouble,' said Jason.

Jenna glared at Jason across the table. 'Are you *serious*, Caroline?'

'Why not? We have the best garden in Kew outside the Botanical, don't we, Theo? Christophe will have it looking its best ever by then.'

'Do you mean it?'

'It would be super fun to show it off at its peak, don't you agree, Theo?'

Theo had paused in mid-spoonful, and was looking slowly around the table. 'Er, yes.'

'That'd be so cool, I mean ... we could *walk*, from the wedding. To here, we wouldn't need cars. I was just saying to you, Jase, wasn't I?'

'You don't like cars but it doesn't stop you having one,' said Jason.

'The offer's there.'

'We'd love it, Caroline, thank you. You must all

191

come of course. And, by the way, while I think of it, can we all have a group photo before the main course arrives?' Jenna rummaged in her bag for her camera.

Molly was miserable. After the butlers had delivered the main course, she was frozen with her smile in the middle of a dinner party cul-de-sac. Christophe, to her left, *still* ignoring her, had been monopolised by Caroline. Carter, to her right, was talking to Jenna about his wedding memories. As she ate her pasta with sorrel, she watched the turquoise layers of folded petal ice slowly melting into nothing.

'Did you ever come across Emma Mandelson, Molly?' Carter suddenly turned to her.

'No – I don't think so.'

'Iz said you were on the holiday programme?'

'Oh – yes, I mean – no. I was.'

'Though come to think of it, all TV companies have an Emma these days, don't they?'

Molly laughed. 'Yes, you're right. Though I'm out of it all now.'

'Aye, that's the way. It's all changing so fast I can't keep up with it. If it weren't for my family I'd have got out long ago.'

'You're a film editor, aren't you?'

'Once. Now I sit clicking a computer keyboard like the rest of the bloody world,' he said sadly.

'It's not like it was, is it?'

'Time. That's what's gone. There's no time with these bloody avid computer editors. It's all got to be done yesterday and up there in an instant.'

192

'I used to love film cutting rooms,' said Molly, 'all those bits of film hanging up on pegs, like laundry.'

'The Steenbeck plates whirring.' Carter looked at her dolefully.

'The clunk of the splicing machine.'

'The tin film cans . . .'

'Aye, all piled up. It's criminal, it is. There's no room to think any more, that's what's wrong. They don't put that in their bloody budgets and profit margins, do they? Reflecting while you were spooling, that was part of it all. And if the Steenbeck bulb went – then bingo, it'd be all down to the bar for a couple of hours till Steenbeck Bulb Replacement-Department could come and change it.'

'It did need to change though, didn't it? ' said Molly.

Carter's watery eyes misted over. 'I never really got my hands on those Steenbecks either. I was an assistant then. When I finally got made up to Editor the whole bloody lot was replaced by computers. Within months there were no cutting rooms left. I was a has-been before I'd even been.'

'Ah, but at least you've got work. I can't even do my job any more. Not with a baby.'

'Take the money and let them get on with it, that's what I say. Do the overtime and run. Back to the kids.'

'Getting overtime's quite something these days,' said Molly.

'Got to count your blessings, haven't you. I've got my overtime and my kids.'

While she was talking to Carter she could hear

Christophe giving Caroline his perfume talk to her left.

'*Moon*-jasmine?' Caroline was saying.

'And wild flowers. It has to be dirty, sexy, earthy – but feminine.'

'But of course,' said Caroline.

'All about pheromones, isn't it,' said Theo loudly across the table. Everyone stopped talking and looked at him. 'From the Greek. *Pheran* – to transfer. *Horman*, to excite.'

'Yes, Theo,' said Christophe, looking at Theo admiringly, 'it is the way we relate to each other.'

'How animals communicate,' said Molly.

'Instead of talking too much,' sighed Carter.

Christophe turned to Molly for the first time with a big smile. 'And so do we. Like animals. Much more than we realise.'

It was like he'd pressed a button on her marked 'flush'. She quickly looked away to the ice sculpture which had taken on the role of Molly's surrogate security blanket for the evening. She found herself wondering vaguely if the red of her face went better with turquoise or cerise. Behind it, from the other side of the table, Izzie gave her a huge, obvious wink.

'Christophe, how do you *know* all this?' She tried to keep her voice level.

'As I told you, perfume school.'

Don't say that, she wanted to hiss, but no one seemed to pick up on it.

'It's all about marketing these days, Christophe, isn't it?' said Theo.

'Of course we learn that. But for the *nez*, the most important thing is memory, to remember the thousands of smells, and we have to learn so many things. The perfume since antiquity, the language of perfume, the raw materials, the culture, the biology. Botany, of course. Zoology, chemistry,' he marked each off his fingers, 'the regulations, beauty care. Containers, equipment. The economy, packaging. Marketing, psychology – very important. And of course art – music, food, the history of fashion. And of course sociology...'

Caroline was visibly swooning, resting her chin low on her hands and gazing up at him.

'A right old arts and science combo,' said Theo, impressed.

'You have to be creative and a scientist at the same time. And of all the thousands of smells, we have to recognise them not only on their own, but how they go together or not go together we have to store in our memory. It is like learning a language. We have to train hard our noses.'

'Where is this school?' said Molly innocently, as the image of a nose galloping around a circus ring floated through her mind.

'Versailles. I aim for something very different, though. I will not be led by the market.'

'Everything's led by the market these days,' said Theo.

'The way it is, the character of the perfume, it is made up by the big fashion houses. Like you say, Theo, by the marketing departments. Then we have to invent the perfume to go with their selling idea.

This is not for me. For me all the creativity goes together, this will produce the best result. It is common sense! If you break them apart you get a weaker, more liquid, result. I will keep myself free to work without this. People don't realise how important smell is every day. It affects you everywhere, your memory, your feelings, it goes to make up the way you are, the way you behave.'

'Sounds like it'd make a good TV series,' said Molly.

'If they made such things as proper documentaries any more,' said Carter.

'The computer can copy the smell of anything,' said Christophe.

'Bloody computers,' said Carter happily, filling everyone's glasses.

'I will have to use this for the orchid, it is the only way, but just for that. The only other synthetic will be the vanillin.'

'Let me get this right,' said Theo slowly. 'You want to compete with the multinationals, by yourself?'

'All perfumers work on their own scents as well. But, with the help of my father, I will concentrate on this alone, using the classic techniques. If it works I will work. If it fails, I fail. My life fails. But I have time. There is a very good orchid perfume already...'

'What's it called?' said Caroline.

'You can't get it outside Japan.'

'Why not?'

'The Japanese do not think the Western nose is sensitive enough for it. In Japan they know. They know all about the power of smell. They even have a competition just for the smell of the orchid. It is all very complex but I will harness this. You will see. '

'How?' said Molly. 'How on earth do you begin to do that?'

'In a perfume there are many layers. First of all, you have to hook the nose, you have to make it so that when you smell you get hit in the face with it. Power. So first you will be hit with a new ... your senses will realise this is something different. But it is underneath that you can't see straightaway, the middle, the base notes. This is what really matters.'

'Like drawers, you mean,' said Izzie.

'Drawers?' Christophe looked at her.

'You know, when you've tidied your drawers, not that I get much chance of that, the room seems clearer, even though it was all shoved away before, out of sight.'

'A lot of women wear men's aftershave these days don't they?' said Molly.

'Elle Macpherson does,' said Jenna knowledge-ably.

'And there's all those unisex ones around now.'

'Ozonic!' shrieked Jenna.

'Exactly. My point is political. Women trying to become men. To show equal status? No! All it shows is a homogenised, post-Aids, dull sexless world. What is missing is a perfume, *my* perfume, which will be for a woman's body. For *her* sex, not for her response to some marketing trick. A woman is a woman, a man is a man. No? They think a male smell will make them tough like a man. This is wrong. So, so wrong.'

'Good for business meetings,' said Molly.

'My perfume will not be for a woman who wants to be a man. It is for the superiority of the feminine. The new woman is strong, she grows and she grows stronger. This is the identity of the new millennium woman. *But*, feminine. All female, with flowers that grow independently. That need no looking after. Survivors. To represent the new woman. The strong woman. This is why it is so good to be with all of you. You will be absorbed into my creation.' He looked at Molly seriously.

'Hey,' said Jason, 'I heard of a weird one the other day. It's called Cash and it smells of freshly printed banknotes.'

'Gimme gimme,' said Izzie.

'Bath oil's my thing,' said Molly, 'those big bottles of supermarket bath stuff; you get a faint whiff in the bottle, but when you put any of them into the bath they don' t smell of anything at all.'

'You're better off with essential oils,' said Jenna, 'just a couple of drops of lavender'll do you.'

'What about the bubbles?' said Izzie. 'You've got to have bubbles. No, I know, a drop of lavender and a couple of squirts of Matey. That's it. I'll try that on Carter. Dum-ditty-dummmm.'

'Here, smell this.' Jenna held open her wrist to Christophe.

'Fig.'

'Right!'

'It's vegan? I got it on the Net.'

'What do you wear, Christophe?'

'Of course, nothing.'

Caroline did an exaggerated shiver.

'I have to keep my senses clear. A smell is as unique as a face.'

'Like wine-tasting,' said Theo.

'A little – yes.'

'The big question, then,' said Theo, 'is have you thought through your *own* marketing?'

'Yeh, chuck us your pitch, man?' said Jason.

'What about the Internet?' said Molly.

'Oh Norah,' said Carter. 'Now we're on to it. It was only a matter of time, I suppose. Everybloody-where you go it's the decline of the BBC and the bloody Internet.'

Christophe was looking at Molly. 'It is an interesting idea.'

'Selfridges perfumery. Sexiest place in London!' said Jason. 'Get it in there, mate, and you'll be doing fine.'

'*When* do you go there, Jase? I only have organic vegan. You don't buy it for me.'

'On the way to the food hall in my lunch hour, Jen, that's all.'

'Bloody Internet. People all over the world sat punching at a bit of plastic staring into space, bloody end of the world it is, the bloody end,' said Carter to his drink.

'I don't know,' said Jenna, looking at Jason, 'it has some pretty good uses.'

'Er yeah, there's some really cool games out there,' said Jason sheepishly.

'When will people cotton on it's just another form of bloody communication,' said Carter, 'like making a telephone call or writing a letter. In all this fuss and bother everyone's forgotten about the message.'

'I don't know,' said Jason, 'I think there are some pretty good messages out there, Carter. You should come and have a look at mine sometime. I'll show you what I mean.'

'Next question. The big companies spend millions on promotion. How can you compete?' said Theo.

'Slowly, slowly. By reputation. This is OK. This is back to how it should be.'

'Has it got a name yet?' asked Jenna.

'Not yet. I have to go back to France at the end of the summer when I have done my research.'

'Does it work on wine, your nose?' said Theo.

Christophe laughed. 'I am French.'

'Are you interested in wines?'

'Yes, of course.'

'Come. I've something to show you.' Theo stood up.

'*Theo!* I don't think so,' said Caroline.

'We'll only be a moment. Come on, follow me.'

'They're off to the basement, his pride and joy, his wine collection. I suppose a man's got to have *some* hobbies.'

'Wine collection?' Carter sat up.

'Go on, Carter, off you go,' said Izzie as if letting a horse out into a field.

'Theo! I do think it's a bit rude...' But they were gone.

Molly pressed the side of her spoon into her filo

200

tartlet, sending baked pineapple and mango splurging out of its sides.

Halfway through her pudding, the baby listener leapt into life with the rattle of snoring.

Molly sat up. 'Excuse me.'

She found Ulé and Daisy asleep. She watched them for a while. Happy to have spent an evening with real live people instead of the TV. Happy she'd managed to leave Daisy for a few hours, happy knowing it would get easier to leave her. She just had to take the plunge. Get on with it. Life, after all, did go on, would go on. Without Max.

She stopped off in the loo on her way down, weeing hard and noisily.

As she left the bathroom, she jumped. Christophe was standing outside. She stood back to let him pass, though she needn't have bothered as the landing was as big as her flat and the only furnishing was a pot with a few twisty sticks in it.

'Is she OK?' he said, stopping opposite her.

'Fine, absolutely fine.'

'Are you OK?'

'Fine, absolutely fine,' Molly repeated.

'It was great. The other day. I really enjoyed it.' He smiled.

'No – well, thank *you* for showing me the place. I'd never have found it, I'd never have known it was th–'

He touched her mouth with his finger. Molly stopped talking and stared back at him. Neither of them moved. He leant forward and kissed her lightly on the lips. She felt a hand lightly touching her waist as he moved closer.

A door opened downstairs.

She jumped away.

'Ahhh CHOO, meeeee hungry,' a strange voice wailed.

It was Izzie, holding onto Carter's back as he fumbled in the coat cupboard.

Christophe raised his eyebrows at Molly, put his finger to his own lips and disappeared into the bathroom.

'Ay up, here you go, love.'

'Big kissssssssss, biiiig kissssssss, Wheeeeeeeeeeeee.'

Carter turned to Molly as she reached the bottom of the stairs. 'It's all right, Iz is off on her Furbie impersonations. She only does it when she's rat-arsed, don't you, love. Come on now, let's be off home.'

'Cock-a-doodle-dooohoooooo. Fooom fooom.'

Despite hating them to pieces moments earlier for interrupting, Molly couldn't help laughing as she watched them tripping out of the door.

CHAPTER THIRTEEN

Molly shook out the last few drops of bath oil under the gushing water, the smell batting her back to her last Shalimar soak. The hysterically laughable impossibility of a Portobello suite now seemed as remote a luxury as time itself.

She hoped that by the time her mum gang arrived, the oil would have done its stuff, wafting the heady Oriental scent through the flat, disguising the worst of the traffic oxide air. The silky water made her skin glisten. She lay back thinking about her mother. Spain? Would it be more stressful or less stressful? Daisy in her mother's arms. That would be something. A bit of a tan. Before Jenna's party. Before the picnic. Get rid of that brain-dead head and back on-line, Molly Warren, she told herself, staring with detached fascination at her tummy flopping around like a beached jellyfish beneath the oily warm.

She pulled out a pair of leggings and a baggy white T-shirt from the drawer – lately promoted to best clothes status by the mere fact of their newness. She'd finally chucked the maternity dresses, but her once razor-sharp charity-shop chic had taken on a floppy feeling of fading desperation since it had become charity-shop necessity.

The lack of money cancelled out the lack of time which cancelled out the lack of money, and everything, not least the flat, had to stay as it was. A little of both could have put cupboards on all the kitchen doors. Got her a proper oven glove. A proper light. A wooden loo seat to replace the cracked brown plastic one that half slid off the bowl. The list was too long to begin doing anything about. But options could be opening up. Maybe a part-time job at the estate agents' could be the gentle kick-start on the road to recovery she needed.

She put Daisy under her play-gym and took her mug of tea out into the garden. The two lilac trees at the end were in full bloom, the purple blossoms shadowing the white. A ribbon of honeysuckle, teeming with bees, was unfurling itself onto the low wire fence which ran all the way round the garden. Bloody hell, bees! She was standing in a fearsome biting, stinging place. What did you do if your baby was stung by a bee? She rushed for her Penelope Leach. B. B. Bee, B for bee at the back – beds and cots, bedwetting, bibs. No bees. Sting! Try sting. Sterilising, Sticky Eye … STINGS. She read the text quickly, the words 'fear' and 'panic' leaping out from Penelope's solid, calm text. OK, Penelope, she said aloud, so the thing to do is not to be afraid and not to panic, but come on, what *do* you do? She read quietly for a moment before snapping the book shut. She looked about her wildly.

Special products?

She didn't have special products. To get them would mean at least an hour walking to the village and back. Oh car, oh little car. Where are you? With three fussy mothers and Tamara about to turn up. Mistake – big time.

Cutting roses calmed her. Calm. Calm down. Right down. Get back.

It'd be sheer bad luck if someone got stung. She watched the bees dipping in and out of the creamy yellow flowers. She went up close, picked up a branchful and shook it. Let them try out a sting on her. Remember the feeling of it, let them attack her, not the babies. The bees busied on, ignoring their mini-Molly-earthquakes.

Back in the kitchen Rod Stewart was singing his heart out. Molly sang 'The First Cut is the Deepest', changing cut to sting. She rinsed the stalks of the heavy pink roses, her first-ever home-grown roses; the music and the sun made her feel warm and optimistic. She thought only good things. Like Spain, the picnic.

Max was still out there, somewhere on Planet Earth. His head still firmly under its blanket. Meantime, it looked like there was a summer fling on the horizon. She must work on that stomach. She filled a vase with water, sniffing deeply into the soft pink rose petals, before snipping the stems at an angle and bashing them to a pulp with a rolling pin.

There was a rustle, then a plop, in the hallway. She went out and faced the mat. The dreaded white window envelope, the old enemy, the Visa bill, was back. Tamara's subject for discussion that day, crying, was going to be very appropriate.

Preferring to know the worst, she opened it immediately. Once she'd started taking little nibbles, it had been hard to stop. The old 'what the hell' guilt she'd had whenever she reached for the old plastic to pay for naughty treats had returned. Except the Japanese restaurant binges and the occasional must-have Whistles dress had been replaced by container-sized knickers, bras and leggings. Followed by other odds and sods, like make-up, and – a new one – Nice 'N' Easy. All of them reclassified from necessities to luxuries.

As part of her preparation for her next meeting with Christophe, whenever and wherever, she'd pushed her way across the great ocean of floor between Boots' now familiar softy powdery baby bit to the alien, hard-sell, glitzy glossy make-up bit. Scowling at the cardboard cut-out, computer-enhanced models grinning at her at every turn, she'd spent hours picking up and putting down hundreds of cellophane-wrapped boxes, bottles and tubes which had all suddenly become horribly anti-wrinklingly, anti-ageingly, eye-creamingly, neck-creamingly *relevant*.

By the time she'd reached lipsticks she was programmed to pick out and poke in the whole jolly Moisture Stay, Continuous Colour, Won't Kiss Off lot. Her final selection in the little tray at the side of her Boots basket seemed minuscule in relation to the marathon bite that one little swipe of the Visa had taken as she guiltily took the receipt, both arms a rainbow of Raging Ruby, Tricky Toffee and Indian Spice.

If Izzie, Jenna or Caroline were shocked at Molly's flat, they hid it well. Tamara had walked through with her nose in the air, but then she always did that anyway and by the time the others arrived she was at the bottom of Molly's garden chattering over the fence with Mrs Constandavalos.

Molly had learnt the ritual. She'd laid the obligatory baby mats, toys and blankets down. She'd double-bleached the loo, bought in a new packet of biscuits, honey and ginger tea for Jenna and Earl Grey for Caroline.

Lavender, Charles and Bob had all changed a lot in the weeks they'd been apart. They were all rolling onto their sides now and Charles was the first to push himself up with his arms. Tamara's suggestion that he'd probably be crawling soon sent Caroline into spasms of delight.

'Just look at the *deepness* of the pink on those foxgloves,' Tamara was saying to Mrs Constandavalos as they settled themselves into the garden under the cherry tree. 'And tell me, how do you get your hydrangeas to stay blue?'

'Buy new ones from Homebase every year,' said Mrs Constandavalos.

'Oh...'

Molly picked at the grass as Jenna launched into the latest on her wedding plans.

'We've still not sorted our honeymoon. Can you believe that? Only twelve weeks till we're married?

Jason likes to book it all last-minute on the Net but I said, Jase, I don't want cheap last-minute deals. This is our honeymoon we're talking about! Would he listen?'

'Where do you *want* to go?' said Caroline.

'That's the hassle. We used to go anywhere at the drop of a hat, Bali, Thailand; now they're all so out, aren't they? My mum offered to have Lu but we'd miss her too much. We don't want any long plane journeys, or mosquitoes. So that cuts out most of the world. It's a real pain.'

'Holidays are *such* a problem now, aren't they?' sighed Caroline.

'What about America?' said Molly.

'Guns.'

'England?'

'England?' Jenna's voice went up high at the end, as if she'd never heard of the place.

'Too risky,' said Caroline. 'You can't even trust France these days. The Dordogne last year was a wash-out. The *gouffres* were *ghastly*, full of *campers* keeping dry. Even Tuscany's a no-no now.'

'I thought that'd be ideal!' said Molly.

'Too many pylons,' Caroline huffed dismissively as if it were last year's news.

'We've got two weeks Camp Warnering in Cornwall,' said Izzie. 'It's just not got to rain, that's all.'

'I wonder how that woman who never came again is getting on, what was her name?' said Molly, changing the subject.

'Becky,' said Izzie.

'The one that went back to work,' said Jenna. 'How could she *do* it with such a young baby?'

'Because she *wanted* to, I expect, Jenna,' said Tamara, stuffing herself into a white plastic garden chair.

'But *so* young?' said Jenna.

'Nothing wrong with that?' said Caroline sternly.

'Maybe she's got her mum on hand. It's not a problem, is it, leaving them with your mum?' said Izzie.

'But it's, what does the baby think about it all? Do you think it matters?' Molly looked up at Tamara.

Tamara had just opened her mouth when Izzie beat her to it.

'A baby knows its own mother. Mothers can't be replaced and that's that.'

'To say you're indispensable is arrogant, and, if you don't mind me saying, a little stupid,' said Caroline.

'But mothers *are* indispensable,' Izzie replied forcefully.

'*Some* people are obviously happy to go back to work,' said Molly.

'I reckon they don't give their maternal instincts a chance to develop,' said Jenna. 'It's an organic process, isn't it? You don't know everything, do you? No one does. You have to let it grow as the baby grows.'

'That's right,' said Izzie. 'In work you're replace-able, it doesn't matter what you do. As a mother you're not. And, let's face it, if your kids are raised by someone else they'll be different people, won't they?'

'Oh don't be so ridiculous,' said Caroline, 'do you think Charles will turn out like *Ulé*?'

Molly tried to imagine podgy Charles with lank dark hair, a Polish accent and a stoop.

'Tests have shown –' began Tamara.

'Nannies play with the children *more*,' Caroline butted in. 'That's what they're paid for!'

Izzie rolled her eyes to the sky.

'Tests have *shown* ...' Tamara's voice went up an octave.

'If you ask me,' said Caroline, taking a sip of Earl Grey, 'too many mothers sit around on their backsides, chewing the cud and drinking cups of tea all day.'

'*Tests have shown*,' said Tamara with authoritative finality, 'mothers who have the choice are the happy, healthy ones. If they *choose* to go back to work, and do so, then they will be happy. If mummy's happy, baby will be happy. If they *choose* to stay at home, and it is their choice, it's not something they're forced into, then all will be well too.'

'Well, I've got to,' said Molly quietly, fiddling with her fingers.

Daisy screamed.

'Got to what? Stop it, Lavender, stop it.' Jenna leant forward and picked up Lulu, who had a fistful of Daisy's hair in her hand.

'Go back. To work.'

They all looked at her as she scooped up Daisy and stroked her head.

A blackbird swooped down from the pear tree at the Constandavalos end of the garden, flying low across to the neighbouring lawn, calling tchk tchk.

Molly looked up. 'And I'm not happy about it. Am I?' she said to Daisy.

There was an awkward silence. They all sat listening to the buzzing of the bees and the wind in the trees. A plane flew overhead.

'Has your maternity leave run out, then?' said Jenna, standing Lulu on her lap and bouncing her up and down.

'I'm not on maternity leave.'

'Oh.'

'I'm a freelance.'

'So?' said Caroline. 'What will you do?'

'Cry probably. Shall we get on with it? I've got to go out later. Anyone want more tea before we begin?'

'I wouldn't mind a glass of juice?' said Jenna.

'Right,' said Molly, standing up and brushing her dress down. Glad for something to do.

'Best get it over with if you've got to go back,' said Izzie, taking her glasses off and wiping them on her T-shirt. 'It'll only get worse.'

'What do you mean?'

'If you wait much longer she's going to hit the six-months mark and that's when they get really clingy.'

'Oh, thanks,' said Molly, looking to Tamara for support.

'At six months baby knows it's not part of mummy any more. He's becoming a person in his own right,' said Tamara. 'They *can* get clingy.'

'It's best you know, isn't it?' said Jenna softly.

211

'Yes, sure. Yes. I – I'll go and get the apple juice. Anyone else?'

They all held their heads down. Tamara picked up her bundle of leaflets which flapped about in the breeze as she handed them out.

'Is everybody all right? Not too chilly for you, is it?'

'Don't wait for me,' Molly said to Tamara, 'I think I know enough about crying as it is.'

'Now now,' said Tamara, 'we wouldn't start without you, would we, ladies?'

Molly stood by herself in the kitchen for a while. Trying to regain her composure. She checked the cups again for cracks and stains, putting the worst one to one side for herself. What was it with Jenna? Why did she always find herself being so sycophantic with her? False sympathy for her unplanned honeymoon. Was she just disguising her jealousy? Was she jealous? Why did some people seem to have it so bloody easy? Stop being so bloody false, Molly Warren, she told herself. It came from a lifetime of not belonging. Trying to fit in. Adapting all the time to different situations. She was an expert at it. Though this was the hardest one yet, she thought as she looked at them from a safe distance through the bathroom window behind the kitchen.

When she returned they all fell silent.

'So does anyone fancy coming to playgroup?' Izzie was saying.

'Where's that?' said Molly.

'Kew!' said Izzie, as if it could have been anywhere else. 'There's music.'

212

'Babies will enjoy that!' said Tamara.

'Bob's clapping, aren't you, mate? Come on, give us a clap, Bob. They do a little bit of art, a little bit of music, there's loads of toys to play with.'

'Aren't they a bit young?' said Jenna.

'What day is it?' said Caroline, 'Charles's calendar is already getting full. He has baby Mozart on Mondays, baby yoga on Wednesday afternoons and sub-aqua aerobics on Saturday mornings.'

'I know what to get him for Christmas then! A baby Psion. Friday mornings any good?' suggested Izzie.

'Splendid! I'll send him with Ulé. Friday is Christophe's morning. It'll stop her swooning about the garden so pathetically. I feel sorry for the poor boy now. I mean, *Ulé*?'

'So you've forgiven Christophe but not Ulé?' said Izzie.

'She *shouldn't* have encouraged him,' said Caroline. 'Theo's commandeering him now, got him going through the whole wine cellar giving marks out of ten!'

'So he's a bit of a Jilly Goolden on the side, is he, our Christophe,' said Izzie.

'It'll take forever. But still, it amuses Theo.'

'Shall we get on?' said Molly.

'Yes, good,' said Tamara, looking at her watch, 'Now. Is anybody having any particular problems with crying?'

'It's all they bloody well do if you ask me,' said Izzie.

'There are many different types of crying. If baby

is crying he is crying for a reason. Is he cold? Is he hungry? Has he pooed? You address the problem, baby will stop. But what if it's a high-pitched wail, a strange different sort of a cry? You mothers know your own baby's voices by now. You'll soon recognise a strange one. And then you must think. Is it colic? Is it pain? Is it wind? Run through all these possibilities. Pick your baby up and – and while I'm here, ladies, I'll say pick baby up whenever you want to. If your instinct is to pick him up, then pick him up.'

'Even if he's just trying it on?' said Izzie.

'A happy baby is a happy mummy, Izzie.'

'Tssh. Like going into the sweetshop every time you pass it.'

'I can't leave Daisy to cry for a minute,' said Molly. 'In fact I try to get to her before she starts crying. She usually starts wriggling first, and her breathing changes...'

'Now that's spoiling her. You'll pay for it later,' said Izzie.

Molly felt like bursting into tears.

'No, I think you're right to do that, Molly. You're following your instincts, aren't you?'

'My instinct is to chuck him out the window when he starts yelling at three in the morning,' said Izzie, 'and that's just Carter.'

'Now, now, Izzie,' said Tamara.

'Who's coming to the Windmill playgroup then?' said Izzie.

'We'd love to come,' said Molly, 'while we still can.'

They all looked at the ground. 'And, anyway, I've got to find a childminder. Tamara – what comes first, the job or the childminder? ' Molly added almost hysterically at the impossibility of it all. Everyone was looking at her sympathetically. 'It's all right, it's not the end of the world, is it?' she said, feeling it was precisely that. 'And anyway. I've got to *get* the job first.' She laughed as convincingly as she could.

'Phew, you had me worried for a minute,' said Izzie, 'I thought we'd be losing you next week or something. One down, three to go, I was thinking. So much for Bob's little gang.'

'*The* job?' said Jenna.

'I don't know if I'm putting the cart before the horse or the horse before the cart or whatever that stupid bloody expression is – but I've got an interview.'

'When?'

'Tomorrow morning. That's what I was going to ask you, Izzie. You know what you said about taking Daisy?'

CHAPTER FOURTEEN

Inside Baxter, Rumbold and Featherington, one of the smaller of Kew's eight estate agencies, tucked in the heart of the village between the bookshop and the station, Celia Sprague turned the pages of Molly's CV with a noisy, dismissive flick.

'This doesn't say which school you went to.' She looked at Molly accusingly across her broad desk which filled most of the room. Molly opened her mouth to reply, closing it again as Celia continued, 'And we were, clearly, looking for somebody with *experience* in the property market.'

Molly nodded, holding one hand firmly on top of the other to stop herself grabbing Celia's complicated switchboard of a phone to call and check on Daisy. Though Izzie had insisted the piercing screams as she left were down to teething, both of them knew otherwise.

'And. Clearly – your CV ... it isn't property oriented, is it?'

Assuming this was another question which needed no reply, Molly sat, stared, she hoped politely, and waited for the next statement. Unlike herself, Celia had been put on earth, clearly, to be nothing but an estate agent. Everything about her from her fake pearls and white blouse to her short blonde bob which looked like a wig, shrieked mortgage interest rates, quantity surveying and dry rot.

'I'm a quick learner,' she offered brightly. Though it was mid-May, the heating was on. Sweat began trickling down Molly's armpits like globs of jelly.

What was she saying? Did she ever in a million years *want* this job?

'Are you familiar with Apple Excell 4000 Version 3?'

Could I put up with this woman for five minutes on a football pitch?

'I'm Word for Windows, but they're all pretty much the same at the end of the day, aren't they – Control plus X, plus V and all that.'

Molly's slow, hesitant answers contrasted strongly with Celia's short, sharp questions. She could see Celia was, clearly, very confused. After all, there she was, this blabbering creature sitting in front of her while her mildly boosted CV and rave references promised a dynamo.

After she'd been shown the tiny dark back room where her desk *would* be, and they'd discussed what her salary *would* be, she'd left without a clue as to whether she had the job or not and with even less of a clue as to whether she wanted it. As soon as she got outside she raced to the call box outside Oddbins, for once not an excuse since she'd stopped paying her monthly mobile rental.

'Izzie!! Just finished the interview, I'm on my way.'

'Hang on, hang on a minute, calm down. Daisy's fine. She put down a whole jar of Heinz chicken purée and has gone out like a light. Giggling away she was, I swear. Listen, why don't you take a break? Give yourself a cup of something wet and naughty in the caff, or whatever. How long does she go down for? Well. There you are.'

'I suppose it'll be good practice. Being on my own.'

'Enjoy! Make the most of it.'

After checking the cards in the newsagent's for childminders, glad to see there weren't any, she did the by now completely automatic glance up at the flats above Oddbins, quickly averting her eyes to the sky. It was one of those late spring days which didn't know whether to be winter or summer – warm and sunny one moment, cloudy and wet the next. She decided to risk it and turned towards the Gardens.

The leaves of Lichfield Road's massive horse chestnuts met in the middle, forming a tunnel-like approach to the Gardens, rustling like shingle in the wind. Smoke rose from a high back-garden wall, transforming the last of the garden's winter debris into wispy clouds. The old-wine smell of autumn felt out of place in the soft spring sun. A child's red glove had been left on a railing spike, its index finger pointing to the sky.

A black cat sat washing, pulling a paw over its ears, one by one, which squashed and popped upright in turn. It ran over with its tail in the air, wrapped itself around her legs and arched its back, purring deeply. Molly ignored it. She was too busy providing food elsewhere to be taken in by a cat. Before, she'd have stopped to have a chat and a tickle. Now she just found it mildly irritating. Any pretence of affection, a ploy to gain favour. A try-on. Like blokes who come on in bars at closing time. Her post-natal instincts still sharp and intact, her whole mental capacity was probably closer to the cat's level than human.

She stood long enough to let it have its rub, reading a sign pinned to one of the big fat tree trunks. A plea from a child called Freya who'd lost her cat called Sweepy. Molly looked down suspiciously, relieved to see it didn't fit the description. She had enough on her plate without carting lost cats around.

Like everyone else walking up to the Gardens, Molly found it impossible not to peer in through the bay windows of the double-fronted Victorian houses, crawling with camellias and wisteria. It all looked so effortless – an antique beaded curtain here, a Chinese fan there, music stands, candles. There were lots of candles. From big creamy fat ones on their own stands to tapered arrangements on complicated-looking candelabras. Someone somewhere was playing Debussy on a piano which made her think of parquet floors and beeswax polish.

The front gardens overflowed into each other, their divides hidden by fountains of ceanothus exploding like intense blue skyrockets across yellow drops of lobelia which dangled over tangles of flowering rosemary and the last of the tulips. Tulips of every size and colour, their crispy petals spread wide like whores, showing more than was decent of their black, furry stamens.

This is the real world, thought Molly. Not Baxter, Rumbold and bloody Featherington. Still, there had been things she'd liked. It'd be fun to have a desk again, with a little pot for pens and a board to stick things on. The smell of stationery, coffee breaks – a salary. And as for Celia, she was off-putting, but, clearly, readable. She just wanted a cheap part-timer. Molly could use the place to pull herself together, to get back into the world again.

Anywhere but Kew Gardens might be an anticlimax after all that, she thought as she flashed her season ticket at the gate. She stopped across the lake from the Palm House. With the clouds drifting fast behind it, it looked like it had just landed from another planet, its gigantic glass curves glistening and tempting her in as always. But she knew where she wanted to go. And she only had so much time. The glasshouses closed at five, the Gardens at five thirty and Daisy would be well awake by six. She passed behind the Princess of Wales Conservatory and hurried through the Rock Gardens and round to the obscure Garden backlands.

She crossed the lawn displays, feeling the spring of a hundred varieties of manicured grasses beneath her feet, pausing at the water lily pond to watch swarms of iridescent electric-blue dragonflies doing their frantic jazz dance across the surface of the water, dodging the flowers and each other without missing a beat. The sound of the wind rattling the bamboo made her shiver; she looked up at the sky, which had turned a startling shade of purple. Hugging herself to keep warm, she crossed to the Orchid House. Seeing it was empty, she stood by the snow gum eucalyptus, not sure what to do. Absent-mindedly stroking its smooth silver bark, she peered into the large windows of the modern Jobell laboratory, feeling like a groupie as she scanned the white-coated technicians for a shaggy brown head.

She decided to go and see the orchids anyway. She took off the loose light cotton jumper she'd been wearing over her dress and dangled it over her bag. Pushchairless, bigbabybagless, and with her old Prada back on her shoulder, she felt good, almost weightless. She'd made an effort. She'd had an interview, if nothing else. She'd started. She was pleased with her dress, too. A real charity-shop find. A silky soft viscose René Derhy, its generous folds of mauve, rust and burgundy magically tucking and hiding her own folds below. She intended to wear it to bits, all summer.

She walked slowly around the Orchid House, trying to remember all that Christophe had said. It was small. Minuscule compared to the other glasshouses, like a large, old-fashioned greenhouse, with fans whirring and clicking above her head. She wanted to smell them. Put her nose close to the elaborate arrangements of petals: the intensive pla-sticky bright white and yellow ones; the delicate pale pink ones, the deep purple ones and the tiny shadowy-looking animal-like ones, their petals a strange, dark orange the colour of sick. But most of them were behind glass, too valuable to be poked and picked at by casual visitors. A wave of recognition flew over her, like finding an old friend, when she saw the swarm of bee orchids. The more she looked the more she could see what he'd meant by calling them sex on stalks. As if in response, her breasts tingled. They felt heavy and full. Molly had manufactured Daisy's next meal and Daisy wasn't there. She felt panicky. She had to get back. She'd had enough alonetime.

She walked back quickly through the grasses; they always made her feel sad, though she didn't know why. A sudden strong gust of wind hissed through the pampas grasses, making her dress billow around her. The clouds had gone from purple to black. She hurried passed a statue, then stopped in her tracks and looked back at it. A young farmer in leather thigh boots throwing seeds from a basket. She read the nameplate below, The Sower, half expecting it to say something else. The delicate but strong face, it was *him*. Then all of a sudden there he was. The Sower come to life. Hurrying across the lawn towards her, his green waterproof jacket pulled tight across his shoulders.

'Hey,' she said guiltily as she looked up from the puddle she'd dissolved into.

'Hey yourself.'

'I, er, was just admiring him.' She nodded towards his bronze double.

This was ridiculous. She felt like a stalker. Caught.

222

Why the hell else would she be in this remotest part of the Gardens?

Come clean, Molly, come clean. 'And I've, er just been looking at the orchids. After what you said about them...'

Christophe pushed his hair back from his face and smiled. 'I – I've been working in the Palm House.'

He's as flustered as I am, she thought.

'They are incredible, aren't they?' Molly waffled on. 'And just like, you know, what you said about them.'

'About the sex?' He did his half-smile.

Stop it, damn you! And don't flush, Molly, you're forty, remember.

'I mean – I don't know why I didn't see them like that before.'

'So you've been looking at orchids, thinking of sex.'

'Well – yes.'

'My favourite thing to do in the world!' he laughed. 'Next to the real thing, of course.'

Molly didn't bother to try taking the smirk off her face.

'Come – I have to show you something.' He touched her arm and turned in the direction of the Orchid House.

'No! I have to get back now. I have to get Daisy.'

'Where is she?'

'She's with Izzie, she'll be waking up soon.'

He stood looking at her.

Molly looked at her watch.

She had an hour.

'This is it,' he whispered, holding a tiny orchid gently in his hand like a butterfly. 'You see how it is.'

'Just like a bee,' said Molly, trying to concentrate.

They were standing very close.

'Look closer, see, here, the male pollen is at the top, the female stigma is underneath. Smell it,' he held his hand up to her.

She ignored the flower and studied the sexiest hand she'd ever seen, roll-up stains, dirty fingernails and all.

'It's the white ones which smell the most.'

She sniffed. 'Can't smell a thing.'

'Because they are fertilised at night. By the moths.'

'Clever things, aren't they?'

'They know the insect is only interested in three things: food, sex and a place to lay its eggs.'

'Let's have another sniff. No, nothing.'

The way that bangle dangled...

'It is not what a bee would say! He smells a female on heat.'

Molly swallowed.

'And then,' Christophe said in a quiet expressionless voice, without looking at her, 'he tries to fuck it.'

'And then,' whispered Molly, 'he realises he's made a big, big mistake!'

Her back arched as she felt his arm slip behind her waist.

'Not this bee,' whispered Christophe into her ear. 'Not this one.'

She sank into his kiss and closed her eyes. She'd jumped into the deep end. She was underwater.

The rain came. Fast and hard. Hammering on the glass roof like a thunderous round of applause. Well done, Molly! it was saying. More! Encore! It was joined by a deeper, different kind of a roar, getting louder and louder and more powerful until it drowned out the rain completely.

This. Is. some. Kiss! She thought. Then she realised the sound was closer to outer space than her inner ear. It was the five o'clock Concorde going over. Five! She had to go. She tried to pull away. Christophe held her tighter. Kissed her harder.

She heard the door open at the other end of the greenhouse. He released his grip.

A distant voice broke the spell, 'Do you not drink lemon verbena tea? Next time I'll bring some in a little bag for you.'

'Ooooh, look at this.'

'That's, that's – whatsitsname?'

They went out into the rain, not looking at the two women in generous folds of batik, crouched over the bucket orchids, carrier bags crooked under elbows.

Christophe took his jacket off and put it round her shoulders; he grabbed her hand and they ran through the grasses to the rockeries. They ran faster, through the twisting paths of the rock garden, past the waterfalls to the peony garden as a low thunder rumbled in the distance. The rain got heavier. They climbed the daffodil hill and sheltered, soaked and giggling, in the Temple of Aeolus.

They kissed again. The lightning and thunder came together.

They held each other, shivering.

'Come – we can't stay here.'

Suddenly he was gone. Molly followed, skidding and sliding down the hill, her dress clinging wet to her body.

They sped on across the lawns, past the lake to the Palm House, its crystal curves flashing like a beacon in the lightning.

Molly tried the door. 'Of course, it's closed!' She rattled it hard.

'Here.' Christophe rummaged in his pocket.

'How did you get hold of that?'

'I work here, remember?' He turned and smiled wickedly at her as he slipped the key into the lock of the heavy iron door.

CHAPTER FIFTEEN

The door slammed shut behind them with a big, iron thud. The sudden transformation from wet cold outside to dry steaming inside sent Molly into a panic.

'Christophe, they'll be locking the main gates any minute, we've got to get out of here!' She turned back for the door.

'You can't go out in this.' Christophe grabbed her arm.

'Can I borrow your mobile a minute?'

Christophe shook his head and lifted his arms out in a shrug.

'I *knew* it, I knew as soon as I cancelled it... Come *on*, we've got to *go*.'

Christophe put his other arm behind her back. 'Half an hour, the storm will pass.'

'Half an *hour*. The gates will be locked, Christophe, they'll be locking them any minute, now come on, let's get out of here.' She struggled to free herself from his grip. 'We could be shut in here all *night*.'

'Your baby is safe and warm. What good will you be to her if you are in hospital with pneumonia?'

Molly stopped struggling. They both froze. Trapped in each other's stare as the rain hit the glass like scrunched polythene at a million beats a second high above their heads.

'I have another key, Molly,' he said quietly. She loved the way he said Molly, letting the 'y' linger like an 'ee'. 'For the staff exit. We can leave when it stops raining, OK. In half an hour?'

Molly looked at him. 'Show me.'

'You don't trust me?'

'Of course I don't trust you, now, show me.'

'The key?'

'*Yes*, the key.'

He took it out of his pocket and pressed it against her stomach, turning it round and round. Molly looked down.

'I'm steaming!' Molly held her arms out to her side. 'And listen to my feet!' She squelched them one after the other.

'Now, you should take your shoes and your stockings off.'

'Are you forward or what?'

'Put them on the hot pipes – they will be dry in minutes.'

'I suppose you're right.'

Molly went behind a big banana leaf to peel off her tights, draping them over a mangrove swamp as she tipped her shoes up against a ventilation grill.

'Now we're here, why not enjoy it? We have the place to ourselves!'

He put his arm round her and they began to walk

slowly along the broad central aisle. Past star fruit and rubber trees, ylang-ylangs and sugar cane. Through the drip-juice leaves and citrus trees, strange flowers, heavy reds, orange spikes and dangling fronds.

'What's that hissing?' Molly, still jumpy and unsure, glanced up to the treetops.

'The hoses of course.'

'They sound like cicadas. What do you think of this one then?' She sniffed at a large, white trumpet flower with almost human-looking pink veins.

'Too sweet and high to be trusted.'

'Like you,' laughed Molly.

'Like *me*?' Christophe said in mock jest.

'I love the smell of this place.' She breathed in deeply.

'Too much disinfectant.'

'It reminds me of the best bits of my past, the travelling in the tropics.'

'What about your boyfriend? He was a good bit of your past?'

'Max?'

'Ah, Max.'

'Ye-es – he was. He was always travelling for his work too. We both lived for our work. But when we were together, we had a good time.'

'Work hard, play hard?'

Molly nodded. 'The problem was, we both thought our work was our life. He still does.'

'So – what happened?'

'He didn't want a baby. I did.'

'And?'

'And then there was his wife.'

'Ahhh.' He smiled.

'Oh, I suppose it kind of works for them, you know, both wanting their independence so they have their own lives and stay together but not together.'

'This is so common.'

'In France, maybe. In Notting Hill, so so. In Kew?'

Christophe laughed, 'In Kew, not so much! So he – you don't see him now?'

'We're not together, no. But...'

'But you wish you were?'

'I don't know what I wish, Christophe.'

'You see this.' He broke away from her and went over to a climbing plant. 'This is one of the most interesting plants in all of Kew.'

Molly looked closer. It looked like any other climbing plant to her, its small white flowers twisting and climbing up to the jungle canopy above.

'It's a Caesalpinia.'

'Is that so?' Molly feigned interest, missing the feel of him close to her.

'What is incredible about this plant is...' He put his arm out towards her and drew her in close. 'Look up. You see, there, about halfway.'

'What?'

'It changes its sex. Half of the flowers are male. Half of the flowers are female.'

'Which is on top?'

'The female of course! Come, let's get closer to the rain.'

He took a step up the spiral staircase which led to the treetop walkway.

Before she could follow, he swung back on the central pole and bent down to kiss her. Not a long kiss, but not a short one either. Just so they both knew what was going to happen.

'Monkey!' She ran her fingers through his hair, suddenly feeling her age as she twisted the wet brown silky ends tight around her fingers.

She dropped her arm as he stood back to let her pass.

By now, Molly's breasts had grown away from her and down, so seriously heavy were they with Daisy's evening meal. She had to carry them up the wrought-iron stairway almost as if they were a separate part of her. Aware that Christophe's eyes were on her from behind, she did this as discreetly as she could, holding one arm across her like Nelson. When they reached the top, they walked along the narrow pathway which ran all the way around the curving roof of the Palm House.

'What are you thinking?' he said.

'I, er...'

'Don't worry about your baby, OK? She's fine. I'm sure she's still having a good sleep.'

'How come you know so much about children?' Molly held out her hand, touching the tops of the palm trees, the fronds of mango trees, the hot, hot jungle right next to the thunder and the rain.

'From my own family, of course.'

'How many?'

'I have three sisters. Younger.'

'Are you Catholic?

'Of course. We take care of our children and our mothers.'

'And your lovers?'

'Don't ask!'

'Am I a mother-figure or a lover-figure or a mixture of both?'

'Mixtures are always the best.' He put his arm round her and squeezed her tight. 'Do you want to fuck?'

Molly kept her walk steady as she had an inner seizure. There was a long silence. Just the sound of their footsteps on the iron walkway and the rain, thundering on the glass above their heads.

'I still don't think you can beat an English garden, though,' Molly said conversationally as if she were taking tea in the conservatory.

'Or a French? Go on, I want to hear you say it.'

'A rose garden in the summer.'

'The Jardins de Bagatelle.'

'Where's that?'

'You are a traveller and haven't heard about it? It's in Paris. Molly – you want to fuck me now?'

She touched the back of his thigh, felt the muscle, firm, hard as he walked.

'No. Yes, I mean, no, I haven't heard of it.'

'It has the biggest collection of roses in the world.'

'Really?' She slipped her arm up to his waist, subtle, slender.

'I will take you there one day.'

'Will you?' she laughed.

'Why are you laughing?'

'Oh – I'm just a cynical old bat, Christophe, I'm sorry.'

'Don't you believe me?' His hand slipped up her back, he gripped the back of her neck, turned her face to him and kissed her hard.

It was a shock after he'd been so gentle. Like he'd changed into someone else. Transformed. He wanted sex. He wanted it badly. So did she, but not like this. Not so – crudely. So quickly.

He slipped the top of her dress down and cupped a gigantic breast in each hand.

'No!' She moved his hands gently but firmly, *'please* – not there. No – I said NO!!! Forget about first base, Christophe! They're not what they seem.'

'We don't have much time,' he whispered in her ear as he pushed her against the railings, touching her through her dress. 'Please.' His voice had changed. 'Please...'

'We can't! We can't!'

She could feel the force of his body against her.

She wanted to go further. All the way, hell, why not? But she had to be sensible. Though her body was telling her otherwise, she managed to say it again. 'Christophe, we *can't.'*

He put his hand in his back jeans pocket and pulled out a tiny packet.

In one swift movement he'd hooked his fingers under her pants and pulled them down, throwing them over the balcony.

He ignored her remonstrations as he quickly and expertly slipped on the condom.

233

'HEY!'

He was rough. His gentle manner had gone. But as he entered her, as he filled her, she melted into his force and let it all happen around her and in her and through her.

After he came he stayed hard inside her. Kissing her neck over and over, saying he loved her. When he came again, so did Molly, and he said it again, repeatedly, and as he pumped into her, her screams echoed like a parrot's through the treetops.

He said he loved her again as they fumbled to straighten their clothes. She knew he didn't mean it. But it was sweet just to hear him – someone – let's face it, *anyone*, say it. And she'd needed it as much as him. It was just sex. Even if it was animal sex. More like going to the gym than making love, but it had reminded her of what she'd been missing.

'So it's true,' she said lightly as they strolled back to the stairway.

'What's that?'

'What they say about big noses.'

'Who are you saying has a big nose?' he called laughingly behind him as he ran ahead and skipped round and round the spiral stairs with a satisfied, cocky bounce.

She felt like another notch on his pole as she followed him meekly down the steps. There was no getting away from it. In this kind of sex there was a strength which the male took away with him, but which the female lost forever.

She winced as she took a sideways glance across

at her lemon-yellow knickers, dangling from a mango tree like a deflated banana.

What have you done, Molly Warren? What have you done now?

CHAPTER SIXTEEN

'Carrier for the baby?' Tap tap tap.

'Is the flight full?'

'I'll just check for you.' Tap, tap. 'Not completely.'

'Is there a window seat next to an aisle that's already taken?' Molly swung her rucksack onto the conveyor.

The hostess smiled to herself. 'I'll just check that for you.'

Caroline's jet-set tip-off worked. Molly got the spare middle seat for Daisy.

Knowing all too well that babies were nothing but lethal noisy pong zones to many of her fellow-travellers, Molly had an ingratiating smile waiting for the owner of their aisle seat, a large, grim-looking Spanish man with sun-worn, pock-marked skin.

Molly's smile began to ache on her face, fixed as it was on his belted trousers, as he spent ages fiddling in the overhead locker before he sat down in a waft of aftershave.

'Well, hello there,' said Molly merrily as he fumbled grumpily for his seat belt.

He looked at her sharply. Molly nodded and smiled encouragingly at him. He gave her a puzzled 'should I know you from somewhere?' frown before a big smile cracked his face open as he noticed Daisy for the first time. He chuckled to himself and tickled her tummy.

'I'll move her to the other side of me, once we've taken off – to the window seat,' Molly began her prepared speech.

'No understand.' He frowned at Molly again and went back to Daisy.

Not only did Molly not have to swap seats, the man and Daisy entertained each other for the whole flight, both of them collapsing in intermittent giggles in between games of peek a boo and funny faces, while Molly, tucked into a double G&T and a new edition of *Red* magazine, threw them the odd glare when they got too noisy. She'd not only finished her magazine by the time they'd landed, but had also read every word of every article of *In Flight With Cheapie Charters Dot Com*. She really felt her holiday had begun.

The ribbon of sea appeared and disappeared through the hills as the old bus crunched noisily through its gears, almost stopping suspended in air as it swivelled round the bends. Up to the top and then down again into the next bay. Molly's eyes squinted behind her sunglasses as she looked down the ravine drops to the valleys below, hoping against hope that Colin wouldn't ruin it for them as usual. Her mother always put it down to jealousy, but if he

237

was like that with her daughter, how would he behave with her first granddaughter? But her mother had to defend him, didn't she? He looked after her well and put up with her eccentricities, loved her for them, even.

Molly stared out of the window, trying not to think bad thoughts, of Colin, of the pain they all suffered when her mother had upped and gone so suddenly. Her mum hadn't done too badly at the end of the day. So long as you didn't look too closely at Colin or ask how he got his income. At each turn, the landscape became sparser and more ragged, until the dots of low, white housing complexes and the orange and blue nylon campsite bubbles disappeared altogether.

Halfway down a deserted valley, the driver pulled up in the middle of the road, hauled her rucksack out of the coach's belly and pointed to a tumble of white bricks a few hundred yards down a sharp, steep path.

The old blue bus spluttered into life and left them alone in the hot, still air. Molly stood and listened as the engine faded into the distance. Cicadas called from the patches of spiky grass and clumps of yellow broom scattered across the dust. The air felt sweet and clear, like she was more in the sky than below it. She crossed the road and let her bag drop to the ground.

'Well, this is it, Daisy,' she said cheerily as she looked down.

It hadn't changed at all. Still the same old scattering of outbuildings tumbling down haphazardly towards the sea amid the scrub, olive and fig groves. She pulled absent-mindedly at her dress, stuck to the sweat on the back of her legs, and craned her neck to see if she could see anyone before heaving the bag onto her shoulder again. The René Derhy, renamed by her *the* dress, was almost all she'd brought. No cruddy clothes allowed. A dress, a sarong, a bikini. Her luxury item, a long, thin cellophane packet of snow-white M&S mini-briefs, awaited her somewhere among the huge bulk of Daisy supplies in the rucksack.

Then again, it was not at all as she remembered. It was so quiet, so still, it appeared to be deserted. There was no car in the drive. She pushed her sunglasses to the top of her head and wiped her brow. 'Don't *do* this to me, Mother, don't say you're not going to be in?' She unzipped her baby bag and pulled out the travel wipes.

'Best get this done before we meet Granny, eh? We don't want her thinking you're a whiny baby, do we?' she said, wiping herself and Daisy down with the cool nursery smell of fresh Wet Wipe.

'And now for the baby torture, ha ha.' Molly pinched Daisy's cheeks and made silly faces as she unscrewed the lid of the sun cream. To no avail; Daisy recognised the bottle and began screaming before a spot touched her skin.

And she screamed. And she screamed.

The house seemed even quieter and stiller.

'You look cuter than ever,' said Molly, screwing the lid back on the tube and plonking Daisy's yellow sunhat on her head. Her short dark curls had magically transformed into long, fair kiss-curls which framed her frown beneath her hat beautifully.

'We can go swimming, Daisy, how about that?'

She dropped the rucksack, tucking it below the roadside to collect later.

She turned to see some movement down below. And then there she was. Standing beneath the big palm tree by the front door. Molly was shocked. She looked tiny. Thin and grey. It looked like she was leaning on the tree to balance herself. Most shocking was her face. It was the face she looked at a hundred times a day – except for the ever-present cigarette dangling from her mouth, it was Daisy. Daisy going on seventy. A flurry of dust whipped around her mother's feet before racing up towards Molly.

'Hello, Spikey!' Molly said brightly, glad to see some things stayed the same but holding Daisy a little tighter. The dog stopped yapping and crouched down low, wiggling its stumpy bottom and circling her ankles. For as long as she could remember there had been a small black wiry Spikey around.

'Down, Spikey, down,' her mother called as she began walking towards them. Another dog, a greyhound cross, walking royally at her side.

She was stooping. Was it the way of the ground or was she limping?

She'd always called her Mother. Now it seemed too formal, but Mum wouldn't have been right, Mummy, or Ma, worse, a cool, hip first-name-terms 'Barbara', just beyond.

'You've changed.'

'So have you.'

'Your hair's different.'

'Yes.'

They stood silently looking at each other.

Molly leant forward self-consciously and kissed her mother on her cheek. They'd never been a kissing family. But it was so common in London to kiss even the mildest acquaintance, and twice, it would have seemed weird not to. It was the first time she could remember kissing her in her life. It was like old friends. To kiss Caroline was fine and well, but to kiss her schoolfriend Julie would have been just weird.

'You travel light, don't you?' Barbara lodged her cigarette into the side of her mouth and bent down to pick up Daisy's nappy bag.

'No,' said Molly quickly. 'Don't do that, there's another case up by the road. I'll go back for it. Or perhaps Colin might...'

'Colin's away for a few days.' She coughed, a deep, rasping smoker's cough.

'Really!'

'I thought you'd be pleased.'

'Surprised!' She hadn't counted on that. Colin was *always* there. Sulking away in the background. Daisy, you clever little Daisy, she thought.

'I'll go back for my bag in a minute.'

'So this is Daisy.' Barbara crouched down. She talked with almost a refined breath as if she were about to cough. Which she often did. 'Aren't you lovely, hey?'

'She looks like you, don't you think?'

'What's her name?'

'Daisy! You know that.'

'Her *other* name.' A familiar old exasperation in her voice. She'd changed but hadn't changed. She was her mum.

'Oh – Jane. Daisy Jane.'

Molly could hear the unasked question fluttering in the silence.

'*Warren*. Daisy Jane Warren.'

'Daisy Jane? Sounds like daisy chain!' she joked.

Don't rise to it, Molly, just don't. Not before you're even through the door.

'Come on, lovely, come and see where Granny lives?' Molly watched in alarm as her mother bent down to pick Daisy up, the long silver lozenge of her cigarette dangling dangerously from the side of her mouth.

'You go and get your bag, Molly, I'll take her inside.'

'Can you manage?' Molly wasn't sure what to do. She had to trust her own mother with her grand-child. Didn't she?

'Manage? Of course I can manage. Come on, sweetheart, come with Granny.'

Molly's heckles rose. 'Put your cigarette out, *please*!'

'Don't fuss, Molly,' Barbara laughed, 'it never did you any harm, did it?'

She tried to put the images of hot ash dropping into Daisy's eyes out of her mind as her mother put her awkwardly over her shoulder and limped slowly off down the path, patting her gently on the back. Daisy snuggled into her neck contentedly.

'See you've still got a Spikey, then,' said Molly as the dog jumped and yapped around her rucksack when she dragged it through the front door.

'Oh, Spikey'll go on for ever, won't you, darling?' Barbara said affectionately. She was jiggling around on the spot, holding Daisy over her shoulder like she'd had her there all her life. Molly exchanged wary looks with the greyhound before it returned to its watch over Barbara, gazing with the eyes of an abandoned child.

'Don't worry about Floss, she wouldn't harm a flea, would you, darling?' Barbara bent down and stroked the dog's nose. Floss licked her hand affectionately.

'And Jellybean?' Molly hardly dared ask if the old grey mare was still going.

'Oh Jellybean's all right, doesn't get out much these days, what with my leg and all. She's a strong old girl though. She's happy enough, Bacco keeps her company. You could take her out if you like. She'd like that.' Barbara put her dog-licked hand back onto Daisy.

Bacco was a grumpy donkey Molly had every intention of avoiding.

'Here.' Molly pulled out a bag from the top of her rucksack.

'Now what's this, dear?'

'Sorry I couldn't get more. I – things are tight now,' said Molly, gently and casually prising Daisy off her mother's shoulder.

243

'They always are when a baby comes along. They take everything from you, don't they? Oh Molly, thank you.' She did a little series of small contented coughs as she piled the already cluttered coffee table with boxes of Pontefract cakes, PG Tips, jars of Oxford English Marmalade, a large bag of parnsips and a stick of duty-free cigarettes.

'I thought about bringing wine, but then, Spain's full of it, isn't it?'

'This is lovely, Moll. Just like Christmas. Cup of tea?'

'Oh yes,' Molly said happily, sinking back into the soft old sofa, letting the warmth and cosiness of the shabby room wrap itself around her. She wouldn't be able to fight the dirt so she'd just have to learn to live with it for a few days. Relax. Chill out, as Jenna would say. At least the air outside was fresh.

Somehow, Barbara had managed to transfer 1950s Sutton to the old fig farm. The room was dark, spliced by two solid-looking shafts of light, swirling with dust, coming from the high small windows on each side of the blue-tiled fireplace. Molly's childhood smell of stale tobacco, dust and dog hair, transported to another country. There was the same shabby furniture, the same dogs. The bulging ashtrays dotted about the place, the newspapers everywhere, the dodgy paintings hung too high and not quite straight. And the ever-present twosome, the packet of Kensitas double-strength and TV remote always at the ready on the right hand side of the mantelpiece. Above it, the same dirty old mirror in which you could hardly see your reflection that she'd spent her angst-ridden teenage years staring into.

She could hear her mother coughing in the kitchen. Deep and gutty. She was home.

'There's nothing like a cup of tea made by somebody else is there?' She took the cup and wrapped her hands around it.

'Aye,' said Barbara softly.

Years of conflict, disharmony and blame over her dad and Colin dissolved in a patch of mutual ground over that cup of thick brown PG tea.

After a lunch of gritty shrimps and fruity red wine, Barbara disappeared for her siesta and Daisy, unaccustomed to the heat, took hers early. Molly couldn't believe her luck. She wasted no time and seized the moment greedily. She emptied the last of the wine into her glass and took a handful of limp old copies of *Woman's Own* out to the garden.

Greeny and leaf-strewn, Barbara's pool was more like a pond than a pool. It couldn't even be called a distant cousin to Caroline's Evian-blue job, but its setting, on a small terrace surrounded by orange trees and deep purple bougainvillea, was unbeatable. She felt as if her bones were melting inside her as she lay back on the sunlounger. But when the timer was on, even relaxing had its own tensions, and for a while she was torn between her magazines, going for a swim, falling asleep or just lying in a happy daze, gazing across the fig orchard to the sea beyond.

In the end it was the heat which decided it. She pushed forward from the edge, letting the water take her. She lay on her back, her feet transformed from sandbags to flippers, floating, feeling the burn of the sun and the white Spanish light through closed eyes. She flipped her feet, making gentle splashing sounds, wishing she could stay there for ever. But then, Colin'd be back and it would all change again.

Those few hours passed by in seconds. All too soon Spain and Daisy stirred as one, heralded by the insect buzz of mopeds on the distant road.

'I can't tell you what it's like to have a meal cooked for me,' Molly sighed. She'd slipped into a teenage-like sloth, but, in their unspoken way, she knew it was OK. It was more than OK. In discovering her new grannyhood, Barbara was enjoying being a mum again, fussing and bothering around her.

'You'll have to come more often,' said Barbara, joining her at the dinner table.

'How's Colin?'

'Just the same. He looks after me well, doesn't he, Daisy? Here.' Barbara held out her arms and Molly passed her over.

'You're lucky,' said Molly, meaning it. Maybe he wasn't as bad as she'd always thought.

'He has his faults, like all of us. Look – she's nearly standing already!'

She held Daisy in a standing position on her lap for a few seconds before her knees buckled.

'I suppose you want to know about Daisy's father,' said Molly casually squeezing a fat wodge of lemon over her grilled fish.

It was time to fill the gaping silence. Molly was stupidly, childishly aware that her mother would now know for sure she'd had sex with someone. They'd never discussed their emotions, let alone their sex lives, ever. When Molly had started school, her mother had gone back to work and she'd quickly adapted to taking herself to school and back from a very early age. There wasn't so much fuss, so much traffic then and parents weren't so hyper-protective. But their lives had separated prematurely. It had made it even more shocking and unforgivable when her mother had, completely out of the blue, given up her all-important job she'd said was everything to her to run off with Colin to Spain. So saying it, saying, 'You want to know about the father?' sounded exactly like, 'You want to know who fucked me? Who fucked your little girl?'

Fourteen-year-old cringey anxieties.

'In your own time, dear, in your own time.'

'He's married.'

"I'd guessed that!' said Barbara cheerfully.

'Had you?'

'A married man or you were gay. It had to be one or the other.'

Molly laughed nervously at her mother's newly revealed worldliness.

'Is he supporting you, that's the main thing?'

'Well – yes, he is... I mean – financially. He's away

in Geneva, he's terribly busy.' She didn't want to go into the whole thing of her reluctance to take money from him. That, she knew, would escalate into a never-ending argument for the rest of her stay.

'Is he a soldier?'

'A journalist.'

'Oooh, is he famous?'

'No – no, no.' Not as much as he'd like to be, she thought, not wanting to begin to go down that road with her mother. She'd be telling the whole of Spain Daisy's dad was a radio star.

'Oh,' Barbara said disappointedly. 'So, you'll be going back to work then?'

'I wish people would stop asking me that!'

'You're going to stay at home then?'

'I'd like to, but I can't, can I?'

'I thought you said he was sending you money?'

Molly ignored her. 'I've just had an interview, at an estate agent's in the village, as it happens.'

'Estate agent's? Good! Colin could give you some tips there.'

'I'm sure he could. So you think it's fine, do you? Going back to work?'

'Most people do these days, don't they? Don't get angry, Moll, come on, we're having a lovely time, let's not spoil it, hey. Cigarette?'

'Well *you* did it, didn't you? One of the pioneers of it, weren't you.'

'We needed the money, Molly. That's why most people work. And you have to think of the future.'

'Pfff, your own future.'

Barbara ignored her, 'I thought it was a good role model for you. I wanted you to know there was more to life than than the kitchen sink and running around after slobby husbands.'

'My father was not slobby '

'Only because I wouldn't let him be. All right, what would have happened then, if I'd stayed home sewing and baking like the rest of them. You'd have thought that was all the opportunity there was for a girl, wouldn't you? This was before all that women's lib stuff, remember. Before Germaine Greer and the Space Girls or whatever they're called.'

Molly sighed, put her fork down and picked up her glass.

'It's an unequal world, Molly, it always has been, always will be. There are tough decisions to make when you get married and have children.'

'There are tougher decisions to make when you don't get married and have children.'

'It's always been harder for women since time began, if you ask me.'

'You don't seem to be doing too badly. Or most of the people I meet these days come to that.'

'When men get married, their lives get easier, don't they? No matter what anyone says, ninety-nine times out of a hundred suddenly they've got someone to make a home with, to be there when they get home from work, to do the shopping.'

'Have their babies...'

'Have their babies. Women are the home-makers. There's nothing new about that. For women it gets harder, doesn't it? And I don't care who says what about women's lib, no man is going to clean toilets and dishes if he can get out of it.'

'You wouldn't catch them doing that in Kew either. They all have cleaners and nannies coming out of their ears. *And* grandparents mucking in.'

Barbara's face froze in mid-chew.

'Sorry, it's just that they *do*.'

'What about Max's parents?'

Molly looked at her. 'D'you know, I haven't really *thought* about them? Isn't that terrible?'

She could have added she had enough preoccupations with Max himself, let alone his parents. But she was right. They *should* know.

'It's another problem. I'll add it to my list.'

She tried to remember what Max had told her about his family. It was, after all, the whole side of his life that wasn't hers, had never been hers, and never would be. Two brothers, a house in the Sussex Downs somewhere? A dog called Lobster he loved deeply. Pitifully little...

'They don't *know* about her?'

'Of course not, he's *married*. I told you!'

'Ah well, I suppose it's one of the advantages of having a girl rather than a boy. At least you're guaranteed to know your grandchildren if you've got any. When will you know if you've got this job?'

'They haven't called, so I probably haven't got it.'

'There'll be a job out there somewhere with your name it,' said Barbara comfortingly.

'Yes.' Molly rallied herself. 'I'm sure I'll get used

to it, it's just the initial leaving of them that's hard, isn't it? That's what they say. We'll get used to it, of course we will.'

'Of course, dear.'

'How old was I when you went back to work?'

'I did stay home with you, you know, till you were – let me think, six it was.'

'Six! Well, that would do me.'

'If he's paying you, why can't you?'

Paying? Because, because *lots* of reasons. 'I want to be independent.'

'I've done a good job then, haven't I?'

'It doesn't work with a baby, though, does it? You need people. People to lean on. To help.'

'You must have friends, Molly, you've always had lots of friends.'

'Of course I've got friends,' Molly snapped.

'You could always move over here.'

'What – *here*?'

'Colin'd get you a place in the village. Or down by the sea if you want. They're almost giving them away at the moment. There's a lovely one...'

Molly let the idea hold for about half a minute, then shook her head. 'No no no, I couldn't.'

'Colin'd set you up, he knows all the property people round here.'

'I'm sure he does.'

All sorts of reasons clashed for space in her mind – Max, Izzie, the other mums even, she was just building a life. Christophe? Even her resistance to the schools prattle was caving. Did Spain have OFSTED reports?

251

'I've ruined enough people's lives, it seems, I don't want to ruin Colin's life as well.'

'You haven't given him a chance.'

'ME! Given *him* a chance!'

'He just gets a little bit jealous sometimes, that's all. The Spanish are fabulous people, you know that, don't you.'

'Colin's from *Hull*!'

'And they *love* children here. Especially babies, you just wait. When we take Daisy into the village tonight, they'll be falling over her. Won't they, beauty?'

'Thanks for suggesting it. I'm really touched, Mum. But I've got to stay at least in the same country as Daisy's dad.' She laughed at the nonsense of this remark. 'I want him to be part of her life.'

'Yes.' Her mother lit another cigarette. 'Yes, of course,' she said quietly, handing Daisy over and picking up Molly's plate, scraping the fishbones onto her own.

Before setting off for the village, Barbara put on her red lipstick and sprayed herself with a squirt of Ma Griffe.

'NO!' Molly jumped forward as she rubbed her wrists together. 'Don't do that!'

'What's the matter with you?'

'Never, *never* rub it in!'

'What are you getting so excited about, Molly? It's only a dab of perfume!'

'Come on, I'll tell you all about it.'

As they set off across Jellybean's field, Molly told

her all about Kew, making it all sound as positive and upbeat as she could. She walked slowly next to her mother, enthusing about her new friends, and Christophe, noticing all the while how her mother's limp, after the wine, had become more pronounced. The dogs darted in and out of their legs, raced on ahead and waited for them, panting happily. They crossed the darkening orchard to the sea, turned left along a narrow sandy pathway beside the beach and soon reached the old beach-houses her mother had been talking about. They peered into the windows of the shabbiest one with a tatty SE VENDE sign stuck to the door. As they crossed the old bridge into the village, the deep green avenues of Kew seemed cramped and very far away, and her flat a positive Colditz compared to that little empty house with its green wooden verandah and white tiled floors. And the village was so pretty too – so unspoilt, undiscovered. *Could* she?

Her mother, despite her limp, had firm control of the pushchair. Molly felt doubly protective as she walked beside them. They walked through the narrow, cobbled main street, stopping every few yards. It wasn't only the old ladies who went ballistic over Daisy, but the young girls and the men; even the youths were stopping, calling from the balconies above, giving their congratulations and admiration. They stopped at the one small bar, buzzing with mopeds, greasy young men and pretty young girls with shining black eyes.

'See what I mean?' said Barbara. For the first time, Molly could see how very much at home her mother was here. She had mellowed too. She was more wrinkled, much older, but softer. Perhaps it was to do with Colin not being there. Or was it she who'd opened up to her mother at last, who felt an affinity?

'I think this is as close as we'll get to a family christening!' said Molly as they sat down at a table on the street.

The barman brought out a jug of wine and an armful of plates of olives and meats.

'I don't remember ordering that? Listen, let me pay for this.' Molly reached for her bag.

'*No no no*,' the barman insisted, '*a casa, a casa*.' He patted Barbara's shoulders. 'Ahora grandma-mammy.' He went off laughing.

'*Couldn't* you live here, Molly?'

'In my dreams.' Molly poured the wine from the rough, earthenware jug. She wanted to hold on to the harmony she'd found with her mother. There was so much still to say.

'Colin'd cope.'

'I don't want anyone "coping".'

'All right, wrong word, he'd get used to it. You know, I think he'd enjoy being a grandad, Moll.'

'*Step*-grandad. Look, it wouldn't work, let's not ruin what time we've got left.'

'He'd—'

'It's not just Colin, Mum. And besides, a tiny Spanish village like this is no place for a single mother.'

'Shhhhuh, keep your voice down.' Barbara looked over her shoulder.

'See?'

254

'Sorry, darling, but my reputation...'

'It'd just be another place I wouldn't fit into. I mean, blimey, Kew's a hard enough nut to crack!'

'It's just that...'

'Catholic Spain. It's all right, I understand. I'm getting used to it. It's like I've done what I've thought is right all my life, worked hard, paid my taxes, paid my National Insurance, got a good flat, got a good job, worked hard. Then I have Daisy which, from all those sort of innuendos which crop up out of the blue everybloodywhere, I take to mean that actually I've stepped out of line here, I've done something terribly, terribly *wrong*! It's all right – I'm learning to live with it, but the thing is, the funniest thing about all of this, I *know* one hundred bloody per cent, and I think *you* know...'

'It's the most rightest thing you've ever done.'

'Precisely, Mum. Precisely.'

The next morning they were outside early, before the heat hit. Barbara made a little playpen for Daisy in the garden, covering it with a sarong on sticks.

'NO – Daisy, don't eat the dirt! You silly girl.' Molly pulled her fingers, covered with dusty soil, out of her mouth.

'Oh, let her be,' said Barbara.

'Mother, this is DIRT!'

'A little bit of dirt never did anyone any harm.'

'Don't be ridiculous, where's that blanket?'

'You ate bucket-loads when you were a baby.'

'Well, that does explain a lot, doesn't it,' said Molly crossly as she spread the blanket underneath

Daisy, getting herself, still wet from the pool, stuck with mud all over.

'For heaven's sakes, relax, Molly! This is your last day.'

'Don't remind me.'

'Why don't you stay on? Colin wouldn't mind.'

'Yes, he would.'

'For a day or so. Go on. It's all gone so quickly.'

'Listen, I don' t want to spend the rest of my time here arguing about how I'm going to spend the rest of my time. OK?' She wished she hadn't as soon as she'd said it. Why did she always snap at her? The time was evaporating before her, and she wanted to cram so much in; hurrying around trying to relax was making her fretful.

'It was only a suggestion.'

'It's a fixed charter.'

'Why don't you take Jellybean out then? I'll look after Daisy. Go on '

Molly looked at her. At Daisy.

'Make the most of it.'

'I haven't got any trousers.'

Barbara laughed. 'The saddle disintegrated years ago, there's a bridle somewhere. Or a halter anyway. You're all right in your bikini, just take her for a gentle walk, she'd love that. Might be the last proper ride she gets.'

'Oh Mum, don't say that.'

On her way to Jellybean's field, Molly mooched around the outbuildings looking for a bridle. She loved outbuildings. She found an old tin of hoof oil and unscrewed the top eagerly. She sniffed hard at the thick black contents. It was one of her big memory smells, she was back in the stableyards of her childhood. She put the tin outside the door to remind her to take a sample back for Christophe.

'Hello, Jellybean old girl,' she said, slipping the old rope halter round the mare's warm, whiskery muzzle. 'Sod off, Bacco, go on – off with you.' She shooed the donkey away so ferociously she almost frightened herself.

The old mare walked steadily and trustingly next to her, snorting and tossing her head like a three-year-old. As soon as they were through the gate and out of Bacco's reach, Molly jumped up.

'You're a fat old thing, Jellybean. Like a warm furry armchair, aren't you?' She patted her neck affectionately. Jellybean's ears twitched like radar.

They ambled across the orchard towards the shore. The warm smell of sweaty fur and the heavy thud of hooves on the soft fudgy sand blended intoxicatingly into the ocean salt air. Molly wished she could put that into a can and take it back as well.

She thought about Christophe as they plodded along. She wondered how he'd be next time they met. Would it happen again? To have been wanted again physically had done her good. If nothing else, she'd thrown off the woolly aura of the unfucked. Unloved. Yes. Of course he didn't love her. But then, at least he'd *fancied* her. That was quite something after feeling so low. She'd probably got as much out of it as him. More, probably. And no harm had been done. So long as the others, so long as Caroline, never found out.

Jellybean flicked the flies with her tail. Molly squeezed her on with her legs. Her slow, lumbering canter turned her from an old comfy armchair to a rocking horse chair, splashing through the waves.

She pulled up at the beach house and slipped down to the ground.

'You have a rest, old bean,' Molly told the horse as she tied her to the verandah.

She peered through the windows again. It was shabby and the kitchen was nothing but an old stone sink and one big, high tap, but the space of it. Full of air and light.

Could she live here? On her own with Daisy but with her mum just across the fields? Where there were no fences around everything, no houses squashed together in tiny roads, no permanent three-lane motorways to wake up to? No safe hot-house jungles, no manicured lawns, no manicured lives, where everything just grew, or didn't grow as nature decided. Where it lived. Or it died.

The bottom line was no. A sad but resounding no. Despite the big, open skies, the ocean, the beach, she'd be swamped and stamped on by the permanent, low-hanging cloud of single motherhood. The local men would think she was loose and the local women would despise her for it. Hadn't humankind moved on from all that, though? Maybe not. Maybe it wasn't even so different in Kew. Maybe it was just more obviously on the surface here? Who knew.

Anyway, there'd be too much she'd miss. There were things to look forward to: Jenna's barbie was coming up. With her tan she'd get herself looking

258

great for that. And the Kew Gardens picnic, and Max should be back from Geneva by now. And Christophe?

What a place for a holiday home, though, she thought, as she leapt onto Jellybean's back and galloped off back towards the farm.

CHAPTER SEVENTEEN

The greenness of England in June was a shock. First the towering, erect, horse chestnuts lining the M3 from Gatwick, then Kew itself, which had grown into one big rose garden. They were everywhere. From pale, papery-white climbers to thick deep folds of burgundy velvet, all fighting for space with the buddleia, sweet peas and honeysuckle, covering the garden fences and papering the walls of the houses. Molly had another surprise when she got home: her answer-machine had taken sixteen messages.

'Where *were* you?'

'At my mother's.'

'*Spain!*'

'Yes – I—'

'By *plane*.'

'Well we didn't go by coach, did we. I know we're broke but even so.'

'You've *been on* an aeroplane?'

'Yes! You know, those things you go on all the time.'

'Why didn't you *tell* me? Why didn't you *call*?'

'Call where?'

'The office of course!'

'You mean you've *been* in the office?'

'Barely, but...'

'Since when did you need to know our every movement?'

'Or you could at least have left an outgoing message.'

'And let all the burglars know?'

'Molly, I've been worried *sick*! How is she?'

'She's fine – we got on really well actually, Creepy Colin was away, luckily.'

'Not your mother! Daisy. How's Daisy?'

Molly smiled to herself. 'Fine.'

'Has she changed?'

'Loads. She's got two teeth.'

'*Teeth?*'

'Yes, you know, those things—' She stopped herself before her sarcasm ran away with her.

'*Bloody* hell!'

'Come and see!'

Sudden silence.

'No strings, Max.'

Silence.

'I'm – I'm back in Venezuela.'

Molly's shoulders fell.

'I'll be back as soon as I can. They're keeping me hanging on, the military are on full alert, might intervene, rumours are flying, difficult to tell.'

'Sure. Give us a call when you're in this hemisphere. Listen, I've got to go, Max.'

'Where are you going now?'

'To a barbecue.'

'To a *barbecue*! Where – *Gibraltar*?'

'Listen, I'm glad to hear you. Glad you're OK. Call me when you get back, all right? Come over and spend as long as you like with her.'

Another silence.

'Where's the barbecue, Molly?'

Oh dear, she thought, he is sounding sorry for himself.

'Kew. All right?'

'Who's looking after Daisy?'

'The person who usually looks after Daisy. She's coming with me. Listen, my taxi's here.'

Molly smiled to herself as she put the phone down. She tried not to speculate too closely, or build up false hopes, but something, at long last, was happening. He'd pulled his neck out of the sand.

'Molly! Where've you been hanging? You look great!' said Jenna.

'Oh, just Spain, for a couple of days.'

'I knew it? I can sense those big ocean ions all over you.'

'I just hope I can hang onto them, that's all.'

She did feel good. Less like a sagging bag of brown water and more loose-limbed, tanned and rested. More wanted. She'd been somewhere. And, with her growing expertise with the Light 'n Easy, she'd upped her shade from mid-brown to golden blonde, her old natural colour, which set off her tan and her dress. Her *the* dress.

Jason bounded across the garden. 'Hey, how you doing?'

'Come on, I'll introduce you to everybody,' said Jenna.

Was Jenna liking her more because she was less shabby? Molly wondered as she followed her pert, perfect arse past the barbecue sizzling on the left and through a laburnum arch to the small, round lawn. Candles hung in jars from a large apple tree. Its brown, faded blossom covered the ground. Next to a high brick wall on the right, water trickled from the hat of a wizard fountain onto a mini beach of coloured pebbles. Three strapless backless girls were sitting hunched together on a white, wooden garden bench. On various heights of garden chairs opposite them, three men, all in baggy shorts with legs spread wide and holding tins of beer, were talking cricket.

'Hey, guys, this is Molly, a new friend of mine?'

The men held up their cans, one said cheers. The girls looked up, one smiled. Molly gripped Daisy's car seat tighter. They all looked about seventeen.

'Come on, I'll show you where to put Daisy,' said Jenna.

The doorbell went.

'Oh, Jase,' said Jenna, 'could you get that?'

'Just turning these sausages, Jen.'

Jenna looked at Molly, raised her pretty eyebrows and rolled her eyes as if to say 'Men!' before she rushed off to open the door. She called back, 'And when you've done that, can you show Molly Lu's room? '

Molly stood watching Jason picking up the

sausages with the tongs and turning them over, every so often looking up and grinning at her.

'I thought you were veggies,' Molly said, searching for something to say.

'*So* real-looking, aren't they?' he said, holding up a sausage with his tongs, 'Come on, I'll show you the bedroom.'

Molly followed Jason down a long narrow corridor and into Lavender's room.

The cloying over-aromatherapised sticky heat of the flat was replaced by the cooler familiar powdery baby smell. The room was dark, lit only by a Humpty-Dumpty night light, but she could see the walls were lavender, with lavender curtains and lavender wallpaper. All sorts of crystals and a mobile of stuffed fairy dolls dangled over the crib. Beneath the window, a wooden changing table stood to the ready with little bowls of multicoloured cotton wool, tubs of Wet Wipes and a pile of neatly ironed and firmly folded white nappies.

'Here,' whispered Jason gently, 'she'll be fine there?' He pointed to a space below Lavender's white, veiled crib. 'Oh, and no worries about coming in whenever you want, Lav sleeps like an ox. Nothing'll wake her now till the morning.'

So it was true. She was sleeping through the night.

Though Daisy wouldn't think about waking till two, Molly hesitated about leaving her there.

''S'allright, look,' Jason whispered, 'there's the baby listener. The other end of it's in the front room.'

'Sure,' said Molly brightly, going to leave but finding six feet six inches of Jason standing in the doorway. There was an awkward pause as they stood together in the dark, quiet room.

'I'd better see how my sausage's doing.' Jason smiled down at her.

'Yes, you'd better had,' said Molly firmly; he turned and bounded with his big, bouncy walk off down the hallway.

Obviously still not getting it, Molly thought as she filled her glass with red wine and parked herself next to the baby listener, sipping and looking around at the strange grown-up party world. A world she'd forgotten existed.

The flat was not so much a blend of new age and high tech as a proximity. Two large, black speakers dominated the front section of the room, one each side of the Edwardian fireplace with a Jenna mantelpiece of candles, lumps of stone and aromatherapy burners. Above it was a large, black-framed poster of the yin yang circle. In the bay, a pink candle burned in the centre, flanked on each side by two large, pink amaryllis flowers.

Molly hovered at the back end of the room, wondering what to do with herself, idly studying the bookshelves. They were neatly stacked with hundreds of CDs, videos and computer games, going on all the way up to the high ceiling. Predictably, the books included travel guides, computer manuals, volumes on vegetarian cookery, yoga, *feng shui* and the I Ching.

Whatever the music was, it was much too loud and she wished she could turn it down. More people arrived, all glittery, ready for fun and all looking about twelve. It was odd seeing people dressed in party clothes again. Clothes they'd obviously bought for pleasure and were wearing for pleasure. That, she knew, meant only one thing; for all her feelings of well-being, she must look about fifty to them. They're probably wondering what Jenna's mum's doing here, she thought wryly as she picked up a crisp and put it in her mouth, trying to create the illusion she was happily partying all by herself there in her corner of the room.

A familiar voice boomed from the hall.

'No, Theo, I don't think so. I *do* apologise, Jenna...'

Caroline, in full-on greeting smile, appeared at the doorway. She looked almost as out of place as Molly felt. Her blonde hair was coiffed up onto the top of her head, with professional-looking wispy curls dangling down her long neck. She spotted Molly and clacked confidently across in her high, pointy-toed heels.

'*Dar*ling, how are you,' she said, as if Molly was that long-lost bosom pal she'd been searching for for years.

'Fine, thanks.' Molly felt a surge of guilt and tried not to think yipes-yelps thoughts about Christophe. No reason, no reason at all she should ever know.

'By yourself?'

'Daisy's in with Lavender.'

'Her first sleepover, how ad*or*able,' said Caroline as she darted doubtful looks around the room. 'Not expressing yet then?'

'I did try, not very successfully I'm afraid. It took hours.'

'Dreadful, isn't it? Nothing makes one feel like a cow more than squirting one's titty into a cup.'

'It was more not having a babysitter. I've started weaning her off, now anyway.'

'*Have* you?'

Theo joined them, handing a glass to Caroline.

'We were just talking about expressing, darling.'

'Gooood.' Theo winked a crinkly eye at Molly, and rubbed his hands together.

'I must say,' Caroline continued, 'I think I'm coming to the end of this breastfeeding business. What do you suppose happens when they get *teeth*?'

'Daisy's got two coming through.'

'No!'

'Think I'll have a look at the garden.' Theo wandered off, hands clasped behind his back.

'As soon as I talk about anything to do with bodily parts, he just glazes over,' she said. Her eyes rolled around the room. 'Izzie!' she called over Molly's shoulder.

'Guess who we just saw?' Izzie came racing across the room. 'Hey, Molly, you're looking *great*!'

'Who?'

'*Mick*! Driving behind us, down Sandycombe Road!'

Caroline and Molly looked at each other.

'You know,' Izzie nodded knowingly, 'Mick!'

'Who's Mick?' said Caroline, uttering the name as if it were sick.

'Jagger! Mick Jagger. Right behind us.' She looked to Carter for confirmation.

'Silver Merc.' Carter nodded.

'When we stopped by the chip shop to let the traffic the other way through—'

'Nightmare it is, driving down Sandycombe,' interrupted Carter.

'He stopped as well! Right behind us! Jerry wasn't with him. Well, she wouldn't be, would she. Now.'

'Where would he be going in Kew?' said Caroline.

'Coach and Horses quiz night?' laughed Molly.

'Molly, bloody hell, Spain's done you good. You look completely different! How's your mum?'

'Great. I've put my Fodor's back on the shelf, right next to Penelope Leach. So I won't forget to get back soon.'

'Good on yer.'

'This is going to be a good night, I can feel it in my bones. Carter, what's the *matter* with you tonight! Get those drinks in. Sorry we're late. Getting out of the house was like breaking out of Fort Knox. God, Gordon wouldn't go down. He was convinced we were going to see Barbie.'

'Izzie, what have you *done*?' said Caroline, looking at her closely.

'You've not got your glasses on!' said Molly, 'and your hair!'

'Finally got to the serum cupboard. It's worth it for going out, isn't it.'

'I think I need glasses,' said Molly.

'I'll get myself some contacts one day,' said Izzie, taking a handful of crisps. 'One day, when I've got a moment – ha ha. Meantime I thought I'd be blind as a bat for a night.'

'Is Bob at home, then?'

'Yep, with his gran.' Izzie flung her arms wide and spun round. Her brown leggings had been replaced by sparkling silver vertical striped ones, with a longer-than-usual baggy T-shirt embroidered with black butterflies. 'Carter. *Drinks!*'

Carter jumped and took his gaze away from the backless, strapless lot dancing in the front half of the room.

'I've had a wonderful, wonderful day,' said Caroline.

'Go on then,' said Izzie, giving Molly a here-we-go look, 'tell us.'

'I've been back at that new underwear shop in Church Street? It's simply *divine…*' Her voice petered out as she looked at Molly and then to Izzie. 'No? Well, you simply must. The good news is I'm back into G-strings, look!' She did a twirl, stroking her pert round bottom beneath her tight pink skirt.

'You've got the figure for it, Caroline,' said Izzie warily.

'And they have *all* the collections there, so I stocked up! The first time since Charles was *born!* Heaven, absolute heaven! They make you feel so *good*, those shops.'

'I'm sure they do,' said Molly curtly. If there was one subject capable of making her envious, this was it.

'I must find Theo. Where are you, Theo?'

'Yeuch, the thought of a G-string makes my teeth

go all peculiar,' said Izzie as they stood watching Caroline's bottom disappearing into the garden.

'My underwear's so disgusting, I'm more embarrassed at anyone seeing my bra than my nipples.'

'I've got about thirty bras in my drawer,' said Izzie.

'*Thirty?* Well I'm not buying any more until I'm back to normal,' said Molly. 'I'm not paying out for any more of those revolting feeding bras.'

'My tits go up and down more bloody times than Richard Branson's balloon. One week I'm 38C, the next I'm 42D.'

'Why don't they make black maternity bras? White ones are useless, they go off so quickly.'

'Here's a good one for you.' Izzie leant forward and whispered conspiratorially into Molly's ear, 'Net White.'

'What do you mean?'

Carter returned and handed her her glass.

'Stick 'em in to soak, they'll come up as good as new.'

'Brilliant!' said Molly with feeling. 'That could change my life. Oh, to have white bras again. Though I'm starting to wean now. Or trying, anyway.'

'Are you?' Izzie looked at her, surprised.

Molly looked at Carter.

'It's all right, don't mind him,' said Izzie, 'he's heard it all before, haven't you, love?'

'You could say that,' said Carter.

Izzie gave him a peck on the cheek, then she froze and looked into the air. 'Oh, I love this song...'

'Who is it?'

'Smashing Pumpkins.' Izzie grabbed Carter's neck. 'Come on, let's see if you've got any rhythm left in you.'

'Who?' said Molly as they danced slowly away, leaving Molly suddenly alone again.

'Right, folks.' Jason was bouncing around behind the barbie, tongs clicking, 'I think we're ready. Grab your plates for the best sausages this side of Perth.'

Glad to have found something to do, Molly joined the queue. Just being in the same room as so much youth and energy was making her feel weary. She looked across at Caroline and Theo, sitting on a bench in front of a bush covered in tiny white flowers and multicoloured fairy lights. She wondered what they were talking about, betting it wasn't grubby bras.

'Mind if I lean over you there?' a soft, Australian voice came from behind.

'No, of course not,' she said, turning round.

Looking ahead, she saw the queue had moved up leaving her still in the same spot. 'I'm so sorry.'

'In your own world there?'

'Well – to be honest, yes.' Molly smiled up at him. 'Best place to be, these days.'

Unlike the other males in the place, at least this one was a man as opposed to an overgrown teenager. And he was big. With a tidy blond crew-cut which made his neck look enormous.

Molly groped desperately for some small talk. 'You must be one of Jason's rugby pals?'

'Rugby, football, cricket, swimming, you name it,

we do it.' He straighted up stiffly and tightened his lips together seriously.

'Is that how you know Jason and Jenna?' she said pathetically, just wanting to keep the conversation going, wanting to talk to someone new, just so she could tell herself later she'd not been a complete party failure.

He touched his ear lobe and held his head to one side. 'I'm having to think here now! What came first, work or play?'

'So you work and play together?'

He nodded.

'Banking?'

'No no,' he laughed as if it were a ridiculous question. Molly felt the conversation slipping into oblivion and tried to rescue it again.

'But you work together?'

'I'm in software.'

'Software, how interesting!'

'My company does all his bank's software.'

'Which bank is it again?'

'Michigan Melvin Inc.'

'Is that so. Barbie looks good, doesn't it.' She nodded towards Jason, speedily opening buns and filling them over the fizzling grill.

'Yes.'

Molly took a spoonful of salad and plonked it on her plate. 'Do you want some bean salad?' She turned helpfully and piled his plate up in a motherly fashion.

When it was Molly's turn, the buns had run out.

'Plenty more where that came from,' Jason leapt

round to the front of the barbecue and crouched down to the cardboard boxes underneath the salad table. A hand came from behind her and stroked the back of his head and neck.

She turned around to look at Mr Crew-cut. He was standing looking around as if nothing had happened. Then Jason stood up and gave her a big, silly, leery grin. Molly looked at the guy again, confused, then back at Jason. He stood to his full height, then rubbed his hands happily on his thighs before going back to the other side of the barbecue.

'Burger, sausage or both?'

'Both,' said Molly.

'That's my girl.' Jason took his time picking up a sausage. He put it in the bun and handed it to Molly, who looked quizzically back at the guy behind her. He smiled pleasantly.

What was going on? Why did he stroke Jason's neck? Had Jason got that desperate? Did Jenna know?

'OK, Dan, what'll it be?'

'Pile it on, Jase, you know me.'

Did he? Typical. Now, this was more like the old days. Dan! She'd homed in on the only gay man in the place. He didn't look gay. Jason looked more camp than he did. Or was he bi? Did she really give a damn here?

Molly stood for a moment with her plate, not knowing which direction to go. Caroline had gone, leaving Theo on his own on the bench. Join him? Better not. She took a forkful of mango salad.

'It's all organic, you know,' Jenna put her hand on

273

Molly's shoulder. Molly, with her mouth full of food, opened her eyes wide in an appreciative nod. Dan joined her.

'Oh, neat one.' Jenna stood back from them and picked up the camera which was dangling round her neck. A neon flash went off in Molly's face. Jenna popped out from behind it. 'Come on, one more, and smile this time, you two.'

Dan stood next to Molly and put his arm, uncle-like, round her. Molly thought, oh, what the hell, and put her arm round his big waist while she smiled brightly for the camera.

Jenna mouthed the word 'trouble' to Molly behind his back before sauntering off into the darkness of the garden.

'How d'you know Jase'n'Jen then?' he asked, taking a big, sideways bite of his burger.

'Kew Post-Natal Group.' Take that for a passion-killer, matey.

'You have kids?'

'Just one. A baby. Same age as Lavender,' said Molly. Rather than sending him further into oblivious disinterest, he seemed to brighten.

'Boy or girl? Hey, are you all right?'

Molly nodded, gulping down the rice salad she'd almost choked on. She'd just seen someone she hadn't expected to see over Dan's shoulder. Christophe was walking over to Theo's bench.

'Yes. Yes – a girl. She's called Daisy. She's five months old,' Molly waffled, 'she's really gorgeous. I – er – I only moved to Kew a few months ago, I mean we moved, of course I mean we...' Molly looked past Dan, who was nodding seriously like he was really taking it all in. Theo was standing up. Christophe was introducing him to a slim, dark girl.

'Nice place to live.'

'Pardon?'

He was with a *girl*!

'Kew?' he said.

'Do you live around here then, Dan?' She was petite, Asian.

Long, straight black hair. Short, silver dress. Amazing legs. She would have, wouldn't she?

'Lawn Crescent.'

He was holding her hand! The *bastard*! She forced herself to defocus to Dan, and found her eyes resting on his nose. Slightly on the fat side, but quite a *big* nose.

'Do you know it?'

At least it wasn't Ulé. Poor, droopy Ulé.

'Oh – I know. That's off Sandycombe, isn't it. I know, we were just talking about Sandycombe as it happens, my friend, she just saw *Mick Jagger* there, and she was saying, we were saying, well, actually, her husband was saying, about, you know, how bad it is for driving and it's true isn't it? Not that I drive any more but when I did I always felt I was going to be mown down, it's the big white vans that are the worst, isn't it? I'm sure they have a sport called Sandycombe, and the buses – the BUSES! Though they've got to have their little bit of fun, haven't they, who'd want to be a one-man bus driver...'

Dan stood listening politely while she tried to collect herself. Keep with Dan, stick by him for a while, protect, protect. One side blocked. Keep it that way. One side occupied...

Then one of the strapless girls came up, grabbed Dan's arm proprietorially and whispered to him.

'Nice meeting you, Molly,' he said politely.

'See you later.'

The girl gave Molly a look which said oh no you won't.

Molly shrugged, took a big glug of wine. Man shortage, same the world over, Kew, Notting Hill, what's the difference?

Go over and join, go over and join, handle it. You're a grown tough woman. It was only a shag. You knew that! Just be friendly. She felt her feet taking her towards them.

Christophe held his arms out. 'Mollee.' He kissed her on both cheeks then stood back and looked at her admiringly, 'Mollee, you look fantastic!'

'Thanks.'

He didn't introduce his new friend. Molly smiled sweetly at her and back at him. She was very pretty. He looked like the cat who had got the cream.

'Christophe, you're here.' Caroline minced over taking kittenish short little high-heeled steps. 'Come on come on come on, I can't wait any longer, we *must* dance.' She took not a blind bit of notice of the girl. Or Theo. He was sitting on the bench, as unruffled as ever. He gave Molly a friendly wink.

'Do you know, however much I drink, I don't seem to get drunk any more!' said Molly.

She was slumped out on the sofa watching the dancing with a sozzled Izzie and a somewhat deflated Caroline. Christophe, his girlfriend and Theo were in deep conversation in the garden, while Carter had taken up position in the booze corner, shuffling happily from one foot to the other as he watched the action through a drunken haze.

'There's something I've got to tell you, now that we're all here,' said Molly.

'Whazzat?' said Izzie.

'I've got a job!'

'Whaaat?'

'Only part-time,' she added quickly, as irrational bad mother feelings rose to the fore.

'Where is it, darling?' said Caroline with a tired voice.

'Baxter, Rumbold and Featherington.'

'The estate agent's?' said Izzie sitting up and coming to her senses slightly.

'Well done you,' said Caroline.

'It's mornings only. Well, until two. And there are still things to arrange, I have to find a childminder and, well, there's lots to work out but...'

'A nanny-share's what you need,' said Izzie, 'and I meant what I said, we'll take Daisy till you get sorted.'

'That's really, really kind of you.'

'I won't pretend there's not something in it for me, though.'

'What? Anything? Tell me?'

'Any inside info on three beds with an SF garden that needs work?'

'What's an SF?'

277

'Molly! And you're going to work in an estate agent's?' said Caroline.

'South-facing,' said Izzie, 'Big south facing gardens, like gold dust in Kew.'

'I'll do what I can. Of course I will. I've been meaning to tell you all evening, to ask you, I mean, about having Daisy, but. . .' Why did she always find it so difficult to ask people to help her?

'What about Ulé?' said Caroline casually. 'You can have a bit of her if you want.'

'What do you mean?'

'All she does is mope around the place, since – you know who – dumped her. It might wake her up a bit, having two.'

'Do you mean it?'

'Why not. It will broaden Charles's horizons. Develop his social skills. Do him good.'

Molly felt like bursting into tears. 'I'll pay you – I mean her. Who do you pay in a nanny-share? The nanny or the mother? Of course she'll have to agree to it.'

'She'll agree,' said Caroline firmly.

'I can lend her my double buggy,' said Izzie before slumping back on the sofa and closing her eyes. 'Oh, I feel ill.'

CHAPTER EIGHTEEN

'She goes down for her nap at one, feed first, finish off with a cuddle and half a bottle, cold not warmed...'

'Is OK.' Flat monotone.

Was it? It was so hard to tell what Ulé was thinking or feeling. Molly left the room, the house, the road, without turning round, her jaw set firm as she walked, heavy-footed, across the Green. Daisy had gone ballistic when her two a.m. drink dispenser had cruelly transformed yet again from soft titty to rubber plastic teat. Which had started Mr and Mrs Constandavalos upstairs marching around with an exaggerated, angry stamp. Molly, by that time crying almost as loudly as Daisy herself, had persisted, refusing to give in like the previous nights. It didn't help that her body was doing its own weird contortions at the sudden shock-change of routine. Her breasts had transformed into two close-to-bursting, granite-hard lumps of rock. She wasn't so much top-heavy as she walked across the Green towards her first day at work that morning as forward-loading.

A cat on full alert slunk past the pond, chest

crouched low, its tummy scraping the ground. It stopped behind a thick clump of of tall yellow irises. Molly quickly looked away from the troop of baby moorhens bobbing like clockwork toys behind their mother, dangerously close to shore. Stupid bird, thought Molly. Revising her thoughts as she turned left into Priory Road – she'd never fob off her babies onto another moorhen to go and help flog desirable nests to yet more moorhens all day. SF or no SF.

She rang the bell of Baxter, Rumbold and Featherington, trying to force herself into a positive, businesslike frame of mind. She had free childcare. Close by. Ulé, for all her aloofness, was a known quantity and Caroline was there, keeping one of her eagle eyes on it all. It was time to stop herself getting weepy over baby moorhens, most of whom would die soon anyway, and all her other post-natal wimpishness. She'd watch *Newsnight* that night, from beginning to end. She'd stamp on her desires to cuddle and say 'there there, never mind,' to the poor politicians and Third World dictators getting the pointy end of Paxo's tongue. Why! Later in the week she'd even have a go at *Question Time*.

She peered through the window in between two photos of cramped ugly cottages, both with SOLD stamped in red across their half-a-million price tags. It was dark and empty. She hung around and watched the village waking up. A big yellow dustcart reversed into the station forecourt, scattering the pigeons. Across the road, the Natural Free Range Meat shop was already well into its morning. A butcher was dipping things in a bowl and lifting them out high and dangly. She squinted. It looked like he was washing his smalls. No – they weren't smalls, escalopes in breadcrumbs, that was probably it. More money out but she had to do something about making an optician's appointment. Were National Health glasses still all the rage?

Young, smart professionals passed, going up to town – cliquey, preoccupied, down at mouth, all looking like they knew exactly what they were doing, exactly where they were going in life. In the other direction, lost-looking tourists poured out of the Tube like toothpaste, with an expectant but hesitant jauntiness. Group by group, they stopped and stood bewildered before spotting the brown sign pointing to the Gardens. By the time they crossed the zebra beside the Greenhouse Café, they'd be marching, purposefully ant-like, away up Lichfield Road to the gates of the Gardens ahead.

A down-at-mouth with a purposeful glint in her eye coming from the tourist direction made Molly jump by stopping next to her.

'I'm Johanna,' said the girl, digging into her floppy brown handbag for her keys.

'Molly Warren.' Molly stretched out her hand.

'Welcome,' she said wearily.

'This is where you sit.' Johanna showed her to the back room. Molly noticed, with disappointment, someone else's postcards and bits on the walls and a row of fluffy donkeys Sellotaped to the top of the computer screen.

'Don't move anything. It's Debbie, the accountant's, desk. She's only in on Mondays. The day you're not here. You'll have to share her computer. Here's a set of keys. I'll show you how the burglar alarm works first. When Celia and I are out on viewings, or lunch, you'll have to cover for us out front. She'll tell you about that.'

Johanna spoke in a deadbeat way which didn't invite any response. Molly listened and scribbled notes as she was taken through the routine. The phone rang.

Johanna looked at her expectantly.

Molly picked up the phone. 'Good morning, can I help you?' she said, her voice disintegrating into cracks as she hunted for her old official telephone ways.

'Molly. Caroline. Just to say everything's fine. She's just stopped crying and Ulé's taken them into the garden.'

'Has she been crying all this time?'

'She's settled. I'm calling to tell you she's settled.'

'Thanks,' said Molly, looking sideways at Johanna and putting the phone down. 'You don't allow private calls, do you?' she went on, not wanting to let this stupid girl get her oar in early. 'Thought as much. It's just, my baby, she hasn't been left before, you see.'

'We rely on the telephones. An important buyer or seller could be trying to get through.'

'Sure,' said Molly, thinking, much more of this honeybunch and I'm out of that door before you can say fixtures and fittings.

'Don't let it ring more than four times, always answer with "Good morning, Baxter, Rumbold and

Featherington. Molly – whateveryournameis speaking, how may I help you?" Do you want to write that down?'

Molly had to forcibly stop herself picking her bag up and leaving there and then. How many times had this girl been through this routine before?

Celia Sprague was a little more pleasant. She emphasised the need for tact and diplomacy, which made Molly want to ask the obvious question as to where Johanna's was hiding. She told her how most Kew residents rarely left the area but tended to move around in circles and were therefore acutely aware of the property market. She warned her of the frenzy, whenever an unmodernised, south-facing came along between a lot of desperate people, clearly ready for a fight. However, Molly wouldn't have to move her brittle old bones about that much, but she would have to be aware of the pressures Celia and Johanna were under, and cover out front when they were at lunch or both out on viewings.

Things got better when Molly was settled behind her desk at the back with Celia and Johanna out of her sight. She found ridiculous pleasure in just typing and things like the little bowl of coloured paper clips on her desk, drawers full of scrummy crispy clean stationery and the stapling machine. Having a desk again. Tapping away at the computer was fun. Restful, even. More relaxing than racing around at home all day. And she was getting paid! She was on her way back into the world. She began to think she was really living when Johanna brought her a mug of real coffee and a biscuit and told her she could have a ten-minute break.

She sat sipping, wondering if this was why mothers went back to work. To have real coffee breaks where you stopped for ten minutes. Without interruption. Where stopping meant stopping. And then, what about people who had really stimulating jobs they loved where they had people to help them? Where there were no pesky office juniors being all superior over them, where they passed their chores on to someone else. Perhaps that could be as unputdownable as your own tiny baby girl? Couldn't it?

She opened her sumptuously tidy handbag and took out an envelope, relishing the novelty of not having to rummage through balls of tissue, stray soggy Wet Wipes and shit-coloured nappy sacks. Jenna's wedding invitation. Well, it had been a change from the pile of bills. She fingered the handmade parchment card, touching the bumpy daisies glued on in the shape of a heart. 'Mr and Mrs Norton invite you to a Flower Wedding in Kew Gardens,' she read. It was addressed to Molly plus one. She had till the end of August to get her plus one sorted out. She'd be a different creature by then. A thin, independent, working girl. She ran her finger down the scented rose-bordered present list. A few months' work at Baxter Rumbold and Featherington would get her closer to a pair of Egyptian combed cotton double beach towels, or the Metro cutlery, maybe? An elaborate PS at the bottom, bordered by two spindly pen and ink lilies, asked for each guest to bring a plant. To be planted out in Jenna and Jason's Love Garden, brackets, soil fine, sandy and sunny but, please, nothing red, close brackets.

Fine, sandy and sunny. How lovely!

'Molly!' Celia called. She looked at the clock. Exactly ten minutes had passed. Celia came through, leant across her, far too close, and clicked her mouse. Molly leant back as Celia clicked pointedly back to the screen, showing her how to type house details.

'Best get on then!' said Molly, pulling her chair up to the screen efficiently.

'Clearly,' said Celia.

Molly worked quickly, for all the unpleasantness wanting to show them she was fast and, beneath her befuddledness, really, clearly, very smart. She'd rummaged through the stationery cupboard, found the right paperheading for house details and printed the lot out before handing it to Celia with a proud, take-that flourish.

'What's this?'

'The new house details.'

'But I haven't checked them yet.'

'That's why I'm giving them to you now.'

'NOnononono.' Celia shook her head seriously. 'Johanna, show Molly how to transfer her files to me. I only check on screen, Molly, never on paper. Waste of paper. Waste of time.'

'Why didn't you tell me that?' Molly said to Johanna as she leant over Molly, clicking quickly on icons. 'You must have heard the printer going.'

'All you have to do is ask,' said Johanna, 'if

you don't know something. Ask. We're only over there.'

'How can I ask about something I don't know about? Oh, forget it.'

Despite the teething problems, at the end of her first working day Molly walked out happy. She'd done it. She'd done it. She'd got a job and a child-minder. The impossible had become possible. Clearly, no one lasted long there, but it didn't matter, she'd use them like they wanted to use her. Use them, use them, she said over and over to herself. Get used to leaving Daisy, to computers again, then leave. They want cheap, part-time, no-responsibility employees, I want to get myself back on the tracks. Use them. Use her. Let the silly girl get her bossy kicks. Molly smiled to herself as she walked along Riverside Drive. She'd barely got her feet under the desk yet and already she was playing office politics.

She hesitated as she approached Caroline's. Christophe's 2CV van was parked in the driveway.

'How did it go?'

'OK,' said Ulé, stepping back to let Molly in. Molly recognised the unique, precious quiet that only houses with sleeping babies have.

'She's asleep now?'

Ulé nodded, both of them.

'Was it much extra work – having the two? I mean, if it's too much for you, just let me know, I don't want to impose on you.'

'Is OK.'

'Where's Caroline?'

'Out.'

'Oh.'

Then Theo appeared at the top of the stair landing. He looked ruffled and sleepy and equally surprised to see Molly.

'I didn't know there was a mothers' meeting today, Molly? Caroline's out somewhere.'

He came down the stairs, stroking the back of his head absent-mindedly.

'No – I've just come to collect Daisy, Ulé's been loking after her.'

'Course course *course*, yes. . . . Good.' He rubbed his hands together, looking no less confused before shuffling off down the hallway.

'Thanks, Ulé,' Molly called out to her as she went up the stairs.

Still standing on the doorstep, she looked at the gateway to the side of the house. Did she dare? What if Caroline came back and caught her? She looked over her shoulder before gently unclicking the gate and going into the garden. She hesitated. He was nowhere to be seen. He must be in the summer house. Or the shed. Or the garage. She stood for a full few minutes. Her curiosity about how he'd be when they next met alone was eating her away. Did she dare go further? If she could see him, if he'd appear, then she could go quickly over to him, then if Theo saw her, it wouldn't look so odd as if he – or Ulé – saw her snooping around their back garden. No. She couldn't. She'd have to wait. She'd be there every day. She'd see him soon enough. Would he still be interested? Or was that it? Was *she* still interested? Why the hell else was she standing there like an idiot in Caroline's side passage? Maybe he'd be interested in a casual but mutually beneficial arrangement. She was old enough for that. Old enough for a Mrs-Robinson-like romance on the side. Even if it was only just sex. It was better than no sex, wasn't it?

The scrunch of gravel made her act. She just got on the right side of the gate before Caroline's maroon BMW convertible screeched to a halt.

CHAPTER NINETEEN

Molly learnt to switch off emotionally when she handed Daisy over. She was fast coming to like and trust Ulé.

In her second week she was late for the first time. Only twenty minutes but she arrived armoured-up for the inevitable Johanna put-down. She was surprised to be greeted with a warm, you're-my-new-best-friend smile. A peculiar smile, more a drawing back of the lip, revealing long, gappy teeth.

It only took a nanosecond to work out why.

Christophe was sprawled on the armless, padded grey reception chair, sipping a mug of coffee.

'You have a visitor, Molly,' said Johanna pleasantly.

'What are *you* doing here?'

'I'll get you a coffee, Molly,' said Johanna sweetly, disappearing into the kitchen.

'I just wanted to check with you.'

'Did you see me?' she said, instantly regretting it. 'Where?'

They looked at each other. No, she realised, he

hadn't seen her lurking in the passageway. Good. Good. 'Just now,' she said vaguely.

'Caroline has invited me, this afternoon, to join you in the garden. At your mothers' group. Is it OK?'

'Why check with me?'

He shrugged sheepishly. 'We, we haven't talked since...'

'There wasn't much chance at the party, was there.'

'I think maybe you have bad thoughts about me now.'

'Why?'

'Well, you know I ...'

'Look, Christophe. It was just a shag.' Molly flipped a look back to the kitchen and lowered her voice. 'Forget it, all right?'

'No bad feeling?'

'No bad feeling.' Go on, go for it now. 'Maybe we'll do it again sometime.'

He gave her a childish, relieved smile. Phew! So it can't have been that bad for him. Phew phew phew.

She nodded back to the kitchen. 'Meantime, I think your next conquest is arriving. I can get her phone number for you if you like?'

Christophe sprawled and looked down at his knees. He'd suddenly turned into the young boy he was, all his premature maturity gone in the pop of an ego bubble.

'I'll see you later then,' Molly said brightly as she spotted Celia's mustard Golf parking up just outside the window.

Christophe sat looking at her intently.

Celia was getting out of her car, someone else was getting out of the passenger side. She had a client with her.

'*Christophe*, haven't you got any seeds to sow?'

Johanna came and stood next to Molly as he crossed over the road towards the chemist's. Molly sensed Johanna's eyes boring into his backside.

'I think he likes you,' Molly whispered to her as Celia came in through the door. 'In fact, he lives just across the street, on the Parade there. I'll take you there for lunch one day, if you're interested. I'm sure he'd like that.'

Johanna looked at her, not knowing if she was serious or not, and gave her another weird smile.

'Bugger,' Molly said to herself as she stared at the computer. She'd been working on updating a rental chart when the table had suddenly disappeared from the screen. She was going to have to ask Johanna for help. Finding her way around the office was like being in someone else's kitchen. Mastering the machine minefield – the telephone answering, the burglar alarm, the computer, the fax. The e-mail. The coffee percolator, the toaster.

She went out to the front office and waited while Johanna was on the phone.

Johanna turned to her. 'Yes?' she said with the old satisfied irritation in her voice.

Bugger it, Molly thought again as she led her back through to the computer.

Johanna sat down and, with a big sigh, put her hand over the mouse and began clicking.

'Which file is it in?'

'It's on the floppy.'

Johanna turned to her sternly. 'Never,' she said, 'never, ever use the floppy disk.'

'I thought, as it's Debbie's computer, that way I'd stay away from her stuff, keep all mine separate.'

'It could get *lost*,' said Johanna.

'What, you think someone's going to come in here and steal it from the drawer?'

'What if we had a burglary?'

'If you had a burglary, the computers would go, hard disk and all.'

Johanna shut up and Molly returned to her work making a mental note to hide her floppy somewhere unsabotageable that night. Just in case.

'Two hours. Two hours to Wimbledon.' Caroline was in a bad mood. 'Damned, damned traffic made me miss virtually the whole match!'

'What one was it?' asked Jenna.

'Henman v. AGASSI!!' She said Agassi in a deep guttural voice which made her sound like she was choking.

They were lying by the pool. A small portable television perched on a stool in front of them. It was their first baby meeting since Tamara's classes had finished.

'You should've taken the Tube?' said Jenna.

'I have my *own* parking, Jenna, in Philippa Oliver's driveway. Parking in Wimbledon when the tournament's on is like gold dust!'

'Fat lot of good if you don't get there,' said Izzie.

The crack of ball on racket, punctuated by smatterings of applause and the murmur of commentary blended into the chatter. Molly leant back in the wooden patio chair, crossed her ankles and looked at the river, as still as mud in the heat. A shifting cloud of mayflies swarmed beside the willows, fluttering up quickly before gradually sinking, rising and falling.

'It's going to go down as an absolute classic!' Caroline moaned. 'I can't believe I missed it. One of the best matches for years. The first week always has better tennis than the second. And where was I? Clutching my ticket for No.1 court on the Putney by-pass.'

'It's better on the telly anyway,' said Izzie.

'I just like the sound,' said Molly. 'I could listen to it all day. Pity you can't turn off the commentary and just have the ping-pong.'

'That's right!' said Caroline. 'When you're *there*...'

'You probably had a better morning than me, anyway,' said Molly.

'How's it all going?' said Izzie.

'Oh, I'm hanging on in there. What I can't get over is how alien the two worlds are to each other. The mother thing, and the work thing. There's no give in either.'

'The main thing is you're trying,' said Caroline.

'If that were all there was to it! I don't know what I can do. I mean, it's not all their fault. I was a bit slow to begin with. And I find it really hard to take orders from people now. Especially when they're half my age.'

'No inside information yet then,' said Izzie.

'Afraid not.'

Caroline stood up lazily and stretched. 'I'm going for a swim.'

Molly sipped at her Pimm's, studying Caroline's lean, bony back as she walked away from them, seemingly oblivious to a frenzied thwack of volleying rackets and gasps from the TV. She opened the little gate to the new low white wooden fence running, kidney-shaped, all the way round the pool.

'I'd be shit-scared to have all this water around,' said Izzie, as the gentle splosh sound of Caroline's dive cracked the silence, 'even with the fence.'

'Jolly good of her to let us use it though,' said Molly. She was beginning to relax. Knowing Christophe would be turning up at any moment was quite delicious in its way.

'Lu, NO.' Jenna leapt up. Too late. By the time she reached her, she was triumphantly stuffing all eight tentacles of Daisy's treasured yellow octopus into her mouth.

While Charles, dangerously naked but for a mini Ralph Lauren polo shirt, looked on, Molly grabbed a gobsmacked Daisy before she'd had a chance to register what had happened and reached for her baby bag.

'I do miss breastfeeding,' she said, expertly flipping the lid off the bottle with one hand.

'It's good to get some energy back though,' said Izzie.

'And you've lost weight,' said Jenna, stretching back in her micro bikini.

'I feel like a beached sea lion next to you. I never realised how much breastfeeding sucks it out of you. Literally, doesn't it?'

'You know, she really should get rid of those willows?' said Jenna quietly. 'Do you think I should tell her?'

'Why? They're beautiful,' said Molly.

'Really bad *feng shui*, they encourage unfaithfulness.'

'What a load of rot,' said Izzie.

Caroline climbed out of the pool and came back, her skin golden and dripping in her high-cut tangerine bikini, her make-up still perfectly intact. She grabbed a big yellow towel from her lounger and threw it around her shoulders.

After patting Daisy's back to wind her Molly leant back on her chair with Daisy dozing off beneath a makeshift sarong tent on her lap.

There they stayed in the comfortable semi-silence of friends relaxing together, until, half an hour later, Caroline, casually rubbing sun cream on her legs, made a surprise announcement.

'Do you know, I think Theo's having an affair,' she said, looking round at them all and holding her gaze on Molly.

'No!' Molly and Izzie sat up as one, looking at Jenna in amazement.

'Why do you all sound so surprised?' She looked down to screw the lid on the cream, then hunched her knees up to her tummy and stared straight ahead. A woman scorned.

'He's not the type,' said Molly confidently.

'What's it got to do with type? Come to think of it, maybe you do know. How do you know if your husband is having an affair? Any clues, Molly?'

'That's a bit below the belt, Caroline,' said Izzie in a low voice.

'No – it's all right,' said Molly in an insincere higher octave, by now used to the cracks coming from all sides when least expected.

'I think we all know each other well enough by now, don't you?'

'Yes, but then I'd be the last to know,' Molly said nervously, 'I've never had a husband.'

'But you have had *affairs*?' said Caroline, slipping her oversized sunglasses up onto her head.

'Caroline!' said Izzie.

'*An* affair. Well, of course, I'm the world expert on that side of the fence.'

'See?' said Caroline to the others. 'Listen and you might learn something.'

'I don't know what to say.' She stopped and turned. A collective gasp, followed by thunderous applause, shouts of disbelief, groans and slow hand-claps came from the television.

'What does his *wife*–' Izzie began.

'Shhh,' said Caroline. 'Action replay.'

They all watched a slow-motion close-up of a ball touching the edge of a white line, and major tantrum tennis rackets thrown in air.

'That was in! It was in, did you see that!'

'Well, what do they, what does he say to you, about . . .' said Izzie.

296

'His wife?' Izzie looked awkward as Molly finished the sentence for her. 'Where to begin?'

'Anything. Tell us anything,' said Caroline quickly. They were all looking at her with rapt attention.

'Are there children involved? In – your...' said Caroline.

'No. He, well, he has now, hasn't he. But what makes you think Theo ...'

'He's been acting *very* peculiarly.'

'Like what?' said Izzie.

'He's been hanging around the house a lot. Looking – er, *strange*.'

'Everything all right at work?'

'As far as I know. But if he carries on like this...'

'Everything all right between the sheets?' said Izzie.

'What more can I do? I'm spending a fortune on underwear. But there's something, like, a *resistance*. That's new. That wasn't there before.'

'It's called a screaming baby,' said Izzie.

Molly's heart leapt as the top garden gate clicked.

'If it's any consolation, they rarely leave their wives.'

'Huh!' said Caroline.

'If they can get away with it they won't. It's, it's like visiting houses, isn't it?'

'What do you mean?'

'You can go around visiting as many people as you like without thinking anything of it, but there are only so many visitors you can take in your own home.'

'I don't think I quite follow you, Molly,' said Caroline.

'If they get found *out* then ...'

'Then?' Caroline was looking at her suspiciously. Molly paused. She was there in the afternoons, collecting Daisy, no – she couldn't possibly think – could she?

'Then?' said Izzie.

'Then there's a lot of shit hitting a lot of fans isn't there, but it usually settles again. Eventually. Just like dogs, really.'

'Faithful but prone to wandering if let off the lead!' said Izzie.

'Naaah,' said Jenna, shaking her head. Molly looked at her. 'Not my Jase. Sex-mad, yes, but...'

'There are many different *breeds*, Jenna,' said Caroline.

'If men are dogs, women are bitches,' said Molly.

'What's this one then,' said Izzie as Christophe, looking stunning in baggy brown shorts tied with a Peruvian woven fabric belt and nothing else, sauntered down the lawn towards them. 'It's not a Yorkshire terrier, is it?'

'Got to be a bloodhound with that nose,' laughed Molly nervously.

'I asked him to join us,' said Caroline. 'Thought it'd be jolly. You see, what I'm thinking, girls, is if *Theo* can have a little *amour de coeur*, I might do a little playing away from home myself. But in my case, perhaps not so far from home!'

'*Caroline!*' said Izzie and Jenna, genuinely shocked.

Molly said nothing.

'Now – who's coming to my hen night?' said Jenna.

'Ooooh, girly night out? I'm in there, when and where?' said Izzie.

'All Bar One? In Richmond?'

Molly shuddered inwardly. She picked up a chilled strawberry from the cut-glass bowl. A wedding she could just about handle. She absent-mindedly brushed its whiskers over her lips. A bar full of twentysomethings, no way.

'Excellent. I'm getting everything organised at last. There's some neat sites on the Internet. And I've got the coolest surprise for everyone at the end of the reception.'

'Wassat?' said Izzie.

'Not saying. It's a surprise. A triangle surprise.'

'Not a flowery fanny?' said Izzie in real alarm.

Jenna glared at her. 'One bit of advance info I can let on about is we're having these neat little gold disposable cameras? Have you seen them? There'll be one at each place setting? So all of you'll be taking our wedding photos for us?'

'Oh,' said Izzie.

'Instead of having a boring bloke with a camera it'll be a bit neater?'

'And you'll have your camera, of course,' said Molly, biting into her strawberry, sensing him getting nearer, not looking up. After the first tart hit, the sweetness filled her mouth: strawberry milkshake, strawberry childhood chews.

'Too right. But what happens is you give us back your camera when you leave. We'll get double prints made of all of them, then we'll send your photos back with our thank-you letters. Neat, hey? I got it off the Net.'

'*Christophe*, how are you!' said Caroline.

'I have a little work to do first. Excuse me.' Head held low, he went down to the summer house.

Molly felt a twinge, more motherly than loverlike.

'What's up with *him*?' said Izzie.

Caroline, frightening the life out him, Molly guessed, lying back down and surrendering to the sun.

'Will you look at that,' said Izzie five minutes later.

Molly sat up slowly, casually.

Caroline had gone down to the summer house, and was talking animatedly, pushing her hair from her forehead, standing with legs stiff and wide apart.

'You don't have to be Desmond Morris to know what's going on there, do you?' said Izzie. 'Ey up, they're coming this way.'

They all sat up self-consciously. Christophe looked around the group, raising an eyebrow at Molly.

'Your babies are growing?' He looked at Molly again, a half-smile on his face. 'How's the job, Molly?'

'Fine.' Stop talking to me, she thought. Keep it general, don't let on. Please don't let on.

'I've invited Christophe to join our picnic party in the Gardens.'

'Good one,' said Izzie.

'If you don't mind me coming.'

Just don't bring Miss Asia, Molly thought.

'Our husbands are coming too!' said Izzie coyly, swallowing it whole.

'Ah.' He laughed.

'Except Molly,' she added brightly.

Caroline fired a look at her.

'I mean, she. . .' Izzie faded away.

'He knows that, Izzie,' said Caroline sharply.

'So we can make a group?'

He looked at her strangely. Stop it, can't you? Stop being so obvious. At the same time she felt pleased at the thought.

'Garden's looking good,' said Jenna.

'Thank you.'

'How's *Ulé* getting along with Daisy, Molly?' said Izzie pointedly, looking at Christophe.

Christophe was looking at Jenna.

'Very well,' said Molly resignedly.

'Now she's over her *trauma*,' said Caroline in a stern voice.

Christophe turned to her sharply.

'Ah, she's just a girl. She's OK,' he said, leaning over Molly and picking up a strawberry.

'Just watch it,' said Caroline. It was hard to tell if she was joking or not.

'How's the perfume coming along?' said Jenna.

Caroline poured him a tumbler of Pimm's.

'I have the name,' he said quietly.

'You *do*?' said Caroline. A loud burst of applause came from the television. Caroline ignored it. 'Well, come on then, out with it.'

'He's not allowed to tell us, it's a secret,' said Molly.

'I don't think there are any perfumers hiding in the bushes here. I think I can trust you. I'm going to call it Q.' He looked at the ground.

'Kew like the Gardens?'

'No, Q. The letter.'

'No, no, I promise. Your secret's safe with me, Christophe,' said Caroline. 'Q,' she whispered to herself. 'Q.'

CHAPTER TWENTY

Molly guessed something was up when, instead of doing her usual march up, Celia turned and gently closed the door behind her. She knew for sure when she lowered herself down on the stool next to her desk with an exaggerated carefulness.

'The thing is, we need you to be more pro*active*, Molly.'

'Excuse me?'

'We expect you to take more initiative, flesh out your role.'

'What?' said Molly in disbelief.

'Complete your tasks...'

'What do you mean?'

'Take your time, think about it. We are proactive creative here, the input we need ...'

'Can I ask what brought this on?' said Molly, knowing what she was going to hear next.

'Yesterday, Johanna had to finish that document.'

'As I thought.'

'It was important.'

'Now, hang on, Celia. You employ me until two o'clock. Right?'

'And you always *leave* at two o'clock. The exchange was at *four*. Clearly, the task had to be completed.'

'Let's get this straight, shall we? I'm paid until two o'clock, two ten-minute coffee breaks, no lunch. Right?'

'It was a three-way *exchange of contracts*, Molly.' Celia got up to leave.

'It is not possible for me to stay beyond two o'clock,' said Molly bluntly.

'Clearly.' Celia twisted her lips, nodded, and took a step backwards towards the door.

'Clearly, Celia, you're looking for a full-time result from part-time hours.'

'I really can't waste any more of my time input arguing with you, Molly.'

Molly spoke calmly. 'I have a baby waiting to be to collected.' Safe in the land of her afternoon nap, she thought, but, then, Celia wasn't to know that.

'Sometimes all of us have to work a little bit beyond what is expected of us, Molly.'

Their eyes met in the chill, suspended light of mis-understanding.

Molly snapped. 'I haven't stopped working for bloody six months! Day and night! Night and day. Twenty-four hours on call. OK?'

'This is how business is these days.'

'And not only a baby to collect,' said Molly, 'but a childminder to relieve.'

Celia tightened her lips. 'We all have our dead-lines, Molly.'

'That's *it*,' said Molly to Debbie the accountant's

fluffy donkeys stuck on top of her computer after Celia had left.

Molly pushed bits of paper around her desk, shaking. Too cross to work. Just when she was beginning to think she was getting the hang of things, too. Or so she'd thought. The only thing stopping Celia firing her, and Molly walking out, was their immediate need of each other.

Just as her first forays into the world of childcare had been working out better than she could have hoped, too. She was getting better at repressing her motherworry-jitters, and trusting Ulé. As Caroline had forbidden her to give Ulé even a token payment, terrified her au pair status would be sabotaged, Molly was taking her bunches of flowers from the Parade greengrocer's and little rocks and stones from the Parade rock shop to add to her collection. Which made her smile and light up. Molly hadn't realised how very lonely she was. Missing home and, probably, Christophe; though she hadn't broached the subject with her yet, she intended to give her some motherly advice when the opportunity arose.

Keep Ulé, find new job. That was the thing to do. Though it had to be local. And it had to be part-time. For all its faults Baxter, Rumbold and Featherington was so damned handy. And she'd just about mastered the coffee percolator and the burglar alarm.

So, Johanna wasn't very bright but how much of it was down to Molly? How dead had her brain become? Was she kidding herself? Was she too far gone to hold down a simple job in a poxy local estate agent's?

Some of it she really enjoyed. Especially when Celia and Johanna cleared off to the Flower and Firkin for their pub lunches and left her in charge. She could sit out front and watch the world go by and deal with the occasional customer, feeling in control and back in the world, a part of it all.

And so it was, on the lunchtime of that same day, that Molly had another, far greater, shock. She'd been gazing out of the window, watching the groups sitting at the wooden tables outside the pub. Chatting, sipping at their golden, sun-warmed beer. She'd become completely fascinated to see people so deep in relaxation, who, seemingly, had nothing to do!

Even her rests were hurried. She didn't as much fall asleep as have it on the agenda as the next thing to do, a passing-out in the full knowledge she'd be rudely kick-started again at some unearthly dark hour of the night.

Her newly emerging estate-agent smile appeared reflexively as the door clicked. Molly jumped and the smile disappeared as quickly as it had formed, before re-forming as Molly banished the bonkers thought from her brain. For a moment she'd thought she was looking at the last person she expected to see in Kew. The very last person she ever wanted to see. Anywhere.

Didn't it look so very much like her, she thought jovially to herself. Fatter though. If it *was*, no – it couldn't possibly be. Molly smiled up into the large, heavily lidded eyes framed by the enormous Chanel – they *were* Chanel glasses ... Was it? Could it be?

306

She had the impossibly well-cut suit. The lip-liner. The big chunky amber jewellery.

'Can I help you?' Molly managed to get the words out somehow.

'Yes, I'd like a property list,' the woman said in a loud, firm voice. The *voice*. She'd know that voice anywhere. It bloody damned well *was* her. Veronica bloody Bulford-Boyd, Max's wife!

She'd seen her enough times on *Despatch Box*, reviewing the next day's newspapers. She'd compulsively played the video to all her friends. Each of whom had sat fascinated, making sympathetic clucks, wondering how Max could be married to *that*, and assuring Molly over and over that she was much better looking, and a much *much* nicer person all round.

'Er – yes.' A hundred thoughts flashed through Molly's mind at once. 'What price range was it you were looking for?'

'Does it matter?'

'If you could just. . .' What the *hell* are you doing in Kew?

'Give me all of them. Quickly if you don't mind. I'm in a hurry.'

'What is it, exactly, you're looking for?' The only positive one of these thoughts was an extreme thankfulness that Veronica didn't know who *she* was.

Veronica began to puff up, shifting from one leg onto the other.

'What I mean is, is it a flat? A house? To buy? To rent? We have different lists, you see.'

Whichever, the consequences of this were unthinkable, and, whatever it was, she had to know.

'How many bedrooms?' She didn't have the patter. Never had. Never would.

She *had* five bedrooms in Hampstead. What the bloody hell was she doing on this side of the river anyway? North Londoners never came West. It was unheard of. Any more than West Londoners went East. Or South Londoners went North. Or maybe. Maybe! Was she leaving Max? Was she looking for a flat? Just for herself? Max would never move to Kew. Or had she been given some tip-off along the media grapevine, had a stray branch somehow spread and spread until it had got to her ears...

No. Impossible. Not even Max knew where she worked. Or maybe she wanted a pied à terre for her little trysts. Maybe she had a lover she wanted to set up out of Max territory. Somewhere Max was never likely to go. Somewhere easily accessible to town. She had to know. She waited with bated breath.

'Four bedrooms. Up to three-quarters of a million.'

'Oh,' said Molly disappointedly.

'Is there something the matter?'

'No, no. To buy? Or rent?'

'Of course to buy,' Veronica said in exasperation.

'Oh.' Molly could see Celia and Johanna coming out of the pub. 'I – er, I'll just see what we've got.'

'Soooo sorry.' Celia was suddenly right in front of Molly's face. 'She's new. Can I be of assistance?'

'Yes. Good. I was just trying to explain to, to, to...'

'Come and sit down and we'll take a few details,'

said Celia, giving Molly a look which Veronica echoed as she turned her full attention to Celia.

Max and Veronica in Kew?

Bumping into them all the time?

It was unthinkable. Molly went into her back office and sat and listened as Celia poured herself over Veronica like syrup. She found something she liked. The detached in Kew Road.

'You can arrange a viewing today?'

'It's a superb property. Just come on our books. Clearly, it looks most suitable for you.'

The one that had been on the books for months. The one directly underneath the flight path.

'Splendid! I'll just give my husband a ring. See if he can get down.'

What! Here? Soon! Buggery. Molly looked around. Should she stay or run? She couldn't not stay. She had to know.

As soon as Veronica had gone, Celia got down to business.

'I'll put a call in to the owner, Johanna, get on to Heathrow, find out the flight path plans for this afternoon. If it's not on we'll have to postpone until we've got clear skies.'

'But I'm in the middle—'

'If you like I could stay on a bit,' Molly leapt in.

Both Celia and Johanna looked at her.

A look of triumph crossed Celia's face. 'Goooooood, Molly. That's more like it.'

'I'll just have to ring the nanny.'

'Yes. Do. Go ahead. Use the phone,' Celia said generously.

If Molly had some forewarning of their impending meeting, Max did not. It was debatable as to which was worse. For while Max was innocently driving across the Thames into the epicentre of marital infidelity hell, Molly was pacing up and down, standing up, sitting down, and leaping out of her skin every time she heard the door out front click. Trying for all the world to behave like a normal human being.

As the appointed time drew nearer, Molly stayed well away from Celia and Johanna as she disintegrated into a fumbling, quivering wreck. From the safety of her back room she could hear the scuffle and bite of Celia on heat as she prepared to sniff and preen around her possible big sale of the week.

The door clicked. Molly wrapped her arms around herself tight, stood up, sat down again, then crept over to stand just behind her carefully prepared half-open door.

'Ah, do come in, would you like to take a seat?'

'I think we'd like to get on with it, if you don't mind.' That was Veronica. We. We? Did that mean her and Max? Or her and Celia? Was Max there?

'Clearly. We just have to wait a few moments, then my colleague will be back with the keys. She's just been showing another client. These properties are very popular at the moment, they don't stay on the market long.'

'We haven't much time,' said Veronica.

'We won't keep you, Mrs Bulford-Boyd, she's just on her way now.'

Johanna had in fact been sent off up the Kew

310

Road. Celia had her abort viewing plan in place should the skies not be on their side.

Molly stood, in morbid fascination, listening to Max and Veronica talking together. It was like reading her own obituary. She bit her lips, straightened herself up and made her entrance.

'Would anyone like a coffee?' she enquired.

Max lifted his eyes from the property details briefly. 'Yes. Thanks.'

'Darling, we don't have time,' said Veronica.

'Black, decaffeinated, one brown sugar?' Molly smiled sweetly down at him.

Max looked up for a moment. 'Yes, thanks,' he answered, then went on reading. A few seconds later he looked up again, sharply, at the same time emitting a strange restrained warble of a squeak, his ice-blue eyes meeting Molly's in a frozen, glacial suspense of disbelief.

'Ah – here's my colleague now,' said Celia, too ravenous for the big sell to notice anything odd.

Veronica was looking at Molly like she was a witch.

'It's all right, I'm psychic.' Molly smiled brightly at her before twisting dramatically on her toes and heading for the kitchen.

As she handed Max his coffee, she deliberately wobbled the cup, just stopping the hot black liquid spilling onto his trousers.

'Oh, I'm *so* sorry. . .' Molly again smiled sweetly at him.

Max gave her a thwarted twisted half-smile. Molly stubbornly stayed in the front, busying herself noisily with a drawerful of obsolete concertina files.

She turned and watched as they left. Max gave her one last look over his shoulder, like a terrified whippet.

'Promising,' said Johanna after they'd gone.

As soon as Molly got home she rang Amanda to see if she could throw any light. She couldn't. She rang everyone she could think of. Who could know? She'd have to ring him. At work. She'd have to get him at work.

As soon as she'd finished her call to Amanda, the phone rang. Molly looked at it, then grabbed it.

'Molly – was that – *you*?'

'Of course it was me.'

'I – we have to talk.'

'Too bloody right we have to talk!'

'Oh Molly.'

'Don't you oh-Molly me. What the *fuck* is going on, Max?'

'It's Veronica. She's got this ridiculous idea. You know what she's like. Since *when* did you become an estate agent, Molly?'

'I'm not, Max. I'm a mother, remember?'

'Well, what the hell were you doing?'

'I think I should be asking you that, Max, don't you?'

'Look. . .'

'Max, Veronica cannot move to Kew. Kew's *mine*. OK?'

'I'm trying to stop her, Molly.'

'Yeah, it looked like it, hotfooting it over, when you can't find time to come and see us but you turn up instantly to see some cruddy house.'

'That was *why*, Molly. I had to dissuade her. Put her off.'

'Kew's all we've got, Max.'

'She's got this crazy idea.'

'So you haven't split up then?'

'No, of course not.'

Molly swallowed.

'Don't you think you'd be the first to know if we had?'

It was the of course more than the no.

'Oh come on...'

'Look, we've got to talk about this.'

'Celia came back saying you were going to buy it!'

'Oh – she was, look – she's looked at hundreds of houses, Molly. You know what she's like. I really shouldn't worry.'

'Why *Kew* of all places, Max? Isn't Hampstead good enough?'

'We've got to talk about all this. When can we meet?'

Molly didn't say anything.

'Please, Molly? Saturday night. Dinner?'

'Get real, Max! I can't just go out to dinner any more!'

'Why not?'

'Max!!'

'Restaurants take babies, don't they?'

'Max ...'

She put the phone back on its cradle slowly and

went through to Daisy, sitting cheerfully chewing a breadstick in her new high chair.

'Guess what, Daisy? Daddy's coming. Daddy's coming to see us!'

There was no more action on Veronica Bulford-Boyd in the office that week. The immediate offer Celia was expecting didn't come in and Molly had to spend the rest of the week listening to Celia and Johanna speculating. By the end of the week they'd put her down as a time-waster.

It was only when Izzie reminded her they weren't meeting that week because of the Bootleg Beatles picnic in Kew Gardens on the Saturday night that Molly realised.

Well he'd just have to go with them. She'd have a plus one. Even if it was only a semi-detached one. Max could see she was getting a life and she could play at being one of them for the night.

When she rang for an extra ticket the woman in the booking office laughed. 'It sold out last April, dear,' she said. 'We've got Kid Creole and the Coconuts on the Thursday. Is that any good?'

'No,' Molly said slowly, putting the phone down. 'No good at all.'

CHAPTER TWENTY-ONE

An uneasy truce hung in the office while Veronica Bulford-Boyd once more unknowingly held Molly's life hostage. Any one of a series of petty incidents could have sent her walking, but she had to stick so she could periodically click Veronica's file to check she was still under Buyer or Time-waster? and hadn't, horror, transferred to the Under Offer, or, worse, Sold file.

Queueing for Celia's sandwich in the Greenhouse, she was idly gazing out of the window when Ulé walked by, pushing Charles and Daisy. She watched them disappear up Sandycombe Road towards playgroup. What the hell was she *doing*, standing there in a queue for bloody Celia Sprague's hummus and mushroom sandwich while that lonely girl from Poland was taking Daisy, her child, *her* baby, to playgroup?

She stomped around for the rest of the day, stopping off at the Greenhouse Café on her way home for a drink and a think. A decision had to be made and followed through. Before she saw Max on Saturday, she must work out what, exactly, she wanted. Should she go looking for another job? Or give it all up and get some proper figures worked out with Max?

Could they get back together on the old basis? Her pride rejected it but her heart yearned for it. She'd have a little bit of him. Daisy would have her dad around sometimes. But she'd never move on, then. Single mother was preferable. Even miserable single mother. Better than miserable kept mistress hoovering up the scraps of Max's life.

The circular tables of the café were crowded, inside and out, with tourists and groups of women, the Scrums, as Johanna sourly called the school-run mums. Crowds of them always gathered for coffee after school drop-off time and tea at school pick-up time. She looked at them, with their pushchairs full of siblings and biscuit tins, laughing and chattering, some in breezy summer frocks, others still in their gym clothes, talking intensively about how 'terribly animated' Alice was, and how Georgia was 'so excited'.

What do you *want*, Molly. As if there was the choice! She had to find another job. She'd made a start, and she *was* already feeling better in some ways. More part of the world, if less a part of Daisy. That was just how it was these days. Did she want to be a school-run mum? Or working independent mum?

She took her hot chocolate with Flake through to the back greenhouse.

'Cooo-eay!'

A hand was waving from behind a weeping fig.

'Izzie!'

'I was just leaving to do a bit of shopping, finished my drink, but, hey, let's live a little, I think I've got room for another hot choccy somewhere in here.'

'Can you watch Bob for a moment?' Izzie pushed her way through the plants to the front of the caff.

Molly looked down at Bob, chewing contentedly on a dummy.

A cold draught ran through her body.

'So – how's work?' said Izzie, settling down opposite her.

Molly went into a moanathon. '...it wasn't even my fault! Because Johanna had to go on a valuation, I was typing house details dictated by Johanna who can't dictate to save her *life so* when Celia complained I was slow, I was ready for her. I told her – I *played* it to her – she'd dictate a whole chunk and then say, "Oh no, scrub that," and go back again after I'd already typed it, it's like trying to do a jigsaw blindfold so ... Celia told Johanna to hone up which means the undeclared war with Johanna is now – well, war!'

Izzie sat quietly looking at her.

Molly's voice fizzled out. 'Well, you did *ask*.'

'I don't know how you put up with it.'

'I won't be for much longer.' She hesitated, then stopped herself before she went into a fresh rant about Veronica and Max.

'So – how was playgroup?'

'Fine. Oh, fine.' Izzie looked at her sideways. 'Listen – I was going to ring you later. It's Findham's open day tomorrow morning.'

'Findham?'

'The state nursery. If you want Daisy to get a place you'll have to be quick and get her name down. Go and see if you like it first.'

'I'm working, aren't I?'

'Can't you take an hour off?'

Molly didn't hesitate, 'Yes. Yes, of course I can.'

'*Ohhhhh*?' said Celia at the end of the phone the next morning.

'I'll only be about half an hour late,' Molly laughed lightly, 'though it depends on the queues. Doctors' surgeries wouldn't be doctors' surgeries if they ran on time, would they, Celia?'

'Clearly.'

Molly breezed in an hour later, not giving a damn, feeling like she'd already done a good day's work. She'd loved the nursery and had Daisy's name registered on the spot.

Celia and Johanna both looked at her suspiciously. She didn't give a hoot.

'I'd best get on then,' said Molly brightly. 'Anyone want a coffee?'

Chilly silence.

'I think you'd better get on, Molly,' said Celia flatly, looking pointedly at her chest then witheringly at Johanna.

'Right. Off I go then.'

As Molly retrieved her floppy disk from its hiding place at the bottom of the brown envelope pile, she looked at her chest and suddenly saw why.

'Oh bog. Ohhhhh bog. Bog. BOG.'

A large white sticker was still stuck to her chest with MOLLY WARREN – VISITOR – FINDHAM NURSERY SCHOOL written in big, black capitals, and, underlined in red, the day's date.

She had the feeling her indecision about what to do about her working life was about to take its own independent turn.

The opportunity presented itself later that day for Molly to have the last word. Before Celia and Johanna went off to the pub for their lunch, Johanna gave her a pile of awkward charts to photocopy and stick together.

On the lid of the photocopier, casually lying at a diagonal, like it had been thrown there, Molly found a photograph of a baby with a dummy in its mouth. She picked it up. It had a white bubble balloon, cut out and carefully stuck on with little cartoon thought circles decreasing in size to the baby's head. Something had been written inside the bubble.

Her face flushed as she read, 'Go home where you are needed.'

As soon as they returned, she was ready for them. Ignoring Johanna, she went straight for Celia.

'See this?'

Molly threw it on the desk in front of Celia.

'*This* is the ignorance-level of your – colleague – here!'

'Molly – keep your voice down, please.'

'Well, go on – look at it!'

Celia picked up the photograph and looked at it.

'And as for you,' she addressed a smirking

Johanna, 'I have never, in my life, worked with such an ignorant, arrogant waste of space.'

'Molly!'

'I could have you. Do you realise that? I could complain about this to the equal opportunities, race relations, or whatever it is, people. You could pay for this, Celia. But – you know? I'm not going to bother myself. I'm not going to bother myself with either of you ever again for the rest of my life. And – do you know? That makes me feel really, REALLY happy!'

She went back to her room, slipped the floppy disk into her bag and left without another word.

CHAPTER TWENTY-TWO

'Sesame, garlic, wheatbran, toasted, toasted cheesy?'

Molly looked at the shelves full of every kind of breadstick the Western world had to offer.

'Ooooof.'

Daisy kicked her in the stomach.

'All right, all right, I know, wait a second.'

She picked open a box, bit at the cellophane and put a stick into Daisy's outstretched hand.

'Come on then, let's get this picnic organised,' she said as she threw the box into the empty trolley. Daisy giggled, still thrilled at her recent promotion from baby-cradle trolley to toddler seat. Molly did a U-turn and headed off back to Vegetables and Fruit, gawping at the trolleys of the stream of Friday shoppers gunning it towards her, each more stashed with goodies than the last.

'This is a bit different from our usual supermarket run, isn't it, Daisy? Wheeeeeee.' She swerved her trolley round a case of wine and a huge bunch of stargazer lilies wheeling towards her at full whack.

Waitrose was a treat in Max's honour. Since selling the car, she normally took the bus to the Bogof deals at Brentford Somerfields, just across Kew Bridge. Though only a river's-width away it might as well have been another country. There, the trolleys drifted slowly around as their pushers stopped to gossip and took their time comparing the prices and filling up with the irresistible Bogofs. There, the word nanny bore no relation to Norland and was more likely to be shortened to nan. As clearly as the young pram-pushers in Kew were the other kind of nanny, in Brentford they were, with their pale complexions, tired eyes and heavy walks, unmistakably mothers. Mothers, like Molly, struggling with the day-by-day effort of getting by and staying awake to do so.

She watched the assistant slicing the parma ham and layering it out into a neat, meat fan. The big question of whether Max would be staying the night or not was taking on a practical rather than romantic element. Did he expect to stay the night? Did she want him to? Would *he* want to? What on earth was she doing even thinking along those lines after the events of the week?

She took the ham and pushed on towards the breakfasty things. But on the other hand. Knowing what they were like. What if? She hedged her bets and chucked in a packet of pain au chocolat and a carton of, unheard of luxury, freshly squeezed orange juice. If he did stay, which of course she wouldn't allow, but just in case he declared his undying love for her and Daisy and announced he'd sorted it all out with Veronica and they'd decided to go their separate ways, then they'd be there, wouldn't they? If he didn't? Well, then she'd have them as a lonesome treat. She'd probably need cheering up by then anyway.

She pulled up at the chickens. If he did. Would he then stay on for lunch? She picked up a small chicken. Then looked at the larger, corn-yellow-coloured ones on the shelf above, plastered with free range labels and cartoons of smiling chickens, costing three times as much as the anaemic blob in her hand. Its white, blood-splattered flesh felt cold and squashy. Expensive happy dead chicken? Or cheap sad dead chicken? Did they know? Were they looking down from chicken heaven? Or up from chicken hell? She dithered before putting it back and walking quickly away. Stop it stop it stop it. Don't get carried away.

Molly's preparations went on until late that evening and through till lunchtime the next day.

'So you prefer Heinz to Mummy's cheesy potato, do you?' she said as she touched the hot spoon to her lips first before popping it into Daisy's wide-open mouth.

Daisy banged on the table of her high chair and threw her cup on the kitchen floor, her furious shrieks drowning The Blessing's 'Soul Lake' at full volume on the radio.

Close to Max's arrival time, the phone rang. She paused in mid-Mr Sheen squirt, quickly peeled a banana, plonked it in front of Daisy and snatched the phone, swearing she'd spend her last penny on arranging a contract killing if it was Max cancelling.

Then she remembered she'd actually spent that and was living on a precarious line of credit boosted by crummy wages not enough for a Waitrose mini-binge, let alone the rent, the council tax ...

It wasn't Max, it was Izzie with last-minute arrangements for the picnic. Her panic thoughts changed from the 'will he won't he stay the night' issue to the other little problem. Christophe at the picnic. How would he react? Should she ring and tell him? She remembered her humiliation at Jenna's.

Molly raced back to the kitchen. In the short time she'd been away, Daisy had managed to get banana everywhere. In her hair, her ears, on the floor, between her toes, stuck all over her bib.

'Oh, Daisy,' said Molly, quickly rinsing a J-cloth under the tap.

As she wiped her down, Daisy became more and more grumpy. By the time she got to her face, her grumbles had turned into a high-pitched, wake-the-neighbours 'my mother is murdering me' scream. Molly unbuckled her and took her through to the back room and laid her on a towel on her bed. She unpeeled her sticky Babygro and took down the new blue velvet Hennes dress hanging on its tiny hanger on the back of the door.

Before dressing her, she held her tight and stroked her soft cheeks with her own.

She undid the packet of miniature blue tights and pulled them onto Daisy's chubby legs. She took her through to the front room and pulled a tiny pair of shoes out of the Mothercare bag next to her cot.

'Look, Daisy. New shoes! Your first pair of shoes to see your daddy.'

She looked out of the window at the traffic. Grey cars crawled past under a grey sky. After weeks of heat, the weather had disintegrated into days of solid drizzle. Max would be seeing them in the worst possible light. In the sun, her flat could work. Out the back. In the rain, even with imagination, it couldn't.

She wondered what he'd have to say for himself. *Why* did Veronica want to move? Was the marriage on the rocks? Could moving be a last-ditch attempt at making it work?

Maybe she could find a job where she could take Daisy? Become a childminder herself. She'd be inspected. Being inspected there on the motorway. She'd never pass. Find a different flat? Impossible at the rent she was paying. Go on the council list? Go back to the real world. Go the whole hog and live on an estate with the other single mums? Would she feel less out of it there? Rather than trying to keep up in the comfort zone. After all, she was poor now. She qualified. They'd all be there, bungling along together. Helping each other out. Having a laugh? The best laughs were usually the saddest ones. But – no. She feared the worst: echoey brick corridors, gangs. Shouting, noise, damp, litter, urine-smelling lifts, heroin needles...

Or should she go on the dole? That's what Amanda had said.

'Take them for every penny, darling, you're entitled to it!'

She put Daisy in her bouncy seat in the front room and went to give herself one last check-over in the bathroom. As soon as she left the room, Daisy started crying. Molly tried to ignore it, as Izzie had told her to. She could hear Izzie's stern voice: *'Don't rush to her every time she cries.'* She put some lipstick on and combed her hair. She put Izzie's stories of leaving Bob to cry himself to sleep right at the front of her mind. She slipped into her dry-cleaned René Derhy. If only she could have herself dry-cleaned, she sighed as she took one last look in the mirror before rushing to Daisy's hysterical yells and screams.

'All right, all right, just having three seconds to myself. Sorry, Daisy. Oh here we go, here we go-ho, Daddy's here, Daddy's here ... Oh please, Daisy, please be quiet.'

There was only one way to shut her up quickly. She shoved a cassette in the video, ignoring Jenna and Caroline's tut-tuts running through her head. If it bought a few minutes' peace she was having it.

'Dipsy, Laa Laa?'

Daisy was instantly silenced.

'Bless you, Teletubbies,' Molly said as she fumbled for the remote control.

'Ah, *good* girl, you know what's coming, don't you?'

She heard the car-door slam.

'Tinky Winky?'

She turned round.

'Oh DAISY. Not again!'

Daisy kicked her legs happily, completely oblivious

of the thick river of milky white sick running down her dress.

Molly grabbed the remote, pressed the on button and raced for the J-cloth.

It'll probably take Max a while to get within smelling-distance anyway, she thought as she hurriedly wiped Daisy down. She didn't exactly expect him to race up and embrace her saying, 'Daughter, oh daughter.'

She looked out of the window. He was bent over the boot of his car, rummaging around.

'Poor Daisy, I'm sorry,' she said. Wiping her cheeks. 'I hurried you, didn't I?'

She rinsed the last of the sick down the plughole, raced to the bathroom and gave herself a liberal squirt of Shalimar just as the bell went for the second time.

She was so relieved to see him as she always saw him, without Veronica at his side. She cleared her throat and stood back. 'Come on in.' Her estate agent voice came out, unbidden.

'Suppose I'd better,' he said. Three words. But they were loaded, not just with nerves. A deep, furious disappointment. Not unexpected but all the same, like being punched in the gut in a Prince Charles 'whatever loves means' kind of a way. Stop it, Molly, stop it, she told herself. Don't try to analyse everything. You're hyper, overreacting. Just play it cool. Take it easy. Be pleasant.

Max leant over and kissed her on the neck. He immediately jumped back, his face distorted and twisted, spitting furiously and wiping his mouth with the back of his hand.

327

'Oh – I am sorry!' Molly dashed into the kitchen for a glass of water.

'Perfume's for smelling, not tasting,' Max spluttered before gulping down the water.

Sod Christophe and his not-rubbing-in rubbish.

'Tubby custard. Laa Laa want Tubby custard,' the television was saying.

Daisy was kicking and staring at the screen intently.

Max knelt down on the floor next to her, looked up at Molly, 'She's grown!'

'They do,' said Molly, going off into the kitchen, trying to gauge his emotions through the mist of her own feelings.

When she returned, they were both glued to the television.

She handed him his drink.

He knelt down next to Dairy and picked up her foot. 'Hello!'

Daisy giggled.

'I've got a present for you! Would you like to see? Pressie pressie?'

He pulled an enormous doll, dressed in Venezuelan national costume, out of his bag.

She kicked her legs and put the doll's legs straight to her mouth.

Molly took it off her. 'I'll keep it for when she's older. It's lovely, Max, thank you. Do you want to come through?' She went towards the back room, cursing her estate-agent-speak again.

'Fascinating, absolutely fascinating,' he said as he stood up and brushed his trousers down. 'I've never

328

seen them before!' He looked at Daisy, who was still transfixed. He paused, seemingly deep in thought. 'Which one is the gay one?' he said as he followed her out of the room.

Give him time, Molly thought. Give him time.

She sat awkwardly on the edge of the bed, indicating for Max to sit on the dressing-table pouffe stool.

'So, come on then, what's going on?' Molly looked up at him sharply.

Max's naughty-boy grin twisted Molly's frown into an involuntary smile. He could play her like a worn-out old computer game and he knew it. He knew all her buttons. Every bloody one of them. She tried to turn her smile into a sarcastic scorn.

'Molly, you're looking good.' He put his hand on her knee.

'You sound surprised.'

She felt the warmth and heaviness of his touch. She looked at him and smiled. Yielding slightly. Just as she'd decided to let him leave it there, he took it back. She felt the coldness of the withdrawal. He'd put himself back in charge again.

'Come on, what the bloody hell's going on?' she said quietly.

'Going on?'

'With *Veronica*, Max. You and Veronica, Veronica and her lover, you, whatever combination. None of you must ever move to Kew, OK? Kew's *mine*, Max.'

'Oh, *that*.'

'Oh *that*?'

'You haven't told me yet what *you* were doing there, Molly.'

'What I spend most of my time doing. Surviving.'

'Where was Daisy?'

'With a nanny.'

'*What* nanny?'

'What does it matter to you?'

'Of course it matters to me. Look, you don't have to work, Molly! Why haven't you been cashing my cheques?'

'Because I don't want your cheques, Max.'

'That's ridiculous.'

'That's exactly why I have to work, Max. I'm living on the bare bones as it is, look at this place, and the car's gone, I'm...'

She could hear her words distorting, flying up and twisting and turning before landing on a different plane. By the time they were out there, they reached his ears as nothing less than a fully formed, slightly hysterical, old crow's nag. He'd managed to convey this with just one minuscule movement of an eyebrow.

As the argument went back and forth, Molly could feel herself wearing down. Even though she could read his interviewing technique like a book. He could turn prime ministers to putty. What hope did she have? And why did she still love this man? Christophe, for all his maturity, was just a boy in comparison. But it was so much more with Max. All the things she'd wanted to shout at him, all her problems, emotional and practical – he seemed to make them seem so trivial. He was so damned persuasive. Maybe she should just go for another bit of living for the moment? No no, stop it stop it.

'... as I said, don't worry about Veronica. She changes her mind every few days, you know what she's like. One minute it's Hoxton, the next, Hammersmith.'

'Hammersmith? *Why*?'

'Restlessness, I suppose. Keen to exploit the property boom.'

'But nobody. Nobody ... Max, she's from *North* London! '

'That's why there's nothing to worry about,' he said matter-of-factly.

Molly paused for a moment as a new thought crossed her mind. 'She doesn't – *know*, does she?'

'Of course not.'

Molly had to say it. She took a deep breath. 'So, everything's all right then. Between you?'

'Nothing's changed.'

Molly tried the silent raised-eyebrow response. He laughed. Molly could hear the Teletubbies saying their bye-byes.

'Nothing's changed, Molly. Nothing at all.'

'Yes it has, Max. Plenty has changed.' She left the room. 'I've got a fat arse, big tits, scraggy skin ... and a beautiful baby girl,' she said as she returned with Daisy.

'Come on, you're looking good, Molly! I like the hair. It suits you.'

Max leant forward and looked into Daisy's eyes. 'Hello.' His cool had left him.

'You can hold her if you want.'

Molly held her out to him. He held her stiffly, cradled lying down. Like a child with a doll. Daisy stared at him. He looked up at Molly, 'She's gone blonde.'

'Just like her dad!'

'That sounds strange. Where shall we have dinner?'

'I've already arranged to go out tonight.'

'Why didn't you say so?' Max held Daisy up a bit higher, too close to his chin, rocking her slowly. 'Where?'

'It's a picnic. With music and stuff. A Bootleg Beatles concert.'

'Bootleg Beatles?'

'It happens every year in Kew. Everybody goes.'

'Where?'

'In Kew Gardens. If you want to come you'll have to buy a ticket from a tout. It shouldn't be too difficult. Apparently. But expensive. Probably.'

'Do we have to?'

'It's been planned for months, Max.'

'Months?'

'That's how things are round here.'

'And what happens to Daisy?'

'She's going over to Caroline's. Her nanny will be looking after her.'

'But I thought the three of us ... who's Caroline?'

'I'd better get the picnic things ready. Shall I take her?' Molly held out her arms.

'No, you can leave her here,' he said quietly.

'You can put her on the bed if you like!' Molly called back as she went into the kitchen.

When she got back, Max and Daisy were playing 'this little piggy'.

Max stared intently at Daisy as he put her gently into his car, strapped and already asleep in her car seat, tucked under a blanket.

'You can't stop looking at her, can you?' said Molly, climbing into the back. She could almost hear his emotions churning away inside him. 'No no, that way,' she laughed and wished she hadn't. Max looked crestfallen.

'How was I to know they go in backwards?'

'She'll be ready for her new car seat soon,' Molly said, helping him turn Daisy round, leaning forward to arrange the seat belt.

'It's like *University Challenge* fitting this thing,' Max said.

'That's just the beginning of it, let me tell you. It's a steep learning curve. You just master one development and they've moved on to the next!'

'What's the next thing then?'

'She'll be crawling any day now.'

'Then walking?'

'That usually follows, yes.'

'Then talking?'

Molly nodded, looking straight ahead.

'Unbelievable. Unbloodybelievable.' Max turned the key in the ignition and revved up the engine.

CHAPTER TWENTY-THREE

Max placed note after note into the ticket tout's sweaty upturned palm. Molly, a little distance away, watched with mild interest then increasing alarm as the money pile grew until she had to hold herself back from bursting into tears and thumping the pavement with her fists screaming about how many packets of Pampers, or how many hours of slavery at Baxter, Rumbold and bloody Featherington, that lot could buy.

They followed the flow of people and hampers through the gates and along the path which twisted through the shadowy trees.

'It's not quite Glastonbury, is it?' said Molly as they reached the concert area.

'Thank Christ,' said Max, eyeing the run of Pimm's and cream sherry stalls.

Molly resisted the urge to snuggle into the warmth of him as they stared across the tarpaulin patchwork of endless picnics. The showers had held off long enough for the last hours of the summer sun to bake the ground springy dry. The smell of rain lingered, mingling with damp leaf, balsamic vinegar and garlic, to give a steamy, tropical undertone to the subdued English carnival atmosphere. The Temperate House terrace had been transformed into a convincing stage, with all the paraphernalia from scuttling roadies to crowd barriers.

'We've to look for a red heart balloon. On a hill, just to the left of the lighting tower.'

They began to pick their way across the picnics to the sound of cork pop and glass chink lit by flickering night lights.

Max touched her arm. 'What about here?' He nodded to a space. 'Why don't we pitch up here, just the two of us?'

'No,' said Molly firmly.

'We've so much to catch up on, Moll.'

'No!'

She wanted him to meet her new friends, she wanted him to know she'd been getting on with her new life. And would. And besides, she wanted to show him off *and* get her own back on Christophe.

'Pretend we didn't come?'

'We're not pretending anything, Max. Anyway, Caroline knows we're here. Ulé's got Daisy, remember.'

'Just the two of us.'

'Daisy is in her *home*, Max.'

'MOLLY! Cooee, Mollleee!'

'There they are,' said Molly, pointing to a frantic Izzie, standing out like a sparkler in glittery T-shirt and silver leggings, waving both arms in the air.

'Good spot, Izzie,' said Molly, looking around.

Blankets had been spread right across the small rise in the landscape, surrounded by a variety of barriers made out of picnic baskets, camper chairs and a red and blue stripy beach wind-shield. At right angles to the stage, flanked by the metal poles of the lighting gantry, Carter, in a large, Daz-white Newcastle Brown T-shirt, stood proprietorially behind a collapsing, collapsible camper table.

'This is the dining area,' said Izzie, 'when the band's on we go down and dance.' She looked at the crowd of young blokes behind. But they didn't seem to care, they were in their own universe, orbiting around a barrel full of ice and beer.

'Look at that,' said Max warmly, looking across at Carter.

Carter beamed proudly. Carefully laid out on the table before him were racks of bottles of wine: white, red and rosé. Whisky, gin, vodka and Bacardi, miniature Schweppes mixers, bottles of beer, cans of beer, Guinness, Coke, 7-up, American ginger and a tiny bottle of Worcester sauce. Two glass dishes, one with a fan of lemon slices, the other with lime, flanked rows of glasses of different shapes and sizes, a cocktail shaker, salt, a jar of cocktail sticks and a silver bucket full of ice. Little bowls of peanuts and olives made a pattern all the way along the front of the table.

'Bloody hell, Izzie! Carter!' said Molly.

'It's our one big night out, isn't it, Carter?'

'Aye.' Carter nodded happily. 'Now,' he said rubbing his hands together barman-style,' what'll it be?'

Jason and Jenna, who were sitting on the rug to

the right of Carter, their backs to the stage, were both looking up at Max expectantly.

'Oh, sorry,' said Molly, introducing them.

Max navigated his way through the food and bent down to shake hands.

'And this. Behind you, Max. Is Caroline. Caroline Symes.'

Caroline looked cold and uncomfortable in her creased trousers and strapless top, perched on a camper chair, arms folded, a crossed leg swinging angrily with a clod of mud stuck halfway up her suede tan heels.

'Where's Theo?' said Molly.

'Working late,' she said agitatedly, taking a large slug of white wine and looking around her, her head darting like a starling.

'And look at all this *food*!' Molly quickly changed the subject.

'What'll it be then?' said Carter.

Max pulled two bottles of champagne out of his holdall.

'Vintage!' said Carter admiringly and nodding with approval.Caroline, with a glass of class in her hands, seemed to cheer up a bit, raising her eyebrows approvingly at Molly and giving her a wry smile. Molly felt a surge of pride. He did look good that evening. Smart in his own scruffy way. At the same time she felt a pang of sympathy at Caroline's aloneness. She knew alone when she saw it.

'Cheers, all,' said Jason, holding up his glass.

'I'd get some food in you now, if I were you,' said Izzie.

'This is a bit different from the banana and honey sandwiches I normally bring with Daisy!' Molly said, looking around at the food. 'What are those?'

'Wild rice griddle cakes with seared tuna and chilli-soy dressing,' said Caroline. 'They're supposed to be starters but I don't think it matters.'

'Chuck it all on your plate,' said Izzie happily.

'And those,' said Caroline, pointing a polished pink crescent of a fingernail, 'are lobster tails with charred asparagus which really should go with the baby new potato and quail's egg salad.'

'Great,' said Max, taking a prosciutto-wrapped breadstick.

'Those over there are grilled figs with prosciutto if you prefer, Max,' said Caroline.

Molly looked across at Jenna.

'Don't mind us,' said Jenna, 'we've brought our organic wraps.'

Molly's cosiness was short-lived. She hadn't been consciously looking for him at all, but her eyes had found him and stuck there all by themselves like a radar beam. As Christophe approached, she grew increasingly alarmed, like a teenager at a school hop. Double-dating – but then not, because neither of them was her date. Max was an old friend and Christophe was a new friend she'd happened to shag once. That's all. And she wasn't going to sleep with Max later anyway. Was she. Though she could pretend and play-act at being with Max for the evening, later he'd disappear. And that'd be that. And she'd have to cope with it. She'd have to go and get solidly drunk with Amanda when it was all over, that was all. As if sensing something was going on, Max suddenly put his arm heavily across her legs. Her thoughts quickly rearranged themselves. She couldn't push him away in front of the others. Oh all right, just an arm across a leg, that's not exactly getting back together again, is it? And she didn't want to, did she? Even if his movement had all the subtlety of a tomcat spraying his territory. How come though, if men were so predictable, how come she'd got it so wrong, so often?

'What did you bring for puds, Moll?' said Izzie.

'What?'

'Puds? Pudding?'

'Oh, er, nothing too fancy.' Glad to have something to do, she unzipped her Tesco blue and white freezer holdall and busied herself unwrapping the cantaloupe halves filled with strawberries, blueberries and raspberries, feeling every single footstep of Christophe's approach.

'Come on, get tucked in, the band'll be on soon,' said Izzie.

'I haven't been to a rock concert in a long, long time,' Max said to no one in particular.

'I wouldn't call it a *rock* concert,' said Carter.

'Hey, what are these?' said Molly, picking up a bamboo skewer of meat and roasted vegetables.

'Splendido of chicken,' said Caroline.

'Caroline, you've been slaving!'

'PicnicToGodotcom I must confess,' said Caroline. 'I was intending to do something – I had Jamie's cous-cous planned but I simply couldn't find the *time*. You know how it is.'

339

Molly noticed Caroline's crossed leg twitching faster.

'Here's Christophe,' said Carter. 'Let's get this other bottle opened. Do you know, someone was telling me the other day champagne makes a special sound, if you pop it in the Palm House here?'

'What sort of a sound?' said Max.

'That's what I asked. He said you have to try it yourself.'

Molly smiled at Christophe, who looked at Max then looked away.

'What is this?'

'Champagne,' said Carter, 'in the Palm House.'

'I have tried it already,' said Christophe, looking directly at Molly.

Stop it, Christophe.

'Go on then, what did it sound like?'

'You'll have to try it yourself.'

Stop it now. Molly tried to convey a blank don't-you-dare look Christophe's way. Oh dear, he doesn't like it, though. She gave him a triumphant, serves-you-right look and took a tiny sip of champagne. Carter poured Christophe a glass. Caroline had stood up. She was talking animatedly to Christophe. So. That's all right then, thought Molly. Wishing it was. She was fed up, weary with so much being so wrong all the time.

'Good evening KEW!' A Liverpudlian voice came from the stage.

The band, dressed in tight grey suits and ties and Beatle wigs launched into 'Love Me Do'. Molly twisted herself round to face the stage, leaning lightly and cosily on Max's legs.

The stage lighting had turned the glasshouse into a blue, red and purple backdrop Pink Floyd would have been proud of, complete with low, moonlit clouds scudding along behind.

Halfway through 'Help!', Theo arrived, striding through the crowd with his legal walk, a march with his arms held out from his sides, leaning slightly as he weaved in and out of the picnics, still in his mustard-brown legal coat with black velvet collar. He stood, stroking his bald patch, looking flustered. Caroline, still talking to Christophe, ignored him.

Theo heaved himself down next to Max, leaning awkwardly on one hand with his legs stretched out to one side with his knees bent.

Molly leant forward. 'All right, Theo,' she said sympathetically. He looked at her blankly. Troubled. She handed him a paper plate and dug around for some cutlery.

'Good! Thank you. Yes.'

'Bad case?' she said politely, then to Max, conversationally, 'Theo is a lawyer.'

'Really?' said Max sarcastically.

'Max's a journalist!' Molly piped up in the cold silence.

'Really.' said Theo.

Oh dear, thought Molly. Perhaps not. 'A very nice lawyer,' she whispered to Max.

'No such thing,' Max whispered back.

'Come on guys, let's have a group photo before we all get too rat-arsed,' said Jenna.

They all gathered around Carter's bar. Max stood

at the back with Molly. As Jenna clicked the shutter, he ducked.

That hurt.

Izzie and Carter clambered away, giggling.

'We're off to dance! Anyone coming?'

'I haven't danced for so long,' said Molly.

'Well, come on then. Now's your chance.'

Caroline grabbed Christophe's hand.

Christophe turned round and gave a wounded-dog look to Molly, Theo and Max as he was dragged off.

'I'm going down,' Molly told Max as she finished off her glass.

'Think I'll have a scrap more to eat...'

Molly went to the back of the crowd standing in front of the stage. Christophe and Caroline had disappeared into the mass. When she returned Max and Theo had both moved to camper chairs and were sitting deep in conversation.

'Seen my wife anywhere?' said Theo.

'I think they went right into the crush. They sound like the real thing, don't they?'

'Oasis aren't a patch, are they,' said Carter, happily going back behind his bar. 'Now. Who's for a top-up?' He reached for the drinks as a sheepish Christophe and a flushed, happy Caroline returned.

'Those of you who aren't dancing,' said John Lennon from the stage, 'you can chew in time to the music. OK? Or – rattle your cutlery.'

Molly and Max sat quietly, listening to 'Norwegian Wood'.

'I think that's my favourite one,' said Molly.

'And mine,' said Max.

'Never heard it,' said Jenna.

Molly and Max exchanged looks.

'She wouldn't have been born when the real lot were around, would she?' Max whispered.

'I don't know these old ones either,' said Jason.

'Well, at least I'm not the only one getting old around here tonight. Come on, Max, I can't sit still any longer.'

They danced close. Well. It was only dancing. No harm in that. Halfway through 'Here Comes the Sun', Molly couldn't ignore the call of nature any longer. She went to the vans at the back and joined the queue of bursting ladies. She hopped from one leg to the other, staring enviously at the queue-free Gents. She had a choice, a few stray penises in a pongy van, the bushes, or the very real possibility of wetting herself on the spot. Without thinking any more she made a run for it and straight into a cubicle before she had time to focus on the stiff-legged, head-bowed row of men. When she'd finished, she sat waiting. Listening. For ages. After reading all the graffiti twice, she unbolted the door, and nonchalantly strolled to the end of the tinny little corridor, down the steps to fresh air and freedom. She glanced into the bushes behind the van, glad she'd made the right choice, as there were more people snogging there. She suddenly stopped.

"Scuse me, love,' the bloke behind her said, pushing past. Molly didn't hear him; she was standing stock-still with her mouth while open. One of the snoggers was Christophe. And it wasn't Caroline he was kissing.

Molly concentrated hard on the stage when Christophe returned. She couldn't look at him. She'd never be able to look at him again. By the time Theo returned, Christophe was all over Caroline again. The dog! The completely utterly shitless dog! And Theo? Who'd have guessed it? He looked so, he was so, so *straight*.

The band had moved into their druggy period, with long wigs, Sergeant Pepper outfits and a small orchestra.

Molly watched Theo, listening intently to 'Lucy In the Sky With Diamonds'. She was so shocked, she wasn't sure if she'd seen what she'd seen or not. But she had, hadn't she?

He caught Molly looking at him. Molly smiled and looked away quickly. Oh dear. Oh dear oh dear, she thought. And I thought I had problems.

The 'Hey Jude' encore sent the whole audience into drunken, swaying song. Molly stayed wrapped in Max as the fireworks exploded all around them. She gave in and stopped thinking about how hard it would be to part at the end of the evening. Everyone else was at it. She was only human. Just one more time, just the once...

'What was that peculiar noise your sparkly friend was making at the end?' asked Max as they were driving home.

'What noise?'

'The sort of meeeeew, fooooo boooooo.'

'Oh, Izzie's Furbie impersonation. She always does it when she's drunk.'

'What's Furbie?'

'Oh never mind, Max. Never mind.'

'It was a good night.'

'It's all pretend though, isn't it? You'll stay, you'll go. What's going to *happen*, Max? I have to know!'

'I know, I know, Molly. Tomorrow. Let's talk tomorrow.'

And would she ... Tomorrow.

Later, as Molly tucked Daisy into her cot, Max came up behind her. 'She's wonderful, Moll.' He put his arms round her. 'Absolutely wonderful.'

'So you're pleased?'

'She's sensational. We have a lot to sort out, Molly, but we'll do it. We'll find a way.'

'We?'

'We.'

He stood close behind her, pressing into her. His arms round her, protecting, warm. He snuffled into the back of her neck. Kissing her over and over with tiny little kisses. Closer to her ear, making her shiver.

She let herself be steered towards the bed.

His hands ran up her leg again. She buried her head into his neck. She kissed him, tasting the salty strength in his sweat. He tilted her chin with his finger and kissed her.

She ran her hand down to his trousers.

'Hey,' he said, kissing her over and over, on her cheek, her neck, 'be careful.'

He moved around and sat on top of her, astride.

He hitched her dress up to her waist, stopped a moment, then hitched it up higher, till it was round her neck. Molly held in her stomach and silently thanked the Visa gods for her new Calvin Klein.

He tucked her bra down, cup by cup.

Back down to a respectable unleakable 34C by 34C, Molly couldn't help but be proud of herself.

He ran his tongue round one nipple, then the other.

He slipped his hand inside her.

'Please, Max. Please. Now. Now ...'

They knew each other so well. He knew what she liked. She knew what he liked. He moved his tongue down to her stomach.

He smothered her squeals with kisses.

He held her and lay on top of her.

She felt his nakedness next to her. In her. Slowly all the way in, then still. Not moving.

'Oh, Molly ...'

They held each other tighter. Molly began to sob. A deep cry of relief, a deep elemental feeling of belonging. That it was right. That it would be right. They were one and the same and together. He began to move, slowly.

'Oh no ...' she whispered.

'Oh yes,' he whispered, pushing even deeper.

'No!' she tensed some more.

'What's wrong?'

She tried to sit up.

Max pushed her back down.

'I can't, Max, I've got to go to her.'

'No.' She felt the yield in herself, which made him push her down harder. Deeper.

Daisy, disgusted at the lack of response, upped pitch.

'Max!'

'Leave her.'

He moved faster.

Daisy was silent for a moment. Max stopped, they exchanged glances. A parental exchange.

In the same moment as she felt Max moving again, in a faster, more urgent rhythm, she heard Daisy yowling in a new voice, a startling high-pitched scream from which the only way forward was down, or repeat. All sense of her own pleasure had gone. As soon as he rolled off her in an ecstatic sweat, she slipped out of bed and back to work.

With Daisy under one arm, she stumbled into the kitchen to get her bottle. She switched the light on, closing her eyes in the pause between the tungsten flickering and bursting into life.

She took Daisy back into bed with them, putting a pillow lengthwise between her and the edge of the bed to stop her falling out.

Max lay crooked on one elbow, put his arm round Molly from behind.

'We'll just have to squeeze up tighter, won't we?' Max slowly massaged the back of her neck.

They both looked down at Daisy, happily guzzling her bottle, looked at each other and kissed again.

CHAPTER TWENTY-FOUR

A waft of perfume followed in Molly's wake as she tiptoed back to bed through the kitchen, naked but for a big fluffy pink bath sheet, wrapped around her like a sarong.

The bedroom filled with Shalimar. Max stirred in his sleep. She pulled back the thick, heavy curtain, screwing her face up as the sudden, sharp sword of sunlight stabbed her eyes. Cursing under her breath, she jiggled at the curtains, trying to loosen the rings which had bunched together on the wooden pole. As she stretched up, the towel fell from her waist. Max stirred again.

'What the—?'

'Sorry.' She turned to look at him.

'Come on back to bed.'

Molly climbed in between Max and Daisy and lay back concertina'd in a warm tangle of arms and legs. Her arms snuggling Daisy, Max's legs wrapped around hers, his arms across both of them. Holding them. Tight in a pool of warmth.

She lay with her eyes open in the stillness of the sweet Sunday morning sun which said that everything was well and would be well.

She felt him pressing into her back. She wriggled her body into the right position. They made slow, almost motionless, tantric love.

As she got the breakfast ready, her mind whirred with all that had happened. Rerunning the image of Christophe and Theo. Caroline, what would she do if she found out? Should she tell her, gently, somehow, rather than let her discover it accidentally? She automatically switched the radio on then snapped it off again, cursing Radio 2's inconsistency. Pickettywitch was going a bit too far.

'Here.' She balanced the bottle on the bedside table on top of the alarm clock, 'just shove that in her mouth.'

'She'll–'

'Do you want the papers or don't you?'

'I'll get them.'

He leapt out of bed.

'I thought I'd never see the day!'

'Now now, Molly.' He bent his legs as he zipped his trousers.

'She doesn't bite, you know. She's only got two teeth!' As the door slammed, she lay down next to Daisy. 'You're the beauty of our love, aren't you? Hey. Why is everything such a mess? Why does anything more need be said or done? Why can't we just have happy sunny days, followed by more happy sunny days?'

She went into the kitchen and tried the radio again. '... *so that's why Heinz changed their recipe for sandwich spread. Now we know, listeners...*'

'And it's something I will never know,' she said to

the radio, peeling off six slices of unsmoked back, to Marvin Gaye's 'What's Going On?'

She threw open the French windows to the sunshine in a positive waft of warm Sunday-morning comfort thoughts. A leisurely breakfast on the lawn. A goss with the papers. Then they'd talk. Or maybe it could wait till lunchtime...

They ate and read in the comfortable mutual silence which only happens after sex which has said everything, in the chink-clatter of coffee cup against saucer and the crackle of croissants and newspapers, crisping and curling in the heat.

Molly managed the whole of *Style* and the magazine before Daisy woke.

'Shall we go to the Gardens today?' she said, coming back up the lawn with Daisy and her play-gym.

'Hnnn?'

'For a walk.'

'Mm-mm.'

'I thought you'd like to see the Japanese garden.'

'Mmmm.'

'It's lovely at this time of year.'

'Mmmm.' He closed the newspaper together and opened it again at the next page.

'We could get sushi.'

'Mm mm.'

'There's a bottle of champers left. Perhaps we could try the cork trick in the Palm House,' she suggested, thinking it would be a good exorcism of the Christophe incident, already far behind her in the uncertain past.

Max put the paper down and looked up. He held out his arms for Daisy. Molly sighed inwardly as she put her gently on his lap.

'What shall we play now?' He looked into her eyes. Then down at her feet in exaggerated movements. 'Ahhhhhgggghrrr! This little piggy went to market, and this little piggy stayed at home...'

And this little piggy's staying at home too, Molly thought as she smiled fondly at them.

'I don't normally come here on a Sunday,' said Molly. 'It's so crowded. In the week you have this place to yourself.'

'"And the wildest dreams of Kew, are the thoughts of Kathmandu,"' Max murmured as they walked up the textured path of the Japanese Garden.

'Who was that?'

'Kipling.'

'I don't think he reckoned on one of these,' said Molly as they approached the enormous mahogany gateway at the top of the garden hill.

'It is pretty amazing, isn't it,' said Max, manoeuvring Daisy's pushchair around a solid block of Japanese girls coming towards them, their pretty, flat faces firing off each other, their voices rising and falling incomprehensibly.

'They sound like the Teletubbies, don't they, Daisy,' said Max.

'You always gets lots of Japanese in this bit.' She held onto his elbow loosely.

'Looking for bits of home away from home.'

'They'll be gone in a minute,' said Molly.

'And another lot will arrive!' laughed Max.

'It makes it authentic, I suppose.'

'The Japanese garden – a place of harmony in nature interspersed with groups going around in chattering clumps.'

Max swiped a bee away from the pushchair.

'Did you know, there are orchids that look so much like female bees, the male bees actually try to screw them?'

'No, I can't say I did know that.'

'I mean, it's funny, isn't it? You'd have thought the bees would have caught on, over the thousands of years of evolution, that they were being hood-winked.'

'It just means that bees are not very bright, Molly. A bit thick.'

'Male bees.'

'Touché,' conceded Max. 'Come on, where shall we set up camp then?'

'Over there?' Molly pointed to a pool of raked sand. 'The closer to the Zen bit of the garden the better. I know just the spot.'

'What about the cork pop in the Palm House?'

'Oh, it's way over there, we'll do it next time.'

'Yes.' Max nodded slowly, suddenly looking serious, 'next time.'

She tried to banish the incredulousness she had felt, the shock of Christophe and Theo which kept lurching up in her mind and concentrate on the moment, drinking in the sight of Max and Daisy finding out about each other, blue eyes meeting blue eyes, thick blonde curls upon thick blond curls.

352

'... gone to fetch a rabbit skin, to wrap the baby bunting in.'

'Max, I'm impressed! Did you learn these songs especially?' Molly chucked their empty sushi trays into a carrier bag and laid out strawberries, sugar and clotted cream.

He looked up, his smile turning to a thoughtful frown. 'No, they, they just come back, don't they? Childhood memories, all banked up in there somewhere.'

'So, does it feel different, then? Being a dad? I mean I feel like a completely different person. I *am*, I know. But is it like that for you?' Molly edged in slowly.

'Yesss ...'

'In what way?' Molly brushed a greenfly off her hand.

'I feel – well, like very protective.'

'Like a lion?'

'Mmm.' Max nodded, taking a sip of champagne.

'Ba ba ba ba,' said Daisy.

'No, Daisy darling, da da da da,' said Max, looking at her intently and mouthing the words widely. Daisy stared back in startled fascination.

'And I'm the lioness, ready to leap to Daisy's defence,' said Molly. 'It's funny, I mean, I don't mind about dying so much now. In a way they get you ready for your own death, don't they? I'd gladly leap in front of a car if necessary.'

'We don't want you doing that, Molly, do we?' He cuddled Daisy tightly on his lap.

'It's like your life isn't your own any more, like it's

353

more – a part of something else, a flow, not just Daisy, it's your own past, your own future – everything. What is the future, Max?'

'This is a perfect spot, Molly, absolutely perfect. Just what Japanese gardens were made for, to retreat from the violent world filled with samurai swordsmen waiting to strike you down.'

'A retreat from the violent world of Kew mothers. What time do you have to go?' Get down to it.

'Five-ish, I suppose.'

The bamboo water-trough clacked, wood against wood, into the silence.

'I don't want to get the weekend traffic.'

'You could stay tonight if you wanted?'

'Veronica's back tonight.'

An electric shock ran through her.

'Do you love her, Max?'

Max stopped playing with Daisy.

'She's my *wife*, Molly.'

'Do you love her?'

'It's – it's not a matter of, I did of course, I *married* her, didn't I?'

'What about now?'

'Now? Well, it's more of a partnership, a friendship ... And, on a level. Look, we're just more realistic about life, Molly. Humans are not swans, they *don't* mate for life.'

'Puh!'

'If they did, I wouldn't have met *you*, would I?'

'She won't buy that house, will she?'

'No.'

'How do you know?'

'It's highly, highly unlikely.'

'Highly highly's not enough.'

'All right, highly highly *highly* unlikely.'

Molly shook her head grimly. Why did Veronica's control of her life seem to bear such a direct relationship to Molly's lack of control of her own?

'It would be a disaster, Max. She can't. You can't.' Something held her back from mentioning the flight path.

'I'll do everything in my power to stop her.'

'I'd have to leave.'

'Well, let's face it. That flat isn't exactly up to much, is it? It'd be no great loss.'

'Kew is my home now. I don't *want* to go anywhere else.'

'I'll do all I can to stop her. That's all I can say, isn't it? *I* certainly don't want to live in Kew.'

Molly felt the stab again.

'Why *not*?'

'Now Molly ...'

'It's the best place to live in the world. Just, just look around you! Where else has all of this plus the whole of London on its doorstep, not that I *go* there any more but still.'

'First you're saying don't move here, then you're asking why not.'

'Oh, forget it.'

It was hopeless.

'All I can do is do all I can to stop her. Right? It'll blow over. She's always talking about moving. It's like a game with her. I shouldn't worry too much.'

'Doesn't she give you any say in this?'

'Why do you think she got me down the other day? And you still haven't told me what you were doing there. Why didn't you *tell* me you were working?'

'Because you were *away*, Max. I needed, I need to get myself sorted. Anyway, I've already chucked that job in.'

'Why?'

'Because it stank, it was the stinkiest most miserable few weeks of my life. And I've had some ...'

'I don't understand what the problem is, Molly. You don't have to work. It's simple, I can afford to ...'

'It's *not* simple, that's exactly it.'

'If you need more, work it out and I'll send you whatever you need.'

'Send? Phhhhh.' Molly picked at the grass. 'I have to sort out what I'm going to do for the rest of my *life*, Max, and not just for my sake.'

'Molly, what *do* you want?'

'You *know* what I want.'

'We can have plenty more weekends like this, Veronica's always got some conference or other to go to.'

'If our future's not going to be together, then we've got to make a break. Properly. I mean, I know Daisy must see you, and you must see her, and last night was amazing as always. But it just gives me false hopes all the time.'

Max lay back on the grass next to Daisy and covered his eyes.

'When's her birthday?' he said through his hands.

'The eleventh of January.' She tried to sound

bright. 'Just think, when she's older, you can take her out.' She bit into a strawberry. 'There's still something odd about it, Max. I mean, Primrose Hill, St John's Wood, I could understand – at a long shot, Chiswick, Richmond even, but *Kew*?'

'It's not so different from Hampstead.'

'It's completely different! Hampstead's on a hill in the north. Kew's in a dip in the south. People just don't do it, Max. Kew's overseas! I *know*, I did it! She can't just be bored with the restaurants, can she? Or does she want to change the colour of her Tube line?'

'Veronica doesn't travel by Tube, you know what she's like.'

'Oh for heaven's sake! Kew is a *family* place, Max.'

'Look – all right. I'll tell you. I suppose you'll have to find out one way or another.'

'What?'

'Sooner or later.'

'WHAT?'

'Veronica. She's pregnant.'

Molly felt the blood rising to her cheeks at the same time as all her strength sank through her body and out in one short, sharp gasp. She stared ahead across the sea of sand. A socking great black hole between her heart and her eyes had opened up, a dismal result of all the hopes and expectations and anticipations sinking down and out of her in silent tears of disbelief and dismay.

'She decided, before it was too late...'

Molly leapt to her feet. 'So you thought you'd come and have a look, did you? See what a baby looks like?'

357

'In her thorough way, you know what she's like, she discovered Kew has some of the best schools...'

'Is it yours?' She turned away from Max, the tranquil rippling sand blurred beyond recognition.

'How do I know?'

'You don't know!!!'

'How does any man know?'

That was it.

'Boy, am I glad she's too young to understand any of this,' said Molly, calmly picking up Daisy and strapping her into her pushchair. 'It's just as well this is all happening now rather than later, that's all I can say.' She clicked together the blue plastic harness with a short, sharp snap. She turned, grabbed hold of two corners of the blue chequered picnic rug and pulled them as hard as she could. One of the glasses smashed on a rock and the other rolled down the hill. The strawberries, the sugar and the cream flew into the air, crash-landing in the middle of the sea of sand while the half-full bottle of champagne tumbled away, lodging itself upside down between two significantly placed boulders.

A group of Japanese tourists in red anoraks stopped and stared, motionless, as the remainder of the champagne trickled onto the strawberry-strewn sand, turning it into a soggy, alcoholic puddle of mud.

CHAPTER TWENTY-FIVE

Her crying all done, Molly shuffled around her garden, bending down to pull at the bindweed. It had been a different kind of crying, the tears filling her eyes all by themselves and plopping out, as if they had little lives all of their own. No convulsions. No feeling of self-pity. No sadness even. Nothing. All gone into a void of used-up emotion like she'd had her life sucked out of her.

She nodded at Mr Constandavalos over the fence. He was sitting on an old car seat with the stuffing hanging out in the shade of his plum tree, sipping raki with a friend and playing backgammon. She liked the melancholic sound of the dice, rattling and landing with regular thuds onto the baize, punctuating the hot, still air like a song.

'There,' she said to Daisy, dangling in her sling, 'I'll be with you now. No more messing around with our lives.'

She snipped off a pink rose from its bush, cupped it in her hands and held the still damp, heavy dripping thing to Daisy's face. The rose. The mother flower. Soft, so soft. And vulnerable. But only allowed to be so by the protection of its thick, thorny stem.

'We're on our own, now, OK, Daisy. I'll fight your corner with my head, not my heart, now. I promise. It's all about survival from now on. Look at this pretty one.' She moved on, snapping off a large pink peony, 'it's a frilly-knickers flower, isn't it? A pink frilly-knickers flower.

'*And* there'll be no more ironing in the evenings,' she said, taking a satisfied side-glance at the washing line full of sheets as she went back inside.

She took the old dead roses out of the vase and poured the slimy yellow water down the sink.

'What's happiness anyway? Hnn? It doesn't last. Not for anyone. Might as well be miserable in the first place. Saves getting disappointed. Poo! What a stink.'

'Poo,' said Daisy.

'Poo.'

'Poo.'

'Poo poo poo poo. You're a giggler, aren't you.'

The phone rang again. He could try as often as he liked, but she wouldn't be picking it up. There was nothing left to discuss. Max, not even Max, could talk his way out of that one. And she wasn't going to let him begin to try.

The rings seemed to get louder as she swayed Daisy to Bill Withers's soulful voice. How could she have been so naive? As naive as the sixties. That's all she'd been. A dreamer, clinging to the raft of life, willing it to work out, following her feelings, her desires, trying to will things that weren't going to work out to work. But not any more. Never again. She'd put a wheel-clamp on her heart. From now on she'd be a hundred per cent straight-down-the-line sensible. Mrs Sensible, that's what she'd be. How could she ever have been so *stupid*? At her age!

Boys and girls come out to play
The moon doth shine as bright as day
Leave your supper and leave your sleep
And come to your playfellows in the street.

The nursery rhyme echoed from generations past, the words inseparably part of the notes as they hit the air. Molly sat in a semi-circle of women gathered around the piano. She clapped with her hands over Daisy's as she rocked her backwards and forwards on her lap. She smiled at Izzie, who was turning and pointing behind her with a scowl, as the rhythms changed and she launched into 'The Grand Old Duke of York'.

She turned to see Ulé and the other nannies sitting on chairs at the back of the church hall, quietly in conversation while their employers amused themselves at their feet.

'I don't think it's so bad,' said Molly to Izzie as they were clearing up afterwards and the nannies were still sitting chattering. 'I mean, why should they sing if they don't want to? We enjoyed it, didn't we, Daisy?'

She had. Like the nursery, the playgroup had filled her with a basic but deep-rooted peace. Something about the women gathered in a circle and singing the old rhymes together had touched a primitive part of her soul.

'All right, "Twinkle, Twinkle" isn't exactly the Ministry of Sound but they could muck in with the tidying up,' muttered Izzie as they pushed their way home. 'It's the same every bloody week.'

Daisy and Bob, side by side in their pushchairs, clapped and made singing noises together. 'Yes, but from Ulé's point of view, it's probably one of the only times when Charles isn't asleep she gets off. I mean, at home she has to be doing things with him all the time, doesn't she? She's not allowed to plonk him in front of the telly like the rest of us.'

'Did you hear Caroline's got her talking to him for an hour a day now? An hour a *day*.'

'Why?'

'She read somewhere it'll make him a faster reader. *Reader* – at six months!'

'It must be hard – living in someone else's life.'

'Imagine, when your reason for being is having them dump their kids and the ironing on you. Oh – hi.'

A small, smartly dressed woman had nudged her pushchair up behind them.

'Molly, this is Annabelle. She quit her job recently, just like you. I meant to introduce you earlier.' The three of them pushed on in a slow drift up Sandycombe Road.

'How long did you last?' said Molly.

'Three months.'

'You did better than me, then.'

'They haven't got it sussed, have they, these employers, I mean, I took work home and all of that but it was hopeless, hopeless...'

'Were you full time?' said Molly.

'And the rest. They think if you're not at your desk you're not working. There's even a name for it now, presenteeism, did you know that?'

'Who looked after Joseph?' said Izzie.

'Ach, and then the nursery! D'you know what the fine was if you were late? Ten pounds for every fifteen minutes! Try telling that to the railways.'

'At least I had the nanny side worked out...'

'I was being pulled one way by the office, the other by the nursery, and that's before poor wee little Joseph here got a look-in. Let alone myself! I was taking my work home as well, making international calls from *my* phone, but did that count?'

'Where did you work?'

'Vernon & Hall. That was the joke of it. Enlightened employers, huh! Equal opportunity's the biggest lie ever, it doesn't fit into the unequal realities of family life, does it? Period. Then they suggested I took a career break. Crap. Take a foot off the ladder and you're off the rung and down that snake before you're out the door.'

They turned left onto the main road. 'It's all fine and OK when you're young with no kids,' said Molly, speaking louder now they had the traffic to compete with.

'It's a con,' said Annabelle. 'You start out all the same then they shift the goalposts – halfway through your life! Crittenden said it all.'

'Crittenwhatenden?' said Izzie.

'I just read about her in a book.'

'You have time to read *books*?' said Molly in admiration.

'The ideological fight for woman's rights, it isn't real, it doesn't add up...'

'We're doomed,' said Izzie in mock gloom.

'It can't be worked out in just a couple of generations, can it?' said Molly.

'When you think how many millions of years we've all been around having babies,' said Annabelle.

'Makes you want to get into politics, doesn't it,' said Izzie.

'Working at home. That's got to be the answer. But at what?' said Molly.

'I'm staying put on the dole, me, till Joseph's at school,' said Annabelle, 'I'm not going through all that form-filling again.

'Er, how, how do you go about that exactly?'

Molly left them at the junction of Marksbury Avenue, thinking hard about what Annabelle had said. She'd insisted Molly had to sign on for benefit straight away, even if she was going to get another job, reeling off a stream of reasons. Who'd get custody if Molly died? Her mother? Which meant – Colin! She had to make a will, she'd get dental, healthcare, training courses, back-to-work incentives, glasses, even, all there to help. She should. She had to...

Three weeks later, Molly set off for Caroline's via the Kew Green post office. She was grateful to turn off the main road and get down into the shade of the avenues. The July heatwave was settling into its third week; the thick, windless air hadn't moved for days. Nothing was moving if it could help it. On the cool of the Green, Frisbees and low-flying ducks criss-crossed in lazy glides. The grass was fading into brown patches now, as were the white chalk grids running across the middle, running tracks for the Church school sports day.

Molly looked behind her nervously as she joined the queue. When she got to the counter, she looked behind her again before she slipped the book underneath the plastic screen, face down, not wanting anyone, not even strangers, to recognise it. She looked at the kind face of the Indian man as he stamped it. A man doing an honest day's work. She expected him to be judgemental, to say something. But he just looked up and gave her a friendly smile.

'Bottled milk or powdered?'

'Sorry?'

'Your milk tokens, love, which do you want?'

'Powdered. No – bottle.'

'You sure?'

Molly swallowed and nodded.

He stamped a little slip of white paper and handed it over to her with the cash.

She shoved it in her purse and hurried outside.

So. That was it!

Phew.

'It was the, one of, the worst experiences of my life!'

said Molly as she bobbed a naked, delighted Daisy up and down in the crystal-clear water.

The whole signing-on procedure had been a nightmare. The hopelessness of it all. The raggedy slow queue, all the signs of desperation there together in one room. Alone, she'd have just got on with it, but she hated having Daisy with her. Poverty stank. She could do nothing to stop the stench of stale alcohol, desperation and dirty clothes seeping into her hair and skin.

'You *poor* darling,' said Caroline, ducking Charles right underneath the water and letting go of him.

Jenna shrieked, 'No! Don't do that!'

'It's all right, he's used to it, we learn it at Aqua Babyland, don't we, Charlieboy?' she said as Charles came up spluttering and gasping before disappearing below the surface again.

Molly held her breath until Caroline grabbed him and threw him up in the air.

'So. I'm a single mum. Official!'

'There goes my inside information,' said Izzie.

'Isn't he going to pay you anything, then?' said Jenna.

'He doesn't have to any more. He can do it through the official channels.'

And then there was the endless, endless form-filling. Told to go here, sit there, take a number, turn into a number, go over there, join another queue.

'I thought you two were getting it together there,' said Izzie.

'So did I. But not now. We're over. Through. So if

any of you can fix me up with a blind date, I'm up for it!' she added lightly.

'So what happened?'

'Oh, you know – one big row too many.'

'What about?' said Izzie.

'I'll get myself back out there eventually. You know...' She smiled bravely around at them. 'No – perhaps you don't.'

And all the questions. Then questions about Max. They'd asked for his name. She'd hesitated. But she had to follow it through. So she'd given it. Max would be hearing from the Child Support Agency. Official. There. She'd drawn a line under it. It was the only thing. Now at least she was a statistic, if nothing else. She couldn't worry about Max's problems any longer. They were his to deal with. And Veronica's.

'So what'll you do then?' said Jenna.

She'd have eighty pounds a week to live on and that would be it. If the only people who were allowed to stay with their children were the very rich and the very poor, then she was just going to have to be very poor.

'Go back to college, take a course.'

And then, when she'd answered all the questions, they'd become really helpful. She'd been given a list of colleges where she could retrain at something she wanted to do. Something to fit around Daisy.

'As what?' said Izzie.

'I haven't decided yet. Computers probably... hairdressing even. I'm even thinking of plumbing! I was talking to someone in the queue, it's quite

easy these days apparently, now it's all plastic pip-
ing.'

'I'll have you when you're trained,' laughed Izzie.

'*Seriously*?' said Caroline.

'Well – why not? I could do my own hours.'

'Maybe we should all get in on it?' said Izzie. 'A
firm of female plumbers'd clean up around here.'

'You could live on the call-out charges alone,' said
Jenna.

'You don't get any women's part-time jobs paying
that kind of money, do you? Anyway, I'm not sure
yet. But the main thing is quite a few of these colleges have a crèche on site.'

'That's super, Molly. Well done,' said Caroline.

Molly watched her playing with Charles, so
secure in her surroundings, her life. Christophe
would be going back to France soon; it'd blow
over, Theo wasn't going anywhere. She'd have a
word with that Christophe, though, if she got the
chance.

'At least I feel I've got an identity to go forward
from. It might be at the bottom of the pile but, you
know, it feels better. Much better,' she said on the
phone to Amanda that evening.

'I don't want to say I told you so, darling, but I did
say...'

'Do you know, Amanda? I think it's one of the
pleasures of getting older. Getting rid of all that silly
love stuff. I'm going to act my age from now on.'

'You sound like you're finished. You've got to get
back out there quick, girl!'

'I've had it with out. If I want anybody, it's some-one to stay in with now, not go out with.'

'And make the cocoa with.'

'Oooh yes.'

'You need a good night out on the tiles, hon,' said Amanda. 'Listen, let's do it, let's make a date.'

'I, er, haven't got a babysitter.'

'Don't give me that one again, Molly. You've got three weeks to get one sorted. The twenty-third, OK? I'm writing it in my diary as I speak.'

CHAPTER TWENTY-SIX

'I didn't say *is* it a joke. I said *I* was joking...'

'We've arranged it now.' Jenna sounded hurt. 'My mum's here... she'll take Daisy if you haven't got a sitter? We've got the Wine & Moussaka on the Green booked for eight-thirty. Table for four.'

Molly hadn't expected anyone to take up her suggestion seriously. Least of all Jenna. It was something she'd said to show she was, ha ha, *out* there. But her sarcasm had got the better of her. Now she was being dropped into it and was floundering for excuses.

'Who is it?'

'What?'

'The datee?'

'Wait and see.'

'You mean I *know* him?'

'Sort of. He's a GSOH.'

'GSOH?' Images of the back pages of *Time Out*, the Lonely Hearts section, surfaced.

'I'm sorry, Jenna, but if anyone has to describe their sense of humour in that way, it guarantees they don't have one.'

'No? Good salary, own home.'

'Oh.' Now, that was a bit different.

She hated dating, she was too *tired* for dating. Too tired to make herself look fantastic when she just didn't look fantastic any more and didn't have the means or the energy to go to any of Richmond's countless beauty salons or spas to try and get herself anywhere near. Apart from anything else, she hadn't a clue how to behave. What were the rules?

Molly's early relationships had usually started off in bed and gone on from there, or not, as the case might be. That's how it was then. And that's what she felt comfortable with. All that stuff in the car with Christophe, well, that was different, she'd been in lust with Christophe.

That call ruined the rest of her week. Instead of narrowing down her college possibilities and inspecting crèches, she found herself raiding every single charity shop in Richmond and Sheen, hunting for something old/new to wear. *Anything* to wear. And finding nothing. It didn't bode well. She'd ended up with the René Derhy as always, like its owner getting a little faded and worn now.

Her feelings of foreboding peaked as she set off with Jason and Jenna down Forest Road and up Gloucester, feeling like a prize cow at a fair, all she needed was a ring in her nose. Being led to the judging ring. To be looked over by some bloke. She didn't *do* dating. Well, stuff those stupid old Molly thoughts. She simply wasn't on the market anyway and that was that. She was past all of that awful twenties/thirties crap. She'd be single for the foreseeable future. Anyone would have thought it was Jason who was the datee, the way he was hovering around her, fussing, grinning, touching her behind lightly when Jenna wasn't looking. She'd worked out why. Since that guy at the party had stroked his hair, he'd thought she fancied him. Jason wasn't remotely gay. It had taken her a while to catch on but she realised he thought it was Molly who'd stroked his hair. Not the guy behind her.

The guy behind her? The guy from the queue she'd so shamelessly flirted with when Christophe had arrived?

A big man with a neat, blond crew-cut stood to greet them. It was him. Molly was relieved. Though younger, at least he was closer to Molly's decade than Jason and Jenna's.

The small, dark, candlelit restaurant was packed. Molly was squashed in next to him at a table by the window.

The waiter brought plate after plate of mezze dishes.

Predictably, and, initially, embarrassingly, the talk had been of weddings and not much else. Dan, it turned out, was Jason's great confidant and mentor and was going to be his best man. Great. Rather than a romantic arrangement, she'd just been tagged onto the fringes of the dreaded wedding planning meeting and Jenna had the perfect excuse to talk of nothing else for the whole evening.

'And, Dan, I've got another little job for you?'

'Whassat, Jen?'

'We need a poem, we've got to have a poem.'

'What for?' said Jason and Dan together.

'Like, like in that film, what was it, Jase?'

'It's all right, Dan, we don't need a poem, she's getting a little overexcited about it all that's all.'

'*Four Weddings and a Funeral*,' said Molly. 'That was the film.'

'That's the one. So – Dan can you...'

Jason and Dan exchanged helpless glances.

'Fine, but I don't know anything about poems!'

'There are books, Dan, lots of books.'

Dan shrugged. 'If that's what you want, Jen, of course, I'd be happy to.'

'I'll need to check it over, when you've chosen one.'

'Shouldn't you be choosing it?' said Molly.

'Oh, do you think so? I don't know, I'll have to look it up in the book and let you know, Dan, all right?'

'All right, Jen. Whatever makes you happy.'

As the retsina flowed, the bouzouki music seemed to get louder and faster, and conversation across the table eventually petered out.

'Have you not been married, then, Dan?' Molly asked as she drained her glass. Dan laughed. He had a funny, high giggle. Like he was laughing quietly to himself.

'What do you think?' he said in his soft, quiet Aussie accent as he leant over and filled her glass again.

'Well, you know what they say, if you've not I'll be immediately suspicious and wonder what's wrong with you,' said Molly. 'It's blatantly obvious what's wrong with *me*, of course, but that's beside the point.'

'Oh, I don't know.' He smiled. 'Marriage is for other people.' He nodded over to Jenna and Jason. 'To me, it doesn't really matter any more. It's a status thing, isn't it? A legal thing these days.'

'It used to be important,' said Molly, gazing out of the window at the floodlit church across the road.

'What do you mean?'

'I mean, before, before, when if you, you know, *did* it…chances were you'd be up the duff. But these days…'

'That's right. I can see why Jen and Jase are doing it. They've got a child to think of.'

'Yes,' said Molly quietly.

The waiter brought fresh figs and honey. They chatted easily. There she was, talking about marriage to someone she'd just met, to someone she was on a *date* with! and it didn't matter. They were just having a grown-up, intelligent conversation.

'It's something we've lost,' she continued. 'I mean, compared to the old days.'

He laughed. 'Listen to you! In the *old* days!'

'All right, in the fifties, say, I mean, the wedding ceremony preceded sex, didn't it!'

'You don't think people did it before marriage?'

'No, yes, well, of course they did, but everyone was more careful, it wasn't exactly New York in the early eighties, was it?'

'OK.'

'That was the whole point of a wedding! The handing over of the girl to start breeding.'

'To put it bluntly, yes, I suppose so.'

'She would formally take on another identity and it prepared her for the big changes. Whereas today, if you want a child, it's a negative, rather than a positive, now we're in such complete control of our fertility. All you do is to stop taking that tiny little tablet.'

'Rather than a thrusting big sexual high after the biggest party of your life.'

'And a few tin cans rattling behind you in your car.'

'I know what you're getting at,' he said, suddenly going quiet as he tipped his bowl and slowly and methodically scraped the last of the honeyed figs and cream onto his spoon.

'No! I'm not – I mean...'

'It's all right. I'm not that kind of guy.'

Well, what kind of a guy are you, then? Molly wondered.

'George!' Jason called, 'can you bring us the bill, mate?'

She'd been dreading this bit. Some rules of the game were still grey and murky. She pulled out her Visa card. Jenna sat and smiled sweetly as Molly went through the argument with Jason and Dan about who should pay what.

They were the last to leave the restaurant. Jason and Jenna tactically walked on ahead, holding hands easily and naturally, leaving Molly and Dan walking along behind, uneasily and glaringly not touching.

*

'Thanks, Jenna, I really enjoyed it.'

Molly got Jenna alone in Lavender's nursery before she left, and she grabbed her opportunity to find out as much as she could about Dan.

'He's a nice guy.'

'He's been really good to us, Jason loves him! I'd say stay the night, but Mum's on the sofa?'

'No, it's all right. I'd rather get back. But, Jenna, tell me. What happened to the girl he was with at your party?'

'Search me. You'd better ask him that!'

I will, thought Molly on her way home, if we meet again. I will.

There was something direct and honest about him that had appealed. Still, all her prattling on about weddings had probably put him off? But no, that was what they were all talking about.

He hadn't asked for her phone number. But then, she hadn't asked for his, had she?

CHAPTER TWENTY-SEVEN

'Plumbing's full.'

Oh well. Maybe scrapping around in the attics and loos of Kew for the rest of her life wasn't such a good idea after all.

Molly was in Richmond at the open day of her chosen college. The one with the nicest, the cosiest, the friendliest crèche. She'd already signed on the dotted line for her computer course and had a little time on her hands to linger before collecting Daisy and going back to Dan's for supper. She'd seen him several times and they'd been having a relaxing, pounce-free time. He was easy to be with, easy to talk to. He liked sport and the outdoors, went to the gym three times a week and worked five days a week as a software sales director. She wasn't in love with him, or in lust with him, he was just a nice, straightforward single *bloke* who seemed to really like her. And he was even more crazy about Daisy. She couldn't believe her luck.

She was so full of optimism about her future that the next time Max called, she picked up the phone.

He was livid. He'd just received a letter from the CSA.

'You could have had the courtesy to warn me!'

'*Courtesy!*'

'It came to my house! Onto my *doormat*!'

'Oh, so you haven't moved yet then. That's good.'

'Molly, stop it.'

'Stop what?'

'Look – we've got to meet.'

'What for? It says it all in the letter, doesn't it?'

'Don't be so cold, Molly.'

'Cold!'

'I know we're in a mess, but...'

'No, Max. You're in a mess.'

'Please, Molly. You can't expect me not to – I'm still her father even if ...'

'Don't say it, Max. Don't say it,' said Molly, a sharp mother voice appearing from nowhere.

'Look. We could meet somewhere. Discuss everything properly.'

'There's nothing left to discuss, Max,' she said wearily.

'You mean I'm not allowed to see Daisy again?'

She could hear his chin wobbling.

'No, I always said you could see her whenever.'

'When is whenever?'

'I'm working hard to reconstruct my *life*, Max, can't you understand that?'

'Do you think it's been any easier for me?'

'I'm not questioning that, Max. I'm trying hard, very hard, not to think about you.'

378

'What about lunch then, that would do no harm, would it?'

Molly didn't say anything.

'Molly? Are you there? Molly!' Panic in his voice.

'Yes, I'm here.'

'Come on. We have to discuss Daisy.'

Molly was quiet again.

'No, no, Max.'

'Oh go on.'

'No!'

'What about Harrods sushi bar?'

'All right, you win, Max. You win.' Molly smiled.

'I should have just said "sushi bar" in the first place, shouldn't I?' He knew only too well her zero resistance level to sashimi and Kirin beer.

Going on the Tube with a pushchair was only the start of it. When she changed trains at Hammersmith, a woman in front of her dropped something. Molly rushed forward and picked it up and gave it to her. The woman looked at her strangely. Molly looked down at her hand. It was an empty caramel wrapper. Embarrassed, she turned away and casually shoved the woman's rubbish into her pocket. What is it about you, Molly? she asked herself as she stood back, terrified of the speed of the approaching Piccadilly Line train after her rumbling old District dinosaur. Back to doing what you've always done, picking up other people's rubbish.

In Knightsbridge, it got worse. She just wasn't part it any more. The city flowed around her at a terrifying speed. She kept bumping into people and doing funny zig-zag dances with her pushchair. She'd lost it. But why was everyone was in such a rush? And everywhere, in doorways, on the Tube, on the station, there were people chattering into their mobiles, some of them with earpieces, walking around looking like they were talking to themselves. It was insane.

By the time she reached Harrods she was a wreck, surprised and completely grateful just to be allowed in. She breathed deeply, feeling a real sense of achievement as she reached the other side of the doorman's scrutinising gaze.

Inside, Molly's jaw dropped even lower. The streets of Knightsbridge were one thing. The dark green interior of Harrodsworld was something else. It was like hitting Disneyland in Antarctica.

Back home in Kew the redrawing of her interior high-street map had been seamless. The old Whistles/Top Shop/Hobbs route had effortlessly been replaced by the Boots, Mothercare and Superdrug run. So after months and months of 'going shopping' meaning just that, with her weekly bus trip to Somerfield, and her occasional flash flashes into Waitrose, the charity shops and the Hounslow Primark, when she was feeling rich, here was the real McCoy.

Molly had a ball. She looked. And she looked. She was hours early. She resisted the automatic-pilot urge to find the baby department and set off in search of ladies' clothing, randomly pressing the second-floor button on the lift, which some hidden memory told her was where department stores put their fashions. She experienced a massive frisson of excitement when David Beckham got into her lift as she got out. She spent ages trying to work out which floor the piano music was coming from, gliding up and down the Egyptian escalators as if in a trance, until she realised it was taped. After an hour of just looking, her Visa card, zipped firmly away in an obscure, *almost* unreachable region of her purse, wasn't as much burning a hole as setting off a continental-sized bush fire in her bag. After getting lost several times and when there was only an hour to go before rendezvous-with-Max time, she decided to limit her wanderings to the ground floor, lingering close to the Food Hall and its sushi bar.

She was too fascinated by everything as she walked around to feel self-conscious. Until she got to the cosmetics. Then it hit her. It couldn't not. There were mirrors everywhere, scattered like a cruel joke among the clear-complexioned, powder-puffed, Cliniqued, Lazartiqued and Chanelled girls. Molly tried to avoid the only-too-real reflections and keep her tourist awayday perspective on things as she studied the utterly impossibly well-groomed perfection of them.

When she reached the Crème de la Mer counter she screeched to a halt. Her David Beckham lift experience faded into insignificance. Here, she was standing a few metres away from a mega A-list celebrity. She'd read enough about it in her *Elle* and *Marie Claire* days. This was *it*. The grout with clout made with seaweed, sound vibrations and light that took twelve years and 6,000 experiments to make.

The £100-plus a tub product so famous it had a counter to itself. She looked at the sample jar sitting invitingly just a few inches away from her on its cardboard stand. *Sample jar!* Asking her, no, *welcoming* her to come into its refined world of beauty and elegance and all things expensively wonderful! This could be it! A fat fingerful of this glob could make her skin as soft as Daisy's bottom. Max would see her looking better than she'd ever looked in her entire life. It would refresh the depletions to her new-found confidence the cosmetics department had so cruelly Brillo'd off. She darted a few looks both ways behind the counter. All clear. She looked sideways, behind her, and then went for it. As casually as if she were in her bathroom at home, she picked up the jar and unscrewed the lid.

'Can I help you?'

A chisel-nosed, white-coated woman popped out of the counter from nowhere like Bradley's jack-in-the-box, with a guardian-of-the-cream smile on her purple-glossed lips.

Molly scuttled off like a crab, dragging Daisy's pushchair behind her. When she opened her eyes again she found herself in Perfumery.

Now, this was more like it. It was like coming home! She even managed a knowledgeable chat with the Guerlain man about bottom and top notes. She returned to Cosmetics so brimming with confidence, she sat herself down on a chromy black leather Prescriptives high stool and asked for a make-over. In no time not one, but two of the perfectly painted girls were fussing over her. And they weren't remotely as frightening as they looked. They were friendly, helpful, and seemed as concerned about Molly's decrepit rhinocerous skin as if it were their own. Standing back as they looked at her, with a strange, once-removed expression in their eyes, as they discussed her colouring. The pampering, just the attention the girls gave her, made her want to burst into tears of gratitude. When they got to work, she relished the cold feel of the toner on her skin, the soft cotton wool brushing, cooling, soothing, cleansing, feeling detached and distant, listening to the harp music, looking sideways, looking up, to order.

She didn't even mind when a tour group of Americans shuffled by, stopped and watched for a while. She was no longer a spectator, but part of the show.

So pleased was she with the result and not least with the complete lack of hard sell from her new best friends, her credit cart erupted from her purse and made her the new owner of fifty pounds' worth of face creams in moments. And worth every penny, she thought happily as the till clicked and whirred its way to Visa Central.

She got hopelessly lost again looking for a place to feed Daisy, and so, having arrived at Harrods three hours early, she was a cool whole quarter of an hour late for Max.

'I feel like I've been on a week's holiday!' she said happily as she settled herself down on a stool and manoeuvred Daisy's pushchair away from the traffic of people passing by through the Food Hall.

Max, stooped on his stool, straightened. 'Do you?'

'Hey, you look like you've been on holiday yourself.'

'I wouldn't call being holed up in a Venezuelan hotel a holiday. She's asleep!' he said accusingly.

'Yeah, good, isn't it! I can't tell you how much I'm looking forward to this.' She ran her eyes greedily over the display of uncut raw fish behind the perspex counter in front of her. A kimono-clad waitress was already hovering, waiting for their order.

Max was slumped in his stool again. Molly nudged him.

'Kirin and sashimi,' she said to at the waitress.

'For two,' said Max.

'Are you in the country long, then?' asked Molly conversationally as the beer arrived seconds later.

'Two days.'

'Then back to Venezuela, is it?' Her mouth watered as she watched a hand reaching into the cabinet and taking out a slab of tuna with her name written on it.

'Geneva.'

'Oooh, that'll be nice.'

She ogled the tiny Japanese man in white hat and overalls, his deft fingers holding the fish, as his razor-sharp knife sliced at a perfect angle.

The American tour group passed by again. She smiled at them. She was in another show now. This was fun.

'Will it?'

'Come on, Max. It's not that bad. I'm getting myself organised, that's all. That's good, isn't it?'

'Veronica could have found that letter.'

'She didn't, did she?'

'No.'

'Well, you're all right then.'

'You could have warned me, Molly.'

'I can't sort your life out for you, Max. I'm sorry. I can't any more.'

'I'm trying to do the best here. I've been sending you cheques, why did you have to go and do that?'

Molly told him why, about the awfulness of the whole going on the dole procedure as she savoured every mouthful of the fresh, creamy raw fish, soy and sharp, green wasimi.

'So, in the long run, it'll be better, Max. I'm about to start retraining.' The ice-cold Kirin beer slipped down her throat as she told him her plans.

'*Virtual assistant*, what's a virtual assistant?'

'I'm not really sure, that's why I'm doing a course. No, well as far as I can make out it's like being a PA except you do it from home.'

'How?'

'Virtually! They send you the stuff they want typed or transcribed or whatever and you e-mail it back to them.'

'You're not a typist, Molly!'

'I can type; that's good enough, isn't it. Apparently you can get yourself set up to receive transcription tapes down the line now, so it's all that kind of computer stuff really... and there's loads of things, technical things, website design's a big part of it, that'll be fun... and...'

'And are you paid virtually as well?'

'Just be grateful I'm not becoming a plumber, that's all.'

'A *plumber*?'

'Never mind.'

'How did you find out about all of this?'

'A friend, a friend who works in computers, he suggested it.'

'He?'

Molly nodded, picking a pink slab of fish up with her wooden chopsticks. 'Mmm, this has to be my favourite place in London. There's a big demand for virtual assistants, apparently. What they call a growth area. And it's something I can do from home.'

'He?'

'And I think it'd be fun. It'll be a while yet. Before I'm ready to go into business. But – Max, what's the *matter*!'

'Everything's the matter.' He was staring at Daisy again, her mouth half-open as she slept.

'Yes, sorry. Right. We have to make arrangements. Look. Come, come whenever you like, Max! She's on the bottle now. You could take her to the Gardens. Take her wherever. I'd be glad of the break apart from anything.'

Max nodded. The waitress was hovering again.

They looked at their empty plates.

'One sake, two cups.'

He leant towards Molly as he poured the warm liquid from the blue and white china jug. He went to pour his own, but she put her hand on top of his to stop him.

'Let's not invite bad luck,' she said as she served him. 'But you must promise... I don't want her – Veronica – to...' she added quickly as sudden horrible thoughts of Max and Veronica frolicking through Kew Gardens with Daisy and new baby came to mind.

'Of course, Molly. Of course.'

'Is she still interested in that house?'

'I – er...'

'*Is* she?'

'I'm doing everything to put her off, believe me, Molly!'

'That means she is!'

'No – I mean, not for much longer. I'm sure.'

'It's right underneath the flight path. Tell her that.'

'Is it?'

'Yup.'

'Well, I hadn't noticed.'

'They time the viewings, Max.'

'Well, we don't worry about things that haven't happened yet. There's enough to worry about as it is.'

'You're not kidding!' Molly refilled his sake. He ignored her as he gazed down at Daisy again.

'Who's he?'

'Who?' Molly looked around.

'No – your friend. You said "he".'

'Oh – just a friend.'

It was true. But not for much longer. They were about to go off on a camping weekend to the New Forest.

'*Just?*'

'At the moment, yes.'
'At the moment?'
'Look, Max, you can't expect me to. . .'
'No no no, I know.'

CHAPTER TWENTY-EIGHT

Molly sat up stiff-straight from her semi-snoozed recline.

'Everything all right?' Dan turned anxiously towards her as he slipped his gearstick into neutral and they cruised to yet another stop.

'Fine!' she said in a high voice.

She forced herself to keep looking his way, her focus shifting from his profile to the high brick wall of Kew Gardens behind before flicking her head back to her left.

She had to face what was coming up on her side of the car, square on. It stood out like a beacon ahead. Behind the row of tired, drooping plane trees, nailed to the fence of Veronica's proposed house, was the bright yellow board of Baxter, Rumbold and Featherington. At first, she refused to believe what she was seeing. But as they got closer – first gear, crawl, neutral, stop, sigh, exaggerated 'yet another' pull into first from Dan – it became increasingly clear. The orange sticker slashed at an angle, almost obliterating the two little words FOR SALE with one short, triumphant slash.

SOLD.

To Molly it said FINISHED. TAKE THAT! KEW'S MINE. PISS
OFF. TRY AGAIN, DARLING.

'Something the matter?' Dan looked at her with
concern, then round at Daisy in the back.

'No – she's fine. So – am I. I forgot something,
that's all.'

'Do we need to turn back?'

'No, it's OK.' She suddenly felt nauseously claus-
trophobic.

'I don't mind if you want to…'

'No.'

'If it's important.'

'NO!'

Dan turned his attention back on the road. Molly
looked at him. 'Sorry, I'm a bit tensed up.'

'You need a holiday.'

'I do.'

'You'll love this place.'

She nodded every so often, trying to look enthusi-
astic as he went into detail about the beauty and
isolation of the Forestry Commission campsite.

Money Box Live came on the radio. Molly was glad
of the silence as they listened to people phoning in
with their investment problems.

'*So you see this ISA hasn't been performing as well and
we were wondering what to do with it…*'

'For fuck's sake, if you don't know what to do
with it, then *spend* it!' Molly shouted at the radio.

Dan looked at her quizzically.

StopitMolly. Stopit.

'Couldn't we have Radio 2?' she said meekly.

'Sure, no problem.'

Molly's mind churned as she stared out of the window at Saturday-morning holiday traffic. The high summer days were melting into each other, glued by the heat. Estates and Espaces stuffed with kids and summer bits and bulging roof-racks, gelled and blonded couples in convertibles with tidy boots and reclinable seats, coaches and trailerfuls of boats and bikes and funky guys with stereos screaming testosterone beats into the heat. Heading west all of them, pumping their exhausts out behind them like slow, continuous farts into the hot, sticky air.

He had aftershave on. That had annoyed her, too. Too achingly, obviously splashed on in a pre-date ritual.

'Once we get past the M25 it'll open up. It's surprisingly quick once we get going. What time do you get up in the morning?'

'It's all down to Daisy here. She's around five, I'm afraid.' Molly tried to calm down.

'That's all right then! Same as me!' Dan smiled and shifted into third gear for the first time in ages.

'This is a big car for a single guy,' said Molly, conversationally digging, as they left the straggly bungalows and last of the 'Yes you really are forty' lamp-posts of London's outer suburbs and shifted into fifth for the open road ahead.

'Good cars. Hold their value. Great for camping. ' said Dan, 'big tent. You'll see.'

This turned out to be something of an understatement. Molly watched in amazement as the rubble of poles and canvas morphed into an orange building the size of Caroline's front room.

'Dan, it's a marquee,' said Molly as he banged the last peg into the ground.

'Sleeps twelve, officially, not that that counts for much. Come on inside and choose where you're going to bed down.'

Now wasn't that a loaded question. So he wasn't just expecting her to sleep with him. He was giving her a choice. Damn!

'Dan. Why?' Molly looked around the tent.

'Why not? All it takes is a bit more space in the car and an extra half an hour or so than building a tiny two-personer. Good value. Lots of space. No extra cost. All pitches cost the same. This room good for you? I'll just get the bedding organised, then how does fish and chips sound?'

'Sounds great, Dan.'

The campsite was spread out in a large clearing. Their pitch was in a secluded grassy, mossy glade. When Dan had driven off, Molly sat outside for a while. Just her and Daisy, alone in the Forest.

Daisy, aware of the change in air, kicked excitedly. 'Ba ba ba, da da da, dada.'

'Ma ma ma, why won't you say ma ma ma?' Molly held her close.

A new carload of campers drove into the glade, stopped, looked aghast at Dan's tent, then drove on. When Daisy fell asleep, Molly settled her into her room, a canvas state room with a large, zipped up window. She peeked into Dan's room, just a zip pull away next to hers. She snuggled Daisy under a navy-blue down sleeping bag. She lay back on the Lilo next to her and watched the moths gather around the light, a reversed torch, dangling from the ceiling. What was it that made her, with barely any hesitation, go all the way with Christophe, that made *everyone* go all the way with Christophe? And yet Dan, who was *such* a nice guy...

'Supper's ready.'

'Coming!' she called back cheerfully.

Zzzzzzip...

The camping table had been transformed by a pink tablecloth and two glass goblets; Dan was crouched down with a bottle of wine held between his knees.

'Ah, my favourite sound!' said Molly as he pulled the cork. She banished thoughts of Max and Veronica from her mind as she settled cosily into her camper chair and looked up at the stars. 'And we have all this space to ourselves!'

'Keeps the other campers away, tent this size too. Something psychological about campsites. Tent territory? The space you get around you bears a direct relationship to the size of your tent. You'll see tomorrow, the smaller tents all grouped up near the entrance. Some of them are only yards apart!'

'They probably think we're a family of twenty!' laughed Molly, unwrapping her newspaper parcel.

'Yeah, that keeps them away too. So – what'd you like to do for the weekend? The walks around here are good, or we could go to the coast.'

'It'll be heaving,' said Molly, shaking vinegar over her chips.

'I know a nice, quiet beach.'

'On an August weekend?'

Dan, his mouth full of fish, nodded.

'In the south of England?'

Dan nodded. Chewing.

'In a heatwave?'

'Or we could go walking. Tons of good walks around here. There's a river we could follow, some good places for swimming there too. Or riding, do you like riding?'

'I *love* riding.'

'Great, so do I.'

'But Daisy ...'

'I'll look after her. We can go one at a time. Here, have a top-up.'

'Sounds good!' Molly smiled and held out her glass to him.

Molly relaxed into the wine-fuelled romantic woodland dinner. As they toasted the weekend, she half expected the *Blind Date* cameras to pop out of the bushes to film them for the perfect ending clip. But what happened next? That's what everyone always wanted to know. She thought she had a pretty good idea. She felt warm with anticipation as they finally made their way into the tent, giggling and stumbling with guy ropes and zips. She made a ladylike pretence of going into her room, listening as he prepared himself for bed on the other side of the dark blue canvas wall. Then, after a sigh and a bit of scuffling, there was silence. Now what?

She lay staring at the tent roof for a while, then thought, sod it, and sat up straight. She leant forward and peeked around the side of the wall; he was lying with his back to her. She slowly unzipped the canvas and crept through, quietly curling her naked body around the contours of his broad back and thighs.

He turned to face her with a concerned look on his face.

'Are you sure you're ready for this?' he whispered as he began massaging her neck.

'Mmmm,' she murmured, 'mmm, I'm sure.'

Slowly, he moved his hand down to her back. As his strong fingers manipulated her shoulder blades, she snuggled in closer.

'Dan,' she murmured as she began to explore his body, 'dear, dear Dan.'

CHAPTER TWENTY-NINE

'I'm sorry, Jenna, I can't make it.'

'But Molly, I thought you never went out?'

'I'm sorry, I can't change it.'

'But I told you *ages* ago.'

'Hen parties are supposed to be on the night before the wedding, aren't they.'

'No one does that any more,' said Jenna witheringly.

'You didn't say exactly when. And look, I'm sorry, but Amanda was booked weeks ago. I can't change it.'

'Oh.'

'If I'd known earlier.'

Ridiculous, thought Molly as she put the phone down. It's not as if I'm her best friend or anything. Molly hadn't been to many weddings as most of her old friends were still very single, and even fewer hen nights. And glad to miss one more.

Amanda had reacted with typical sarcasm when she'd mentioned it.

'You're really getting in there, aren't you?'

They were sitting in a nook of a Richmond pub. It was full of big, thick-necked, thick-thighed blokes. A few tarty girls were sitting on the high bar stools, nonchalantly smoking and eyeing up the talent. Molly had chosen the venue carefully; she'd thought a rugby groupies' pick-up joint might amuse Amanda.

'Nothing between their ears, of course,' said Molly.

'That's not the bit I'm interested in,' said Amanda, happily hitching up her short black skirt and crossing her legs with a swoosh of her stockings.

'I'm not going to drink too much at this wedding.'

'But it's part of the ritual, darling, the fun part, the only fun part.'

'And I always go too far, don't I.' Molly picked up her glass of Guinness. 'What are you laughing at?' She looked up at Amanda, wiping the white frothy moustache off her top lip with her wrist.

'You.'

'All right. Which one?'

There hadn't been many, but Molly's wedding binges had been a running gag going back years.

'The cab company?'

'After getting so drunk I'd gone upstairs to lie down.'

'Mmmmmm.' Amanda nodded, her lips tightening.

'Well, how was I to know it was the honeymoon bed?'

'White linen sheets?'

397

'I didn't know I was going to be sick.'

'Red wine sick?' Amanda screwed up her face even more.

'Ouch,' Molly winced. 'And then I got Oliver at the end of the line.' She remembered how gobsmacked she'd been when, in her drunken haze, she'd mixed up the automatic phone number memory part of her brain and dialled her ex-boyfriend by mistake.

'And you said, "Oliver, what are you *doing* in a cab company?"'

'I really thought he was there, I thought, "Oh no, he's lost his job in Penguin marketing and has had to resort to minicabbing." I had the whole picture! I could see him, in this tiny little room with all these blokes sitting around on plastic chairs, smoking rollups, waiting for a job.'

'And he came all the way to Barnet to pick you up.'

'And it took me another two months to get rid of him. The mess that's my life, Amanda! Then as now.'

'He was a nice boy, Oliver.'

'Oh leave it out. What is it with me, Amanda?'

'It's universal, darling. You go for the wrong ones and the wrong ones go for you. That's why it's always amazing when two right wires connect.'

'I'm so glad the sex bit is over with Dan. And he's not only a nice guy, it was *all right* in bed!'

'All *right*? What's that supposed to mean?'

'Do you know, Amanda, I think I've cracked it. I've finally been and gone and cracked it!'

'Yeah, yeah.'

'He's fantastic, Amanda. We had a good time. He let me have a *lie-in*! He gave Daisy her morning feed and changed her after bringing me a cup of tea in bed! He's even lent me his *car*.'

'Where is he then?'

'Rome. On business. Two days. I mean, I hardly know him, well, I do know him now of course but ... Amanda, he's so brilliant with Daisy. When I eventually got up we went to the beach, I had a ride.'

Amanda raised her eyebrows.

'On a horse, Amanda...'

'So you're off Max now. Well at least that's something.'

'That's the trouble, all the time that bloody red SOLD sign was flashing in my brain.'

'It's early days, hon. It'll take you a while longer to get over Max.'

'But how can I if they move around here? Imagine it! Imagine seeing her at the school gates every morning. Seeing Max at the nativity play. Sports day! I'll be racing against her in the mothers' race!'

'Don't think so far ahead.'

'Only a few years, Amanda. And at the rate time's suddenly decided all by itself to race ahead, that's virtually tomorrow in my book. I'm going to have to bloody move, aren't I?'

'Well, let's face it, that...'

'I *like* my flat, Amanda. It's got...'

'Character?' Amanda said drily, picking up Molly's empty glass and going to the bar.

'I could do without the traffic of course.'

'It's not only that you don't love this Dan guy,' said Amanda, plonking a pint of Guinness in front of Molly.

'No – but still.'

'You're not even in lust with him, are you?' She said it as if this were an even worse fate.

'I've *had* all that, Amanda. I'm forty! People used to *die* at forty!'

'Listen to her!'

'They still do in some parts of the world.'

'What's the difference between a bimboy gagging for it and a *hearthrug*?'

'Well, I think a hearthrug is a pretty good thing to have around. Far better than Cup-a-Soup sex with whatever builder happens to be passing, and, and, it's just *childish* to wait for the next real love to come along. Or to expect a fling with someone like Christophe to go anywhere. If I get the chance to hook Dan I tell you, I'm going for it.'

'And live your days in comfort and security.'

'Absobloodylutely! He's a really nice guy anyway! He's crazy about Daisy. She likes him – a*nd* he's away a lot on business.'

'Molly, you don't decide you're going to hitch up with someone because they're going to be *away* a lot!'

'I've decided. I'm not leaving Kew.'

'I'm going to get drunk,' said Amanda, emptying her glass. 'Do you want another one?'

'I'm driving.'

'You're allowed one more then.'

'All right, but it's juice after this. At least I can hold my drink these days. My body's so used to booze now it doesn't as much as murmur.'

'Know what you mean, honey,' said Amanda. 'I just get mellower and mellower and then fall over.'

'None of that hey-ho high and laughing state then throwing-up state.'

'We must be getting old.' Amanda swivelled to look at a noisy group of men who had just come into the bar.

'Oh no!' Molly smacked her hand flat to her forehead.

'Looks good to me. Hey! Look, one of them's waving to us.' Amanda held up her hand and tickled the air with her talons.

'Amanda, stop that.'

'Just because you've landed Mr Right, don't spoil my fun, hon.'

'I don't believe this,' said Molly.

'Molly, I'm impressed,' said Amanda, smiling broadly as the tallest guy in the group, now at the bar, came bouncing across towards them.

'Don't even begin to think it, Amanda. He's getting married on Saturday.'

'Oh?'

'And he hasn't had sex for months,' Molly couldn't help adding, giggling.

'Makes two of us.' Amanda smiled up at Jason.

'Thought you'd catch me 's a single bloke, Moll!'

'I, we, didn't know you'd be here.'

'Thought you'd be out with Jen.' A sudden look of

sheer terror crossed his face, 'Hey she's not, this sis-in't some kind of a wind-up?'

He sat down next to Molly sideways, half-falling. His flies were half undone, his broad striped T-shirt with embroidered crest was half untucked.

He suddenly sat up straight. 'It's a set-up,' hiccup, 'set-up?'

'No. Jenna's not here. Don't worry. This is my old friend.'

'Not so old.' Amanda smiled widely at him.

'Just leave him alone or I'm dogmeat. OK?' she whispered to Amanda, 'and take that predatory look off your face.'

Jason leant back heavily. His friends were looking at him from the bar.

'Good on yer, Jase?' one called out.

'We must get the girls!' said Amanda as they all came over, reaching in her jacket pocket for her phone. 'Man-watch alert – pub in Richmond chocka...'

'*Don't*!' said Molly firmly, putting her hand on Amanda's.

Two girls in sparkly vests sitting on the bar stools were scowling at them.

'Cheers, mates.' Jason draped his hand over Molly's lap. She removed it firmly and quickly.

'Now, Jase,' said a bald man in a leather jacket, squeezing past Jason and sitting himself between Molly and Amanda.

'Amanda, I think we'd better go.'

'You must be joking!'

'This is a stag night. '

402

'Exactly!' said Amanda happily.

'We've got lots to catch up on.'

'We can do that another time.' She waved her arm dismissively.

'Chill out, girl,' said Bald Leather Jacket.

Molly hated him instantly.

She spent the rest of the evening practising for the rest of her life. Sober. While everyone else got rat-arsed and became increasingly mind-numbingly boring. This was how it was going to be. Boring. While Amanda had got chummier and chummier with the bald leather jacket man, Molly, fed up with Jason's attentions, had taken him up to the bar, and propped him on a stool next to one of the glitter-tops. It had worked a treat and Molly had listened fascinated as Jason did nothing to dispel the girl's belief that he was a visiting half-back from the Western Australian Under-21s. Not long afterwards one of the girls had very loudly invited him outside for a rocket-polish and he'd followed her meekly out of the pub while his mates, and Amanda, jeered him on. They didn't see him again before closing time.

'Damn!'

Molly and Amanda were standing in the Paradise Road multi-storey.

'I d'n'see why we couldn't've gone on with them?' said Amanda.

'Because I have to be back so that Izzie can go to bed and you have to get back home. Now, come on, this is serious, can you help me find this bloody car!'

'What?'

'We've lost the bloody car,' said Molly looking at the empty space in the Paradise Road multi-storey where she'd sworn she left it. 'Either that, or it's been stolen. In which case, my whole future's in ruins. Come on, help me.'

'Whassit look like?'

Molly looked at her staggering, drunken friend. 'That's the trouble. I don't really know!'

'Let's go, then.' They began walking up and down the rows of cars.

'It's dark, it's got four doors, it's big, it's a Ford something-or-other.'

They took the lift to the next level.

'Bloody company cars. What happened to individuality?'

'I don't believe this,' wailed Molly ten minutes later. 'It's been stolen!'

'Naah, it must be here somewhere, Moll?'

'I'm *sure* it was on Level Four? It's *got* to be here somewhere. It *has* to be!' wailed Molly, a hollow chill gripping her stomach as she saw her happy, secure future with Dan slipping away down the slope marked EXIT.

'Hey!' she said as Amanda grabbed the key off her. She held it up and pressed the remote button.

'Genius, Amanda, genius!' said Molly as they went through the car park like a pair of water diviners, the key held out straight ahead of them. After a few minutes, the missing car's headlights flashed and beeped at them.

'My future's assured!' said Molly, welcoming the

odour of Dan as she climbed, and Amanda fell, into the car. 'Though I must do something about his aftershave,' she added happily as she pushed the gear down into reverse.

CHAPTER THIRTY

Molly quickened her step as she turned off the main road, rehearsing her lines. The terraces grew grander and the hollyhocks taller, until the houses were solitary Gothic piles with gables and church-like porches, peculiar corners and secret gardens behind high brick walls. As had become her habit on any walk in Kew, Molly looked in at each garden as she passed, all under the influence of the Big One spilling out of and over the long brick wall, and seeding itself in the surrounding avenues.

She peeped round Lion Gate Gardens and looked furtively down the Kew Road, hoping she'd find it was all a terrible mistake and the board would have changed back to its old FOR SALE status. Her heart beat faster as she stopped outside No. 496. It was an ugly, double-fronted modern house with a wide, heavily carved wooden door out of all proportion to the small, leaded windows. Her estate-agent summing-up concluded the house was spacious inside, and, by the look of the tall trees behind, probably had a wonderful, mature garden at the back.

There was a gardener mowing the crescent-shaped front lawn. Maybe it was empty already? She hesitated before unclicking the front gate. No. She had to know. After all, someone else might have bought it. She could be losing what little sleep was being granted to her under false pretences. Perhaps the new buyer wasn't Veronica Bulford-Boyd at all. Anyone could have bought it.

She stood up straight as she heard footsteps in the hallway.

Bolts slid back. Locks unlocked.

'Yes?' A small, dark-skinned woman, dwarfed by the door, looked up at her suspiciously.

Molly stood and looked. For a moment she forgot why she was there, finding herself hypnotically impressed at how beautifully made up this woman was for that time in the morning.

'Yes?'

'Good morning. I'm sorry to trouble you, I, I'm from Baxter, Rumbold and Featherington?'

'Yes?'

'Celia Sprague asked me to just call to ask if....'

The woman looked at her, then at Daisy in her pushchair.

'If – I could just check that your buyer, Mrs, Mrs er...'

The woman looked back at her.

'If Mrs Bulford-Boyd – BULFORD-BOYD? – could possibly come and – and measure for curtains some-time.'

'Yes?'

Was that a yes yes? Or a yes? yes.

407

'later...' A plane arrived, drowning her last words '...in the week?'

Molly waited as the roar reached its peak before fading, giving her a moment's thinking time to consider where to take it next.

'Mrs Bulford-Boyd? The lady with the large glasses, you remember her? Your buyer?'

'Yes.'

Stuff it, let's get this clear, 'She *is* your buyer, isn't she – the lady with large glasses?'

'Blond husband, very nice – yes, yes, yes.'

Molly swallowed. *Shit!*

'Excuse me?'

'Oh – nothing. I'll telephone you later with a time,' she said quickly, turning away, her eyes smarting.

Oh everything, Molly muttered under her breath as she retreated as elegantly as she could.

She walked the long way home via Boots perfumery department.

'Molly, you *shouldn't* have!' Dan took the neat shop-wrapped parcel from her with exaggerated care.

They were sitting at opposite ends of Dan's patio table in between the soggy remains of a Niçoise salad and a half-empty bottle of Badoit.

Molly smiled. 'Don't mention it.'

'It's not even my birthday or anything.'

'No, it's just to say thank you. For the weekend. For lending me your car, for everything, Dan, you've been really, really kind.'

'Shall I go and put it on?'

'Yes, Dan, why don't you do that?'

Molly took a sip of water and looked down the neat green rectangle of a garden. They only had wine at weekends. When he returned he'd be out of his work clothes and into his clean jeans and T-shirt.

'What do you think?' he stood looking at her, smiling.

Molly smelt the air around his face, 'Mmmmm, Dan, that's lovely. Really lovely.' Her insides churned as Vetiver, Max's aftershave, zapped straight through her nostrils to the bull's-eye in her brain.

'You shouldn't spend your money on me, Molly. You can't afford to!'

'I know, but … sometimes…'

'Thank you.' He gave her a kiss on the cheek before disappearing into the kitchen. 'How was college today?' he called back.

'Really, really good. We've each got to do a project.'

'Oh?' Dan returned with a glass bowl of fruit salad and put it on the central table mat of the polished dark wood table.

'I've got to come up with a website idea, and then design it!'

'They don't give you any client bases to work on, then?'

'Second term. First term we're given our heads to make our own sites. It gives us a chance to explore what's out there.'

'Difficult!'

'I think it's rather exciting actually.'

What'll you do then?'

'I haven't a clue. Any suggestions? What's needed out there in Internetland?'

'Retail's a no-no for starters.'

'What about Amazon and all?'

'Services, that's where the future is; and you need a USP.'

'You just said selling was out!' Molly spooned the fruit salad into bowls.

'USP for the site, stupid.'

'All right, all right. I'm new to this, remember. What's new, what's the latest geek chat then? What are your computer mates getting worked up about on their chatlines?'

'I can't quite see it myself, but they say the next thing'll be e-smell.'

'E-smell?'

'By the end of the year, they reckon every computer will be able to receive smell over the Internet!'

Molly had stopped eating and was staring at him.

'All right, maybe a couple of years. It'll be there, right down the web. Like you have e-mail now, you'll have e-smell!'

He looked for a response from Molly. She sat. Staring.

'You know, for things like computer games, burning rubber for Formula One. A polymer disk is bolted onto your computer.' He paused while the clock in the centre of the mantelpiece chimed seven

410

times. 'Then you get special command software which triggers the smells. Only half an hour to *Coronation Street*. I'll put the coffee on, shall I? Molly, are you all right?'

CHAPTER THIRTY-ONE

Christophe's bedsit smelt deliciously Continental tangy – a blend of tobacco, olives and coffee. Molly sat beneath the big window overlooking the Parade on the only piece of furniture, a double mattress, draped in a dark blue velvet cover, scattered with cushions. She looked around, trying to gauge whether his flat had more of the tidy gay genes or the hetero mucky bloke ones. She couldn't really tell as, apart from a tiny kitchenette, the only other furniture was a small TV and a masterblaster music centre. It wasn't very clean, though: dusty rather than dirty but the cushions, all spots and stripes and frills, were definitely on the girly side.

Molly sat listening to the music coming softly out of the speakers. She'd never quite made up her mind about jazz; she liked it when she came across it in clubs but hated it on the radio. But here, this was all right, this sounded good.

Christophe came over with two small tumblers of whisky and sat down heavily beside her, his legs spread thigh-taut as he leant forward and rolled a cigarette.

'I have to go back to France at the end of the summer when I have done my research. But – yes, I like it, I think this is worth finding out.' He clinked his glass to hers.

'It won't be going on-line or anything like that. It's just for my course.'

'But if I like it at the end of the day?'

'Who knows? '

'What you have to remember is sixty per cent of the buying decision is made from the marketing image. So it has to be strong.'

'Well, what I was thinking was we could have something about your father's farm, about the jasmine being harvested at full moon. Moon jasmine! We could call it moon jasmine. And, you know, make a link maybe with your wild flowers and the wild, you-know, individual woman.'

'The twenty-first-century woman, independent, strong, all female!'

'Yes! Oh, and I have something for you!' Molly rummaged in her bag and handed him a small olive jar. 'I'm not suggesting you use it, it's ...'

He smiled warily as he took it. 'You want to test me?'

'No no no! It's one of my favourite smells, that's all. I got it in Spain for you, I completely forgot about it.' She stared at him, willing him to love it as much as she did. 'What do you think?'

'Ha, easy. It is the oil for horses' hooves.'

'Hole in one!'

'Perhaps I could put a twist of this in, somewhere deep at the base.'

413

'Oh, I wasn't thinking you could use it!'

'I think I have to now.'

'The name Q.com will already have been taken. So, well, if you don't mind, as a working title, I thought, just for my course, I'd call it www.dot-pong.com.'

He laughed. 'Whatever you say. And – thank you for this.' He put the bottle on the floor next to their feet, leant over and kissed her lightly on the cheek, holding his face close to her before kissing her lightly again, a delicate tickle which touched far more than just her cheek.

Molly quickly sipped at her whisky.

'You see, the question of getting people to look at our site will be solved by the sheer novelty value of this Internet smelly technology thingy.'

'After the experiment comes the commerce.'

'That's right,' she said, praying inwardly for the will to resist him.

Their conversation dried up.

He put his hand on top of hers.

'I haven't seen you lately,' he said.

'I've been busy.'

'Very busy, from what I have heard.'

'What have you heard?'

He smiled.

'Whaat, go on, tell me.'

'That you have a boyfriend now?'

Their fingers entwined.

Molly did think about taking her hand away. She did. But she didn't want to. So she left it there and struggled on.

'Who's this?'

'Miles Davis.'

'It's good.'

'The best.'

His fingers played with hers, her fingers began playing back with his.

'I missed you, Molly.'

'Pah, come on! You're too busy for all that missing stuff, Christophe!'

He looked down to his knees.

'And stop that stupid mock-hurt look. You haven't exactly been sitting up here in your bedsit pining, now have you?'

He looked up at her.

'Christophe, I *saw* you. With Theo.'

He played with her fingers.

'I also, if you remember, saw you with that girl at Jenna's!'

He played with her fingers.

'*And* with Ulé!'

She wished he'd stop doing it. It was turning her on something rotten.

'It's all right, I don't mind. You're a young, amazing-looking bloke, Christophe. In fact, it's a wonder for womankind that you're only bi.' She was already feeling horribly unfaithful. 'But you really should watch it with Theo. Just be careful, OK? Don't go and wreck their lives. Please,Christophe.'

'How could I?'

'Very, very easily. Just listen to me for a moment. She's vulnerable, Christophe. Her whole life turns around Theo and Charles, her house, her garden...'

Christophe raised his eyebrows. 'It's only a little adventure for him. Everyone must try something adventurous.'

'For you. Maybe. In England, in *this* part of England, these things are harder to take.'

He looked at her meaningfully.

'For some people. I mean, I've been around a bit, I don't deny it. For us, we had a little fun and can be friends. But be careful, Christophe, it could be serious.'

'He needed to break out! He was in a prison. She was his only lover all his *life*!' he said in a high kind of 'of course' whine.

'And now look at him! The poor man's going around looking suicidal most of the time. She knows something's up, Christophe. And, what's more, I think she thinks it's me.'

He laughed at this, and she laughed with him.

'Males, they need more sex than the females, this is just how it is.'

She couldn't resist it. 'So, which do you prefer?'

'They are both nice people.'

'No, not them, I mean, men, women, you know...'

'I love people for what they are. Not for what sex they are. It is a waste to be any other way, you are missing out half the human race!'

'You don't have to screw all of the human race, Christophe.'

'Yes, but sometimes, some people, like Theo, they need to open out, they can't stay shut up forever. That's all. And besides, in two weeks' time I will be gone. Hey, don't look sad!'

'Believe me, I'm glad! I'm really glad you're going back so soon. You can stop messing up all our lives so deliciously.'

He pushed her back into the cushions before kissing her long and hard.

CHAPTER THIRTY-TWO

Molly went back to her flat that afternoon, thanking the heavens it was Dan's five-a-side night.

The blisteringly hot day had cooled into warm early evening as she lowered Daisy into a bubble-bath paddling pool in the garden. Daisy had never seen anything like it and laughed and screeched and splashed, covering Molly in thousands of little meringue puffs of foam.

While she'd been with Christophe, Daisy had been with Dan. That was the grippingly awfulest thing of it all. Not that he'd minded. He'd leapt at the chance. So had Daisy. If she'd taken Daisy with her, then nothing would have happened. But then. But then, she'd wanted it to happen. Was one last fling before she settled for the rest of her life so bad?

She unscrewed a bottle of bubbles. Christophe would be gone in a few days. She wasn't a bad person. She'd been faithful to Max all those years.

She dipped the stick in and blew. The little round skin of liquid flew out into a mass of bubbles. A final goodbye embrace is something that happens to a lot of people, after all. And when it's being offered by someone like Christophe, well, what chance has a woman got?

Daisy reached out eagerly for the bubbles, trying to touch them, to pick them up. Molly laughed at the look of astonishment on her face as they pinged into oblivion.

Dan'd never know. Daisy'd never know.

Compartmentalise, compartmentalise, she told herself, do what men do, they don't go down the guilt-ridden path, so get off it. That was it, though, she told herself as she pulled silly faces at Daisy through a foamy beard and nose, she'd do nothing ever again to jeopardise her relationship with Dan. Daisy deserved a secure future, even if she herself didn't.

She put blobby spots all over Daisy's face and showed her how she looked in a mirror. Daisy banged the foam in hysterical delight. Molly picked up the mirror and pulled silly faces at herself. Suddenly she went very still and quiet. Her expression had changed so much Daisy stopped playing too, looking at her with a sideways frown.

In the reflection, there was a tall figure, standing at the garden gate behind her, watching them and laughing.

Molly grabbed her sarong from her garden chair as she stood up and quickly wrapped it around herself.

'What the bloody hell are *you* doing here?'

'Can I come in?' He was still smiling.

She looked at him, aghast. 'My, you've got a nerve!!'

'You did say I could come and see—'

'If you want to see Daisy, Max, you telephone, you make an appointment, you don't just *turn up* on your way to the airport. Or are you just back from the airport?'

'Actually, I—'

'No – don't answer that.'

'Can I—'

'NO!'

'It wasn't Daisy I came to see, actually. I mean, not specifically.'

'OH!!! You came to see ME, did you! Why can't you get it into your head, I don't want to see you. We're talked out, Max.'

'You might, I think you *might* want to know…'

Molly paused for a moment. 'No.' She quashed the familiar fleeting hope which crossed her mind, before it had a chance to take hold. Then rallied before it could take hold again. 'No, absolutely not, no way. I don't want to listen to you, Max. I don't want *any more* of your excuses.'

He unclicked the gate to the garden.

'DON'T touch that! How dare you!!! Now – get out of here. Go on. OUT!'

'Please, Molly, just listen to me for a moment.'

'NO!'

She flew at him and slammed the gate.

'Molly, I—'

Daisy let out a strange wail.

'NOW look what you've done. This is exactly the sort of scene I don't want to happen, Max. I trusted you at least to call if you wanted to come over.'

420

'I have been calling. You haven't been *here*.'

'Ahh, that's it, is it, coming to check up on me. Now, please go before you give Daisy any more stress. If you want to see her, ring, Max. RING.'

'Molly, calm down and just listen a moment.'

'NO!'

'If you'd—'

'No, no, and NO. Now GET OUT. And you might as well know, if you're here to tell me you've bought that house...'

Max opened his mouth to reply but she was already talking again before he could speak.

'Don't bother, Max. I already know. And I'm not leaving Kew. All right? Never. Never, never, *ever*.'

Daisy's crying intensified. Molly picked her up and wrapped her in a towel, clutching her, as if scared Max might make a grab for her and take her away to happy Veronicaland.

Max turned to go.

Phew Molly, well done, girl, she told herself, stamping on each little twig of empathy which dared to surface as she watched him walking away.

'Phone and make an appointment next time,' she called weakly after him before going into the flat and collapsing in a heap on her bed.

CHAPTER THIRTY-THREE

The last Saturday of August was nearing and speculation and gossip, hoses and sprinklers, hissed in the gardens and allotments all over Kew. By the time the day arrived, the posters for the Horticultural Show, pinned to trees all over the village for weeks, had started to look faded and sun-worn. It was the same day as Jenna's wedding and Molly wasn't going to go, but when she saw the large white marquee going up on the Green she determined to squeeze in a couple of hours on her way.

All done up in all her charity-shop wedding gear, she felt, for once, like a native Kewite in her head-hugging twenties-style straw hat and, a new find, a baggy linen Hobbs dress. The distant sound of music made her feel she was missing something. She pushed a little faster down Gloucester Road, ignoring the roses nodding out of the gardens, begging to be sniffed, wobbling on her heels, overtaking a woman cycling slowly along with a sunflower in her front basket.

She'd been feeling a bit self-conscious about her headgear, but when she got to the Green she relaxed as she saw nearly every head sprouted a hat. Mostly of the gardening straw variety, but also baby bonnets and Gap caps, floppy flowerys, big-boy baseball jobs turned back to front and a sea of deerstalkers, each propped at various angles on tweedy old men with walking sticks, stooped from a lifetime of digging.

Molly wandered, glad she could go where she wished without having to talk or listen to anyone. Dan, by now her well-established plus-one, was busy fulfilling his best-man duties over in Forest Road.

She ambled past plant and vegetable stalls, bric-à-brac, embroidery, home-made chutneys and antiques. Ducks dozed like decoys on the lichen-covered pond. In the centre of the Green, the Barnes Concert Band and Kew Wind Orchestra were grouped in a circle playing 'Always Something There To Remind Me' at a brisk speed. There's no way I'm going to give all this up, she thought, Veronica Bulford-Boyd or no Veronica Bulford-Boyd. She bought Daisy a teddy from a woman with freckled arms and herself a hot dog from the Rotary Club barbecue. She flipped through a box of old postcards and browsed through a table of sunwarmed second-hand books, listening to snatches of conversations about extensions, conservatories and plants, plants, plants. As she got to the Kew Bridge corner of the Green, she noticed the familiar blue T-shirts on a stall up ahead, then, as she approached, the sign Students of Kew Gardens dangling in front of the table.

'Can I interest you in some carrots?' said a young girl.

'How much are they?' This was always Molly's first question now as she picked one up.

'Grown on our allotments. We're not allowed to use fertilisers or anything artificial; that's a pedigree organic carrot you're holding in your hand there.'

She bought a large bag. As she was putting it in her holdall with Jenna's wedding present, she spotted Christophe working at the back.

He feigned surprise.

'I didn't recognise it was you, Molly!' he said, lifting her hat slightly and looking into her eyes before kissing her on both cheeks. He stood back, put his hands on his hips and looked her up and down.

'It's Jenna's wedding this afternoon.'

'I've been getting the garden ready.'

'Yes, of course, silly me. So you'll be along then?'

'To the reception.'

Molly looked at him meaningfully.

'You'll be with your boyfriend.'

She nodded.

'Am I allowed to have a little dance, perhaps?'

She smiled and nodded.

'I'll look forward to it!' he called after her as she walked on. From a safe distance she turned and watched him serving beetroot. He even managed to make that look exotic, switching on his charm, joking, laughing.

He'd be gone soon. The summer would be over.

She turned and crossed to the big white marquee. She passed the Priory Road old folks, all parked in their wheelchairs in the shadow of the largest plane tree, sitting, watching, reflecting, remembering.

What would she be remembering when she got to their age? Forty years of mad chaos followed by forty years even madder chaos? Or forty years of settled contentment? With a man she didn't love?

But Dan was hauling her in gently but firmly. Seducing her with his kind ways, cooking for her. Letting her rest! *Any*one who let her rest could have her for the rest of their lives. If only he'd start being awful and unobtainable and as selfish as all the other men she'd ever fallen heavily for, then she'd probably be all over him like a rash.

She looked down at Daisy. Apart from the obvious benefits for Daisy, she couldn't help having the terrible, terrible thought that as it did look like Max and Veronica really were moving to Kew, she'd be able to cope so much better with it all if she wasn't alone. And, who knows?, she thought as she paid her 20p at the marquee entrance, she really might learn to love him with all her heart.

Inside, it was a sauna, the air musty with the smell of trampled grass, flowers and tent. Molly walked along the rows of trestle tables looking at potatoes, shallots and onions arranged symmetrically in little bowls of sand; sunflowers; geraniums; jams; children's miniature gardens with tiny moss lawns and little mirror ponds with plasticine ducks; cakes; pies and lace. Certificates for first, second and third places lay next to the winning entries. Two names in the vegetable section seemed to dominate: Douglas Colletman and Tamara Worstenburt. Tamara! Of course. This was her big day.

With her floor-length billowing silk rose-red

kaftan-style dress with enormous paste-rose earrings, Tamara was easy to spot in the crowd. Molly hovered in Onions and Shallots, waiting for Tamara to finish her conversation with a jolly-looking man with his arm in a sling.

'I know what you are saying, Douglas, but four centimetres of stalk means four centimetres of *stalk*. It's all in the nurturing in my opinion, treat a seed well and your plant will perform for you ... don't do beans ...' and, at last, 'Ah hello! Do excuse me,' she said to the man who stood back with a big smile on his face.

'Nice to see you, Tamara.'

Molly meant it. She rather missed Tamara at the meetings. She owed her a lot. Without her classes where would Molly be? Sitting in that flat on her own? Trying to make it with plumbers' mates in the Warwick?

'You look splendid, dear.'

'So do you. And all this is absolutely wonderful. I thought fêtes like this only appeared in Barbara Pym novels and old black and white films, yet here it is. In full colour!'

'Fête?' Tamara screwed up her nose.

'Well, show, whatever it is. It's Jenna's wedding today!'

'Over at St Anne's?'

'Kew Gardens.'

'Oh ...'

'A flower wedding.'

'Ah,' she said distractedly, 'splendid, splendid. Let's see little Dahlia.'

'Daisy.'

'Yes, of course.' Tamara bent over the pushchair. 'How is she?'

'Wonderful. Asleep.'

'Lovely when they're like that, aren't they?'

'By the way, congratulations on all your prizes.' Molly waved her arm around the marquee.

'Oh.' Tamara's face fell. 'It's quite a controversial year if you want the truth of it. I've beaten Phyllis Gibbs in the loganberries, and Phyllis always wins loganberries, she *is* the loganberry queen of Kew, you know.'

'Well – well done then to you!'

Tamara looked serious. 'It could have repercussions,' she whispered. 'Now, please excuse me, I must talk compost with Mrs Etches.'

Molly wandered on. The chocolate cakes oozed and dripped in the heat. Breads in plaits, in buns, with seeds, with raisins, without raisins. Monsters made out of vegetables. Vegetables that looked like monsters. Daisy'll be able to do all this in a few years' time. Competing against – argh, don't even think of it. In a few years, when she had the time, she'd have a go. Baking bread, making cakes. That's what she thought it'd be like. Full-time motherhood. After the housework done, a morning coffee and a gentle flick through *Woman's Own*, before putting on a slow soup for supper and out into the garden.

If only life could all be like the insides of that tent, she thought, gazing at the marmalades, chutneys, pickles and biscuits. But where would she have been as a single mum then? Completely ostracised. It wasn't allowed. She was beginning to see why. But then there'd been no questions about going back to work or not going back to work. And it wasn't just in the 1950s. It was ever since the year dot. She'd look after Dan, go to his corporate dos and make conversation. She'd be happy to do that. Wouldn't she?

She bought a programme to show to Dan. Next year she'd try and enter. Dahlias maybe. She had plenty of those.

Barely glancing at Christophe's stall, she made her way across the Green to the Gardens and Jenna's wedding.

CHAPTER THIRTY-FOUR

'I hope they're paying you well for this,' said Molly to Ulé, who was hugging Daisy.

'Yes. Very well.' She put her down next to Charles. They both laughed as Daisy took one look at Charles and set off in a backwards crawl towards the door of the makeshift crèche.

'She is crawling too!' said Ulé, scooping her up again.

'I expect she'll find the forward gear sooner or later. Look at Lulu – and Bob!'

Bob shuffled past them in a crab-like movement, kicking one leg forward and jerking it back to bring his bottom up in line. Daisy looked down at him and kicked and struggled in Ulé's arms.

'But Charles ...' They both looked at him, sitting in the middle of the tent, oblivious to the cachet of his blue Dior romper suit with custom-crawl knee- and arm-pads, chewing his fists.

'He's not interested, is he.'

'He couldn't care. Neither do I. The longer he stays in one place, the easier it makes my job,' said Ulé, smiling. 'But his mother!' She shook her head.

'I can imagine,' said Molly.

'Daisy is looking more like a little girl now than a baby,' said Ulé smiling down at her. Daisy, her white-blonde kiss-curls peeping out each side of her yellow sunhat, smiled back at her. Ulé set her down on the ground and they both watched as she determinedly made her way backwards to the door, octopus in hand, making her look like she had some kind of a strange yellow claw.

'Are you sure you can manage, Ulé?' said Molly, kissing Daisy goodbye and brushing herself down.

'Yes yes, there will be my friend coming to help.'

Whatever you do, don't get drunk, Molly told herself as she stepped out into the old walled garden of Queen Charlotte's Cottage.

She found Izzie and Carter, looking itchy in his suit, standing beside a small lily pond.

'Hey,' said Molly going up to them, 'you'll never guess who I just saw! Tamara Worstenburt. This is nice, Iz.' She touched the frock of her long orange dress. 'It matches your hair.'

'She looks like a soul singer, doesn't she?' beamed Carter, putting a protective arm across her shoulder.

Izzie winced with embarrassment. 'Get off, Carter!'

'We should get out more, I was just saying that to Izzie before you arrived,' said Carter, taking a large slug of champagne, 'Here, what are you drinking?'

'It's all right, I can go.'

'No, no no no, what'll it be?'

Molly thought hard. Perhaps just one now wouldn't hurt. 'I have to be careful, I always get drunk at weddings.'

'You're in the right company here then,' laughed Izzie.

'It's not drunk I get, it's totally rat-arsed.'

'Where's Dan? Bradley and Gordon, will you stop that this minute,' said Izzie as soon as Carter had left.

'Oh, doing all his best-man stuff,' said Molly, watching the children poking sticks at the lichen-covered merchild in the lily pond. 'Where's Caroline?'

'Over there looking like thunder.'

Caroline and Theo were sitting on a bench outside the house, apart from the main crowd. There was a visible gap between them and both were staring straight ahead.

'Oh dear.'

'I wouldn't go over there if I were you. You missed a night at All Bar One!' said Izzie.

'Wait till I tell you what happened to me,' said Molly. 'We crashed into Jason's stag night!'

'No!'

'Don't tell Jenna. Don't tell Caroline either, she'll think I planned it.'

'He'll have told Jenna, won't he?'

'Don't bank on it!'

'Why? What happened?' Izzie said, with heightened interest.

Molly paused for a moment. Before Carter returned, she filled Izzie in on the rugby groupies but left out the details. When he came back, she stayed in the safe shelter of their orbit and took the opportunity to look around at the other guests.

Jenna's mother, tall and cool, an early-forties version of Jenna, was instantly spottable, showing, thought Molly wistfully, how it could be done if you put in the effort, the time and the cash.

Jason's mother didn't as much look like him as sound like him. Her voice, a megaphone of a Sydney accent, rose above all the other murmuring conversations.

Izzie was getting excited. 'What's she going to be wearing, that's what I want to know. How she managed to keep it a secret all this time I'll never know, the way she's been blabbing about everything else.'

'I'm wondering what the surprise triangle packages will be at the end?'

'It must be some kind of grown-up party bag. But what do you get that's triangle-shaped?'

'Now, let's see, something down there maybe ...' Carter nodded down at Izzie's waist.

'NO! Carter,' Izzie growled.

'I wasn't!'

'You were.'

'I was going to say Toblerone ...'

'Oh yeah.' She paused, then said smiling, 'that'd be a let down wouldn't it. Expecting some great triangular glitzy party bag ...'

'You don't know it's a party bag ...'

'It's a surprise, it's a party bag, has to be.'

'You're as bad as the kids, you are. What's in it for me? That's you.'

Ignoring Carter, she spoke to Molly directly, 'Imagine. You're expecting something and all you get is a Toblerone.'

'Like the kids when they get a bottle of bubbles that don't work and a packet of raisins,' said Carter. 'Let down like a cheap pair of tights ...'

Molly turned to see Jason bobbing his way through the crowd towards them.

'Hi!' He smiled peculiarly at Molly.

Izzie looked at Molly. Jason had hold of her arm.

'Excuse me a moment,' she said to Izzie.

'Be careful, Jason, don't draw attention,' Molly whispered.

'I only want to tell you ...'

'It's OK, I won't say anything.'

'*Nothing happened* outside that pub. All right?'

'Of course, Jason.'

'It *didn't*, right?'

'I've forgotten about it already.'

'You won't say anything?'

'Jason, I'm not going to ruin your wedding day. Or any other day. Don't worry.'

Molly was nearly knocked over as a large woman in an enormous red straw hat suddenly pushed herself between Molly and Jason. 'Glad to see you've invited all your exes along, Jason, I was just talking to Jane over there. *Such* a nice girl. Now, I don't think we've met, have we? I said it to Jane, I'll say it to you, and I mean it, *good luck* next time, dear, there's someone for everybody out there, isn't there.'

Molly smiled and nodded at her, turning round to confirm what she could feel, Izzie and Carter watching them intently.

'This isn't an ex-girlfriend – Mum,' said Jason.

'Pleased to meet you,' said Molly, holding out her hand.

'Well, *who* is she?'

'I'm – I'm a visiting member of the Canadian swimming team.'

'Is that so?'

'Butterfly. I specialise in the butterfly.' Molly nodded at her.

'Ah, how nice, dear.' She put her nose back in the air and moved on to Carter and Izzie behind them. 'Now, *who* are *you*?'

'As a matter of fact, Jason,' Molly whispered, 'I think you lasted out amazingly well.'

Jason looked at her.

'Good luck, sport,' said Molly, putting her hand on his arm in a gesture of Australian mateyness. 'I must get another one in.'

She went back to Izzie and Carter.

'What was *that* about?' said Izzie.

'Oh, nothing.' Molly sipped.

'Yes it was!'

'I'll tell you later. When I've had a few more drinks.'

The wedding ceremony, led by a woman, took place inside the house in a large room with parquet floors. The floor to ceiling windows looked out onto the walled clover lawns, the epitome of an English country garden except for the huge banana leaves sprouting out of the borders.

Molly found herself following Caroline and Theo as they filed inside. Caroline still looked like thunder. Theo gave Molly a sheepish smile as she sat down next to them in the wedding room. Had Christophe told him she'd seen them?

When everyone was seated, there was a shuffling and banging at the back as doors were closed. The air took on the solemnity of waiting.

Jason bobbed around at the front, looking like he was about to go in for eight rounds rather than get married. Dan, next to him, turned and gave Molly a peek-a-boo wave. Molly smiled and waggled her fingers back at him and turned to look at the door.

They waited. And waited.

The doors at the back opened again.

Jenna's mother, with Lavender in her arms, tip-toed her way as best she could in her heels down to the front.

The doors at the back closed again.

Just when everyone's amusement had passed the mild annoyance stage and was verging on real anxiety, the doors opened again.

The collective sigh of relief transformed without pause into a gasp of amazement as Jenna, clinging to the arm of her father, made her appearance.

The tannoy speakers crackled into life.

Jenna's worried frown dissolved into a broad, sparkling smile as she straightened herself. At the first note of Roberta Flack's 'The First Time Ever I Saw Your Face' she started to walk.

Smatterings of spontaneous applause broke out as she moved, like a sliding magnet doll towards her by-now manically bobbing betrothed. Her dress tumbled in Princess Diana proportions out from her tiny waist – fold upon fold of pale yellow satin petals lapped and curled and twisted on top of one another in imitation of a perfect summer rose, while real yellow and cream roses covered her strapless gold lamé bodice, studded with glistening metal thorns. The three bridesmaids, in their floppier, less thorny roses, each carried a gold hula-hoop twisted with flowers and bows, and a teddy bear covered in yellow ribbons.

Molly's jaw stayed dropped open in amazement, only closing her mouth to breathe in deeply as the Disneyesque parade passed by. What was that divine smell? It smelt of light and purity and innocence. The roses?

Molly daydreamed for a moment, imagining it was her up there, all skin-glowingly fresh and new life ahead. She found herself idly wondering if they'd do it that night. Would Jenna finally relent? Would she get into it or lie back and think of Australia? Her eyes wandered across to Dan. He really looked quite good in his crumply linen suit. She could see he was nervous. He'd been so worried about the poem. He'd spent ages finding it, rejecting all Molly's offers of help in case it was bad luck.

As the ceremony came to an end, and Jenna and Jason had magically transformed into a Mr and Mrs for the rest of their lives, Dan stepped forward to do his bit.

Molly did an involuntary pelvic clench. Good! she thought. Those nerves of hers were for Dan. Real feelings for Dan!

'Ladies and gentlemen, before we proceed, there

436

are just a few words I'd like to read to you.' He unrolled a parchment scroll. 'This is for Jenna and for Jason.'

Dan stood straight and read:

'Set me as a seal upon your heart
as a seal upon your arm;
for love is as strong as death
passion fierce as the grave.
Its flashes are flashes of fire,
a raging flame.
Many waters cannot quench love,
neither can floods drown it.
So come – eat, friends, drink,
and be drunk with love.'

Molly sucked in her lips and looked brightly around.

There was a loud snort as Jason's mother went for her hanky. Jason's dad put his arm round her.

After lots of awkward shuffling about they set off in convoy, with Jenna and Jason leading, through the Gardens to the reception.

Dan held back and waited for Molly.

'Was I all right?'

'Yes, fine,' said Molly crisply. 'Fine.'

They left the cottage grounds and were back in the main Gardens, weaving their way through the Sensual Garden. When they got to the small greenhouse, Jason turned round and put his arms up into the air. Everyone stopped, the ones at the rear bumping into the ones at the front.

The greenhouse door slid open and out came a jazz band, led by a man playing the tuba. The band led the party across the Gardens to the Green.

There was a slight hold-up as they all tried to get out of the grounds at once. Some went through the little EXIT turnstile, others through the entrance gate. A coachload of surprised tourists stood back as they crossed to the ice-cream van and onto the Green beyond.

The church bell was ringing wildly.

'Did you arrange that?' Molly asked Dan.

'No. I think that's for someone else's wedding.' Dan smiled at her.

Oh dear, thought Molly. Oh dear. I'm sorry, Dan. I'm so sorry.

They crossed the road that cut through the middle of the Green, stopping the traffic. Horns tooted in time to the music. People leant out of their windows and waved and cheered.

On the other side of the Green the stalls were packing up and the band were putting away their instruments. A ripple of applause floated across from a group gathered outside the white marquee. They all had their backs to the party, facing a small table full of silver cups. As the wedding group neared, they all turned and began clapping again. Some stood up. Some of the band members picked up their trumpets and flutes and jammed with the band.

Tamara rushed forward and waved frantically. Jenna went over to her and invited her to the party, pulling her by the arm. She resisted firmly.

The man at the microphone continued. 'And for his enormous blackberries – genetically modified...'

'The *Championship Cup* is coming up. I may have won, you know,' Tamara mouthed.

'Come on, Tamara, leave your stuffy old vegetables and come and have a drink,' said a voice from the crowd.

A sea of purple glares turned to the offending voice. Izzie ducked behind Carter.

Tamara stood as rigid as a tree as her face turned beetroot.

The band started up again.

'Come on over afterwards, then,' Jenna called back as they processed across the Green and down to Riverside Drive.

The nannies followed on behind pushing the pushchairs, chattering away. As always, there but not there. In their own nanny universe.

Caroline may still have looked like thunder but her garden looked wonderful. Organza-covered tables, scattered with white rose petals and red jelly babies, had been arranged on the lawn below the patio. In the centre of each was a large bowl of cream and white roses and on each place setting a white orchid lay on the napkin.

The musicians, expanded by a large chunk of the Kew Wind Orchestra and Barnes Concert Band, made their way down to the riverside. There was a scramble as everyone went around looking for their places. Molly found her place name written in gold pen on a leaf.

Don't get drunk, don't get drunk, she repeated to

herself as the waitresses begin pouring the champagne.

The tables had been arranged in a large square: Jason, Jenna, their parents and Dan were seated at the head. There were two packages on each plate beside the orchid. One was a golden rectangle. Jenna's gold single-use camera. The other was a triangular box with a large sign saying STRICT ORDERS – DO NOT OPEN UNTIL TOLD on it.

Molly made conversation with Hazel and Phil, from Jenna's old job, on one side of her, until they all ascertained they had nothing whatsoever in common and she turned gratefully Izzie and Carter on her right.

Molly was squeezing lemon on her vegetable skewer when there was a shriek as Caroline, a few places away, stood up and stalked off up to the house.

Theo sat sheepishly.

'I think he's been rumbled,' Izzie whispered to Molly.

'Oh dear!' said Molly.

There was a loud crashing of cutlery onto glass and the speeches began. Molly watched Caroline trying to control her fixed smile as she returned to her seat.

'And now, ladies and gentlemen. Please raise your glasses,' said Dan. 'And take your triangle boxes. After the count of three – PULL THE TAB!'

Jenna had her camera to her eye.

Izzie nudged Molly. 'She can't stop, can she? Even at her own wedding.'

'One,' everyone shouted.

'Two,' everyone shouted.

'THREE!'

There were shrieks of delight and amazement as the air filled with shimmering blue feathery flickers. Darting up and down and all over the table. Hundreds and hundreds of obsidian butterflies. They scattered then grouped, flying off towards the river. The bridesmaids and the children began chasing them. For a moment the band was obscured by a blue cloud. Then it shifted before rising into the air and scattering into fragments across the Thames.

There was a shout from the patio above them. Coming down the steps was Tamara, waving a silver cup in the air.

'I won it! I won it! I beat the Colletman!'

She picked her way across the lawn and pulled up a chair next to Molly.

'Congratulations,' Molly whispered.

The sun was getting lower, the heat less stifling.

Theo got up and wandered down to the riverside. Molly, fuelled by a mixture of alcohol and genuine concern, took the opportunity to go and sit next to Caroline.

'Are you all right, Caroline?'

'No, I am not all right. I'm seeing my lawyers on Monday. We've discussed it. It's over,' she sobbed.

'No?'

'He *had* been having an affair. I was right all along. I knew it.'

'Oh.'

'It's all over between us.'

'You *can't*, Caroline. Not just because of an affair, espec—' Molly stopped herself.

'That's what I'd expect from you, Molly, *you* don't mind if people have affairs. You think it's fine, don't you?'

'Well, no – yes, I mean. I mean it's just that people *do*, Caroline.'

'Not in my life they don't.'

'But Theo's a *wonderful* husband!'

'How do *you* know?'

'You'd never... '

'Oh yes,' Caroline said with a low laugh, 'he's "wonderful" all right. Lovely lovey-dovey Theo.'

'You can work it out!'

'For a while I must admit I thought it was you,' Caroline said.

'I know.' Molly laughed weakly.

'He says it's over. It won't happen again.'

'Well. *Believe* him, Caroline. Believe him. A lot of men stray. At some time.'

'Yes, but there's straying and... straying.' Caroline's eyes filled with tears again.

'What do you mean?'

'It wasn't another woman.'

Molly got ready for her response. 'Come on, get it out.'

'Christophe! It was Christophe!'

'Oh, Christophe! Not too much to worry about then!'

'What are you saying? My husband goes off with, with a man!'

442

'He's not having an affair, Caroline! That's good news.'

'Yes, but, he's, my husband's...'

'More than likely not, Caroline. It was just a little adventure, an experiment?'

'But I thought Christophe was interested in *me* ...' Caroline wailed, as she dabbed repeatedly at her eyes with a crunched-up handkerchief.

'Hang on there a minute.' Molly excused herself.

She found Christophe sprawled at a table by the swimming pool, engrossed in a conversation with Jason's mother. Molly hovered awkwardly, looking at the mesh sailing ships, covered with white orchids, bobbing on the pool.

'Yes, yes, Christophe.' Mrs Jason nodded. 'That's it, that's what I was getting at. Exactly.' She picked up a large bunch of fat, green grapes, held up her fists to her face and took a large mouthful.

Molly watched, as layers of the woman's chins wobbled like an accordion as the grapes slid down her neck.

'You see, I don't want people to be pleasant and polite to me. It saves me the trouble of doing the same to them, that's what I say.'

Molly took this as her cue. 'Christophe, I need to speak to you.'

Jason's mother nodded and grunted, unable to speak for the enormous melon which she was biting into like it was a standard-sized apple.

I don't know why I think I'm so adept at sorting out other people's lives when my own is such a mess, she thought as she went back up the garden so deep in thought, she jumped when Dan grabbed her. 'Time to dance.'

It was a slow one; she felt Dan's arms around her.

'What did you think?'

'Of what?'

'Of the poem?' he whispered.

'I told you, it was good, Dan. Very good.' She moved mechanically from leg to leg, looking over his shoulder. It wouldn't be fair, she thought, it wouldn't be fair to tell him now.

She didn't miss a beat as she saw Christophe and Caroline take to the floor. She winked back at Christophe as they danced by.

CHAPTER THIRTY-FIVE

A strong mid-September southwesterly blew out the summer with one long, tree-rattling gust. By the end of the month, the blackberries had darkened and the gardens were sprouting clusters of bright berries, the fruits of their dying flowers' beauty work.

With Christophe back in Grasse, peace was restored between Caroline and Theo. Charles finally discovered the joy of movement and delighted his parents by suddenly getting up and walking across the playroom one day, thus confirming his genius by not bothering with the crawling interim.

Jason returned from his Greek isle honeymoon and, by the mellowing of his pent-up bounce, and the smile on Jenna's face, was obviously enjoying a full married life. Izzie shocked everyone, not least Carter, by announcing she was pregnant again. This set Carter off on a new au pair/loft extension campaign and Jenna and Caroline into broody moochings. Moochings which passed Molly completely by. Her days had settled into a rhythm of college and homework, playgroups and baby groups, punctuated by long walks in the Gardens. Daisy began sleeping through until seven a.m. For that alone, she was deeply, deeply grateful and content with the feeling that her life was beginning to take on a shape of her own making.

Almost.

If it wasn't raining, she always walked back from college the long way. Through the Gardens, then home via the Kew Road with a casual side ways glance at No. 496. Then on to the village and home across the railway bridge, avoiding Lawn Crescent and all things Dan. He'd taken it badly. And it hadn't made it any easier for Molly knowing his grief at their parting was as much to do with Daisy as her.

She walked slowly down the twisted avenue of hornbeam trees behind Kew Palace. The sun lit the paths behind the high Palace walls with a crunchy golden light.

Dan'd get over it, just as she'd get over Max. Daisy was the one she felt guilty about more than anything. Poor Daisy. Had she lost the perfect step-dad? No. Whatever sensible Molly shouted at herself ... above all, above everything else, for his own sake. He needed his own children, he'd make a perfect dad, a wonderful husband. For somebody. If only he'd stop being so nice to girls, he'd have them all running after him.

But what would sort her out?

She was preparing to take Max and Veronica's arrival in Kew on the nose, if and when. It had become so all-pervading she'd started to wish they'd get a bloody move on and move in. Then, at least, she could get used to it, instead of going through all the anticipation.

She turned left by the Pan statue and stopped for a moment, taking deep breaths of the leaf-rot air. As she walked, Daisy held her arm out of the pushchair to the wall, running her fingertips through the trails of deep red ivy and old man's beard. She giggled and grabbed at the soft white puffs laced with curly tangled leaves.

Molly sat down on the camomile seat and rummaged in Daisy's string bag dangling on the pushchair for her breadsticks. She looked around at the fading plants. What was it Christophe had said about beauty being a trap set by nature to perpetuate the species? Was that why it was so peaceful? Was it because the plants had stopped their battles with each other, had learnt to live together as they died together? She lifted Daisy out of her pushchair and sat her on her lap. Was love like that? Not the primitive, instinctive love she felt for Daisy, but sexual love? Was it different? Did it grow, bloom and fade like a flower? Didn't it have to? Otherwise no one would ever get over anyone, and that would be some mess. Had mother nature built that into her plan somewhere? Is that why she was called mother? Because she had to let go?

How long was it going to take?

She walked past 496 Kew Road with the usual trepidation.

'One from the top, Carol, and three from the bottom.'

Molly took advantage of *Countdown's* mental arithmetical impossibles to nip into the kitchen and put the kettle on for a second cup of tea, leaving Daisy on the floor with her cube box, trying to fit orange stars into blue cube shapes, and blue cube shapes into pink moon shapes.

She poured the hot water onto the teabag.

'Ho,' chuckled Carol Vorderman.

'Oh, shut up.' Molly took three chocolate digestives out of the packet, then looked back at the packet before picking it up and taking the whole lot in.

She'd raced home with her nerves standing on end, glancing around everywhere fully expecting Veronica to pop out from behind every wall and go 'Boo!' or 'Nah nah ner nah nah.'

He'd moved in.

There. To Kew.

All done.

So used was she to seeing the place always empty, it took her a while to believe what she was seeing. But no, there they were. There were already curtains up in some of the windows. Others were having double – or was it triple? – glazing fitted. And there, in the drive. Not just Max's black Audi. But, parked proprietorially next to it, a brand new shiny red Volvo estate. Complete with baby seat and new Baby on Board sticker. She'd got the family car in already. Had she *had* it then?

'*Consonant, please, Carol*,' said the contestant in a matey voice.

Molly leant back onto her bed, tucked her legs

sideways and under her and tried to concentrate on the television.

Her appreciation of *Countdown* existed on several levels. She got as much pleasure from the Carol Vorderman transformations as solving the word puzzles. Sometimes she looked fantastic, other times not so, as her no-expense-spared struggle with the onset of middle age was played out daily for all to see.

What she found even more odd was how, in contrast, the presenter, Richard Madeley always stayed exactly the same. Week after week after month after year. Except for the awful ties which changed daily.

She tried making a word out of JNCEHOGE but the sheer damned bloody cheek of it all, the fact that Max and Veronica were *there*, just up the road, kept getting in the way. She did no better than HEN, cursed herself, and went into the hall, closing the door on Daisy behind her.

She listened to the dialling tone for a while, chewing her cheek.

He *could* be away? Veronica could be away? All the old familiar second-hand thoughts resurfaced. Just as she was doing so well, too. But a shout would do her good. Just to let him know she wasn't leaving.

She went out to the telephone and looked at it. He'd have taken his number with him, wouldn't he? She stood for a while before slowly picking up the receiver. She held her nose, screwed up her eyes and dialled it quick.

No reply.

She listened to double buzz, double buzz. Transforming it into a double ring in that house. In that hallway behind the large front door. Knowing Max, all over the house, in the bathroom, the bedroom, the nursery? What colour was the nursery?

As she was about to put the phone down, he answered, taking her completely by surprise.

'Max – Molly,' she said. And waited.

Without a pause, friendly, warm, pleased even. 'Molly!'

She didn't know what to say.

'I guess I've got some explaining to do,' he laughed.

'Don't laugh, Max, this isn't funny.'

'Molly, listen.'

'Max – *you* listen. You promised, you said not in a million years would you, would Veronica ...'

'Molly, don't move, OK?' He put the phone down.

No, I bloody well won't. *Bastard!* She stabbed angrily at redial.

No reply.

Before *Countdown* had even reached its final conundrum, he was on her doorstep.

Molly barricaded herself and Daisy into the back room. Letting him bash on the door, on the windows, until Mrs Constandavalos came downstairs to see what was going on and inadvertently let him into the outer hallway in the process.

Molly opened her door a crack. 'Go away, Max. Just go.'

450

'Molly, listen ...'

'I don't want to know, Max. Just leave us alone.'

'Listen!'

'No! Now go away.'

'The house ... I ...'

'I hope the planes are driving you *nuts.*'

'Molly, Veronica's not there.'

'GET OUT!'

'Molly – she's gone. I bought the house for – I mean if you ...'

Molly opened the door a little wider and looked up at him.

'If you and Daisy would ... It was going to be a surprise, I mean, I was getting it ready for – it's still a hell of a mess, Molly, but ...'

'*Gone?*'

'I've left her, Molly.'

'Where?'

'We sold the house. She's moved to St John's Wood. She's, she's, it's – it ...'

'It's not yours?'

'No! I mean, I kind of knew that.'

'What about her car?'

'What car?'

'The *car*, in your drive. The big red Volvo.'

'Oh, that's the double glazing man's.'

'Are you sure?'

'Of course I'm sure. Look, I mean you *know* it was a sham of a marriage, Molly. I'm just grateful, I mean, it was the catalyst which set us free to go our separate ways. I mean, Molly, I'm free now!'

'Oh no you're not,' said Molly, pulling him

through the crack of the door by his arm, 'oh no you're not.'

Mrs Constandavalos crept quietly away up the stairs, shaking her head and smiling to herself.

Also available from Piatkus

NINE MONTHS
Sarah Ball

Holly's plans have just hit a bump!
It isn't until her boyfriend Tom heads off for his year abroad
that Holly realises just how much she's going to miss him.
But Tom's left her with rather more than just a passionate
memory of their last night together – Holly discovers she's
pregnant with no way of contacting the father-to-be. A year
is a long time for Tom to be away. But for Holly, the first
nine months are going to be the hardest ...

WOULD I LIE TO YOU?
Francesca Clementis

Lauren Connor doesn't usually tell lies. She's really only
trying to make conversation when she meets Chris Fallon at
a party. But somewhere between running out of small talk
and agreeing to a date, she ends up telling a few
inconsequential lies to make herself seem more likeable.
Only Lauren's lies are going to have far reaching
consequences ...

'A tangle of lies and lives worthy of *Cold Feet* ...
perceptive and funny' *Mirror*

STRICTLY BUSINESS
Francesca Clementis

Kate Harris wants nothing more than to be liked. She never
criticises, never delegates and feels guilty asking her
secretary to type letters ... But when her leaving present
turns out to be a doormat, Kate decides enough is enough.
No more Ms Nice Girl. From now on, she's going to be
mean, tough and ruthless. And where better to debut her

act than in her new job? Only playing Cruella de Vil by day and Julie Andrews by night is giving Kate an identity crisis, to say nothing of the effect it's having on her love life ...

'Hugely enjoyable' *Marie Claire*

BUMPS
Zoë Barnes

Just when Taz Norton's life is on a smooth upward glide – youngest sales manager at a flagship department store, own flat, cat and vintage motorbike – her lover leaves her for her ex-best friend. Then she discovers she's pregnant! Typically, Taz decides to be Superwoman. No one is going to tell *her* she can't get to the top and be a single mum as well. But no one told her it was going to be so damned hard ...

Fresh, funny and deadly accurate – *Bumps* is the essential career girl's guide to having it all.

LOVE BUG
Zoë Barnes

If love is a bug then Laurel Page is immune. All she wants now is a quiet life. And while running a dating agency may not seem like the logical career path for a woman who has so fervently sworn off romance, for Laurel it's perfect. Until Gabriel Jouet walks into her office. Tall, dark and oozing with Gallic charm, he's an unlikely client and enough to make even Laurel contemplate abandoning her vow of singledom ...

WHY NOT?
Shari Low

Jess Latham has her priorities right. High priority: Career, ambition, friends and Prada. Low priority: men, love and marriage. But when her closest friends succumb to domesticated bliss, she begins to wonder if maybe she's missing out on something. Maybe it's time to dip her pedicured toes in the waters of personal relationships. Surely one affair can't do any harm?

'more fun than a girls' night out!' *OK Magazine*

THE CUPID EFFECT
Dorothy Koomson

Ceri decides to take Oprah's advice and follow her heart's desire. Unfortunately, her new start seems to involve disrupting lives: within days she's reunited a happily uncoupled couple, encouraged her new flatmate to do something about his unrequited love, and outed the secret relationship of her two colleagues. Somethng needs to be done, but can Ceri stick to her vow to give up her accidental matchmaking for good ...?

'One of the funniest, most unusual books you'll ever read' Mark Barrowcliffe, author of *Girlfriend 44* and *Infidelity For First-Time Fathers*

GIRLS' POKER NIGHT
Jill A Davis

Dissatisfied both with writing a 'Single Girl on the Edge' column and with her boyfriend (who has a name for his car and compulsively collects plastic bread ties), Ruby Capote gets herself a new job in the big city. In New York, Ruby undertakes the venerable tradition of Poker Night with her three best friends – a way (as men have always known) to eat, drink, smoke, share stories, and, most of all, raise the stakes. But when Ruby starts falling for her enigmatic boss, Michael, all bets are off ...

'funny, sad, and full of perfect little truths ... one of those rare books that you read and think, I know that woman. She's me.' Laura Zigman

IT'S HOW YOU PLAY THE GAME
Jimmy Gleacher

Jack's got problems. First there's his ex-girlfriend, Breach: a girl who even his mother adores. Then there's his current girlfriend Hope. She's gorgeous, smart, rich and quite possibly crazy. And Hope's psychotic mother and a seductive older woman aren't making Jack's life any easier ...

'hilarious and insightful ... an all around good time' Gwyneth Paltrow

A SELECTION OF NOVELS AVAILABLE FROM PIATKUS BOOKS

THE PRICES BELOW WERE CORRECT AT THE TIME OF
GOING TO PRESS. HOWEVER PIATKUS BOOKS RESERVE
THE RIGHT TO SHOW NEW RETAIL PRICES ON COVERS
WHICH MAY DIFFER FROM THOSE PREVIOUSLY
ADVERTISED IN THE TEXT OR ELSEWHERE.